Kicks
for
a Sinner

by

Lynn Shurr

The Sinners Series, Book 4

Kicks for a Sinner

Cover Art by *Diana Carlile*

The Wild Rose Press, Inc.
PO Box 708
Adams Basin, NY 14410-0708
Visit us at www.thewildrosepress.com

Publishing History
First Champagne Rose Edition, 2014
Print ISBN 978-1-62830-318-6
Digital ISBN 978-1-62830-319-3

The Sinners Series, Book 4

"Joe says dinner is about ready, ma'am."

She scowled at him. "Ma'am? We're exactly the same age."

He lowered his blue eyes, but his glance skimmed across her tight sweater on the way. "My grandparents raised me, and they were kind of old-timey. They taught me to address all grown women as ma'am until told otherwise."

True, when Nell introduced them with such a hopeful look on her pixie face, Cassie had barely given him a once over, let alone told him to call her by her first name. Instead, she'd flounced off to sit under the oaks even though in January, fair-skinned or not, she hardly needed to sit in the shade to watch the children ride. This guy, Howdy, introduced by his real and not much better name of Howard McCoy, took the hint and tamely followed Joe to the grill. So not an alpha male, the Sinners' rookie kicker lacked any aggressive attitude at all, it seemed. Cassie wondered how he survived on the football field, but then, all he did there was boot field goals and try to stay out of the way of the real players.

"Fine! Call me Cassie," she snapped.

"Yes, ma'am, I mean Cassie. Dinner is served." In a boyish gesture, he swiped away the hair hanging in his eyes and reset the baseball cap on his head.
Having done his butler duty by her, he ambled over to the others to deliver his message again. She would say one thing for Howdy, he did fill out his dark blue jeans very nicely under that ugly shirt—but not any better than Joe.

Praise for Lynn Shurr

Dedication

To my terrific editor, Cindy Davis,
and to Lisa Smith and Linda Houle,
who love the Sinners series

Chapter One

"If your mama mentions our little frozen babies one more time, I swear I will brain her with her own cast-iron skillet!" Nell removed the bacon tray from the microwave oven and slammed the door.

Joe Dean Billodeaux, star quarterback of the New Orleans Sinners, reformed womanizer and good family man, hunkered down behind his newspaper in a time-honored way learned from his father. Only now the newspaper, thin, crinkly, and rolling up at both ends, did not provide much shelter from a woman's wrath. Who knew they made any paper cheaper than newsprint? Not exactly the way he'd planned to spend the first day of the off-season. The kids in school, Corazon's day off. No *huevos rancheros* for breakfast this morning. He simply wanted a hearty meal followed by a return to the bedroom with his feisty little wife tucked under his arm. Did not look like he would get his wish *this* time.

"Our twins are in kindergarten," Nell raged, "Tommy in first grade, and Dean in second. We've earned our time without dirty diapers and baby puke. Nadine has seventeen grandchildren already. If she wants more, let your sisters have them."

The toaster popped. Nell took four pieces of browned whole wheat bread from the slots, buttered them, and lacerated the stack of slices in half. He waited until she put down the knife.

"You know how Mama loves babies, and the grandchildren haven't started producing yet. Allie, Eenie, Lizzie, and Izzy are all older than us and say they're done having kids. Catholic or not, if the Pope wants more children in this world, he should have them himself. That's what Allie said."

"I agree with her wholeheartedly."

Nell pushed the mass of yellow eggs around in the non-stick pan. Not a chance in the world she would add a little bacon grease the way his mama did. His wife believed in healthy eating that did keep her petite figure slim and perky. No, she would pour that grease into a paper cup and dispose of it. At least she hadn't inflicted turkey bacon on him yet.

He'd told Mama he would talk to Nell, a dangerous play to call. "It's just that she knows we have those three frozen embryos sitting in a container in Phoenix. We did promise Father Ardoin we would use 'em all."

"You promised and she promised, but not me." Nell slid the scrambled eggs onto a large plate, garnished them with a heap of bacon and a pile of toast, and slapped his breakfast in front of him. The table jiggled causing his glasses of orange juice and milk to slosh over, which made him very glad he held the cup of hot coffee in his hand.

"You know how I feel about keeping my vows," he mumbled into the mug.

She hadn't finished yet. "Do you remember how difficult those days were before we implanted the twins? Do you know how hard it is to carry twins, and now you want to try for triplets?"

"I've been reading up. It won't be as bad this time.

2

You take the drugs that get you ready, and we can have as much sex as we want beforehand since I don't have to save up for the fertilization process. We won't have Emily to cope with this time either. She might be your sister and our egg donor, but that woman doesn't make anything easier. Besides, having twins didn't hurt you any. You only got more voluptuous, sugar."

Her breasts were bigger and her hips a little fuller, but she wouldn't want to hear that last observation. Joe Dean gave his wife one of his patented sure-to-get-you-laid grins. She put her hands on her hips. Those big, brown eyes of hers narrowed and her usually full, tender lips thinned. She still reminded him of a tiny, infuriated, brunette fairy with her hair always worn in a pixie cut. Once, he'd talked her into letting her locks grow out. She'd reminded him eerily of the bitchy, conniving Emily, and he hadn't minded a bit when she cut them off, donating her ponytail to make wigs for cancer victims.

"Don't think you are going to get around me with sex, Joe Dean Billodeaux."

"Around you, over you, and under you." He half rose from the table.

She pushed his broad shoulders down. "Eat your breakfast. We have another problem to discuss."

"This can't be good for the digestion, Tink." He used her pet name. But, he sat and dug into the eggs.

"Cassie is coming over again this weekend."

"So what? She is Tommy's birth mother. We do have an open adoption with her."

"In case you haven't noticed, Cassie is past twenty-one. She's not a scared, pregnant teenager anymore, but a very attractive young woman with a college degree in child psychology going straight on for her master's exactly like I did. Joe, I think she believes she's in love with you, and that's why she hangs around here so much, not simply to visit Tommy."

"In love wit' *moi*? *Mais, cher,* I'm all beat up from playing football and ten year older den her. Me, I don't notice she grown up, no." He tried to humor her with his cute Cajun routine.

Truthfully, he had noticed. His total fidelity to Nell didn't mean he couldn't look at other women now and again. Cassie Thomas had morphed into a blue-eyed, red-haired beauty, though she toned down that hair with blonde streaks and covered her freckles with makeup. She had legs way longer than Nell's and a nice rack, too. Cassie rode their quarter horses around the barrel-racing course with spirit and style, showing off for the children and maybe for him, while Nell could barely stay in a saddle. Still, Cassie seemed more like a daughter to be proud of rather than a woman on the make.

The trouble with Nell when she got an idea in her head, no matter how wrong, she let it build like a hurricane in the Gulf, until it led to disaster as it had when she gave birth to their twins. She needed to be distracted, the sooner the better.

"Put on that cute Cajun routine all you want, Joe. I know what I see when she looks at you. And dammit, you are still a very tall, dark, and handsome man."

Nell leaned from her place beside him at the table where she'd sat to have this discussion with a cup of black coffee not nearly as strong as his Mama made. She smoothed away that black curl on his forehead, gazed into those dark chocolate eyes, and ran her pinkie along his full, delicious lips. That was all it took. He was up and ready. She should have known better than to succumb to touching him when they needed to have a serious discussion.

Joe grasped her around the waist and headed for the kitchen counter. Her barely over five feet tall, about one-hundred pounds body never could resist his six-three, over two-hundred pounds of incredibly toned flesh. He could pretty much do what he wanted with her when he wanted. Still, she protested, pushing against his chest with her hands.

"Joe, put me down! We need to talk about this situation with Cassie. We cannot have counter sex. Someone might walk in."

He gave her that white-toothed grin blazing out of his tanned Cajun complexion, no stopping him now. To love Joe Dean was to have frequent sex with Joe Dean. Not that Nell minded most of the time. They had barely moved into his white-columned mansion when he discovered the kitchen counter had the perfect height to make up for the disparity in theirs. When the children were babies, she hadn't minded at all, but now counter sex had become riskier. You never knew when someone would interrupt.

"Like who? Everyone is gone."

He sat her between the butter and the remaining bacon draining on a paper towel. Moving fast, he had her snug jeans unsnapped and those long thumbs of his inserted in her panties, pushing both garments down around her ankles. His hands moved up under her stretchy red top and unsnapped her bra. He dabbed a finger in the soft butter and rubbed it on her nipples, all the while kissing her neck from ear lobe to collarbone and beyond. The top and bra, too much in the way, came off. He sucked a nipple, paused, and said, "I am so, so glad we haven't switched to margarine."

Nell gave him a light punch in the bicep, not that he cared. She was no three-hundred pound lineman beating up on him. Nothing more to do than close her eyes, lean back on her hands, and enjoy the moment. She spread her legs to take him inside her body. Bracing her hips with his hands, he went long and deep. He kept up a steady rhythm until the two-minute warning came with her small scream. He picked up the pace and scored a big one. Nell collapsed with her head on his shoulder. She'd put her hand down in the butter somewhere along the way and overturned the dish. Joe licked it off her palm.

"Stop that! We still need to talk."

"Nell, even if Cassie does have crush on me, I just proved how much I love you. She's never getting none of this."

"Easy for you to say…"

The kitchen doorknob turned. A person stood outside trying to peek through the crack in the little frill of curtains over the pane in the door.

"You in there, Joe Dean? What for you lockin' your doors now? I brung y'all a nice bread pudding wit' the high meringue the way you like it. Okay, you still in bed. For shame, so late in the day. I'm gonna get the key and set this on the table, you hear."

"Jesus God, it's Mama!" Joe hiked Nell off the counter and gave her a tiny swat on the rear. "Run, Tink."

Nell gathered up the jeans around her ankles and snatched her bra and top from the counter. Admiring her sweet, naked behind, Joe watched his wife retreat to the powder room in the hall. Leisurely, he tucked himself in and buckled his belt. By the time his mother had foraged the hidden key from the shrubbery, he stood at the door ready to take her on.

"Hi, Ma." Joe pecked her cheek. "Let me take that. Looks delicious." He deposited the pan of bread pudding topped with lightly browned meringue and drizzled with rum sauce on the kitchen table.

"Did I interrupt anything?"

Nadine eyed the overturned butter dish and a few strips of bacon that had fallen to the floor. She sniffed the air. Joe sure hoped the scent of the bacon trumped the smell of sex.

"Nope, only breakfast."

"It's okay. You married now." Nadine helped herself to a triangle of toast and shoved some of Joe's food onto it. "These eggs is cold. Speaking of which, you talk to Nell about our little frozen babies, yet?"

"Sure. I promised. She says she isn't ready for more kids yet."

"What? Been five years since you had any. You got this great big house to fill, son, and we did swear we'd use all them eggs instead of waiting on God to do the job if He'd bless our going with doctors and test tubes and such. I thought a little dessert might sweeten Nell up, but I can see you got your own way of doing that."

With a big smile plastered on her face, Nell entered the kitchen. "Hi, Nadine, you're out early this morning. Want some coffee?"

In the past five years, her sturdy mother-in-law had gotten more iron gray in her black hair, but her strong features hadn't softened a bit. Though Joe Dean had gotten his daddy's height and build, he resembled this woman more than she liked to admit. She supposed they could both be described as handsome.

"I never turn down coffee, *cher*. You got grease stains on your shirt, here and here."

"Um, so I do. Must have happened when I made the bacon." Nell filled a mug for her mother-in-law and hastened to take a bottle of disinfectant from a cabinet and begin vigorously wiping down the counter. The smashed butter went into the trash, the dish into the washer and the fallen bacon into a dustpan.

Nadine all but spit out her coffee. "What, you don't use dark roast no more? This stuff is weak enough to water plants wit'."

"It's decaf."

"Figures. So, about your little frozen babies."

Nell clutched the handle of the dustpan like she would raise it as a weapon. Joe pried it from her hand, disposed of the bacon, and put it in its place. "We have embryos, not babies, only a collection of cells."

"You wouldn't say that if you was Cat'lic, dear. You should convert. Less confusing for the children than going to two churches."

"They can choose what religion they want when they get old enough," Nell growled.

Joe slid his arms around his wife and held her tight. "Touchy, touchy. I thought you liked Father Ardoin."

"I do. He's a fine old man, but our babies—I mean embryos—are none of his business. I might add that none of your daughters have more than four children either."

"Well, they don't got to carry on the Billodeaux

name. You have two daughters and Dean, but little Tommy ain't Joe's blood. Not like I don't love him as much as the rest. Still, a few more sons wouldn't hurt."

"Tommy *is* a Billodeaux. His natural father is Joe's rotten cousin, Bijou, remember? And I'm the one who will suffer having more babies."

"Oh, *cher*, it went hard wit' you las' time, the babies coming in the accident the way they did. We gonna have another novena to make sure that don't happen again. We'll pray for three nice healthy babies and a normal birth."

"There is nothing normal about in vitro or triplets. Look Nadine, thanks for the bread pudding, but you need to leave now."

Over Nell's head, Joe nodded and mouthed, "Leave it to me."

"I understand. You need a tee-tiny bit more time. I'm going. Hug my grandbabies for me." Nadine moved her interfering self out the door.

"Easy, easy," Joe said as if he were gentling one of the horses. He turned Nell in his arms and held her against his broad chest. At least, his mama had taken her mind off Cassie.

"Say, I forgot to tell you I invited a guest for the weekend."

"Just what I need right now, another houseguest."

"It's our rookie kicker, Howdy."

"Are you still calling that poor kid Howdy?"

"Aw, come on. He walks into training camp wearing his cowboy boots and hat and greets all the guys with a big ole howdy like he's some country hick. Plus, he looks exactly like that dummy from back in the fifties, the one who ran around with a clown and an

Indian princess. Sort of reddish-brown hair flopping in his face over big blue eyes, freckles across his nose, all lanky and loose-jointed, a huge stupid grin on his face. And he's a kicker. He just begged to be called that."

"Come on. He's a sweet, good looking boy, and he got the Sinners into the playoffs with his field goal. You should treat him with more respect. But must we have him over this weekend? I was looking forward to being alone with you and the children—and Cassie, I suppose."

"Nell, the kid has no family. His grandparents raised him, and they've both passed on. I asked his plans for the off-season, and he said he'd just go back to Oklahoma and knock around the little ranch his grandpa left him, try to fix it up all alone."

He watched the hard, angry line of Nell's mouth soften and her brown eyes fill with sympathy. Nothing like a kid in need to melt her heart. "Fine, let him visit."

"I got an idea. Since you're so concerned about how Cassie might feel about me, why don't we nudge the two together? He's a real nice guy, Baptist, doesn't drink hard liquor, smoke, or run around with bad women. Cassie comes from a huge family, and he needs a family. Not everyone is lucky enough to have lots of relatives, brothers and sisters. Having a big family is great."

"Enough, Joe. Don't push. We'll introduce them, and I'd better not hear one more word about frozen babies today."

"I swear you won't."

There, one problem solved, get Cassie fixated on another man. As for more babies, Joe did not remind Nell of the prediction made by the old *traiteur*,

Madame Leleux, who had the sight. They would have twelve children and get them this way, that way, all ways. Madame Leleux, now dead and gone, had never gotten the future wrong. More Billodeaux babies were on the way for sure, and Nell couldn't stop them from coming.

Chapter Two

Cassie Thomas sat beneath one of the massive live oaks dotting Joe's ranch and watched the redheaded boy she'd given birth to as a teenager six years ago circle the riding ring on a pinto pony named Boo. She could stand another typical Billodeaux family weekend with a smile on her face as long as she managed to be close to Joe.

Sure, as a kid recovering from leukemia, she'd had a crush on his former wide receiver, Connor Riley, a really good guy devoted to his wife, Stevie. Who could compete with tall, blonde Stevie Dodd, glamorous sports photographer? That couple didn't want children interfering with their fabulous lives. At least, they had none so far. But Joe married Nell only so he could make a home for his illegitimate son, Dean, and then convinced Nell to adopt her Tommy.

Tommy could not have better parents, she granted. Once Joe Dean Billodeaux settled down, he'd done so with the same kind of concentration and joy he brought to the game of football. His teammates often called him Daddy Joe, but barely over thirty and hardly an old man Cassie still found him so very attractive. His love of children made him even more desirable in her eyes.

Nell, being a child psychologist unable to have children in the normal way, did love her Tommy as well as Dean and the twin girls produced from her sister's eggs and Joe's sperm, but she had to be the organizer and the disciplinarian because Joe preferred to have fun with the kids whenever he spent time at home. And Nell had been beyond kind to her, always allowing Cassie to be part of Tommy's life.

She did feel some qualms about trying to lure Joe away from Nell, but she could offer the quarterback so much more. Coming from a family with eleven offspring and outstanding fertility, she could give him as many children as he wanted. She'd overheard Nell again today tell Joe she thought they had a big enough family and to shut up about those little frozen babies. The dispute had been going on for some time, the first wedge in their marriage. As a Catholic exactly like Joe, Cassie understood how he felt while Nell obviously did not.

When she first decided to follow in Nell's footsteps and become a child psychologist, she gave her reasons as a desire to be closer to Tommy and to help other foolish girls lured into sex with older men, then abandoned as Bijou had done to her in Arizona. Okay, Nell had saved her and lost one of her newly implanted babies in the process, but she'd given Nell her son in reparation. That made them even.

As she grew up, Joe became the attraction, a perfect match for her with their mutual love of horses. Nell could barely ride no matter how often her husband took her out on long excursions. Sometimes, Cassie watched the children for them until they returned with Nell always looking disheveled as if she'd fallen from her mount a few times. Joe said Cassie sat a horse tighter than a cocklebur.

Since Bijou and all through college, she'd given

herself to no other man, saving herself for Joe, she believed. Nell, she knew from a few frank conversations between only the two of them, had been with at least four men before marrying Joe, maybe more. Of course, Joe probably had been with hundreds of bed partners back when he prided himself on womanizing, but that's the way God created young men. He'd settled down now and deserved someone younger and fresher than Nell. Once Joe divorced his wife, she and he could take Tommy and Dean, leaving Nell with the girls so she wouldn't be all alone. They'd all remain friends like Demi Moore, Ashton Kutcher and Bruce Willis. She did love reading about situations like that in the tabloids, her secret guilty pleasure.

"Lookit, Mama Nell! Lookit, Mama Cassie!"

Tommy dropped his knotted reins over the horn, stood up in his saddle, and raised his arms toward a chilly blue January sky. The patient Boo continued on around the ring at a steady pace. Dean shot by Tom riding his chestnut half-Arabian, Drummer Boy, and obscuring his brother's feat in a cloud of dust.

The twins on older ponies cried out, "Mom, make Deanie stop that!" Despite being very young, all the Billodeaux children rode better than their mother.

"Dean, you come over here at once," Nell commanded from her seat on a fence rail.

Cassie uncurled her long legs. Foolishly, she'd worn heels high enough to make Nell seem like a dwarf beside her and skinny jeans so tight the word "comfort" could not have squeezed into them. Now, she hobbled across the rough lawn to the ring where Dean's chewing out progressed.

"You saw Tommy showing us his trick. How

unkind and dangerous to try to upstage him. What if he had fallen and gotten hurt? Then how would you feel? I think you owe your brother an apology," Nell chastised.

Dean hung his head a little and glanced sideways at Tommy who had come to a stop beside him. "Sorry, bro. It's just Drummer Boy is so much faster and bigger than Boo. He likes to run."

"S'okay, Dean. I'm glad I don't have to ride a girlie horse anymore since you let me have Boo. Besides, I didn't fall off. Daddy says I'm like a tick on a long-eared dog when it comes to riding." Tommy's happy grin squinched all his freckles together and crinkled the corners of his dark brown Billodeaux eyes. Cassie preferred to think his ability to stay on a horse came from her, not Bijou, the former bull rider.

"Poor Buttercup, you learned your lessons on her," Nell said with some disapproval.

"Cowboys don't ride horses with names like Buttercup, Mama Nell. Do they, Mama Cassie?"

Cassie's heart filled with warmth as she answered her natural-born son. "No, they don't."

"Come on, Deanie. Let's race." Tommy took an illegal head start on his short-legged pony. Dish-faced Drummer Boy caught up in one stride.

Nell shouted to the little girls to pull to the side. "Watch out for your brothers!"

Cassie stayed back from the rails and the dust. She smoothed the pastel blue cashmere sweater over her chest and took a quick peek toward the barbecue pavilion—where Joe manned the grill—to see if he noticed how great she looked in her latest purchase guaranteed to draw the male eye. It fit snugly over a seamless Victoria's Secret bra that made her breasts look like perfect globes and shoved all she had into a deep cleavage in the v-neck of the garment. A small gold crucifix dangling exactly the right amount above this display pointed the way.

As a grad student and teaching assistant her income really did not stretch to include such luxuries. Their cost swelled her credit card bills, swamping her with growing interest payments. Oh well, Joe would take care of that someday—if he ever noticed she'd grown up. His eyes stayed on the burgers, hotdogs, and steaks he supervised on the grill. But that guy standing next to Joe, that Howdy they were trying to push on her, did see and went all wide-eyed, a wonder he didn't have to blot the drool from his lips with a napkin. How could Nell possibly think she would ever go for another cowboy type after Bijou?

Cassie twisted a strawberry blonde curl around her finger. Toning down her bright red hair at a fancy salon had cost, but the results did please men. Many had told her so, but they didn't count. She'd let her hair grow long and trained it into smooth curls. She might have been a mixed-up kid when she first met Joe, but she did remember that before Nell he'd preferred busty blondes and redheads who flipped their hair over their shoulders to show off their breasts. The tabloids once featured plenty of pictures of the quarterback with exactly that kind of woman. She kept an album of them. Even without the miracle bra, her boobs were way bigger than Nell's round little tits. Cassie flipped her hair over her shoulders and inhaled to expand her chest. Joe flipped the hamburgers. Howdy smiled so broadly he could have caught the flies trying to get into the screened pavilion with his grin.

Freckles gone, hidden under carefully applied makeup, her blue eyes enhanced with long, darkened lashes and dramatic liner, her lips all pouty and glossy, but did Joe Dean Billodeaux notice? Apparently not. He stuck a finger into his special steak sauce, tasted, then added a few more drops of hot sauce. Being too spicy for the children, Nell always made him serve it on the side. Cassie planned to show her appreciation of his culinary skills by slathering the concoction on her meat as soon as they sat down to eat. Joe said something to the new guy who loped from the pavilion and headed her way. He pulled up in front of her nervous as a shying horse.

"Joe says dinner is about ready, ma'am."

She scowled at him. "Ma'am? We're exactly the same age."

He lowered his blue eyes, but his glance skimmed across her tight sweater on the way. "My grandparents raised me, and they were kind of old-timey. They taught me to address all grown women as ma'am until told otherwise."

True, when Nell introduced them with such a hopeful look on her pixie face, Cassie had barely given him a once over, let alone told him to call her by her first name. Instead, she'd flounced off to sit under the oaks even though in January, fair-skinned or not, she hardly needed to sit in the shade to watch the children ride. This guy, Howdy, introduced by his real and not much better name of Howard McCoy, took the hint and tamely followed Joe to the grill. So not an alpha male, the Sinners' rookie kicker lacked any aggressive attitude at all, it seemed. Cassie wondered how he survived on the football field, but then, all he did there was boot field goals and try to stay out of the way of the real players.

"Fine! Call me Cassie," she snapped.

"Yes, ma'am, I mean Cassie. Dinner is served." In a boyish gesture, he swiped away the hair hanging in his eyes and reset the baseball cap on his head.

Having done his butler duty by her, he ambled over to the others to deliver his message again. She would say one thing for Howdy, he did fill out his dark blue jeans very nicely under that ugly shirt—but not any better than Joe. Nell directed the children to tie up their ponies and wash their hands.

In the pavilion, the twins asked for someone to boost them up to sink level. Howdy tucked one under each arm and raised them to the faucet. The curly-headed little girls took advantage to engage in a splashing game that left him with wet splotches on the front of his red Sinners T-shirt worn under an open green plaid flannel shirt. He looked like a Christmas tree, a wet and dripping Christmas tree. Joe always wore the black version of the Sinners' shirt and covered it today with a gray hoodie that stretched across his broad shoulders.

Still, she could tell the other guy exercised more than his legs as the damp T-shirt clung to a smoothly muscled chest. Cassie shook her own curls and turned to grab the seat at the picnic table closest to Joe, who sat at its head in a folding chair. Dean beat her to the spot. Nell took a seat on Joe's left and slid down the bench to allow Howdy to deposit their daughters between them in case either girl needed help with their food.

"You two are like hauling a sack full of giggles,"

the cowboy said. Jude and Annie giggled some more.

"You're very good with children, Howard," Nell said as she distributed plastic plates, cheerful with a sunflower pattern, on the table covered with a dark green cloth, weighted down with pitchers of iced tea and lemonade. Purposefully, she placed the extra plate on Cassie's side of the table leaving the kicker no choice but to sit next to her as Tommy had already slipped into the end place. As he slung his long legs over the bench, Cassie lifted Dean and plopped him between them.

"I haven't had a chance to talk to your daddy all day, Dean. Why don't you sit next to nice Mr. Howdy."

"Okay." Dean reached for a burger already enrobed in a whole wheat bun and put a splotch of ketchup from a squeeze bottle under its lid before digging into his meal.

Nell, slightly pursing her lips, appeared displeased by the change in sitting arrangements, but that was just too bad. Ever plucky, she continued to pimp for Howard, pointing out again what a way he had with children.

"Did you come from a large family? Cassie belongs to an enormous family of eleven children." Nell squeezed a line of mustard onto Jude's hotdog and tucked some relish into the side of the bun.

"Don't you remember, I told you Howdy doesn't have any family." Joe drew a frustrated sigh from his wife and shrugged, puzzled. Impaling a thick, grilled t-bone from a platter, he asked, "Who wants one of these babies?"

Cassie immediately held out her plate. Howdy sent his up to be filled by red meat, and Nell asked her husband to cut off half a portion for her. "Some of my special steak sauce?" Joe asked, passing around a yellow ceramic bowl brimming with the stuff.

Cassie ladled it over her steak until the t-bone swam in sauce. "Dean, do you want some on your burger?"

"No, Dad makes it too hot. Pass the chips, please."

Howard McCoy accepted the bowl from Cassie's hands and cautiously spooned some on the side. "How about you, Tommy?"

"Little bit." The kicker applied a dab to the boy's burger and handed the bowl across to Nell who sent it straight back to Joe.

Nell offered a plate of foil-wrapped baked potatoes and her own homemade yogurt topping flecked with fresh chopped chives as well as little dishes of bacon bits and grated cheese, a concession to her husband's tastes. Since the children ignored the vegetable platter, she piled grape tomatoes, baby carrots, and celery sticks on their plates, along with some of the yogurt and nodded to Joe to do the same. He took a big handful of veggies and bathed his potato in all the toppings.

Nell tried to jump-start the conversation again. "Now that everyone is settled, Howard tell me how you know so much about children if you have no brothers and sisters."

"Well, ma'am, I used to babysit for pocket money when I went to middle school. But after I got involved in football, I didn't have the time. I do like kids." He carved off a portion of tender pink steak, dipped it cautiously in the sauce and chewed.

"Please call me Nell. Ma'am makes me feel so old."

"See?" Cassie hissed.

"Sure, Nell. Joe, this is a fine steak sauce." He cut and dipped another piece.

Cassie sawed a chunk from her t-bone and shoved it into her mouth. Her eyes began to water, making her liner run a bit. She blotted the tears carefully with her napkin and chewed gamely until she could swallow. A coughing fit followed the swallow. Howdy reached over Dean and walloped her on the back a few times making her breasts wobble like a gelatin mold.

"Need the Heimlich?" he asked.

"No, no, I'm fine," she gasped. It should have been Joe who patted her back. After all, she gagged on his sauce.

"Try the yogurt. It will kill the burn," the cowboy suggested with a cheesy ear-to-ear grin. "Joe, I am enjoying your recipe. Next time I pass through Albuquerque I'll bring you some fresh red and green chili powder to try. My grandpa cooked a lot of Mexican dishes."

"I'd like that. Sorry we couldn't take a Super Bowl while he was still alive," Joe said.

"He got to see the field goal that got us into the playoffs. I'm glad he wasn't around to watch me miss the one that lost the division title." He set down his utensils as if his appetite suddenly failed.

"I saw that one. You blew it," Cassie said, knowing how heartless and unfair she sounded.

Joe's black brows snapped together. He chastised her like one of his children. "He missed an impossible sixty-three yard field goal by a whisper in Green Bay with the snow coming down during the last five seconds of the game because I asked him to give it a try. If I had played a better game that field goal wouldn't have been necessary. Next year, we'll get them, Howdy."

"Yes, sir." Howard picked up his fork and delved into the baked potato. Silence thick as a sour cream topping enveloped the table.

"Maybe after lunch, you could show the boys how to kick a football," Nell said with all the brightness she could bring to the suggestion.

"Not me," Dean replied. "I'm gonna be a quarterback like Dad."

Even knowing her face still burned from Joe's reprimand and how badly in the wrong she was, Cassie blurted out, "That's right, Dean. Kickers are just glorified soccer players."

"We used to call her Sassy Cassie not so very long ago," Joe answered, scowling her way. "Her mouth isn't as cute now."

"That's okay. Lots of folks feel that way, like kickers aren't real football players. I did start out as a soccer player in high school. The football coach saw one of my kicks and before I knew it, I'd made the team and had a special trainer. Oh, and I think your mouth is cute, very cute, ma'am." He continued eating his steak while Cassie's cheeks burned even brighter.

"This kid is cool as ice on the field, and we did have some in Green Bay," Joe told Nell while disregarding Cassie. "You wouldn't know it to look at him. He has that boy-next-door kind of face, you see."

"Takes a lot to rile me, Grandpa always said." Howdy glanced at Tommy who tugged on the sleeve of his flannel shirt. "What can I do for you little man? Need more lemonade?"

"Nope. I play soccer 'cause Mama Nell says we're too young for football. Daddy says I might grow up tall and skinny like Mama Cassie and not be able to play pro, but I could be a kicker, couldn't I?"

Before Howdy answered, Cassie spewed again as if Joe's steak sauce had set her on fire. Oh, why couldn't she stop herself? "I am not skinny! I was thin and sickly as a child, but now I'm very well built."

The cowboy's big, blue eyes, all wide and innocent looking, swept across her bosom. "Yes, I'd say you are—ma'am."

She gritted her teeth. "I told you to call me Cassie."

"I call friends by their first name, but you don't seem to want to be friends—ma'am. It doesn't matter if your mama likes me, buddy. I want to teach you how to kick."

Tommy's small forehead wrinkled under a shock of red hair. "Maybe not if Mama Cassie doesn't want me to learn."

"Oh, Tommy, no. I didn't mean that at all. You go play with Mr. Howdy after dinner." Cassie blotted her eyes again.

Nell sat up straight very suddenly as if someone's long leg had prodded her thigh. Joe leaned over the twins and whispered to his wife loud enough for Cassie to hear every single word. "Ice, baby, ice."

Chapter Three

Howard McCoy sat cross-legged in the grass beside the barn. Cassie watched him from a deep shadow cast by the late afternoon sun. Surrounded by childish objects—a box of chalk, a kid-sized soccer ball, a small football with a plastic tee—he tore off a long strip of adhesive tape Nell had provided and wrapped it lengthwise around the football. A smaller piece went around the swollen middle of the ball. Then, he quartered the space with more tape. Satisfied with his work, he tossed the football into the air and caught it, a small object swallowed by large hands.

All four children raced from the barn where they'd been rubbing down their ponies as Joe expected them to do after riding. They left a whiff of horsey sweat in the air as they blew past her. Ordinarily, she would have helped with the chore, would have been riding herself, but she had dressed for seduction, not a trail ride, and could ill afford to soil the expensive cashmere sweater.

Nell came along carrying a lawn chair from the pavilion. "Grab a seat, Cassie. Let's watch the kicking lesson."

"No thanks, I'll stand." After forcing down all that meat to show Joe she wasn't a prissy eater like Nell, she doubted if she could sit without popping the snap on her jeans. How embarrassing would that be, especially since she'd tucked in the sweater to show she possessed a flatter belly than Nell?

Howdy unfolded from his place on the lawn, his legs carrying him up to his six-foot height, three inches shorter than Joe, and not so broad in the shoulders. But, his thighs pulled the denim jeans tight, and his calf muscles strained the cloth. Cassie saw where Nell's eyes had gone, too, that dirty old woman lusting after this young guy when she had Joe. Disgusting. How could she want anyone else?

"Okay, Tommy. Let me see your soccer kick." Howdy tossed the boy the round, white ball well-scuffed with use.

"I thought we were gonna kick a football?"

"I started learning by kicking a soccer ball over and over again against a barn wall. It's good practice. Show me what you got."

Tommy placed the ball and stepped back a little, then gave it a good strong wallop that sent it crashing midway up the barn wall. Both girls took a turn, but even at this young age, anyone could see they would never be power kickers. Both were bitty like their mother and the aunt who donated the eggs for Joe to inseminate. The only thing inherited from their father appeared to be their curls and lovely brown eyes. Nell had brown eyes, too, but not nearly as beautiful as the dark chocolate shade of the Billodeauxs. Dean, who had his dad's eyes and curled thick lashes, hung back by his mother's chair until Joe arrived and rested his hands on Nell's shoulders.

"Go on, son. Give it a try. A good quarterback understands all the positions and what they bring to the game. No better way to do that than experience it yourself."

With that encouragement, Dean smacked the soccer ball a good one. It soared higher than Tommy's try and rebounded with a vengeance. Cassie cringed a little for her boy. At seven, Dean Billodeaux showed an inborn, natural athleticism that would be hard to top at any age.

"What you want to go for is smooth and long, not so hard and bouncy, kiddo. Hit with your instep, not your toe," Howdy said.

Right then and there, she could have thrown her arms around the kicker and kissed those ridiculous cinnamon freckles across the bridge of the man's nose. One thing nice she could say about Dean, he took constructive criticism well having heard since birth to "man up" from his dad. The boy nodded and asked for another turn, but the kicker told him he'd only wanted to get a feel for their style before moving on to the football.

He started with a demonstration using the child's plastic tee to hold the undersized football. Setting up way back, he approached the ball in three smooth steps: one forward, one to plant his left foot firmly, and then a smooth, solid kick off the instep of his athletic shoe that sent the small object soaring over the barn roof and tumbling down the other side. Most eyes followed the arc of the ball as if the audience sat in a large stadium and watched the extra point being scored. Cassie's eyes stayed on the kicker, his head down, his arms extended into the air and one powerful leg stretched upward in balletic perfection, a beautiful sight to see.

And then, he became loose-limbed, grinning Howdy again. "A mighty small target to hit. Glad I didn't flub it."

"Golly!" Tommy led the pack of children around the barn to find and retrieve the ball like a pack of eager puppies being trained to hunt. Nell and Joe applauded. Cassie kept her hands locked in a tight knot. She would not give this hick any encouragement. She wanted Joe, Joe, Joe, no one else.

One of the girls returned with the football tucked tight against her flat chest since both boys attempted to steal it. Tiny but quick, she already knew how to protect what she had.

"That's the way, Jude. Don't let the guys strip the ball," Joe shouted. "And she scores!"

Jude handed the football to Howdy and executed a prim princess curtsey as if she wore a ball gown and not jeans and sneakers, her triumphant demonstration of victory over her brothers. Then, practice began in earnest.

Howdy chalked the insteps of the children's shoes and showed them after each kick where their foot should have hit in the right quadrant. Cassie thought Tommy did the best. The girls were feeble kickers, and Dean always approached the ball too aggressively and shanked it. Annie, the quietest of the Billodeaux kids, cried when she missed the ball altogether and sniffed, "I want to be a ballerina, anyhow."

"They say punters and kickers are the ballerinas of football," Howdy told her. He followed that comforting statement with a silly pirouette on the tips of his big toes that got them all laughing. Cassie couldn't keep in the smile no matter how hard she tried. Okay, so he was a nice guy just as Nell said when she'd told her another guest would be coming. You could detect the fix-up in her words. Cassie guessed she preferred bad boys like

Bijou and Joe before he became a devoted family man because she had a bad streak herself and wanted another woman's husband.

Howdy coaxed Annie to try again. This time she managed to hit the broad side of the barn a few feet off the ground. The children continued to take turns until the early winter dusk descended and the cold air prickled their skin. The pro kicker sent one last ball over the barn for the fun of it and let the kids scramble for its return. This time Dean brought back the ball with Tommy shadowing behind him as he so often did.

Cassie hugged her son and whispered too low for the other children to hear, "You were the best, the very best." She did not lie. Dean and Jude always kicked too hard and Annie too soft. Her boy performed perfectly. He beamed at her, so proud.

She swallowed her hostility and forced herself to walk over to where Howdy waited by his shiny, new red truck with the double cab and extended bed, much like the one Joe used at the ranch. Nell had gone to make up a box of leftovers for which the cowboy said he would be "mighty obliged." Did anyone actually talk that way, like the star in an old western movie?

"Thanks for teaching Tommy to kick. Dean is such a natural leader sometimes my son gets left his the dust. I thought he did really, really well. Joe might be right about his not being built for football, so this means a lot to him."

The cowboy shrugged and leaned his length back against the truck's cab. "Once the football coach tapped me, my grandpa built me a regulation goalpost in the cornfield. I had a talent for kicking, but I practiced all year round in wind and snow and into the sun to get better in all conditions. Drop a word and I'll bet Joe would build the right-sized goalpost for Tommy, too. The good thing is kickers tend to have long careers and don't get beat up as much—even if we are only glorified soccer players. If that doesn't work out, plenty of other careers to choose from in this big, wide world, ma'am."

She had the grace to blush again and apologize. "I am sorry I was so rude. You are a vital part of the team. What will you do when you are done playing? Coach other kickers?"

Another loose-shouldered shrug. "Maybe, but I do have a degree in psychology. I thought I might counsel troubled boys."

"Really? I'm getting my master's in psychology. I thought I'd like to work with troubled girls."

He showed no surprise, nor had he about her being Tommy's birthmother. Probably, Nell filled him in before introducing them. He hadn't cringed or lost interest because she had an illegitimate son the way some men did. A nice guy and kinda cute.

He gave her that ear-to-ear grin. "Maybe we could go into practice together. Ma'am."

That raised her temper. "Cut that out! Call me Cassie."

"So we're friends now? Friendly enough for you to give me your phone number and maybe go out on a date?"

Panic fluttered inside her like the huge flock of starlings rising into the blue-black evening sky from the fallow cane field across the bayou. Push him away, push him away right now, or you will never be held in Joe's safe arms. Her mind scrambled for the words to fend him off and they came to her all at once. Something Joe had said very offhand about the Sinners' punter, Brian Lightfoot.

"Oh, I thought you were gay! I mean you room with Brian Lightfoot, and I understand he's…" She fluttered her hand back and forth.

Howdy took a turn at blushing and did it very well. "Only on the road. I mean, I'm not gay anytime. The kicker always rooms with the punter. I have my own place, a condo, same building where Joe has his, not the penthouse though, but still real nice." He stumbled on, all of his cool evaporating like dry ice exposed to the air. "Honest to God, I'm not gay."

"Are you sure? For a man, you *are* very graceful."

"Only when I'm kicking. Otherwise, I'm a real klutz."

"You know what they say about psychology majors—they're trying to work out their own problems."

"Maybe I do have some problems, but my sexual identity isn't one of them. And how about you, Miss Going for her Masters? You must have twice the problems I do."

Nell got between them, running interference with a plastic bag clutched in her hand. "Here you go, Howard. I put a couple of steaks in there and some baked potatoes, a sack of the veggies, and little containers of my yogurt topping and Joe's steak sauce. Did you really like it?"

"Sure. I don't lie about important things—like steak sauce. Just needs to be taken with a little moderation. You surely know how to make a man feel at home, Nell. Thanks for inviting me." He climbed into the high cab with ease, giving Cassie one last glimpse of his fine, tight ass. To her, he said before he slammed the truck's heavy door, "Evening, ma'am."

A gay guy might covet that ass, and a straight girl could appreciate it every bit as much. Cassie exhaled with relief as he drove away.

Nell said all eager and excited, "Isn't Howard McCoy the nicest young man ever? Cute, too, and the way he has with children. He won't be single long. What do you think of him?"

"I think I will never see that man again."

Chapter Four

Howard McCoy left Joe's Lorena Ranch and Chapelle, Louisiana in a cloud of dust and a mighty roar of his truck's engine. He breezed through Morgan City and across the swampy region south of there that brought him out on I-10 and back to New Orleans again. All the way, he muttered, "She thinks I'm gay," and ran a mental inventory of any characteristics making Cassie Thomas think that. Other than having to room with Brian Lightfoot, he couldn't think of a thing, but men saw stuff like that differently. He should ask Brian. No! The last thing he should do was pal with the punter.

Gregory, the doorman at the condos, raised his eyebrows when Howdy pounded through the front doors without waiting for him to open them. Mumbling under his breath, the kicker stalked by swinging a white plastic bag and gave him only a curt nod instead of the usual cordial greeting. At the elevator, Howdy turned back and pressed a dollar into the concierge's hand.

"Thank you, sir, but I've done nothing for you."

"Back home when I was a kid, we had a cuss jar. If Grandpa or me said a bad word, we put a quarter in the jar. Tonight, you are my cuss jar. I figured for inflation."

"I do appreciate the tip, but you did not swear at me, sir."

"I did. You just didn't hear me. Don't make it right as Grandma would say. Tell me, Gregory, do I seem gay to you?"

Gregory took the requests of his patrons very seriously. He gave Howdy a good once over and back again, shook his head. "No, not at all, though your western demeanor might be attractive to men of that persuasion. You know in a *Midnight Cowboy*, *Brokeback Mountain* sort of way."

"Thanks, I needed to hear that. Evening, Gregory." He returned to wait for the elevator. As the doors slid soundlessly open, someone called, "Hold it for me, Howdy." He winced without turning, got inside, and held the button down to wait for the new arrival because that was the way Grandma had raised him. "Always be polite, Howie. Polite goes a far way in getting along with people."

He got along with everyone including Brian Lightfoot who had just invaded his space. Joe put in a word for both of them with the condo board. Now, Howdy had a place two floors beneath Joe's city penthouse and two flights above Brian Lightfoot's apartment. Inevitable they would run into each other frequently, sometimes share rides to and from practice, but they didn't room together!

"So, how went the day at Joe's ranch?" Lightfoot inquired.

The man did have a beautiful, flawless smile, a smooth olive complexion, liquid dark eyes, and artfully tousled black curls. Shorter and slimmer than McCoy, he exuded a fruity scent of cologne into the small space. Howdy hesitated to inhale too deeply lest the punter think he enjoyed the aroma and bought him a bottle.

Brian had a reputation for being a generous and spontaneous giver of gifts often accepted rather reluctantly by the straight men on the team.

"Fine," Howdy answered shortly, keeping a good space between them.

"Not so fine, then. I've gotten to know you well, Howard McCoy, after all those days we spent together on the road. Something has you 'riled' as you would say in your charmingly old-fashioned way. I am here to listen, all ears, really."

"You don't know me *that* well!"

"Give me a try." Brian smirked suggestively.

"See, that's why she thinks I'm gay, that right there."

"Ah, a woman of course. I might have known. They can be such bitches. Tell your friend Bri all about it. Was it Joe's wife? I can't imagine Nell bringing up the subject, especially with all those children hanging around."

He wanted to spill to Brian, he really did. The youngest man on the Sinners' team, a replacement for the venerable and legendary Ancient Andy Mortenson, he didn't quite feel like one of the gang yet. The punter, starting a couple of years before him, had settled in as well as any kicker with the rest of the team. A lot of the guys actually thought of these special team players as only one step up from the soccer field just like Cassie. Not Joe. Joe treated everyone equally, though he could show temper if anyone of them failed to deliver during a game.

"Joe and Nell introduced me to this girl, young lady, woman, tall, slim but with a—a…"

"Big rack?"

"Nice bosom and sorta reddish-blonde hair."

"Strawberry blonde."

"I guess. Well, she took a dislike to me before I could say howdy and stomped off to sit under a tree."

"What? She didn't immediately fall for your rustic charm? A suggestion, try practicing 'hello, nice to meet you' instead of saying 'howdy' to everyone. That's how you got your nickname which will stick to you forever unless you stop saying it."

The door opened on Brian's floor. He held the button to keep the elevator from moving. "Stop by my place, and I will give you a few more pointers."

The heat of a blush climbed the column of Howdy's long neck and suffused his face. "She thinks I'm gay because I room with you on the road, so this isn't going to help. Cassie is really homophobic. Kept taking verbal swipes at me all through dinner."

"Tell Uncle Brian how you responded to that."

"I handled it like trash talk. You know when a guy on the other team says, 'I'm coming to get you, Howdy, and break that pretty leg of yours.' I say, 'Try it. The Sinners have the best protectors in the league. You're the one who will end up in the hospital.' Then, I put it behind me and go on about my business."

Brian gave him an arch smile. "So you told this be-otch you would put her in the hospital?"

"No, no! Don't be ridiculous. I paid her some pretty hot compliments like I heard Joe would do back in the day. That shut her down. After I taught her son how to kick, she became downright friendly."

"Nice move. You can always get to a broad through their kid."

"Hey, I like teaching kids kicking, but how would

35

you know about broads, women, I mean?"

"Let's say I'm not exclusive in my tastes. Now stop being silly, come to my place, have some wine, and we'll work this out.

"I don't think so."

The elevator bell dinged, someone else demanding its use on another floor.

"Howdy, did I ever hit on you?"

"No."

"Well, I'm not trying to seduce you now. Come along. That's probably the grande dame on the ninth floor. Any minute now, she's going to call Gregory and say the elevator is out of order. You don't want to enrage her. She already hates having the building and I quote, 'overrun with athletes of questionable moral character.' Don't give her more ammunition to have us tossed out."

Howdy stepped into the small, marble-floored and perfectly maintained foyer. A spindly table held a golden urn filled with two dozen obscenely beautiful cream and pink-edged hothouse roses, each one perfectly formed and in the act of unfolding to reveal its tight inner core like the labia of a naked woman.

"Hey, how come I don't have flowers in my entry?" Howdy questioned.

"I pay extra for them. After a hot, sweaty practice, I like to be welcomed home by a pleasant scent and a beautiful form."

"Okay, I think I can do without the flowers."

Brian unlocked his door and stood aside to let Howdy pass. The kicker took a few long strides into the center of the room, but hesitated to sit on the white microfiber sofa or sully the sheepskin rug under the glass-topped coffee table with his dirty sneakers.

"Sit," Brian ordered. "What do you have in the bag?"

"Leftovers. The thickest steaks you ever did see, baked potatoes, some of Joe's steak sauce and Nell's yogurt topping. Want some?"

"That would call for a nice pinot noir." Brian made a graceful pivot toward the wine rack sitting on the breakfast bar and took down two inverted glasses from an overhead rack. He selected, opened, and poured a bottle with panache. "We'll allow that to breathe while I heat up the steak and potatoes in the microwave. Let's dine here at the bar. Hand over the food."

"Okay." Howdy took a seat atop a red leather and chrome stool while Brian fussed in the kitchen getting out utensils and plates, disrobing the potatoes from their foil wrappings, and popping them into the microwave.

"Talk while I cook," Brian directed.

"So, this girl thinks I'm gay because I have to room with you on the road. Do I look gay to you?"

"Absolutely not! Horrible flannel shirt, nice snug jeans and tight T-shirt, but your outfit really doesn't come together." Brian poured the wine and gestured to Howdy to drink.

He took a big swallow. "Good. The T-shirt is kind of an accident. I shrunk it in the wash."

Brian studied the kicker's hands wrapped around the globe of the wineglass. "When did you last have a manicure?"

"Um, never. 'Keep your nails short and clean, that's all you need to do,' Grandpa said."

"See, so not gay."

"Great! And that's why you never hit on me."

"Howdy, even if you were gay, I wouldn't hit on you. I require a certain level of sophistication that you simply do not have. You are not my type."

"Who is? Don't answer me. I already know. If he swung that way, you'd want Joe Dean Billodeaux. Cassie wants him, too. She preened for him in this pretty blue sweater. I thought maybe she intended that for me, but I figured it out by the end of the day."

"Well, Joe is the man of my dreams, but approaching someone so ragingly hetero usually results in getting beaten. Besides, I would never hook up with anyone on the team. I am tolerated for my elegant and precise punting abilities, but nothing more. Sometimes, I'm lonely. You know Ancient Andy wouldn't stay with me, and he had enough clout to get a private room like Joe. Had it put in his contract."

"Hey, they told me I had no choice. The punter and the kicker room together, no exceptions."

"Newbie. Just the owner wanting to save on housing costs, the economics of the game." The microwave dinged. Brian plated a steak on a pure white ceramic dish and switched it with the steaming potatoes. "I should toss a salad to go with this."

"Not for me. I'll dip some carrots in the yogurt sauce."

"Thanks."

"For not having to make a salad?"

"No, for rooming with me without making a fuss."

"Maybe I should have. Then, I wouldn't have everyone thinking I'm gay."

"Howdy, listen to me. No one thinks you are gay, not even this woman you seem so taken with. She wanted to shake you off, and alas, one sure way to do that is to accuse a straight guy of being homosexual. That kind of guy will either stomp off mad as hell like you, or try to prove he's not by giving her the best sex of her life. Too bad you chose the first."

"I couldn't hardly do anything else with Joe, Nell, and the little ones standing around. Was I supposed to drag her into the barn?"

Brian nuked the second steak. "I don't know. Some women love that kind of macho display. I'd have to meet her to say."

"Not much chance of that. Watch out for the steak sauce. It's got some bite to it."

The punter leered at him. "Oh, I do like it hot and spicy."

Howdy shifted uncomfortably on the barstool. "Bri, don't do that. We're pals, okay? Only pals."

"Yanking your chain, that's all. What can I do to make you feel more comfortable in my presence?"

"How about not getting full body waxes anymore? A man with no hair on his chest or legs, and who knows where else freaks me out."

"Sorry, pal. No can do. It's part of my bodily maintenance routine. Name something else."

"Help get Cassie interested in me and not Joe Dean."

"Now why would you want a woman who treats you like dog crap, Howdy?"

"Well, I figure Nell and Joe thought we'd hit it off like they sort of hand-picked her for me. She's kind of a challenge like a sixty-yard field goal. You know I have trouble meeting nice girls. Nothing bothers me on the field, but when I get face to face with a beautiful woman, I don't do so well."

"I keep telling you the New Orleans bars are full of willing gals. You only have to say you're a Sinners player."

"Trouble is I don't look much like a football player, too lanky. Neither do you. But is that what you do?"

Brian peered over the rim of his wineglass. "Sometimes. As for being slim and shorter than most of the guys, people believe what they want to believe."

"I don't think I want the kind of girl who hangs out in bars looking for football players. Maybe I'd be able to meet someone in church, but that's pretty hard when we play every Sunday."

"Forgot you were raised Baptist. Every time the team hits a bar I keep expecting you to ask for a sarsaparilla."

To make a point, Howdy helped himself to more pinot noir. "'Jesus drank wine and would have appreciated a cold beer in the wilderness,' Grandpa always said. He made some wicked peach brandy on the back porch, too. Grandma didn't approve."

"I suppose she would have said I'm going to hell for my sexual preferences."

"Nope. Granny felt God had enough love to go around for every kind of person he put on this earth and said so often. We only need to ask for forgiveness."

"Good woman."

"Yeah." Howdy tossed back the last of his wine. "She died when I was fourteen. Grandpa and me batched it until I left for college. He's gone now, too. My mom left me on their doorstep when I was three. Never saw her again. Don't know who my daddy was. I know what lonely is, Brian. So are you going to help me? Cassie, she's gorgeous."

Brian twinkled his bright, perfect smile at Howdy. "Now *that* I understand. We need to start with a personal makeover and a game plan."

Chapter Five

"I'd call that a failure, a colossal failure." Nell paced their spacious bedroom, from the French doors to the fireplace where a small blaze provided the only light, and back to the doors again. "Cassie accused that sweet boy of being gay. I overheard."

"My fault. I gave her the idea when I touted Howdy's good points before he showed up. I said he roomed with Brian Lightfoot who is light in the loafers, yeah, bad joke, and never complained. What I meant was McCoy is so good-natured he gets along with everyone. Might have helped if you hadn't referred to him as sweet like you did just now." Hands behind his head on the pillows, Joe stretched out on their king-sized bed watched his wife go back and forth.

"So now it's my fault they didn't get along!" Nell threw up her hands.

Joe patted the mattress. "Hop up here and be a good little psychologist. We don't play the blame game anymore, remember?"

"Sorry, you're right."

The bed, made to fit Joe's six-three, two hundred pound dimensions and not her petite form, presented a challenge. They'd found an antique four-poster and had it artfully expanded to fit modern bedding. It sat high above a thick oriental rug. She kept a wooden stepstool on her side to make access to the raised mattress easier.

Nell often thought a small trampoline would serve even better. At least, sliding down the side to get out presented no problem. She climbed up beside Joe.

"Roll over and let me rub your back. You gave Corazon the whole weekend off. With all the children to take care of and the cooking to do, no wonder you are tense, sugar. Let Daddy Joe make you feel better, sweetheart."

Those quick hands, those magical fingers dug into her shoulders. She sighed. "And you want more babies."

"We can always hire another nanny. Besides, that's not all I want." He put those sculpted lips against her neck and gave her a light nip.

She felt him growing hard against her thighs, the old backrub about to become sex routine—not that she minded. The kids slept, worn out by riding and kicking footballs. Cassie, stowed away in a distant guestroom, wouldn't hear, though it might be good if she did. They still had a vital sex life and a close marriage that left no space for her to come between them.

Joe massaged harder and pushed more urgently against her legs. One of his hands went AWOL in order to unsnap and lower his zipper and showed up again at the same place on her anatomy. Jeans and underwear cast aside, he worked his way under her top and deftly unhooked her bra, an old skill he'd never lost. Nell calculated he'd gotten them both naked in less than thirty seconds, but didn't bother to change positions or pull down the covers. He simply delved between her legs with his erection and filled her with his warm, hard length. One clever hand massaged her breasts, and one long thumb stroked her cleft and held him tight against her as he picked up his rhythm.

Joe would make sure she came before he did. He was generous that way. Women wept when they ran off to Vegas to marry and the news came out in the tabloids. Some of them possibly prayed the marriage would not last. But it had, oh, it had. Married and monogamous, no condoms came between them. Not being able to conceive naturally because of all her chemotherapy treatments and the bone marrow transplant proved to be an unexpected blessing when it came to spontaneous and joyous sex. Together, they raised Joe's son by another woman, the boy Cassie had given them, and twin girls she'd carried thanks to her sister's eggs and in vitro fertilization. If she weren't sterile, they would most likely have brought several more children into the world in the last five years.

Her mind shut down as her pleasure swelled, growing and growing until she tightened and burst free. Joe never ceased moving, simply quickened his pace, building on her orgasm, making it rise again until he brought them both to a stunningly explosive completion. Nell lay there limp, still with her back pressed against his broad, steaming hot chest.

"You know," he whispered in her ear. "If we lived a hundred years ago and were both Catholic, we'd probably have six or seven kids by now because I can't keep my hands off you, sugar."

Nell kept her eyes closed and tried to strengthen her will, but it, too, had gone soft and lax. "We don't live a hundred years ago, and I will never be Catholic. People have small families now."

"Because they can't afford big ones. But we can. Don't you ever wonder about those three frozen babies, how they'd turn out? Would they be boys or girls, have curly hair like mine or straighter like the Abbott family, be tall or tiny?" His breath warmed that vulnerable space between her cheek and collarbone.

"They are embryos, Joe, just embryos, but yes, sometimes I wonder."

"I been reading up again. After five years, most likely not all of them would implant. Maybe we'd only get one more. After having twins that would be real easy on you, *cher* heart."

Nell butted him and his flaccid penis away. She rolled over to face her husband of seven years. "Don't you believe it! I know your mother. She'll get another novena going with your four sisters and the old church ladies involved. She'll pray and pray for all those embryos to implant, and they will. It's like she has a direct hotline to God. Last time, she asked for girls, and we got two of them."

"Come on Nell." Joe stroked her cheek. "I'm the superstitious one, not you. You're all about science. The odds aren't good three will make it. They didn't last time."

"My fault because I got between Cassie and the man trying to molest her, and he slammed me against a pillar. Don't remind me!"

"I never blamed you, Tink. Stuff happens. We don't really know why." Joe stroked her short, sleek hair like he would a nervous kitten held in the palm of his hand.

Nell sniffed and squeezed her eyes shut trying to hold back the tears. "You know how crazy I get on the hormones. Last time, I nearly went nuts when the doctor put me to bed for the last six weeks of the pregnancy. I got so jealous of Norma Jean Scruggs I stowed away in her motor home to catch you two in the act and ended up having my babies in the bathroom after she wrecked that bus. I'm not good at carrying children."

"Sure you are. I couldn't do it any better." That made her laugh. He suspected a tee-tiny crack in her resistance. "I do recall how crazy for sex you were last time, and I couldn't do anything about it because I had to save up my sperm to inseminate Emily's eggs. This time we could have all the sex we want beforehand. Of course, there's that long dry spell afterwards while the embryos settle in." He sighed so plaintively Nell chuckled again. "But we all got to make sacrifices for this to work."

"I haven't agreed," she reminded him.

He went for a quick changeup so rapid the opposition would never see it coming. Rolling onto his back, he tucked Nell against his side. "I saw what you meant today about Cassie having a crush on me."

Nell shoved herself half way up and planted her hands on his sweaty chest. She stared into those deep chocolate brown Billodeaux eyes reflecting little licks of flame from the fireplace opposite the bed. "This is more than a crush. She means to destroy our marriage and take you and the kids away from me."

"Ain't gonna happen, Tink, but having her here is making you tense. I say we go away for a while, just the two of us. We'll go to Phoenix, and you start taking those drugs to make the implantation work."

"Joe!" She slapped one solid pec and doubted if he felt the blow at all. It took a three-hundred pound lineman to get his attention.

"Hear me out. Then, we travel to the Grand Canyon and stay at that old lodge at Bright Angel. We hike, watch sunsets, drink mojitos, relax. We don't come back until the procedure is done, and Cassie has to face the fact we are having more children made from our love for each other. Let's send her that message, Nell. Let's do it."

"What about the children we already have?"

"You know Corazon and Knox Polk will take good care of them. Cassie can be here every weekend and not get on your nerves. And I just might ask Howdy to stay here and help out with the ranch while I'm gone. He grew up on one and knows the ropes. He and Cassie could keep the horses exercised."

"Cassie will see right through that."

"So, she can stay away if she wants. What do you say, my tiny Tink?"

She burrowed her face into his chest hair. "Joe, what if I lose all three babies?"

"I thought you were afraid to have three? But it don't make no never mind to me. I suspect we got a big, strong angel watching over us."

"Yeah, bribed by your mother. Fine, let's do it."

Chapter Six

His discomfort growing by the minute, Howard McCoy sat sweating under a plastic salon cape. He clutched a cup of strong espresso in a cup so small it made his hands seem huge and clumsy. Playing in the background, show tunes from *Mamma Mia!* brought back ABBA and disco from oblivion. More than one person in the various booths, both hairdressers and clients, sang along to *Dancing Queen.* Brian Lightfoot hummed the tune from his self-assigned seat on a café chair to Howdy's left rear.

"Could you shut up?" Howdy growled, showing his nerves.

"But it's such a great song from a fantastic movie starring Colin Firth as a gay man who might have fathered a daughter. What's not to love?" Brian sang the chorus aloud.

Joaquin, the stylist assigned to the kicker at the unisex salon, sank his thin, artistic fingers deep into Howdy's scalp and began massaging conditioner into the roots of his damp hair. "Such lovely thick hair ju got. Ju never go bald," he raved in his heavy Latino accent. "An' my favorite color, ches-nut. Ches-nut. Not auburn, doan you think, Brian? Auburn got more red."

"Yes," Brian replied. "I think you nailed it." Howdy squirmed in the barber chair and slopped some of the coffee on his bib.

"Ju must sit still now. Finish drinking, and we begin to cut." Joaquin peeled off the transparent gloves he'd used to apply the treatment and flung them into a tall, red waste can, an accent piece in the mostly black and silver décor. He lifted a few locks of hair and considered his next move. "What ju think, Brian?"

Howdy swallowed the coffee in one gulp. He prayed he wouldn't need to use the restroom in this place, though not everyone here was gay. Perfectly at ease women filled some of the booths, but all the stylists and even the shampoo boys, especially the shampoo boys, swished when they walked. He didn't think he'd be able to go if they only had urinals on the wall and not private stalls, the least of his worries right now. What did Joaquin and Brian have planned for him—maybe little spikes and red highlights, God forbid!

"Ah, can't we just put some goop in it and comb it straight back if you want it out of my eyes?" he suggested, trying to escape anything worse.

"No, that is so last year and does not suit ju. Your fabulous look is All American Boy, no, Brian?

"Nailed it again, Joaquin." Brian kept saying "nailed" to irk him, Howdy knew it. "How about a razor thin semi-part low on the right, then an angled sweep across the brow ending with the hint of a curl on the left?"

"That would work. I must do some thinning first, then blend in the back and sides. We begin. Ju doan wince. Be a good boy, and I give you a lollipop."

Howdy wrinkled his face again. He couldn't think of anything to be sucked or licked that didn't bring an obscene picture to his mind. He drew on his considerable powers of concentration to stay still and get through the ordeal. In the end, he had to admit he looked pretty sharp and smelled pleasantly of the scented powder whisked over his bare neck with a feather-light brush.

"Thanks. You did a good job," he told Joaquin who appeared offended.

"No, I did a great job! I save ju from looking like a hick, a hayseed, a…"

"Fantastic work, Joaquin. I am sure Howdy will be a regular customer from now on," Brian said as he moved his pal from the booth to the register, picking up the scribbled tab in the process. "Here you go. I got you a special rate for newcomers." He handed over the bill.

"Three-hundred dollars for a haircut!"

"Joaquin usually charges more. And he worked you in as a favor to me. Don't forget to add the tip. He'll expect twenty percent. Some goes to the shampoo boy."

"A sixty dollar tip? You think Joe Dean pays this much to have his hair cut?"

"Oh, honey chile, I know he does, but he uses a different salon."

"Next time, can I go there?"

"Up to you, but Joaquin did stunning work." Brian gave an eloquent shrug implying he'd be a fool to change hairdressers.

"So are you and Joaquin—involved?"

"No, he's far too flaming for me. Nor do I care for longshoremen or the hairy backsides of linebackers. Think Will as in *Will and Grace*, the old TV show, someone sophisticated and stylish who can cook a nice meal. I haven't found that man yet—or perhaps a woman with the same qualities. But, could I be true to her? I'd have to ask myself."

"Never watched that show."

"I imagine it would be banned in the McCoy household, but very, very funny if you like gay jokes."

"What next?"

"Shopping, dear boy. Shopping!"

"Must I? I have plenty of clothes."

"Howard, you signed for over a million dollars in the draft, yet you still dress like a college kid, all grungy and unkempt."

"Well, I do my own laundry and sometimes I forget."

"You forget you can afford to send your laundry out. Gregory will arrange it for you. Once we buy nicer clothes, you must take better care of them."

"Okay, what kind of clothes? Mostly, I wear jeans when we're off. I already got a nice suit. My college coach at Oklahoma State made us dress up with a tie and everything when we traveled. The Sinners aren't nearly so picky."

"They should be, but Coach Buck doesn't care as long as you can play football. Wear diamond earrings the size of plum pits in both lobes, so tasteless, he won't blink an eye."

"No earrings, no piercings of any kind!"

"Of course not. It wouldn't fit the image we are building for this Cassie. Maybe a tattoo, though."

"No!"

"Howdy, you are so easy to tease."

Brian steered him into a plush department store on Canal Street and directly to menswear. "First, we need to upgrade your underwear. Bet you five you still wear tighty-whities. You wouldn't want to strip for Cassie and have her find out the hard way."

"Nothing wrong with a plain pair of men's briefs. My Grandpa wore them."

"Exactly." Brian stopped in front of a display that proclaimed *Imagine your Man in These on Valentine's Day*. He eyed a selection of boxers patterned with red hearts and lipstick kisses, then shot out a quick hand that came up dangling a red silk men's thong.

Howdy couldn't contain his blush, but he said coolly enough, "Now I know you're kidding me again. I'd be dead and buried before I wore that."

Mischief twinkling in his big, dark eyes, Brian said, "Even if Cassie gave this to you for Valentine's Day and asked you to pose for her?"

In the mirror behind the display, Howdy watched his blush deepening. "Sure, I'd put it on for *her* once. Next day, I'd make sure my dog ate it."

"You don't have a dog."

"Be worth buying one to get rid of that thing. Put it down and be serious."

"Very well. Let's make it black boxer briefs then. What size?"

"Ah, I'm not sure." His flush about matched the Valentine hearts on the boxers now.

"There, I wasn't even trying that time. They go by waist size. Who bought your underwear for you?"

"Grandpa. He stocked me up with briefs, undershirts, and tube socks before I left for training camp."

"Howdy, Howdy, Howdy. Undershirts, really? Although V-neck or sleeveless can be sexy. Since you prefer chest hair on a man, a little fluff showing out of a

V-neck might be appealing to some women."

"I don't prefer chest hair. It's just the other way seems mighty unnatural, all that waxing and shaving. 'If God meant a man to have a bald chest, he would have made us that way,' Grandpa said. My undershirts are all crewneck and have sleeves. Think we should get some V-necks?"

"Definitely, if you must wear them at all. Moving along to jeans."

"I got a new pair before I went to visit Joe. Don't need any more."

"Sure you do. Though I must say I did like the ones you had on last weekend."

"I…"

Brian held up a hand. "Don't tell me. Let me guess. You shrunk them in the wash."

"That is true, but I was going to say I noticed Cassie checking out my ass."

"Ass, you do surprise me, Howdy. We'll get a few more pairs of those then, some in black, and wash them in hot water. What designer?"

"Levi's button fly jeans."

"No designer then, but button flies can be very erotic. It's the slow reveal rather than the quick unzip. Fantastic if your lover does it for you." Brian fanned his face with a hand. "I'm nearly as flushed as you at the thought."

They found the folded piles of jeans and loaded Howdy's arms with them. Brian added a stack of crisp shirts in shades of gray and green. His hand hovered over a display of spring pinks and lavenders.

"No!" Howdy said.

"Got you again. Pastels really aren't for you. I on

the other hand look stunning in pink. Look over there. I cannot believe they have blue chambray shirts. That's so cowboy chic. We'll need a dozen of those. I might get some for myself." Brian cleaned out the all the pale blue shirts in Howdy's size and added a couple in his own to their heap.

"Are we finished here?"

"A jacket. You need a good casual jacket even if you won't wear it much after the weather gets hot in April. Something that shouts HOWDY McCOY in capital letters. Leather! Definitely leather, but not black leather. That's more Joe Dean's style."

"Isn't my team jacket good enough?"

"It's redundant. This Cassie knows you kick for the Sinners. Now if you did troll the bars for women, it would work. But, you don't. I got it—buckskin, like Robert Redford in *Midnight Cowboy.*"

"Why does that movie keep coming up? Never seen it, don't want to."

"The main character goes to New York to become a stud, to service rich women. You want Cassie to notice how studly you are, right?"

"I want her to like me."

"Okay, same thing, sort of."

"Did Redford's jacket have fringe?"

"Oh, yes."

"No fringe."

"Don't be difficult. I can see you now at Joe's ranch wearing that cowboy hat and boots you wore your first day at camp and your new duds. Whatever became of the hat, the boots? You should definitely wear the white hat and pointy boots."

Howdy stared at the mound of clothes he held.

"People in New Orleans gawked at me and laughed when I passed by so I shelved them. In Oklahoma, they were normal. I was normal. And my hat is gray and my boots aren't that pointy. Besides, I thought you told me not to wear a hat."

"Just for today so as not to offend Joaquin by covering his work. Get the cowboy hat and boots out of storage, but no more grubby green John Deere caps or stinking sneakers. Maybe a black Sinners cap if you must." Brian made a viewfinder with his fingers. "I see it all now. You with one foot up on a fence rail, staring at cows…or buffalo. Cassie comes up behind you. You turn and say…"

"Howdy, ma'am?"

"Yes, you would. Might work if she likes lingo."

"I'm not so sure she does. I think her ex was a bull rider. Hard to compete with that."

"Come on, you're a Sinner. Act like one."

"I'll try."

"Good. Get out your credit card and pay for our haul, then it's on to leather goods." Brian checked his stainless steel Rolex watch. "We have exactly enough time if we don't dawdle. We mustn't be late for our appointment with Guido, my tailor. A half-dozen custom-made suits should complete your wardrobe. Or maybe you still need some chinos and Italian loafers."

"No loafers."

"Joe wears them."

"Remember, I don't want to be Joe. I want to be HOWARD McCOY in capital letters."

"Right. Gotcha. Oxfords and new athletic shoes, it is."

Chapter Seven

Nell, hopped up on the hormones and drugs needed
to convince her sterile body to build a nice cushy
placenta for the embryos, hugged and kissed each one
of her existing children ferociously. Tears dribbled
down her cheeks.

"Come on Tink, we'll only be gone a month.
They're old enough to know we'll be back. They can
call us anytime. Right, guys?" Joe addressed both his
sons and his daughters all lined up on the lower
verandah to say good-bye.

MawMaw Nadine pried Nell's fingers from
Annie's shoulders. "You doing the right thing, *cher.*
When your mama comes home, she's gonna bring some
babies with her," she informed her grandchildren.

"Bring girls," Jude demanded.

"Boys!" Dean countered. Those two always went
at it.

"Maybe she brings some of bot'," Nadine said.
"Only God knows what you gonna get."

"Don't be disappointed if I don't bring any at all,"
Nell cautioned.

"Then can we have a puppy instead?" Tommy
asked as he had often since failing to get one for
Christmas.

"Go on now. We got the schedule all worked out.
Your folks will alternate weeks with us, and Cassie is

taking the weekends. Knox and Corazon aren't even gonna take their days off while you're gone." Nadine gestured to the ranch manager and housekeeper standing nearby. "We all set. Shoo!" She waved her hands toward the waiting airport limo.

Nadine followed them to the open door of the vehicle holding their already stowed baggage and leaned over Nell as she slid into the backseat. "This is good for you to get away and make babies. I seen that girl making eyes at Joe like she did at Bijou. She's trouble, always been trouble." Nadine cast a backwards glance at Cassie who stood directly behind Tommy with her hands resting on the little boy's shoulders.

"I know Bijou is your nephew, Nadine, but he is also a dirty old man who took advantage of the naïve teenage girl by convincing her she could have a big career as a barrel-racer if only she'd run away with him. If he'd had his way, Tommy wouldn't exist. Then, he tried to kidnap his own son to squeeze money out of Joe, so don't be blaming Cassie—even if you are right about her in some ways." Nell looked past Nadine, Cassie, and the line of children to where Howdy McCoy rounded the side of the house and stood quietly behind the group.

Joe whispered, "There is the answer to our problem." He aimed a big wink at the young man, but Cassie intercepted it and returned the same.

"Let's get out of here before I deck her," Nell said, teeth gritted.

"That's the spirit! We be praying for you, all Joe's sisters, Miss Lolly and Miss Maxine. We are powerful prayers, I tell you me."

"Thanks, Nadine," Nell answered with a tad of

ungratefulness in her voice.

Her mother-in-law slammed the limo door, and Nell and Joe were off to Phoenix to take their babies out of the freezer. Corazon and Nadine herded the children inside for an early lunch. Knox Polk, who still retained a stiff posture that revealed him as ex-military, headed back to the barn. Howdy stayed where he was as the members of the group began to go their way.

Shucks, Brian had provided coaching on how to strike a casual but arresting pose with one boot placed on a fence rail the next time he encountered Cassie, but here he stood with nothing but a fat, white column to brace himself. He slouched back against it and raised one knee so his boot heel rested on the pillar. Made him feel like some kind of hokey male model, and he guessed that's what Brian intended. He did catch Cassie's eye immediately as she turned to follow her son.

She went right for his soft, exposed parts like a fox taking a rooster for its dinner. "What are you doing here?" The chill in her voice could have frostbitten his nose.

"Ice, baby. Stay cool," he thought. "Helping out just like you, ma'am." He tipped the worn, gray Stetson his grandfather had given him years ago and Brian made him practice tipping only yesterday. "I got in last night. They put me up in the cabin next to Corazon and Knox so I can assist with the ranch while Joe is gone."

"Knox never needed any help in the past." Suspicion tinged her statement.

"Well, ma'am, the Charolais cows are dropping their calves this month. Sometimes that keeps Knox up all night. If that happens, I'll see to the stock during the day so he can get some rest."

"I wouldn't call seven horses and a small herd of beef cattle 'the stock'."

"We call it that in Oklahoma where I come from, and they do need care every single day, ma'am." Howdy tipped his hat again and hoped he wasn't overdoing it.

"Would you stop with the ma'am! I told you to call me Cassie."

"I don't feel we're that friendly, ma'am." He resisted the urge to tip his hat again.

She stepped closer as if she wanted to kick away the boot that rested on the pillar and send him sprawling, but she stopped a foot away. Still with those long legs clad in skinny jeans, she could probably do it from there if she wanted.

Instead, she stared at him hard. "You look different."

"New haircut. Now it doesn't get into my eyes." Pretty sure he hadn't worn it long enough to have hat head he removed the cowboy hat to show her.

"That's an improvement," she granted. "Nice jacket. New?"

"Yep."

"I'm surprised it doesn't have fringe considering your orientation."

"Told you before, I'm straight as they come. What I can't figure is why you don't like me."

"Maybe it's your freckles. I can't stand freckles on a man."

Tarnation! He knew he should have gotten some goop to cover them up even if he only had a few across the bridge of his nose. He noticed Tommy standing behind his young mother, heartbreak all over his face. The boy had come up on them while they were engrossed in each other.

"I got freckles," the kid said. "Lots more than Mr. Howdy."

Cassie spun around and immediately stooped down to hug her child. "No, Tommy. I didn't mean you. It's cinnamon freckles I don't like. You have orange, my favorite color."

"The nuns at school say people shouldn't be hated because of the color of their skin. Mama Nell says so, too."

"They are right, absolutely right. Maybe Mr. Howdy's freckles aren't so bad, and I really love yours."

McCoy took the opportunity to tip his hat at her again. "Thank you, ma'am. Somehow, I suspect you might have hidden freckles of your own, and I do like the orange ones, too."

"She does!" Tommy answered for his mother. "But she puts stuff on them to make them disappear because she's a girl. But we're men, and we don't wear makeup. Right, Mr. Howdy?"

"Right," he answered, so glad he hadn't gotten that goop after all. He offered Tommy a high five enthusiastically accepted.

"Corazon says lunch is ready. Are you two coming? You can sit next to me, Mr. Howdy, and maybe after you can help me with my kicking."

"Sure," he said, carefully sliding his boot down the pillar in order not to go pitching forward. His calf muscle had gone to sleep, and he limped after mother and child.

Cassie tossed a venomous glance over her shoulder. "Don't you have stock to see about in the barn?"

"I will after we eat. Maybe Tommy can help me muck out those stalls so we can get down to kicking practice earlier. That was the rule at my grandpa's ranch."

Tommy held out the hand not being gripped by his mother. Howdy took it, and like a happy family, they went into have lunch.

Chapter Eight

"I'm sorry," Joe said.

Nell moved her eyes from the view of falling snow that covered the entire Grand Canyon like an opaque white bed sheet hung out to dry. Nothing could be seen beyond it. They had a rim cabin possessing a funky sort of fake adobe charm at Bright Angel Lodge. Plain furnishings, a double bed, small private bath, and a television made up the amenities. The wood in the fireplace popped merrily making the room cozy and bright if by no means as luxurious as the bedroom they shared at home. Their vast Jacuzzi overhung with a crystal chandelier back at Lorena Ranch would have overflowed the space allotted for bathing here.

Nell smiled slightly at the thought. She and Joe had broken up while he built his pseudo-ante-bellum mansion at the ranch, and his often questionable taste in furnishings had come into play in the bathroom. Really, what woman wanted a thousand watts of light illuminating her when she lay naked in the tub? And he'd put in another bidet, never used, but a great spot to raise African violets. Oh, Joe, how she did love him, bad taste and all.

"There, I saw that smile! This place isn't so bad. I mean not nearly as nice as our suite at the Sheraton in Phoenix, but kinda cute, huh? I didn't know about the weather. It's like spring in the south of Arizona and here we got snow. Who would have thunk it?" He poked at the logs in the fireplace and sent sparks spiraling up the chimney.

"It does get cold at this elevation. I guess we should have expected some snow."

"Some! We can't see a damned thing out that window. We could get lost and fall right off the rim on our way to the lodge for dinner. Don't think they have room service for the cabins."

"Most likely not. Really, I don't care." Nell sighed and returned to watching snow fall.

"Since we're snowed in, how about some sex— anyway you want it? A few more days, and we'll have to hold off until we're sure the babies are settled. We can watch the Super Bowl tomorrow and have a drunken orgy. Last call for alcohol before you get pregnant."

"That's your idea of fun, not mine. Besides, I doubt alcohol is such a good idea with all the drugs in my system right now."

"So. No sex?" He gave her that pitiful puppy dog look he could pull off so well with his large, dark eyes.

"I didn't say that. It's just I thought we'd be taking pictures of the canyon and e-mailing them to the children, not sitting around in a whiteout."

Joe stopped aggravating the fire and moved closer to his wife to attempt stirring up another kind of spark. He wrapped one big arm around her and drew her to the bed. The mattress wasn't the best but after a while, they wouldn't notice.

"Ah, ah, ah! My choice." Nell pulled him to the fireplace and gestured to the probably faux Navajo rug in front of the hearth. "Take off your clothes and lie down."

Joe did a mini-striptease for her, taking one button at a time, inching his zipper down. She reciprocated by slowly raising her top and slinging it aside, then shimmying out of her own jeans so her breasts in a low-cut, pretty pink bra jiggled in the process. She stood there in lacy matching panties and pushed him down using one palm. Not that she could have done it without his cooperation since he outweighed her by a hundred pounds, but when it came to sex, Joe always cooperated. He'd already erupted from the black briefs that stretched across his pelvic bones. She knelt between his knees and took them off.

"I bet I know what comes next," he said eagerly.

"And you would be wrong. Switch places with me."

He did. "Okay, old school then."

"Nope. Down there, between my knees. I want some tongue."

Joe had a tongue almost as talented as his throwing arm, but he didn't rush to the spot. He disposed of her panties and teased his way there, starting at the navel and working down until he arrived at the swollen nub already anticipating a good licking. He did his best, making Nell purr until she came with an unexpected upheaval that almost split his lip.

With one hand grasping the short, black curls on his head, she said, "Sorry. I guess I need to make that up to you."

"I won't last long, sugar. Why don't you mount up?"

They reversed positions again. Nell rode astride. Her breasts weren't big, but they still had a nice bounce to them when he unhooked that little pink bra. He watched their rhythm as his orgasm built, then shut his eyes and let go with a gasp. Nell collapsed on his chest. Joe rubbed her back.

"Reminds me of the first time we made love. You got right up on top and stayed there." He'd long learned to replace the word "fucked" with "made love". It worked so much better with women. The two of them lay there, lazy and half-asleep until a sunbeam penetrated the window and a passing tourist heading for the lodge shielded her son's face from the sight.

"Hey, the sun is out. Guess we should have closed the curtains, but I mean who knew when the blizzard would end." Joe put on his briefs and went to the window. "Tink, you gotta see this, *cher.*"

Nell got completely dressed before standing up and going to his side. The Grand Canyon capped in snow spread out before them. Small, bristly pines growing in crevices lent the scene a Christmas card look with their white branches. The late afternoon sun bought out bands of pink, gold and purple in the rocks, and every cranny glistened with snowflakes. A college girl passed on the footpath and eyed Joe's muscular body up and down. Nell ripped the curtains shut, trading one nice view for another.

"Joe, we need to take pictures for the kids. Get dressed right now—all the way dressed."

They bundled up and went out into the frigid air, slipped and slid to the best overlook in their athletic shoes, and took a bunch of pictures to put on their laptop in the evening when they had a Skype session planned with their family. After that, a raid of the souvenir shop for trinkets for the kids. Nell picked out

Zuni fetishes appropriate for each child, a black bear for Dean, a red fox for Tommy, and two cute but not quite identical jet ravens with red berries in their beaks for their twin girls.

Joe sorted through stacks of T-shirts hoping to find one that said "We Did It at the Grand Canyon" without any luck. He asked the middle-aged sales clerk who said the National Park Service did not stock things like that and to try one of the shops outside the park, maybe one of the biker places. Given such a casual response, he suspected she'd been asked the question many times. He and Nell mushed to the rustic lodge for hot chocolate to drink before the vast fireplace and stayed on for dinner.

On the way back to their cabin, they took more digital photos of the moon over the snowy, glowing canyon and loaded them all immediately into their laptop to send home. Allowed to stay up late because of the time difference, the children, all talking at once, crowded the computer screen when they connected for a Skype visit.

"Snow, you have snow to play in, and we gotta stay home and go to school. Not fair," Dean complained.

"Did you get those babies yet? What kind are they?" Jude asked.

"Not yet, honey. And we won't know for a while what kind they are," Nell answered.

"Why not?" Annie questioned in her quiet but always perceptive way.

"We'll discuss that when your dad and I get home. How about you, Tommy? What are you doing?"

"Getting better at kicking. Wait until you see,

Dad!"

"Can't wait, son. Be home in two more weeks."

A pair of competent hands lifted one of the twins aside. Must have been Annie since Jude would have protested loudly. Nadine's strong face filled the screen. "We finished up our novena las' night, so you all set with God and Mother Mary. You go get my grandbabies outta the freezer and bring them on home, you hear."

"We're all set up for Tuesday, Mama."

"Off to bed, children," Nell prompted. "Nighty-night."

A chorus of nighty-nights echoed back. As the children departed for bed, they could see Cassie lurking behind them. She slipped in front of the screen for a moment. She looked fresh and young, perfectly made up, and beautifully clothed in a draped turquoise blouse.

"Joe, what great pictures. I've never been to the Grand Canyon. It would be a wonderful place to spend a honeymoon, don't you think?"

Nell elbowed her husband aside and took over. "Yes, we sort of had a second honeymoon in front of the fireplace while the snow came down this afternoon." She delighted in seeing Cassie blush from so far away. "Now we're going nighty-night, too. Sleep tight, Cassie."

Nell disconnected and looked at Joe. "Between that conniving little bitch and your mother, I think I *will* get drunk at the Super Bowl party tomorrow."

Joe grinned at her, one of those wicked grins that melted the bones of so many women. "Aw, you don't mean that, sugar. It's just the hormones talking."

****

She did mean it. Didn't take much to get Nell drunk, she was such a little thing. Three glasses of champagne, and she grew tiddly. Two more after their favored team won left her with a hell of a headache in the morning. She had little memory of the orgy that followed. Joe, having more or less sworn off champagne after winning his first Super Bowl and conceiving Dean with the repugnant Margaret Stutes, stuck to beer and did enjoy the festivities. The aftermath, not so much.

As he steered the rented car from the snowy verge of the canyon toward Phoenix, Nell sat beside him with her eyes covered by oversized sunglasses purchased when they stopped for gas. Periodically, she rubbed a cool, damp bottle of water across her forehead. "No music," she'd begged, unless he put on something classical or maybe easy listening. Anything else made her head throb. So, they rode along in silence, utter silence, as they passed from the uplands to the red rock region and on to the desert saguaro cactus forest outside of Phoenix. Nell slept a good part of the way, and he took care not to wake her.

Bored, Joe got out his cell phone and thumbed out a message while throwing quick glances at his sleeping wife. She did not approve of texting while driving, but he always figured his superior coordination let him get away with it. One arm relaxed on the steering wheel, he texted Howdy.

How R U and Cassie getting along?

An answer returned promptly: Better.

Good news. In what way?

Tommy likes me, so she does. Showed me her barrel-racing. She's good.

Yes. Take her riding.

Have done. All the kids went with us.

Without kids!

Nell stirred and raised her sunglasses. Gotta go. Joe disconnected in a hurry and shoved the phone into a slot.

"Were you texting while driving? And you want more children. I could end up a widow with seven babies to rear."

He started to say he'd just kill them both in the accident, then she wouldn't have to worry about it. The old Joe might have said something like that. Instead he sucked it up like trash talk from an opponent. The hormones and drugs she took to implant those embryos always made her bitchy, not to mention the current hangover. He ignored her show of temper.

"Say, that pie place we stopped at last time is coming up. Remember, you wouldn't admit the first implants took, that you were pregnant, and you kept blaming bad tamales for your upset stomach when all along you had morning sickness."

"I do recall."

"Want to stop there again? Last chance for some hot chili before it gives you heartburn again."

Nell swallowed. "I think I'll pass this time. Let's get to the hotel, order some soup, and have a nice quiet evening together."

"Wish I could make you feel better, sugar." His large hand crept across the space dividing them. It moved under her stretchy red top and deftly unhooked her bra. His fingertips, lightly calloused from gripping footballs, found her nipple, gently tweaked and massaged. He waited for her to swat him away, but Nell simply closed her eyes again and sighed.

"You still know all the moves, Joe Dean Billodeaux."

"A man has to practice his skills to stay in the game, sugar." He expected her to snap at him about calling her that as she did when she got tetchy.

"Well, it takes my mind off my headache."

So, petting while driving—okay, but texting, no way. Entirely fine by him. If Nell felt well enough for this, the evening seemed promising. Not only the last chance for spicy Mexican or Cajun food, but for sex for some weeks to come. He wanted them to make the most of it, and they would.

Chapter Nine

The thing Nell hated most about whole implantation process was how people treated her afterward. She and Joe stayed in Phoenix for two weeks after the procedure to make sure all went well—in other words, no miscarriages since she'd lost one before by being careless. Joe grabbed her elbow at the least chance of a stumble as they toured museums and took in concerts and plays. He refused to clamber around ancient Native American ruins, citing the possibility of falls, rattlesnake bites, or crumbling adobe bricks conking her on the head. Forbidden to swim in the golf club pool while Joe played a few rounds, she basked in the sun like a desert tortoise full of eggs to be expelled and buried in the sand. No horseback riding, absolutely not, nor overland Jeep trips.

Sadistically, she made her husband sit in a high-end maternity wear shop while she tried on a panoply of clothes from tight little tops that would show off her baby bump to the tent-like dresses she knew she would need if all three babies stayed in place. Joe smiled like a happy idiot and told her to buy them all while the saleswomen fluttered around offering him coffee or bottled water or a more comfortable chair than the little-lady-seat his large frame overwhelmed. In the dressing room, her glorified shopping assistant went on and on about what a handsome, strong and understanding man she'd married.

"Don't forget rich and famous," Nell added with a growl.

The hormones made her emotional and insecure. All the old feelings of inadequacy she'd experienced when first married to the legendary womanizer, Joe Dean Billodeaux, surfaced again. What if she lost all these babies? What if Joe strayed while she grew big as a harvest moon and got confined to bed for the last weeks of the pregnancy? She took it out on the clerk, sending the thin, nervous woman scrambling for other sizes, other colors, and endless accessories. In the end, Nell apologized for her rudeness, but the salesperson merely said pregnant women tended to be high-strung. She understood entirely, undoubtedly soothed by a huge commission and Joe's compliments on the clerk's good taste. By the end of their stay in Phoenix, their luggage increased by three bags, Joe cheerfully paid the extra fee for them all.

She simply did not like being pushed and told what not to do as if she were a child herself. Joe said that just made her human like everyone else, but as a psychologist she ought to do better. Why did he have to be so damned understanding? She knew before she took the test she'd gotten pregnant again and burst into tears when the results confirmed the fact. Joe beamed and cuddled her to his great chest where she did feel safe and very well loved.

Home again the children soothed her, crammed up against her, boys on one side, girls on the other, while Nadine and Cassie got on her nerves. Her mother-in-law gave her a tour of their freezer stacked to the top with bland, nourishing foods Cajun style: gumbo dumbed down to tourist spiciness, venison stew with no garlic, smothered pork cutlets made with the mildest of onions, all contributed by Joe's sisters and Nadine, as if Corazon couldn't cook for them. Nell figured the supply would last the entire pregnancy.

"Now Joe, he can add his own hot sauce to all this," Nadine said. "You the one we takin' care of, *cher* heart." How could Nell retaliate against the well-meaning?

As for Cassie, her blue eyes filled with tears, saying, "I guess you don't need me to stay here anymore—but I'd be willing to come every weekend to help out regardless." That, Nell could answer with a small smile. "Thanks, Cassie, we'll be fine. Go out and enjoy yourself. You are too young to be tied down yet."

"I guess I'll just go say good-bye to Copperhead, then," the girl said, referring to the barrel horse Joe kept for her to ride.

Joe had gone to check on the animals while Nell got the gourmet tour of the freezer contents. "No!" Nell said urgently, but Cassie went out the door as if she were deaf in one ear.

Nadine patted her daughter-in-law's shoulder. "Don't you worry about her. Howdy is out there putting down some straw. Won't nothing happen." Sometimes Nadine for all her pushiness could be very understanding.

"Sure. Who wants presents?" Nell said to her flock of children, but her eyes followed Cassie's progress from the open kitchen door toward Joe in the barn.

***

Cassie entered the dimness of the barn and glanced around for the ever-present Howdy. That guy seemed to be everywhere when she helped out with the children on the weekends. He took the kids trail riding, inviting her along. And how could she refuse when Tommy begged her to come? The kicker coaxed her into a barrel-racing demonstration, doling out lots of compliments on her fine seat and sharp edges as she ran the cloverleaf course on Copperhead. As if she would ever fall for that line again after her experience with Bijou.

Then, she'd found him in Joe's weight room one morning since her son insisted they find the man and ask when the next kicking lesson would be. He wore nothing but a pair of red gym shorts as he executed leg presses and extensions on one of the machines. Sweat flattened the light covering of reddish-brown hair covering his pecs and arrowing toward his groin. She imagined when newly showered and dry it would feel fluffy to the fingertips and smell of the body wash she'd come to associate with him—a grassy scent like a new-mown meadow.

His legs were objects of beauty, the shapely calves, the strong thighs, bunching for two counts and pushing back their full length for two more. He'd have stamina, lots of stamina in those quads. Unlike most football players, he had no bulk, but owned arms with long, smooth muscles and a chest and belly of flat planes most men would envy if they didn't play for the Sinners.

She stayed back while Tommy charged ahead and got right in the man's face. "Whatcha doing?"

"Strengthening my legs. I do this routine every other day and practice kicking in between."

"Should I be doing that?"

"Not on machines, not at your age, but you can do squats on your own."

He stood up, clear of the apparatus, to show Tommy a squat. They did a few together. Howdy didn't appear to be trying to impress her as he stretched out his arms, folded his knees, and rose fluidly up and down, but he did.

"Whoa now, pardner. Easy does it. You don't want to rush the exercises. Usually I do these with weights. You can use a couple of soup cans if you want, but I'd just rely on your leg muscles until you build up some."

Whoa, pardner? Had he been raised by Roy Rogers and Dale Evans? She snorted at his quaintness.

"You getting a cold, Mama Cassie?" Tommy asked.

"No. Maybe a fever." Had he actually flushed when she said that? "Look, let the man exercise. Stop bothering him."

"He's no trouble, ma'am. I always wanted a little brother. Let me shower, then we do can some kicking."

Cassie knew Joe's shower off the weight room. She used it sometimes after working out on the treadmill to strengthen her legs for riding. His soap had a stronger, more exotic and less innocent scent than whatever Howdy used. The shower stall itself could fit two and had multiple nozzles easily aimed at sore spots or elsewhere. The things she'd done with Joe's soap and a strong stream of water while imaging herself with the quarterback made her color a little now. Howdy presented her with that stupid grin of his, probably believing she thought of sharing the bath with him. No chance of that. The man was so squeaky clean already he probably didn't even beat off like normal guys.

"We'll see you later." She got the hell out of there.

Her eyes adjusted to the low light filtering through the barn. No sign of Howdy, but Joe stood by the large box stall at the end feeding carrots to his stud quarter horse, Lazy Boy.

"Glad to see me, big fellow?" he asked the huge red animal with the flashy blaze and four white socks. Lazy Boy never stopped chomping the carrots to give even a nicker of appreciation as Joe scratched the horse between the ears. What she would give to have Joe's hands on her, right here, right now. She'd been holding in her feelings so long.

"I'm glad to see you, Joe." Cassie advanced toward him in what she hoped was a slow and sexy gait.

"Always good to see you, too, Cassie. Thanks for helping out with my brood while Nell and me were away. You know she's expecting again. I think all three babies took, but we won't know for sure for a while."

"I realize how you felt about using all the embryos since I'm Catholic, too." She placed a tentative hand on his bicep.

Joe took a step back and let his eyes wander anywhere but on her. "Howdy sure did a great job of keeping this barn clean. You can't even smell the manure."

"Knox Polk helped him and me and all the kids. He didn't do it single-handedly."

"Well, he didn't have to do it at all. He has his own ranch inherited from his grandfather in Oklahoma to take care of and stayed here as a favor to me."

"So now he can go there. Joe, you know Nell didn't want to get pregnant again."

"She did it for me."

"Reluctantly. I'm used to big families. I want one of my own."

She moved closer again. The tension in the air upset Lazy Boy who tossed his big head up and down, sending his unshorn chestnut mane and forelock flying. Usually docile if headstrong, still the stallion could be unpredictable, especially around mares in heat. Only Joe rode him, and he hadn't gotten much exercise while his master made babies in Arizona. Howdy had - permission to take the animal out, but he'd said "no" to riding a valuable stud and instead displaced a resentful Dean on Drummer Boy and relegated the boy back to a pony. The cowboy kicker hadn't made any friends there. Why did Howdy have come to mind now, now when she finally had a chance alone with Joe—no Nell, no kids, no Nadine?

"Joe, you must know how I feel about you. I'd lie in the hay with you right now if you wanted. I haven't been with any other man since Bijou. You are all I want, a strong man who loves children and would never fail me."

Joe, as nervous as his favorite mount, shook his head and made that problematic black curl he so despised drift across his forehead. Cassie moved her hand to bush it back into place, but he shied before she touched him. She swore his nostrils flared and his eyes widened like a wild mustang cornered in a box canyon.

"Cassie, you're a great girl, but I'm married to Nell. We got three more babies on the way. Would you really want a man who cheated on his pregnant wife, who failed *her*? I said my vows with Nell, twice, both in and out of the Church. When a Billodeaux says his vows, that's it. I'm done foolin' around."

"But I'm younger than Nell. I'm prettier and better built and just as smart."

"Not in my eyes. Look, I think you need to go back to grad school and stay there for a while until you cool off. You can call Tommy and Skype with him, but I don't want you around here upsetting Nell. The babies are due in October. Let's say we'll see you again for Thanksgiving."

"But that's ten months away!"

"Sounds about right to me. Stay away from me until you leave."

He was gone, turning on a dime, out the far end of the barn, escaping from the pocket to run free. Lazy Boy snapped at her, something he'd never done in all the time she'd spent at Lorena Ranch. Cassie drew back and let her tears come. She heard a creaking of the hayloft ladder, the thud of a body jumping the last few rungs, and tried to stop her shoulders from heaving. There Howdy stood, the last person on earth she wanted to see right now.

"Ouch. That must have hurt," he said, not grinning now.

"You eavesdropped!" she accused, using anger to quell her anguish.

"I couldn't hardly help it. This is an old barn even if Joe refurbished it, and the cracks between the boards are fairly wide. I went up to the loft to throw down some hay for Lazy Boy. I guess I was standing right above you when you made a fool of yourself. Everybody but you knows Nell and Joe are forever. Why, the team gets that and steers the groupies away from him because he doesn't want to be bothered."

"I bet even the groupies don't want you," she

lashed out, determined to wound someone else.

He smiled, not a grin, but small and rueful. "A few have come my way, but they aren't the kind of woman I want. A gal who has been with a lot of men, not my type."

Cassie raised her chin and pulled back her shoulders to show off her chest. "You think I'm attractive, don't you?"

"Sure. Beautiful, actually."

"Okay, then. Right here, right now, up in the loft. Show me how much you want me."

"No. Thank you, ma'am."

"What! You moon around me for a month, and now it's 'no thanks'. I can't believe I've been turned down by a kicker! You are gay, aren't you?"

Temper replaced humiliation in her voice. She kicked at the barn floor and sent a cloud of chaff swirling into his face. Howdy didn't flinch, didn't move one muscle. He stood his ground and met her infuriated blue eyes.

"Nope. You know I'm not. If you'd made me that offer last week, I guess I would have taken you up on it, but I don't want to be Joe Dean Billodeaux's temporary replacement."

"Oh, God! No one wants me." Her hands covered her face. She rocked back and forth as she cried like those sad, motherless little monkeys they studied in her psych classes. She knew how pathetic she must look, but she felt much worse.

Howdy approached her carefully, shyly. "If you need a shoulder to cry on though, I'm here for you." He opened his arms, and she entered their shelter. His good, blue chambray shirt grew wet with her tears, soaked clear through to his v-necked undershirt, but he didn't let her go. He kept patting her back and rocking her gently.

"There, there, Cassie. Everything will be fine and dandy soon. You'll see. I'm leaving here, too, going back to my place in New Orleans. I'll miss seeing you every day even if Joe doesn't. Anytime you want to talk, you call me," he said so slowly, so gently, his words barely registered over her sobs.

Finally, she pulled herself together and stepped back. He let his arms fall, making no attempt to keep her. "Thank you. Sorry I made a mess of your shirt."

He glanced down at the pale blue chambray, not only drenched with tears but smeared with eye makeup and a splotch of peach lipstick. "Don't matter. Grandpa always said men had flat chests just so they could hold women closer when they needed comfort. Besides, Brian made me buy a whole bunch of these before I came here. Cowboy chic he called it."

A smile wobbled across her lips, swollen from being bitten to stop the trembling. "I think I would have liked your grandpa."

"Most people did."

"I might even like Brian Lightfoot if I knew him."

"Sure, if you love gay guys. We can set something up if you get lonely. He *is* good company."

"Maybe. I should pack and say good-bye to Tommy, try to explain I won't be around for a long time, and that it isn't his fault."

"Right. You should do that. I need to get my things together, too. Say, wait a minute." Howdy delved into the hip pocket of those snug jeans and took out a piece of folded paper so soft around edges it looked as if he'd been carrying it around quite a while, maybe as long as a month. "Here's my phone number. Use it whenever you want to talk."

Cassie accepted his offering. A day ago, she would have thrown it away, but now she put it in her own back pocket. "Thanks, I might do that. See you around, Howdy."

Hoping her despair didn't show, she sashayed out of the barn and into exile from Joe Dean Billodeaux.

****

Extremely agitated, Brian Lightfoot paced before Howdy like a sleek, black leopard seeking escape from a trap. "I cannot believe it! After all my hard work, you made a friend of a woman you had the hots for."

"What do you mean?" Howdy had an imported beer in hand and his booted feet hooked around the rungs of Brian's chrome barstool.

"You told her to call if she wanted to talk. You offered to introduce her to your gay friend. That's what girls do with their gal pals, not a guy they intend to take to bed."

"She offered to do that—in the hay, I mean. I turned her down. You can't take advantage of a woman when she's that broken up over another man."

"Men can and do. But not you. You are hopeless."

Howdy set the beer down carefully on the coaster provided. "Sorry I disappointed you. Guess I'll go to my own place now. Just thought you'd want to hear what happened at the ranch."

"Don't go away angry. Yes, I can tell you are. You simply stuff it down inside like some kind of John Wayne hero. Not good. You should vent once in a while. Maybe we can salvage this. Let me think."

Brian took a sip of his sparkling water. Hydrating today and avoiding alcohol, he claimed, for the sake of his skin and internal organs. "I have it. You call this Cassie. You invite her to meet *moi*." He patted his own chest.

"An evening of fine dining and good wine ensues. Later, jazz in a moody bar, more liquor. I see someone I fancy and slip away. You tell her sincerely—and I know you can do sincere—how beautiful she is, how Joe Dean doesn't know what he threw away, how you wish you had taken up her offer in the barn, but sensitive guy that you are, didn't want to take advantage of her at a low moment. Never fear, I won't coming knocking on your apartment door later that evening because you will be involved, deeply involved." Brian finished with a flourish of manicured fingernails coated with a clear varnish.

Howdy raised the beer to his lips and mumbled around the neck. "Only one problem. I don't have her number."

"Say what?"

"She didn't give me her number."

"Well." Brian poised his hands on his muscular hips. "Given the circumstances, I think Joe Dean will share that information with you. He's been trying to set you up with Cassie for months. If not, there's always the internet."

"I think she only has a cell and maybe stays with her parents when she's not bugging Joe and Nell. Besides, she's not over Joe. I should give her time."

"Strike now, I tell you, while she's feeling down and wants revenge on he who scorned her."

"That wouldn't be right. I'll wait and hope she'll

82

come to me. Yeah, that's what I'll do."

****

To Brian's astonishment, Howdy's patience paid off. Cassie did call to cry on his shoulder about her exile from Lorena Ranch.

"There, there, there," he said softly because when you wanted to train a filly to trust you, you spoke quietly and made no sudden moves. Brian might know about fast women and party boys, but his experience didn't run to taming a woman for the long run. Brian found his escorts wild and left them that way.

Howdy suggested they all go out to a place of Brian's choice, get a good meal and take in a little jazz afterward one Saturday night. Even when Brian left them alone in a dark club with a sultry singer on the bandstand, he made no moves. He might not be the best dresser or adept at flirting, but he had a plan now and would stick with it until she was ready to be mounted. When she gave him the right signs, he'd know, but would still go slow, nice and easy, because that's what Cassie needed after being abused by a man like Bijou.

Chapter Ten

Tommy sat apart from the crowd of Billodeauxs celebrating Good Friday with a crawfish boil at MawMaw Nadine's house. The holiday came late this year, falling at the end of April and delaying Easter a good long time. Joe tried to keep an eye on his adopted son, his twin daughters, and Dean, who had gone off with some of the older boys into the cane fields to hunt for toads and snakes. Hell, with Nell lying down in his sisters' old bedroom because the smell of beer and crawfish made her nauseous, he needed eyes in the back of his head to watch them all. If he'd allowed Cassie to attend, that would have been a help, but he couldn't permit anymore incidents with her, not with Nell in a delicate condition and a pretty bad mood.

He had invited Howdy, but the boy had other plans. Too bad since Tommy could have shown off his kicking skills to the other kids instead of brooding over there on the edge of the deep drainage ditch by the side of the road where the winner of the live crawfish race had been freed moments ago. Wasn't Tom's crawfish. Dean's choice, a huge mossy-backed creature with pinchers nearly big as a lobster, backed from the circle first. While his uncles paid off their small bets, the rest of the crustaceans, tossed back into a sack, prepared to meet their fate around dinnertime in a tall, aluminum pot boiling over a gas flame.

He'd told his red-haired son, "You can't win them all. Get over it," but sensed something else bothered the boy. Probably some idiot had pointed out his red hair or mentioned about Tommy being adopted. The kid was sensitive about that even though Joe said over and over he had to get tough and ignore trash talk. Nell would have scolded the ignorant sonnabitches, gone for their throats in fact, but she couldn't handle a fight right now.

Tommy knew all about where he came from because Nell always told the truth when asked. As soon as the boy could understand, she'd explained the terms "birth mother" and "adopted child". Mama Cassie carried Tommy in her belly, but although she loved him very much, she was too young to give him a good home. So, Daddy and Mama had chosen him as their wonderful adopted son. Being a psychologist, Nell excelled at stuff like this.

His "birth father" was a Billodeaux, a cousin of his dad's who looked sort of like Joe. Tommy understood about cousins, the children of your aunts and uncles. His cousin, Randi, about the same age as Tom, had dark bobbing curls, but everyone remembered she'd been bald as a baby. Randi hated being reminded of that, just as he couldn't stand having his red hair and freckles pointed out by strangers, so everyone had something they didn't like about themselves. At least, he did have the same dark chocolate brown eyes as the rest of them, inherited from his birth dad who lived in Mexico and could not come to see him because he had done some bad things—to put it mildly. Nell glossed over that, never giving any details, simply saying the man had to live in exile which meant he could never come home again, even to see his "natural" son. But not to worry. Tommy was his own person and would not have the same problems.

They had a special family, she explained, with Daddy Joe being Dean's real father but Mama Nell being his adoptive mother since Dean's birth mother had died. She'd grown his twin sisters in her own belly, but they came from people eggs donated by his Aunt Emily who also lived in exile, but voluntarily. That meant she could come home if she wanted, but didn't.

"Is that why you call Jude and Annie your "little chicks" all the time? Did it hurt to have eggs shoved into your belly?" the boy asked, making Joe laugh.

Nell kept a straight face. "No, Tommy. I am growing our new babies the same way but they won't come out for a long time yet." She let the child feel her baby bump. He'd found all this knowledge fascinating enough to try and share it at first grade Show-and-Tell, but Sr. Ursula told him to sit down immediately. Later, she called Nell about Tom's sharing precocious knowledge. Joe stayed out of it, especially when Nell started talking about the repression of Catholicism with the nun. He'd convinced her to send Dean and Tom to parochial school, the same he'd attended, mostly to please his mother, but no way would he get between her and a Sister.

Okay, his little girls played hopscotch in the driveway on a grid drawn in chalk by older female cousins. They weren't very good at it yet, but their tiny feet fit easily in all the boxes so they seldom crossed a line. Lots of the Billodeaux teenage cousins did some babysitting, and they cheered the tykes on encouragingly. Joe wished Tom had gone into the cane fields with Dean and the others boys so he had only the two to watch.

The kids knew enough to avoid cottonmouths. They'd look for the little hog-nosed snakes, totally harmless reptiles the kids called puff adders. He'd had one as a child, but Nell didn't care for snakes and made the boys release any they caught. She said they were too young for a puppy, too, when he'd wanted to get a dog for the family last Christmas. He would not press the issue this year either, not with three new babies in the house. Tommy kicked so hard at the side of the ditch that dirt gave way and plopped into the muddy water filling its depths. He need to learn to get over his mad by himself, Joe figured, and let him alone.

His sister Lizzie's husband pressed an icy beer from the cooler into his hand, and a ring of men formed around him encouraging him to tell one of his Super Bowl stories. He finished his brew in one long swallow and used the bottle to illustrate the play. Cocking back his famous throwing arm, he launched the bottle deep into the cane field. The remaining amber drops glittered from the neck as it began its descent. His daughters squealed and left their game. Encouraged by their uncles, they raced down a cane row to see how far the glass missile had gone and if it busted on landing. Joe went to the edge of the field and told them to stay in plain sight, not to get lost in there. They were a problem that way, always climbing trees too high up because they were tiny and light or going into the tall cane and then not being able to see their way out and having to be rescued. The cane was still spring short, so he really didn't have to fuss at them this time.

He seldom worried about the boys that way. If

Tom or Dean climbed too high, why they'd just jump down and risk a broken leg because they were boys. Boys didn't cry for help in a cane field. They always found their way home eventually. They manned up, got tough, did what had to be done like their father on the gridiron. Boys—so much easier to raise.

Chapter Eleven

While all eyes—even those of the aunts and babies sitting in the shade—watched the sailing beer bottle, Tommy jumped the ditch and headed out along the narrow dirt edge beside the hardtop road. He got as far as a bend that hid him from the gathering when a double cab, silver pickup truck with a year's worth of mud caked on its sides glided up and crossed to his side of the road. The driver rolled down a window and leaned out. A purple LSU cap pulled low shaded his face. Several big rings on the man's fingers flashed in the sun.

"Hey, kid, you know how to get to the Joe Dean Billodeaux place?"

Cautiously, Tommy moved across a culvert the tractors used as a bridge in order to get farther away from the truck. Someone had told him about kidnappers and other bad people who stole children. Probably Nell or the nuns said never to talk to strangers, and the kid wasn't dumb. He could make a dash into the field if he needed to escape and stayed far enough away that he felt safe enough to answer politely.

"It's down the road but says Lorena Ranch, not Billodeaux, on the gate."

"Yeah, I tried to get in there, but the place is locked up." The driver smiled, exposing a gold tooth.

"Everyone is at the crawfish boil. It's Good

Friday," Tommy said, which explained the situation entirely to anyone from around Chapelle, Louisiana. He continued to stay out of reach.

The man in the LSU cap slapped his forehead. "So it is. How could I forget? I been down in Mexico too long. Here I come to visit my son and bring him a little gift, but no one's home. You know a kid named Thomas Cassidy Billodeaux? I think he has cool red hair and freckles like his pretty mother."

"That's me!" Tommy squinted, trying to see the man better. The stranger had Billodeaux eyes—dark, dark brown, surrounded by short curly lashes. When he tipped his LSU cap back to show his face better, a strand of dark, greasy hair showing some gray fell forward over his brow. Tommy moved closer.

"Then, you're my son. I come all the way from Mexico to bring you this."

He held up a squirming yellow puppy with over-sized white paws by the loose scruff of its neck. A pink tongue flicked out from its black muzzle as the pup tried to lick the man's face. A funny tail curled over the tiny dog's backside and waggled back and forth. "It's a boy dog, the only kind a man should own. See, it has *cojones* like the spicks say, balls, that is."

Tommy stepped to the cab of the pickup and held up his arms. The man known to the law by his alias of Bijou dropped the dog into his outstretched hands, and the animal laved its pink tongue against Tommy's cheek.

"Look, son. I got to move out of the road or someone will come along and hit my truck. Hop on in, and we'll drive down to Lorena Ranch, okay?"

Keeping a careful eye out for traffic, Tommy

moved around the front of the truck, but on Good Friday, the roads were empty. Everyone spent the day with family, not out in the fields. Bijou stretched out a hand to pull him up into the high cab, and Tommy settled in on a seat that smelled like puppy pee and cigarette smoke. His feet didn't quite reach the floorboard covered with fast food wrappers, empty beer cans, and brown bottles. They went exactly where his natural father said they would go—to Lorena Ranch—and parked in front of the locked gates.

"Daddy Joe has a clicker to open them. So does Mama, Corazon and Mr. Polk, but I know a place where we can get in," Tommy volunteered. "If you don't mind going through some thorns and climbing a fence."

"Kid, in Mexico, we got cactus with thorns so big they could put your eyes out. A puny hedge of Cherokee roses and a fence ain't gonna stop me. Show me your place. Just leave the pup in the truck."

"No, you must never leave a pet in a hot car. That's what they say on TV. I'm practicing to be a good dog owner so Mama Nell will let me have one."

Tommy slid out of the truck and brought his gift with him. He moved along the fencing until he came to a spot where the natural deterrent of wild white roses thinned a little. The fence stood higher than most and the wrought iron pales had been placed close together so no one could slip through them, not even skinny little girls, but the puppy fit and popped out on the other side easily. Even though he could do it himself, the man, not as tall as his dad, lifted him up to the first crossbar. Tommy mounted the second from there and swung over the pointed pales to the other side with no trouble at all. Using long legs with not half of Joe's muscle clad in worn blue jeans, Bijou followed his son over the fence and cursed when the spikes on top poked him in the ass. That made Tommy laugh.

Bijou shook a finger at him. "You better learn some respect for your old man."

"Sorry, didn't mean to laugh. It's just we aren't supposed to swear, but sometimes Dean and me do it anyhow. Then, Mama Nell asks where we heard those words, but we never tell."

"Good, I like a boy who can keep a secret. Let's go enjoy some of Joe Dean's hospitality."

They made their way through the oak grove to the mansion sitting above the bayou. The puppy gamboled along at their feet. "Close your eyes," Tommy requested when they got to the house.

"What for?"

"I have to get the key. We aren't allowed to show where it is."

"Sure, I'll just turn my back. My, my, this place has grown since the last time I visited. You got that high fence and a swimming pool, all those little cottages among the trees."

"Yep, the fence is for our protection, the pool is for fun, and the cottages are where sick kids stay with their families when we have summer camp for them." Tommy carefully removed the shell from an ornamental turtle sitting deep among the azalea bushes. He took the key from the hollow inside and replaced the top. "You can turn around now. Mama Nell hides a key so we can always get in if we're playing outside and it rains or something."

"Good idea. That Nell is a smart woman. Always

could put two and two together. That a camera over the door?"

"Yeah, for safety, Mr. Polk says."

"*Buenos dias,* Joe Dean." Bijou grinned showing his gold tooth again and waved at the lens. "Still got the dental work you paid for." He tapped the cap with a grimy fingernail.

Tommy struggled with the key. Bijou took it, turned the lock, and threw the door wide open in his eagerness to enter his Cousin Joe's domain.

"We got to shut off the security real quick." He punched in four numbers on the key pad.

"What might those numbers be, son?"

"Can't tell you, but it's the year my other dad won his first Super Bowl. Would you like a cold drink?" Tommy asked courteously. The kid, his kid, had nice manners.

"I would, but first, I'd like to see your room. Bet it's real nice."

"Sure. It's upstairs. It's decorated with horses. I love horses—and dogs." He whistled, a new accomplishment learned from Mr. Howdy, to the pup and led the way up a sweeping staircase grand enough for Scarlett O'Hara to ascend in Rhett Butler's arms.

"If you love horses, I got plenty you could ride. Why, I train racehorses. I could make a jockey out of you. You'd like that, wouldn't you? No pissant ponies anymore, but long-legged thoroughbreds."

Tommy considered the offer. "That would be great! My room is over here next to Dean's bedroom. He got football players on his walls."

"Yes, I remember. Last time I stood in this room, you were sleeping in a crib. How about that? The fat

Mexican maid tried to stop me from seeing you."

"Corazon? She's real nice and not that fat." Tommy's forehead wrinkled as if turbulent thoughts galloped across his mind like the multicolored horses in the wall frieze. "My mom said you did bad things and had to go live in Mexico, that you couldn't come back here ever."

"Cassie bad-mouthing me? She wanted what she done as bad as I did." Bijou stretched out in the oversized, tan leather chair and put his dirty boots up on the matching hassock.

Tommy frowned. "That's our story reading place. You shouldn't get mud on it. We have to take our boots off in the house. Mama Nell told me you did bad things. Mama Cassie never talks about you."

Bijou ignored him. His eyes found the pictures of Cassie, a double frame of her in a graduation cap and gown from college and another of her with Copperhead. "Grown up to be a real nice piece of ass, my sassy Cassie. Not that she wasn't prime before, but a little too skinny back then. I have a new woman now, all curves and pretty black eyes. You know, you have a Mexican half-sister down across the border. I'd sure like you to meet her. Want to go on a vacation with me? Your spring break is coming up. Hard to believe I went to the same parochial school as you."

"You know a lot about me."

"Your grandparents drop me a line now and again."

"Which ones? I have four sets."

"Hal and Flo Billodeaux who live up by Toledo Bend Lake. Your real mom and me hid out there once when we were on the run."

"Running from what?" Tommy asked, eyes wide.

He squirmed like the puppy at his feet.

"Oh, we were in love, but your mama was kinda young. Joe Dean and the cops tried to stop us from being together like Romeo and Juliet. You know who they were?"

"No, sir."

"Sir, I like that. Doesn't matter. Seems a man can be put in jail for loving too young a girl. Now that ain't right as I see it. I can't go near your real mama anymore, but things are different in Mexico. Soon as they're ripe, they fall from the tree and anyone can pick them up. So, you ready for an adventure? Got a bag we can pack?"

Tommy nodded. "In the closet—but I have to ask permission from my parents before I go anywhere."

Bijou got up and folded back the doors of a large closet. He whistled, and the pup yapped. "Must be nice to have a rich step-daddy. What you got here, like ten pairs of shoes? Cowboy boots, flip-flops, sandals, church shoes, a pile of sneakers. Xochi would love to have all this. Xochi, that's my daughter."

He found a red Sinners duffel bag on a shelf and threw in the boots, flip-flops, sandals and a pair of sneakers, then removed several pairs of jeans neatly folded over hangers. "No need for school uniforms since we'll be on vacation. Where do you keep your T-shirts?"

"In the dresser. Xochi, that's a funny name. I understand how she would be my half-sister, but Daddy Joe is my adoptive father, not my stepfather."

"Yeah, Joe Dean always did take away what was mine. My job, my girl, my glory. I was a championship bull rider once. They tell you that?" He stuffed shirts from the dresser drawers into the duffle and topped off the load with underwear and socks. "Go get your toothbrush and a comb, and we'll be all ready to go. Jesus H. Christ, a six-year-old with his own bathroom."

Tommy retrieved the items and watched his natural daddy shove them into the bag. "I need to ask permission," he repeated.

"No, you don't. Just write a note saying where you are going."

"I can't do cursive yet."

"Then print it out. What's this, you got a laptop already? Forget it. I'll do it." Bijou sat at the small desk and brought the computer to life. He tapped out, "I am going to visit my real dad in Mexico. Tommy," while repeating the words.

"Say 'Love, Tommy'. Mama Nell tells us we should always write 'love' at the end of thank you notes to our grandparents. She makes us write them by hand."

"Yeah, classy broad. But in this case, we'll just print this one out. I think we should get going soon. Almost dinnertime. We'll catch a burger on the way and get one for your new puppy, too."

Tommy placed the note spit from the printer carefully on his pillow and followed his real dad into the hall. They didn't go directly downstairs. Instead, Bijou poked into his parents' room and sorted through a small jewelry box.

"Nothing much worth takin'," he said in disgust. He palmed a pair of small gold hoop earrings channeled with diamond chips into the breast pocket of his western shirt, but couldn't resist jamming a silver ring set with a garnet onto his pinkie though it wouldn't go over his second joint. "Freakin' little pixie, your second mom."

"She doesn't like to be called a pixie or a fairy or anything like that. The good stuff is in the safe, anyhow. That's where Dad keeps his third Super Bowl ring," Tommy offered.

"No time for safe cracking now."

Bijou poked into the girls' pink, frilly bedroom, and threw some shiny Sunday shoes, fancy flip-flops with flowers on the bands, and neon-bright orange sneakers into the sack. He stripped several pretty dresses, some hand-smocked, some ruffled, some floral-printed, from their hangers and folded them on top. "Your sisters won't mind giving some of their stuff to a poor Mexican girl, will they?"

"Mama says we have so much we should always share."

"I figured that. She won't miss anything we're taking. Let's vamoose."

They moved out so fast the puppy couldn't keep up, and Bijou grabbed it by the scruff and shoved it under the arm not holding the duffle over his shoulder. The pup yelped, and Tommy scrunched his face in concern.

"I'll carry him. We need to set the alarm before we go."

"You go on with the dog. I'll take care of the alarm."

Tommy cuddled the puppy and moved out. Bijou shut the door but didn't bother to reset the alarm. He posed before the security camera and shot the bird at Joe Dean with one bejeweled finger instead. "We're on our way to Mexico, big shot."

Chapter Twelve

Nell sat at the picnic table with a twin on either side. "Joe, where are the boys?"

"Gone into the fields to look for snakes and toads."

PawPaw Frank dumped a heap of deep red crawfish onto the newspaper covering the table and said, "I'll give dem a holler, me," and ambled off on long legs like Joe's to make good on his promise.

Jude shot out a hand to seize a big mudbug, but her mother held her back. "They're still steaming, honey. Let them cool down a bit. Besides, we should wait until everyone is seated."

The gang of boys summoned by a shout emerged from the cane field. Triumphantly, Dean held up an old pillowcase with something large bumping inside. "Caught a pretty king snake, Mom. Want to see it?"

"No! Go inside and wash the toad and snake slime off your hands before you eat."

"I keep telling you snakes aren't slimy, just toads, and they aren't so much except for their poison glands."

"Yuck," Annie said. "Don't let him bring it home."

"It's not poisonous. It eats other snakes and would be good to have around the barn."

"Then we should keep it," Jude declared and snagged a boiled crawfish, deftly twisting off the tail.

"I said to wait," her mother repeated.

Jude made a face. "We're all here except Tommy,

and I'm hungry."

"Dean, where is your brother? You didn't lose him out there on purpose, did you?"

"Don't know where he is. He didn't go snake hunting with us. I invited him," the boy said defensively, implying, "Play one little trick on your brother and you are suspected forever." He trotted off to wash his hands.

Across the table his cousin Randi with her black curls drawn to the sides of her head into two pigtails tattled, "Tommy was over by the ditch *boudering* because someone made fun of his red hair and freckles again."

Nell's usually wide brown eyes narrowed. "Who?"

"No one I know," Randi said and started in on her own pile of mudbugs. "I saw Tommy walking home alone. That's not allowed, is it? He's gonna be in big, big trouble."

"Joe!" Nell called.

Joe had acquired a tray of boiled corn on the cob and small red potatoes to feed his brood. He set the tray down in his best waiter style. "I live to serve you, Madame." His girls giggled. Their mother did not.

"Tommy got angry and walked home alone. I've told him time and again he must learn to deal with looking different from the rest of the family. He's supposed to say he's our special adopted child and let it go."

"I've told him to ignore trash talk, too, but he's young yet. It got worse when he started first grade. New kids who don't know him see he doesn't resemble Dean. They can be cruel."

"I will speak with Sister Ursula about this, but Joe,

you have to go after him and bring him back here right now. He can't be allowed to go into a sulk and worry us."

"I'm on my way."

A pair of firm hands pushed him down on the picnic bench. "No, you don't. Let my boy sit and enjoy his meal. I'll send one of my grandsons to fetch Tommy. A couple of them can drive now," MawMaw Nadine intervened.

"Thanks, Ma, but if Tommy set the alarm system and they try to get in, we'll end up with the police coming out to check. Easier if I go."

Dean returned, took an ear of corn and sank his front teeth into it. When he opened his mouth, both remained stuck in the cob. A trickle of blood sauced the corn. "Hey, I lost my two front teef. They were loose anyhow. Do I get a dollar now? No, two dollars, huh?"

Nell tore a corner from a roll of paper towels in the can on the table and dipped it into her glass of ice water. "Here, hold this against your gums to stop the bleeding. What next? That's all I can say is, 'What next?' How can I cope with three more on the way?" She burst into tears and reeled off more paper towels to blot her eyes.

"Now, now, *cher* heart. That's just them babies makin' you nervous. You feed them some crawfish, and they'll settle down." Strong as a stranglehold, Nadine squeezed her daughter-in-law's shoulder.

"If only it were that simple. Joe?"

"I'm going. Save some crawfish for us."

He loped toward the new red van he'd purchased in anticipation of a larger family. It sat twelve passengers. Nell said the change in vehicles came too soon. She hadn't had her first ultrasound yet. Yes, she acknowledged she was pregnant, and judging by the bulge with more than one, but why the rush? Why not wait and see? So much could happen between now and October. He brushed her protests aside. He'd been to church on the sly and lit a hundred candles to draw attention to his prayers that all his babies would survive. He had no doubt they would. But first to retrieve Tommy and give him a good talking to about scaring his mother when she had bad baby nerves already.

He drove to the gates of Lorena Ranch lickety-split and used the remote on the dash to open them. Before he had children, before Bijou had tried to kidnap the infant Tommy for money, he'd been much more casual about security, but Knox Polk had urged him to take more care. The gates still being locked meant nothing. Small boys could and did slip in and out of the - compound. He never came down hard on Dean and Tommy about that because he wanted them to have the same sort of childhood he'd experienced before football took over his life—the freedom to rove the countryside in search of harmless snakes and bugs to terrify their sisters, to fish in the bayou anywhere along its length, to pop into the homes of relatives for a cold drink and a visit before heading home, beating darkness and a possible punishment by minutes. His sons knew the rules. Never get into a car with a stranger. Call and tell their mother where they'd ended up.

The first bad vibe came when he found the front door open, the alarm unset. If anything, Tommy was more conscientious than Dean about such matters. Joe called out his son's name and heard it echo through the vastness of the large house. No answer. He turned on his heels and checked the barn, a favorite sulking place as the animals always offered a sympathetic nuzzle, especially if offered a treat. No sign of a red-haired boy inside or up in the loft. Joe shouted outside using the same voice he drew upon when he called an audible and the other team's fans tried to drown out his commands and cause confusion while the play clock ran down. No answer.

He returned to the house and took the steps upstairs two at a time. Maybe the kid had been worn out and come home to take a nap away from the noisy crowd of Billodeauxs gathered to eat crawfish on Good Friday. He knew the feeling of wanting to get away from his relatives sometimes. They could be overwhelming. Good thing Nell had proved to be tough enough to stand up to his four sisters and especially his mother, one of the many reasons he loved his wife.

No Tommy asleep in the bed, but the laptop on the desk burst into life when he jostled the chair. Strange it was turned on. Joe saw the note, a white piece of paper propped on the pillow sham depicting a palomino horse's head, neck curved, ears pricked, wild, white mane flying. A short, clear message and all wrong to his way of thinking. He pulled out his cell phone and poked in a number.

"Knox, sorry to disturb you when you're with your people, but we have a problem. Seems Tommy has run away from home. He got into snit over someone making fun of his red hair and freckles and took off." Joe roved the room as he talked to his ranch manager and security officer. "Yeah, lots of his clothes are gone and that Sinners duffel he uses for sleepovers and camping. Seems like way more than a small boy would take along or could carry. Yes, he left a note, but I don't like the looks of it."

"How so?" asked the man on the other end of the conversation.

"Well, he says he is going to find his real dad, and he spelled Mexico right. You think a six-year-old could do that?"

"Spell check? All the kids use it."

"Maybe, but all the kids would use I M instead of typing out 'am', too."

"Good point. I'll be there in fifteen minutes. We'll check the security tapes, but I wouldn't worry too much. A boy his age toting a big duffle won't get far. We'll probably find him hot and tired and sorry sitting under a tree. How long you think he's been gone?"

"No more than an hour, probably less."

"Notify the sheriff's office. They might find him before I get back to the ranch."

"Say, don't tell Corazon yet. No sense in upsetting her or Nell right away."

"She's helping my nieces decorate Easter eggs. I'll tell her some stock got out and we have to round 'em up."

"Thanks. As quickly as you can, okay?"

"Roger that."

Joe placed the call to the cops who assured him good-naturedly they'd probably have the boy back in no time. After all, how many red-haired, freckled kids did a Cajun town like Chapelle have or even the whole area of Ste. Jeanne d'Arc parish? The boy would stick out like the proverbial sore thumb.

Joe paced the bedroom. He had that same prickling

feeling he got when a tackle came from behind to sack him during a game and took him down with a heavy thud. No sense wasting time. He knew inevitably that Bijou had come back. He placed another call to Toledo Bend and got an answer in two rings.

"Joe Dean, what a nice Good Friday surprise. Just a second, let me get my gardening gloves off. You know how I believe in planting on holy days. If you want your uncle, he's out on the lake."

He imagined his elderly aunt with a big floppy gardening hat covering her tightly-permed blue-gray curls, the knees of her stretch pants dirty, her large breasts covered with a flowered muumuu top. Hal had given her one of those phones she could program to identify the caller for an anniversary gift. Despite playing for the Sinners, he knew she'd chosen *When the Saints go Marchin' In* for his I.D. For Tommy, she'd picked the theme from the rock opera by the same name. Despite his own anxiety, he did not want to alarm her. No better people on earth than Flo and Hal. How they had produced a rotten apple like Bijou, no one knew. All their other kids turned out fine. No reason to pass time with pleasantries.

"No, Aunt Flo. You can tell me what I need to know. Where is Bijou hiding out these days?"

His aunt hesitated. "Why do you need to know? You promised you wouldn't send him to jail if he stayed in Mexico."

Certain his aunt stayed in touch with her worthless son, Joe guessed Bijou's ring tone might be *Chain Gang*. "Tommy is missing."

"Oh, no! Bijou can't be involved. He's settled down on a ranch south of Nuevo Laredo and has a beautiful Mexican wife and a pretty little daughter the same age as your girls. He trains racehorses, you know. He's reformed, Joe."

"Sounds like you stay in touch. He ever talk about Tommy?" He kept his voice calm and casual like he did when the Sinners were down two touchdowns, no big deal. They could catch up. He did not want to scare or hurt her anymore than Bijou already had, but could he catch up with Bijou if he'd taken the boy?

Again, that hesitation in her voice. "At first, he didn't show much interest in his son. You know lots of men don't care about babies, not the way you do, doting on them and all. But lately he asked me how Tommy was doing. He said Pilar couldn't have more children, and Tommy would be his only son. He asked for a picture so I sent him one of the school photos from this year. Was that so bad? A man should be able to recognize his own son."

"Sure, Aunt Flo. Look, I need the name and location of that ranch in Mexico just in case."

"In case what?"

"In case I need to go there to get my son."

Flo heaved a sigh into the phone so heavy he knew it came laden with tears like a raincloud about to burst. "I'll get that information for you. Don't hurt my boy, Joe."

"I'll try to restrain myself. I promise not to kill him."

He listened patiently as his aunt made her way inside, measuring her progress by the slam of a screen door, the tap of her athletic shoes crossing the hardwood floor to the kitchen. He took a piece of paper from the computer printer and wrote out what she told him, where she'd sent the school picture.

"Thanks, Aunt Flo. I hope this turns out well for all of us. Happy Easter."

"And to you and your family. Tell Nell and Nadine, I pray every day for those little frozen babies to survive."

"I will. Bye."

Joe heard Knox Polk arrive driving the big-engined farm truck. He raced to join him in the surveillance room designed to look like all the other cottages on the ranch but smaller and always locked. As efficiently as he'd carried out military missions, Knox already had the images of the last hour up on the screens. The ranch manager's disconcerting green eyes set in the mahogany-colored skin of his face scanned the progress of the break-in while Joe watched over his shoulder. Here the culprits came: dog, boy, and man crossing the fence, approaching the house, no attempt to hide his face, flaunting that gold tooth, giving Joe the finger. Damn fuckin' Bijou!

Chapter Thirteen

Ignoring the whining of both the pup and the boy, Bijou didn't stop for food until they crossed the Texas border two hours after leaving the vicinity of Chapelle. He should have resisted the temptation to stick it to Joe Dean and snuck in and out of Lorena Ranch. That would have given him more time to escape, but he figured they didn't have his license plates, carefully obscured by mud, just another Cajun off-roading to celebrate the holiday. He felt safer in Texas. Hell, the Great State had thousands of big-ass double cab trucks on the road even if his cousin did recognize this one as the same stolen from him six years ago along with Cassie.

As darkness fell, he used a drive-up window at a restaurant just off the interstate to get a burger and fries and a cheap toy for the boy, a cheeseburger for the dog, and a quarter-pound burger for himself. He stopped for gas at a convenience store with no other customers in the lot, let Tommy use the bathroom, and put the puppy down in a patch of weeds to piddle. Tanking himself up with one of those energy drinks and buying a few extra bottles because he planned to drive all night, Bijou made a bed with a blanket in the back seat and told his son to take a nap since with night coming on there wouldn't be much to see outside.

He let the pup curl up on top of the blanket, too.

"Aww, ain't that cute." That's what the border guards would say when he approached the bridge in Laredo crossing over into Mexico, father and son going home after a trip to the states. Thanks to that school photo his always gullible mother sent, he had a passport for Tommy. It bore the name Thomas Charles Deaux, son of Juan Deaux. Age, birth date, place of birth, color of hair and eyes, all true. Shouldn't be any trouble to gull the authorities while the Barney Fifes of Ste. Jeanne Parish ran around tripping over their own feet and shooting off toes.

He crossed the border regularly hauling racehorses belonging to his boss to various tracks. Many of the guards knew him. He hauled other stuff as well. Funny how no one wanted to search steaming piles of manure for illegal substances. Since the nasty job of uncovering the plastic sacks full of white powder and wrapping the bags again in brown paper to make them less noticeable fell to him and a pair of rubber gloves, Bijou figured Esteban Miro owed him more than a paycheck and a place to live. He skimmed a little from each of those white sacks and made up one to sell through his own contacts, a small gratuity considering he took the risk of being arrested while the boss stayed safe in Old Mexico. Still, he suspected the drug lord greased palms on both sides of the border because he'd never been stopped or questioned. This would work in his favor, too, when it came to Tommy.

Dawn lit a furtive glow in the eastern sky and sneaked over the horizon by the time the three of them reached Laredo. Bijou skipped the commercial bridge with its lines of big rigs since he was hauling nothing back into the country but his very own son. He'd never signed over any parental rights to Joe Dean either. Damn Cassie for handing the child over to his cousin who had everything. If she didn't want the kid she'd refused to abort, she should have kept it or given the baby to someone else.

No harm would come to Tommy if Joe Dean played along and delivered the ransom, no, call that a voluntary donation—to help out a relative in need—in need to get out of Mexico. He'd mailed the letter with his demands and directions in some no-name Texas town with a post office drop right on the main street when the gas guzzling truck needed refueling yet again. Tommy woke when he stopped, but went right back to sleep with a vague, "That's nice" when he told the kid he'd just sent a postcard home to his parents so they wouldn't worry. Couple of days, Joe and his smart little wife would know for sure where Tommy was, but until then, he hoped they both sprouted as many gray hairs as he had. Life had not been kind: he wanted the rest of his to be nice and easy.

Bijou had a gut feeling Esteban was on to his skimming, and bad, bad things happened to people who crossed the boss. They ended up beheaded, their bodies dissolved in acid if not left as an example to others. Time to turn in his resignation and take off for Brazil with Pilar and Xochi. Now, that country had some righteous bull riders, and he knew a few who'd made it big back in his day and owned vast ranches and fine restaurants now. Could be they'd give a job to one of their kind who hadn't made a fortune on the circuit like them. He was near to topping off his latest bag of white powder, and the sale from that should buy his family first class plane tickets to Rio and keep them in style for a while. Too bad he'd frittered away the cash from earlier scores on rings with real jewels and then lost them gambling. No big deal. With Joe's contribution, they could live for years on the cheap if he didn't feel like working, but a man liked to be busy.

Bijou glanced back at Tommy still fast asleep on the back seat. The shadows of morning dulled his son's red hair and obscured his freckles. The guard wouldn't get a good look at the boy. The puppy, however, scrambled down and lifted an unpracticed, wobbly leg against the front seat where he sat. Jesus God, he should throw the animal out a window before the kid woke, but then the boy might howl when he found it gone, and they were too close to crossing the border now to create an attention getting ruckus.

He'd picked the pissant little cur from a cardboard box of mongrel pups bearing a sign saying, "Free to Good Homes." Two kids, a boy and a girl almost as cute as his own, sat beside the container under an oak tree and looked up hopefully at every passing car. Far as he knew, Bijou Billodeaux took the only pup that day.

The girl with tearful blue eyes and a quivering lip told him their dad would give the pups to the animal shelter if no one took them. "They might be put to death, mister."

Youngsters, so gullible. He could have taken the whole box and sold them to Mexican dogfighters for bait to train their animals, but he didn't have the time or want the trouble. Just one would lure his son to him. He made sure he chose a male. No red-blooded boy wanted a bitch—until he turned into a teenager. His wit made him laugh. Only now, he had a problem. Often enough, he'd brought back pit bulls and fighting cocks for his boss on a return trip. No law against transporting them to other countries so long as you had a health certificate from a vet. This dog had none. He knew Tommy would wail if he woke to find his puppy gone.

Bijou pulled to the side of the road and let other vehicles precede him to the checkpoint. He had a little observing to do and in the meantime would take care of the pup. Rummaging in the trash on the floorboard, he found one of Xochi's red hair ribbons, forever slipping out of her curls, and used his pocketknife to cut it into three pieces. One made a tight muzzle around the pup's nose, and the other two hog-tied its front and back legs. Cowboy skills, a man never forgot them. He shoved the shaking small dog under Tommy's blanket, then cracked open another energy drink and swigged it down while watching the guards at work.

He selected the one he wanted, a short overweight woman with brown skin and thick, cropped black hair under her hat. By the slump of her shoulders and weary wave of her hand to drive on as she returned a set of passports, she'd been on duty all night and waited for her relief to arrive shortly. Passports ready, he got back in line.

"Your business in Mexico," the guard asked dully as she scanned the passports.

"Vacation. Got a place south of the border. I'm taking my boy down there for his spring break. Try not to wake him now. We left north Texas last night so we could have more time together. Divorced. You know how that goes."

She nodded as if she wouldn't be doing this job at all if she were married to a man who made good money. "Juan Deaux, strange name," she commented, pronouncing the last like Dew.

"I say it Doe, Juan Deaux. My mother was Mexican, my dad a randy Cajun." Bijou honored her with a broad smile and a twinkle of his gold tooth. "Guess I am, too. Like to see my place in Nuevo Laredo when you get off? I got a taste for brown beauties."

She handed back the passports and shook a stubby finger at him. "No flirting with the border patrol." She liked him, he could tell. That didn't stop her from checking the box of his truck or its undercarriage. She pawed through Tommy's duffle, too, but very quietly. "Some girls' clothes?" she questioned.

"Castoffs for the orphanage," he ad-libbed.

"Nice of you. These hardly look worn."

Bijou wished she'd hurry before the boy woke up or the puppy whimpered, but Tommy didn't stir. Very little of his face showed with the blanket drawn up. The female guard took care to speak softly just above a whisper. Finally, the broad gave them that tired wave and let them go.

Ah! Good to be back in Nuevo Laredo, the city squatting in a hump of the Rio Grande where industry thrived and all tastes could be satisfied. He steered past the monument to mothers in front of the Crowne Plaza hotel where he never stayed and chuckled to himself. The stout Mexican woman portrayed in the sculpture sheltered a boy and a girl in her skirts. Could be his new family, only Pilar wasn't so fat.

Flush with cash one night, he'd bought her from a bordello owner. Fourteen and fresh, broken in but not yet jaded or diseased, she made a good wife, not that he'd ever married her in the church, just a civil ceremony one afternoon in a weak moment. After a few months, Pilar started upchucking and complaining of sore breasts. That caught him by surprise. He figured her pimp took care of keeping his girls on the pill, but he hadn't given a thought to birth control, not even condoms since a doctor declared her clean. Damn his sentimental heart after losing Tommy to Joe Dean and failing to get him back, he'd let her have the baby, then took care of the matter of her having another. "Tie those tubes in knots, doc," he'd said. "*No mas muchachas, comprende?*"

He snaked the truck toward the very edge of the city where the land turned to arid earth and the bushes grew brittle and scrubby and often covered with thorns. Off in the distance, he could see Esteban Miro's lavish hacienda surrounded by irrigated green fields where high class broodmares grazed with the spring foals by their sides. He'd have a say about which colts and fillies to cultivate and which to sell off as yearlings—if he hung around that long. Parking the truck in his front yard not much different from the xeriscape surrounding it, Bijou got down from the cab and took the duffle with him. The small whirlwind that was Xochi burst from the front door and engulfed his legs.

"Papi, you bring me something pretty?" his daughter asked just like all women.

He spread the top of the bag like a merry Santa Claus and took out the first of the frilly dresses. His little girl squealed with delight and rooted in the sack for other treasures.

Tommy sat up in the truck's cab and put down the window. "We there yet?" he asked, wiping his eyes.

"Hey, who tied my puppy up in ribbons?" He removed the red ribbon from the dog's jaws. "There, now you can breathe better."

The pink tongue lolled out immediately, and the pup's small sides heaved in rapid panting. Tommy freed the paws and received several grateful licks right on the lips. "Stop that!"

He wiped his face on his forearm and leaned out the window. "Hey, this looks just like the Grand Canyon without the big hole in the ground and the pretty rocks. Are we really in Mexico? Is your house made of mud, Dad? Boy, you have a lot of cactus in your yard. Must make it hard to play here. You got some of those red flowers in pots like my mom has. Geraniums? That a satellite dish on the roof? What channels do you get here?"

"Jesus, you got more questions than a wife after a boy's night out, son. This here is your baby sister, Xochi."

The little girl wore a faded blue outfit but danced away with a lacy white pinafore embroidered across the yoke with multicolored flowers and shouted, "*Soy una princesa!*" She twirled and the red ribbon holding back her long, black curls came undone and flew away to land in a thorn bush like a bright bird. She had big, brown eyes with curly lashes, Billodeaux eyes, and was brown-skinned with a small, tight belly straining a dress a little too small.

"Yeah, I understand that. Jude and Annie think they're princesses, too, and sure act like it. Just what I needed, another princess," Tommy said with disgust. He tried the truck door and found it locked. "Hey, hey, let us out of here."

Bijou sauntered over in no hurry to release him. The pup scrambled out first and began nosing around at once, still panting, probably looking for water. Tommy followed not allowing his new daddy to help him down. "I can get out myself. We have a truck just as big at Lorena Ranch."

"Sure you do. You got everything at Lorena Ranch." Except a redheaded little boy. Shove that up your ass, Joe Dean, Bijou thought. "You hungry, kid?"

"Daddy Joe and Mr. Polk always say to tend to your stock first. Macho needs some water. Somebody tied him up and put him under that hot blanket. He coulda died."

Bijou grinned showing off his gold tooth again. "No way. See, if I hadn't of hidden him, the customs people would have taken him away because he has no papers. We smuggled him across the border into Mexico." He winked as if they were partners in a serious crime. "So his name is Macho. How'd you come up with that?"

"Corazon always says Daddy Joe is *mucho macho* so that must be good. She says it means manly and then some."

"Sounds like your maid has a crush on Joe Dean, but don't all women?"

"No, she doesn't. Corazon is married to Mr. Polk who says he likes his women with some meat on their bones."

Someone laughed inside the house. A beautiful woman came to lean in the doorway. She had dark eyes outlined in black, long hair hanging straight down her back like a silken cape, and lips painted red showing up brilliantly against her tan skin. "I would like to meet this Joe," she said.

Bijou scowled. "You ain't never gonna have the chance. Here, I brought you these earrings with real diamonds in them. Put 'em on, then get water for the dog. Pilar is your new mom, Tommy." But she sure didn't look like anyone's mother. Way younger than either Nell or even Cassie, that's what he liked about her most, that and her big tits.

"I like," his woman said, hooking them in her ears. She turned and went inside moving her hips the way Joe Dean's puny wife never would and never could. By the time he took his eyes off her swaying behind, his daughter had the puppy clutched tightly in her arms.

"You bring me a dog, too, Papi?"

What a greedy little thing she was—exactly like Pilar. Bijou nodded at Tommy. "Well, son, you gonna stand up to her or not?"

"No, he's mine. You have a funny name." He answered the challenge with an insult.

"Xochi means flower in Aztec. Aztecs cut out people's hearts. Papi says so. *Como se llamo*?" She didn't release his puppy.

Tommy had taken a step back at the heart comment, but now he got right in her face. "*Me llamo* Tommy. Let me have my dog. I can speak Spanish and English exactly like you. Our housekeeper, Corazon, taught me lots of words in Mexican." He crossed his arms with a "so there" defiance.

Xochi gave him a sly, sideways glance. "What you give me for him?"

Bijou shook his head. "Just like her mama. This is your new brother, Tomas. The dog belongs to him. Go see what else I got for you in that bag. Dig out some of

116

them pretty shoes."

She dropped the puppy and raced for the bag again. Her feet were bare and dirty. She needed shoes much more than a dog.

Pilar returned and put down a plastic dish of water for Macho who slurped it up right away. She had on the dress printed with red roses, the one her breasts nearly fell out of when she bent over, a homecoming invitation if Bijou ever saw one. She'd been to the salon. Red polish covered the nails of her hands and feet. She wore his wedding ring on one slender finger and a toe ring with a tiny green palm tree showing from the open front of her sandals. He wanted to suck her nipples and each one of those digits, the kids be damned. They could play in the yard a while.

Tommy made an astute observation, smart kid just like his daddy, his real daddy. "You look like you could be Xochi's big sister, not her mom."

That laughter came again, not like church bells, more like the chimes on an ice cream truck full of goodies. "*Gracias*. I know my husband have another child up north. Nice you come stay with us, Tomas. Maybe you go to Brazil with us, eh?"

"Brazil, where's that?"

"Shut up about Brazil," Bijou commanded. He looked all around though not a single person was in sight, the hour still being early. He adjusted the swelling in his crotch. Nope, he should tend to business first. "I'm going over to the hacienda to tell the boss I'm back. You make sure Tommy feels at home, Pilar."

"Sure, Bijou. Come, Tomas. I make breakfast. Maybe you stay with us a long, long time."

Chapter Fourteen

"We should have let Tommy get a puppy for Christmas. Nell talked me out of it. Said he was too young, but it's all he wanted. That's how Bijou got to him. We have piles of barn cats for the girls to chase, what difference would one dog have made?" Joe Dean Billodeaux hunched over at the long kitchen table and buried his face in his hands.

His friend and teammate, the best cornerback in the league, Revelation Bullock sat with his quarterback. He'd gotten the call and come right over as soon as the AME's Good Friday service ended. The Rev, only a few credits shy of his divinity degree, assisted his father at the church. With the Rev about ready to quit football and give his service to the Lord, Joe couldn't think of a better man to have his back now.

Connor Riley, Joe's favorite wide receiver who had retired after a devastating knee injury at the end of season, was on his way as they spoke. Stevie, his wife, would probably be doing the driving since Connor hadn't finished his post-surgery physical therapy yet. The couple had no kids, no commitments, but would have come regardless. He called upon these men when he needed support on or off the field.

His wide, black face somber with sympathy, the Rev put a massive pass-intercepting hand on Joe's shoulder. "You can't beat yourself up about not giving the kid a dog. Nell neither. The fault lies with Bijou. The good Lord looked after Tommy last time Bijou tried to steal him and will again."

"But this time Bijou succeeded."

Sheriff LeDoux, still in Madras plaid Bermuda shorts and a red golf shirt that betrayed how he spent his holiday, finished off the pot of coffee Knox Polk made right after they viewed the security tapes. He added his usual two sugars, a large dollop of milk and stirred his cup, but spoke before raising it to his lips.

"You know we're always short-staffed on holidays. It's usually quiet on Good Friday. We put on extra men at night to watch for anybody coming home from crawfish boils loaded with beer. Bijou would know that and get away before sunset. Not that I'm making any excuses, but he was probably out of the parish with Tommy before you called us. My guess is he fled the state while we were still considering this a simple runaway case."

The sheriff took a seat. His belly pooched out over his belt, but his bare legs showed some muscle and a great tan. He sipped and wiped his bristly gray mustache with a paper napkin. "The Amber Alert is out now since you got proof of a kidnapping in those tapes, but that cousin of yours is so *canaille*, he's probably halfway across Texas by now. Let's hope the border patrol catches him."

"And pray," the Rev added.

A car door slammed. Joe did pray—that Connor had arrived, but three more doors slammed. He knew Nell had come roaring home with all the kids stuffed into the little sub-compact she used for work and plenty angry because he hadn't returned with Tommy or given her a call to say why. Fearless on the football field, he dreaded telling his little, very pregnant wife that his rotten cousin had struck again and despite the best in security, made off with their son.

Dean opened the door for his mother, but his daughters flowed in around her and stopped dead in their little red sneakers confronted with a room full of big men. Loving to climb on his broad back, they knew the Rev well, and Knox of course, but the sheriff would have to be introduced and explained. Nell kept right on coming though, and tossed down in front of Joe a soggy roll of newspaper with a few red claws protruding where they'd punctured the wrapper.

"Your mother sent your dinner and some for Tommy since you didn't return. There's cake in the car, too, if the kids haven't crushed it. Wait. Sheriff LeDoux. Was Tommy hit by a car on his way over here? My God! Rev, is that why you're here? Tommy is dead!"

Almost relieved the truth wasn't quite as bad as that, Joe took her onto his knee and held her tight. "As far as we know, Tommy is fine. Bijou came back and took him to Mexico, we believe. No word from the bastard yet."

"What's a bastard?" Jude asked.

"I am," said Dean. "Because my mother and dad didn't get married, but that doesn't matter now because Mama Nell adopted me after my birth mother died."

Nell and her "always tell the truth policy," sometimes Joe could do without it. He saw the Rev suppressing his grin, but the sheriff seemed impressed by the explanation. "Smart boy," he said and patted Dean on the head.

Dean shook off the pat. "Why is Tommy in Mexico?"

Smart and quick, quarterback material for sure, Joe thought for only a second before his thoughts veered back to his second son. Nell sank against his chest and murmured, "My God, my God, awful things happen to small children in Mexico."

"As a law enforcement officer, I can tell you bad things happen to kids everywhere. Now, I've arrested Bijou a time or two and can say he is no child molester, though he does have an eye for younger women than he should. I don't believe anyone raised by Hal and Flo Billodeaux would harm his own son, so let's not worry about that now. My guess is we'll get a ransom call or note. That's what we're waiting for right now. Want me to get that cake out of the car for you?" Sheriff LeDoux offered.

"I'll fetch it." Knox walked outside without further remark.

Another car pulled up, one door slammed. The other opened quietly and shut gently. A few moments later, six-foot-five, blond, and Nordic Connor Riley hobbled in pushing open the door with his cane. He'd made great progress since the last time Joe saw him on a walker days after knee surgery. His equally blond, tall wife Stevie caught the door before it rebounded. Almost model pretty, but too athletic for strutting runways, Stevie did look mighty attractive today, her complexion glowing, her fine breasts pushing out of a snug blue top that brought out the color of her eyes. Sometimes, Joe couldn't help himself when it came to sizing up every woman he laid eyes on, but he did keep his thoughts to himself since marrying Nell. Still, he suspected his wife knew and gave him a pass on an old habit that hadn't died yet. Now, he felt Nell's back stiffen against him.

"You called Connor before telling *me*?"

"He had farther to drive, but I guess Stevie was behind the wheel. You must have put the pedal to the metal, girl." Nell regarded Stevie as her best friend next to the Rev's wife, Dr. Arminta Green Bullock, one reason Joe had summoned them both.

"We were in Baton Rouge. Connor was signing autographs at a charity event for homeless kids. We did make real good time crossing the swamp causeway."

"Yeah, the state trooper let us go after we explained the situation and signed his ticket book. Even gave us an escort all the way to Breaux Bridge. At least my autograph is still good for some things. Next time we drive in a rush like that, I'll be behind the wheel. The doc says so." Connor squeezed Stevie against his hip with the hand not holding onto the cane. She blushed, tough Stevie Dowd Riley, who jostled shoulder to shoulder with male sports photographers and came up with great shots, blushed.

The Rev got up and pushed two chairs forward. "Take a seat, Connor. Take a seat, Mama," he said to the couple.

Nell pushed from Joe's lap and went to hug Stevie. "You're pregnant. How wonderful! How far along are you?"

"Going into my fourth month."

"And not even showing. Look at me, not even three months yet, and I am bulging already. You look great."

"Thanks, I'm taller than you, that's all. So sorry about Tommy. Tell us how we can help, and we will."

"Tommy." Nell burst into tears. Stevie embraced her friend and cried along with her.

Great, now he had two emotional pregnant women to worry about. He'd called Connor and Stevie to have his friend and one usually very sensible woman on hand. "I don't understand how this happened, Con, with your surgery and rehab. How?"

Stevie mopped her tears on the sleeve of Connor's white dress shirt. "What Joe, you never heard of the woman on top position? You can get pregnant that way, too."

Good, Stevie hadn't lost her moxie in a sea of female hormones. Now if only Dr. Mintay Bullock, as the Rev's wife was also known, would arrive and put a lid on all the tears, using tranquilizers if she must. No, that would be bad for the babies.

As if reading Joe's mind, the Rev said, "Mintay will be here soon. She had to stay behind to organize the placing of the Easter lilies for Sunday. The sisters of the church listen to her. Otherwise, they get into spats when it comes to decorating, the lot of a preacher's wife."

On cue, Arminta Green Bullock, slim, light-skinned and still dressed for church, arrived with her hands clutching a potted white lily with four huge blooms. Their fragrance filled the room. "I thought these might bring you hope and comfort." She placed the flowers on the table where their scent helped to mask the boiled crawfish aroma. Her twins and Little Joe followed her, making Nell suddenly aware of the other children, her children, standing wide-eyed in the kitchen.

"Dean, you and the girls take Connor and Riley

and Little Joe to the game room. You can play until bedtime."

"I wanna stay and help save Tommy."

"You can't do that now. Go play. We'll let you know what you can do later."

Accustomed to obeying their mother and wheedling their father, the children left. The second the kids disappeared, Mintay joined the huddle of women and started to cry. "Oh, poor, poor Tommy."

"You aren't pregnant, are you?" Joe asked.

"I'd better not be," the doctor answered, shooting a green-eyed stare at her husband. "I told Rev with Little Joe coming right on the heels of those two big twins, I was done reproducing."

"That's a relief." Joe looked around. Knox Polk silently cut the coconut cake on the counter. For some reason he seemed a little sheepish. Knox sheepish? That didn't make any sense. Had he stolen a lick of icing? No big deal.

"Anyone want cake? Shame to waste it. It's the kind with the sugar syrup soaked in between the layers and fresh grated coconut on top," Knox said.

"What is this, *Cake Boss*? No, we're all here to figure out how to get Tommy back safe and sound," Joe insisted.

"Um, I'll have a piece of that. Missed my dinner coming over here," the sheriff explained. "Got any more coffee?"

Stevie's stomach gurgled. "Sorry, I'm always hungry these days. I'd like a piece, but no coffee unless you have decaf."

Yet another car arrived. Only one slam. Corazon, back from Easter egg decorating with her husband's family, entered the kitchen full of good cheer as usual.

"You all have a good Good Friday, no? You having a party without me? Oh, cake! MawMaw Nadine's coconut, I bet. Cut me a big slice, *querido*. I make coffee for everyone."

"Not decaf," Joe implored.

Corazon waved a chubby hand his way. "Oh, you been drinking decaf since the little frozen babies come out of the icebox."

"Never mind. Corazon, my cousin came back and took Tommy to Mexico, kidnapped him."

"Not my *Rojito*, my little *Rojito,* and this time I not here to save him!"

More tears, they'd soon drown in them like that chick, Alice in Wonderland. Joe sized up his housekeeper, Knox's wife of several years. Always on the heavy side, she'd lost her waistline again. The tears flowed down her round, brown face and dripped off her short chin. She had a few threads of gray in her thick, black Latina hair now. One thing Joe knew about Corazon for sure. She adored children, especially his children, and wanted her own more than anything. So far, this wish had been denied as she aged. Knox didn't care one way or the other. He'd been in the military long enough to appreciate a good meal and a warm bed shared with a loving woman, but evidently, he'd finally fulfilled his wife's one desire.

"You're pregnant, right?" Joe asked.

"We were gonna tell you soon. I asked your mama to include me in her novena for the little frozen babies. Your mama, her prayers got power. I think Mother Mary might be a little bit afraid of her."

"Ah, that would be blasphemy, I think," the Rev

125

said.

"I mean no disrespect, Reverend Rev."

"When are you due?" Stevie asked.

"A little after the *senora* in October, but she might be early." Corazon eyed Nell's belly.

"Why don't we just open a maternity ward on the second floor? Look, I'm happy for all y'all, but we have to make plans to get Tommy. That's why you're here."

"Now, Joe, don't go rushing into anything. We should turn this over to the FBI," Sheriff LeDoux said, brushing a few shreds of coconut from his mustache.

"I don't want them involved. We can handle Bijou. Aunt Flo told me where he is, right across the border in Nuevo Laredo working on some horse farm."

"Think again, Joe. Lots of nasty people in Mexico, and my bet is Bijou knows them all." The sheriff held out his plate for another slice of cake. Corazon obliged him with a large wedge.

Nell put up a hand. "Yes, think again. Much as I hate to say this, you left one person out, Joe. Have you called Cassie?"

His discomfort showed in a wince. "No. I told her not to come here until Thanksgiving. You always say to be consistent with children, Nell."

"Unfortunately, she's not a child anymore. Call her."

The group in the kitchen maintained a silence broken only by the dripping of the coffee Corazon had started. Wanting to be entirely open, Joe put the call on speaker phone as soon as someone picked up at the Thomas house because that is where she'd be on Good Friday if not at Lorena Ranch.

"Who is this?" a small boy asked over the noise of

many, many children. It sounded as if all of Cassie's ten brothers and sisters, their wives and offspring filled the background with noise.

"Joe Dean Billodeaux. Put Cassie on please."

"Cass-eeee!" he screamed. "It's for you."

"Some phone manners you have, Declan," they heard Cassie say. "Sorry, one of my nephews got to the phone first. Joe, have you changed your mind? I'd love to come see Tommy on Easter."

The hope in her voice embarrassed him. "No, it's something else. Something bad. Bijou has Tommy. We think he's gone to Mexico, but we're working on a plan to get him back soon. Just wanted you to know."

"Wanted me to know! Don't make any plans without me. We're on our way."

"We? How many Thomases are comimg?"

"Just me—and Howdy. We're friends now. That's all. Seemed sad he was alone on a holiday weekend. Even Brian Lightfoot went home, so Mom said to bring him over. One more doesn't make any difference."

Oh, but it could if that person were Cassie.

Chapter Fifteen

Near ten p.m., Howdy's huge red truck roared down the lane. Why the boy needed a big rig like that when he lived in New Orleans mystified Joe. Must be hell to find a parking space. He'd gone for a Porsche with his first bonus check back when he was young and dumb. His own truck had come later along with the ranch and Nell. Joe had some fond memories of putting that long bed to use before Bijou made off with it. God damn Bijou in a hundred different ways!

"We could have been here sooner, but Howdy wouldn't let me drive!" Cassie declared as she flung herself into the kitchen.

"You were too upset to drive. I probably saved your life by keeping you from behind the wheel," Howdy retorted. "She drives the way she barrel-races."

"You are so slow about everything! Absolutely everything, Howard McCoy."

"So, you two are friends now. I'm glad to hear that," Nell said. "Sit down. Coffee? It's decaf."

"Nothing. We had dinner before you called. How are we going to save Tommy?"

"I'd appreciate some, Miss Nell," Howdy said in that quiet way of his. He found a free chair and sat.

"Just Nell. I'm glad you came along."

"Good luck with that. He still calls me ma'am. His good manners keep getting in the way." Cassie's eyes searched the kitchen.

The Rev overflowed a chair next to his slim wife. Connor Riley, one arm draped around Stevie, sat with his bad leg outstretched. Corazon, out of character, perched on a cushioned seat and had her legs propped up. Knox stood protectively at her side, and Nell, already showing her pregnancy, poured the coffee. Joe kept his distance when Cassie's gaze settled on him.

"Where are the police? Why isn't the FBI here getting ready to record and trace any phone calls?"

Joe filled her in. "The sheriff left a while ago. He says he doesn't want to know if we plan to do anything illegal. We'll call him if we hear from Bijou or get a note, but we'd rather handle this situation ourselves. We know where my cousin is living. It's just a matter of going there, giving him a bunch of money when we know how much, and bringing Tommy home. I'm sure he has no intention of keeping our boy."

"We should be on our way to Mexico tonight."

"I think considering the violence that sometimes breaks out in border towns, we need to go armed. I have to get licenses to take weapons. We'll make it look like we're going on a hunting trip for javelinas on a private ranch. I've done that before."

"Exactly what is a javelina?"

"A peccary," Nell answered.

"Like a wild pig. They can be a real nuisance. It's not huntin' season, though," Howdy said.

"Private land, nuisance animals, Mexico, I doubt we'll be stopped."

"Are you planning to shoot Bijou—because I'd volunteer to do it?" Clearly, Cassie meant what she said.

"No, I promised Aunt Flo I wouldn't harm him too badly, but I will put the fear of God into the man to keep him from trying this again."

"I'm going along to provide some restraint," the Rev replied.

"Me, too, for moral support," Connor promised.

"And me. I'm the best shot," Knox claimed.

Cassie got that stubborn set to her jaw. "Then take me. Tommy will want one of his moms after his ordeal, and heaven knows Nell is in no condition to travel."

"No way! If Cassie goes, I go!"

Joe embraced his wife and rested his chin on her head. "Remember last time, Tink, when you tried to rescue Cassie all on your own? You lost one of the babies you carried. We can't let that happen again." Before Stevie, Mintay, or Corazon could speak up, he added, "All pregnant women stay home, lady doctors and children, too. Go back to bed, Dean."

The small boy peering into the kitchen hitched up his football player pajamas. "I want to help."

"You can help by taking care of the women while I'm gone. I want you to make sure everyone behaves, including your mother. She shouldn't lift anything heavy or go riding. Corazon is having a baby also, so no sassing her or making extra work. You see the girls clean up their own messes and you, too."

Dean's dark Billodeaux eyes widened. "Aren't you too old to have babies, Corazon?"

"Not if Mother Mary walks with me all the way, Dino."

"Dean, go back to bed."

"It's weird having T-Connor and Little Joe sleeping in Tommy's room. I can hear Riley snoring in her room all the way down the hall."

"Takes after her father," Dr. Arminta Green Bullock said. "But we'll have to get those adenoids and tonsils taken out soon. I do agree that all women and children should stay home."

"Not me. I'm going if I have to follow you in my own car." Cassie crossed her arms.

"I'd like to go along and help," Howdy offered.

"This isn't your fight, son," Joe told him.

"Tommy is a cool kid, like the baby brother I never had. I grew up on a ranch. I can shoot varmints. Besides, someone has to keep Cassie in line."

"As if *you* ever could!" the woman in question fumed at him.

"I might surprise you. I think it's a given you won't be able to leave her behind. She'll get in more trouble trying to do something on her own, I suspect." Howdy leaned back in his chair and folded his arms behind his head.

"Getting to know her pretty well, I'd say," Nell replied.

"Yep. But just friends like she says."

"Okay. Me, Connor, Rev, Howdy, and Cassie make up this team. Knox, I'd rather leave you here to look after the women and children."

"What is this, the nineteenth century? The women can look after themselves and the children and the farm exactly the way they do every time men go off to war," Stevie informed him. "Take Knox if he is the best shot. I can stick around and help here. You should only be gone for a few days, right, not four or five years."

"You know, Stevie, you can be as big a problem as Cassie. Fine, we'll take Knox, but every single one of you must still be pregnant when we get back—except Mintay. Deal?"

"Deal," they all said.

****

Tuesday morning Joe and Nell waited beside their mailbox outside the iron gates of the ranch. The holiday messed with the delivery schedule and not a word had come from Bijou by any means. Joe grew restless with the inaction. His wife knew the signs.

Nell put a hand on his arm as he clenched and unclenched his fist, most likely thinking of how he'd like to drive it into Bijou's face. "Maybe today. Strange Easter," she said, trying to distract him.

"Why? The kids always complain about dressing up and having to go to church twice, Catholic services with my mother and Episcopalian with you. Same thing every year only Tommy isn't here to add to the protests."

"They got to make a cross of flowers at my church and march with it in the processional, better than having to wait forever while all the holiday Christians lined up for communion at yours."

"Not according to Dean who said he didn't want to be a flower girl. Jude and Annie liked it. I was touched when they promised not to eat any of their Easter candy until Tommy comes home. They wanted to delay the egg hunt and egg *paqueing* until he got back, but all those Billodeaux cousins of theirs voted them down. They think Tom is on vacation with Flo and Hal." Joe's fist pounded on the top of the oversized black metal mailbox mounted on top of a brick pillar and its door flew open revealing the empty interior.

"No sense in ruining everyone's fun or letting all

those eggs spoil. We'll have our own hunt and egg bumping contest when our son returns. I swear Dean channeled all his anger into bashing his cousins' boiled eggs to pieces. That's how he won the big chocolate bunny for Tommy."

"Yeah, I taught him that, to direct your anger toward your opponents. Mail is late today."

"Catching up. Look, here comes the truck now."

The pint-sized white, red, and blue mail vehicle pulled up beside them, and their carrier leaned out with a substantial bundle. "Not often I get to deliver to you in person, Joe Dean. Got some envelopes from Mexico."

Ungraciously, Joe grabbed the heap of catalogs and junk mail and began sorting through the stack. "My hunting licenses and gun permits from the place where I shoot javelinas. I asked they send them as fast as possible, and here it is Tuesday."

"They celebrate Easter in Mexico exactly like we do, Joe," Nell soothed.

Beneath the large brown envelopes and above a ladies' lingerie catalog lay a grungy letter postmarked in Texas. "This is it. I recognize that rat's scrawl."

"If you're having any trouble with hate mail, I should report it to the postmaster. Some fans can get violent," the carrier said.

Joe struggled, but finally plastered a cordial smile on his face. "Only an annoying relative asking for money. I can handle it."

"We all got those," the postman agreed. "Y'all have a good day now."

They wished him the same as his small vehicle puttered down the country road to the next mailbox.

Immediately, Joe hit the remote control on his keychain and rushed Nell inside the gates. He handed her the bulk of the mail and strode toward the house while he tore at the cheap drugstore stationary. Nell had difficulty keeping up. Catalogs offering premium chocolate, costly jewelry, high-tech toys, and ranch supplies fell from her arms and spattered open in the driveway. "Joe, wait!"

"Sorry, sorry. Don't overexert yourself." He paused by the huge live oak with the low-hanging limbs, the same one where he'd first courted Nell, sitting beside her on one of the thick, sturdy branches and homing in for a kiss he never received. He did the same now, raising his little pregnant fairy of a wife onto a secure perch among the new spring-green leaves and climbing up next to her. Joe kissed Nell on the lips before showing his wife the letter.

"Seems two million dollars is always the going rate for our children. Same amount I gave your sister for her eggs. The money isn't the problem. I'd pay twice that for Tommy, for any of them, but I don't trust Bijou. He says to wire the money to this account number and show up on Sunday at International Bridge #1 to pick up our son. Claims Tommy has a passport and can walk across to meet me on the other side."

"Do as he asks, Joe. Low as Bijou is, I don't think he means Tommy any harm. His ego is too big to kill his own son. In a way, I think he is proud of having fathered a boy."

"A fine boy who thankfully looks more like his birth mother and is being raised by wonderful woman."

"Thank you. Now, promise me you won't do anything to endanger yourself or Tommy."

"How about Bijou? Can I endanger him—a couple of black eyes, a broken arm, a smashed kneecap?"

"I thought you promised Aunt Flo you wouldn't harm him."

"Said I wouldn't kill her rotten son to get mine back. No promises not to rough him up. Bijou has to understand this is the last time I will tolerate his interference with my family. I need a face-to-face to tell him to take the money in the form of a check and get his ass as far from us as the cash will take him. Any next times, and he'll end up dead or in jail for life."

Nell placed his hand on her belly. "Joe, we have babies on the way. Border towns are dangerous right now. People get shot there all the time."

"Mostly they kill their own in drug wars, not American tourists. This is only Bijou we're talking about. He may be ten years older than me, but I could take him since I was seventeen. He never reached the top as a bull rider because he didn't keep in shape, just got on and hung on and trusted to luck. Bijou rarely thinks ahead much farther than the next poker game. Let's tell the others."

"Yes, the same Bijou who stabbed you in the shoulder last time he tried to take Tommy. Don't underestimate him. He's a snake."

Joe helped his wife down from the branch and walked more slowly to the house where he found Connor and Howdy in the gym, both working on their legs. Breasts bobbing beneath a slick exercise outfit and probably driving the kicker crazy, Cassie ran on the treadmill. All action stopped when Joe entered waving the letter. He read it aloud to the group.

"I'm going down there a few days early to surprise

my cousin with a visit. Anyone wants out say so, because we leave at dawn. We should be ready to cross the border early Thursday. I got the gun and hunting licenses today. We'll take high-powered hunting rifles with scopes, four of them. The Rev won't want one and Cassie has never held a weapon as far as I know. Should scare the shit out of the shit bag. Connor, Howdy, you coming?"

Connor nodded. "I've taken a few deer in my time."

"Big guns to shoot vermin, but yeah, I'm in." Howdy said his words so coldly Cassie did a double take with her head as if the nice guy she knew had vanished and left Billy the Kid in his place.

"Good. I'm going to fill in Knox. Get some rest."

Joe approached his ranch manager who sat on the rail of the exercise ring and watched the children ride their ponies. Horses needed exercise even during Easter vacations, he'd told them, mostly to get the gang out of the way and occupied as they waited for word on Tommy. He let Knox read the letter and explained his plan.

"Sounds good. You're the officer in charge."

"If you see anything wrong with this, I'd appreciate your input. You have the combat experience."

"Other than possibly provoking a fire fight, it sounds okay. I know Nell will care for Corazon and the baby if anything happens to me. My wife will have my military benefits if I take the big one. We can't let scum rule the world."

"Come on, Knox. It won't come to that. We're only going to scare my cousin."

"You never know, sir. You never know."

****

Joe drove the new red family van, not exactly an intimidating vehicle, but the one that could hold the most big men.

The Rev, out of training and packing on the pounds as he did every year on his mama's cooking despite Mintay's best efforts, took up two seats alone. Knox rode shotgun, literally, keeping one of the rifle cases at his feet while they stowed rest of the weapons in the back. Connor took the bench seat in the rear in order to stretch out his bad leg, and Cassie and Howdy sat across the aisle from each other.

Nell made one last effort to stop Joe and convince him to wire the money and pick up Tommy on Sunday, but could not sway his "stubborn Cajun, mule-headed mind," her words.

"Tink, I'm the luckiest man alive," he told her. "Nothing will go wrong, but if it does, I know you are strong enough to carry on. Now, Mama says she's sending Lizzie's boys to do the ranch work. They're off this week, and we'll be home by Sunday. She said not to pay them because they should to this for family, but you give them something for their trouble. With that unreliable drunk Lizzie has for a husband, they always need cash. Show the ransom letter to Sheriff LeDoux after we get to Mexico. I don't want to be stopped at the border."

"I will. Joe, be careful."

"Ain't I always?"

"No, no you're not, especially when playing games. You only think you are."

"Give Daddy Joe a kiss. Hug the kids for me. Tell them we've gone to get their brother."

She did kiss him long and well because it could be their last. A person should always be aware of that. Joe Dean drove the van into darkness with the sunrise at his back.

Chapter Sixteen

Sitting on a lawn chair in front of his modern adobe as nice as ones he'd seen up around Santa Fe, whole developments full of them, Bijou sucked on a bottle of Dos Equis beer and checked his bank account on the iPhone he'd bought with the proceeds of his last purloined kilo of cocaine. Handy gadget, but it told him Joe Dean hadn't put the ransom money in his account yet and here it was, Thursday. He would though. The big deal quarterback could wipe his ass with hundred dollar bills if he wanted.

Besides, everyone knew nothing meant more to the head Sinner than his children, any children really. Didn't his team and his fans all call him Daddy Joe now? Even Tommy used that term a lot when talking about the man who raised him, not his real father. He'd heard enough about his cousin's work with sick kids to make him puke. Bijou remembered how Joe Dean had pleaded on the TV for Cassie's return, but in the end that cunt simply ran away from the man who fathered her child.

On the fourth of the six-pack of beer, Bijou thought fondly of Cassie's coltish legs wrapped around his waist when they did it. She had freckles all over and twat hair the same color red as what she had on her head when not dyed to escape detection. Not much in the way of tits back then, but her breasts ballooned when she got knocked up. For a while he'd enjoyed them until her belly grew to the same size and made sex a chore.

Fool bitch if she really thought he wouldn't come back for her the next day after he'd lost her for a night in a poker game to three other men. Hell, he couldn't lose his truck, so easily stolen from Joe Dean's ranch exactly like the girl, because they needed it to get to Mexico. All she had to do was spread her legs until the gamblers at the motel got tired of her and left. With that big belly full of baby, not likely they'd linger. But no, Cassie went whining to Nell and Joe, save me, save me from big, bad Bijou, and paid them off for her rescue by giving them his son.

Where had that redheaded little flea gone? Xochi, a year younger and already quite the spitfire, pushed him around. The boy needed to grow some *cojones*. He raised his daughter to be tough. Good bet Nell made Tommy share his toys and be nice to his baby sisters even when they deserved a boot in the butt. A woman needed to be put in her place every now and again.

"Pilar!" he shouted. "Supper about ready? Where are the kids?"

With flour on her hands, his wife came to the doorway. What a pair of tits *she* owned, and she made a pretty good tortilla, too. Cassie couldn't cook worth a damn back then, always needed to buy her dinner.

"Soon supper be ready. The kids playing around Senor Gonzales' place." Pilar gestured down the road and flecked her bright red dress with specks of flour.

"They better not break any of his pottery or that fat slob will be coming here wanting money for the trash he sells to tourists like the last time Xochi broke a chimenea."

"I tell them be careful." Her face grew somber, maybe remembering the last time Xochi cost her father money and got the belt for it.

"Go on inside and get cracking. A man gets hungry after training horses all day."

She did as ordered. This time of the day the sinking sun cast enough shadow on this side of the house for a man to enjoy. The temperature hovered around seventy-five, not stinking hot like it would be in summer. Not a bad life right now, but about to get a whole lot better. Bijou checked his bank account again. Nope, still lacking a two-million dollar deposit. Joe Dean better not be playing any games because he could do stuff to Tommy, bad stuff like sell him to the same bordello where he'd found Pilar. A red-haired white boy would bring in good money from the fudge packers and bone smokers.

Or maybe he'd take Tommy along to Brazil and raise him right. He had a certain fondness for the boy, his own flesh and blood. Train him up to be a bull rider. He'd put the kid up on one of the lesser thoroughbreds and let him ride around the practice track. The child had a good seat already. He could make a jockey if those long Billodeaux legs didn't grow out, but bull riding would be Bijou's first choice.

If Joe didn't come through with the cash, and soon, maybe he'd sell that personal sack of cocaine he'd recently topped off from the last haul and shoved under the back seat of the truck. No sense in covering it with horse shit until he must. Should bring enough to get all four of them to another continent. He'd never given up his parental rights to Tommy, so let Joe Dean try and get him back from a foreign place where Bijou had friends with money. If that failed, he imagined it would be easy to get lost in a country big as Brazil. He if changed his mind about keeping Tommy, Rio had plenty of places offering kinky sex of all kinds, he guessed.

In the distance, a black Cadillac Escalade left the rancho where he worked. No telling who drove with the heavily tinted windows. Most likely the boss coming into town for some recreation, but the big vehicle slowed as it approached his home and turned in to park next to the truck. Bijou got up and sauntered toward the opening doors. One of the trio of bodyguards got out and held the door for Esteban Miro.

"*Hola, Jefe*," Bijou said cordially. "Can I interest you in a beer?"

"No, *gracias.* I would be more interested in my missing cocaine."

Miro snapped his fingers. A diamond ring with a stone the size of quail egg gave off a blinding flash. Bijou always admired that ring and with two million in his account could afford one soon, but first to bullshit his way out of trouble. One of the three bodyguards pinned his arms. His beer bottle fell and disgorged its amber contents into the soil. The smell of hops and malt and flop sweat rose into the air.

Another henchman placed a cigarette in a short gold holder, lit it, and put it in Miro's mouth. Not a good sign. *El Jefe* liked to set afire the homes of persons who mildly displeased him.

"Don't know what you mean, boss." Bijou bent his legs in order not to tower over Miro. His height always irritated the guy; they usually talked sitting down. His employer looked like any other greaser, brown and slick-haired, short and a bit bandy-legged, but inside the innocuous body that could belong to any day laborer dwelt a true hard case. The word merciless came to mind as he tried to look the man in his blank, ebony eyes.

"I have received a call from one of my buyers most displeased about short weights in his deliveries. I tell you this in English so you understand every word, no?"

"Sure, I appreciate that, *Jefe*, but I got nothing to do with it." Bijou managed a gold-toothed grin of confidence in his innocence.

"Search the house." Miro took a few puffs from the cigarette and handed the holder over to his main man who carried it carefully inside the adobe and took a second goon with him.

First came the sounds of glass breaking and wooden furniture splintering, then Pilar's screams, followed by the sizzling scent of a kitchen fire wafting from the open door. Still shrieking, his wife ran into the yard. The bodyguards continued to trash the house until the smoke thickened to the point of driving them out into the fresh air.

"*Nada*," the head bodyguard said.

"Kill them."

"Now, you can't condemn a guy without any proof, *Jefe*, and my wife, she ain't done nothing. Why, I'm sure she'd be pleased to entertain you over at your place, anything you want. She ain't forgotten her old tricks, have you, honey?" Bijou sank a little lower, sagging against his captor, hoping to use his dead weight to fight free, but the boss could afford to hire the biggest, most muscular and ruthless men south of the border. The goon simply jerked him upright again.

"Anything, anything," Pilar offered, distraught and desperate. Her eyes scanned the road toward the Gonzales place.

"Look here in my pocket. Use my phone to check my bank account. Not much in there, but I expect a large inheritance soon. Though I ain't cheated you, boss, it's all yours if you let us go. I only need enough money to get out of your sight if you don't trust me no more." Moisture beaded on Bijou's brow. For a moment, he hoped for a reprieve when the guard frisked him for the iPhone, but the bully boy simply put it in his own pocket.

Miro showed no interest. "*La nina*, where is she? I don't like to leave orphans behind for the church to raise. Then, the nuns expect me to make big donations."

Pilar pleaded in Spanish for the life of her child. The ebony eyes of Esteban Miro did not blink as if they were lidless like those of a snake. He held out his hand for the golden holder and sucked the remains of the cigarette down to the ash which he flicked in Bijou's face.

"We find her and the cocaine later."

Another snap of the finger and the last thing Bijou saw was the flash of the ring he coveted. Pilar spied her daughter's slight form among the acre of giant pots down the road and quickly turned her eyes away lest she betray her child. Xochi stayed safe in her thoughts and unvoiced prayer as the bullet entered her heart with a quiet pop from the silenced gun.

"A waste of a beautiful woman, *Jefe*," her slayer said with regret. "We might have kept her for a while."

"Revenge must be swift and complete, Miguel, and

loyalty absolute," Miro answered. "I think I would rather have the red-haired boy tonight. Find him for me, and the cocaine. Kill the girl." Flanked by two bodyguards, the boss walked to the black car with the heavily tinted windows and ordered his driver to return to the picture-perfect ranch in the distance.

Miguel rifled the truck keys from Bijou's pocket. At least, the side shot to the head did not leave too messy a corpse though he had some blowback on his shirt. He flicked off what he could, unlocked the truck and found the evidence all too easily under the back seat of the double cab. The cocaine would not go anywhere while he searched for the children. Using Bijou's very nice phone, Miguel called in the location of the stolen drugs and asked for a couple of men to come get the truck and him. Then, he tossed the keys onto the front seat, and leading with his prominent Mayan nose, set out at a lope for the field full of pottery. Where else would a child hide?

****

Tommy tagged Xochi on the shoulder. "You're it," he said. Usually she hid way better than this, often curling into a small ball inside a chimenea or overturning one of Mr. Gonzales' big urns in order to escape detection. Xochi, peering out from behind a tall chimney decorated with Aztec symbols, did not move, not even when Macho jumped up on her bare legs and licked her knees.

"Not now, *Rojito*."

"Don't call me that! Only Corazon is allowed to use that baby name, I told you. You never do what I ask you. You're just jealous because Papi let me ride the thoroughbred and you only got to watch. Either you're

145

it, or we're done playing, Xochi. I'm hungry anyhow."

"Tomas, our house is on fire."

"Yikes, we'd better get home and help put it out."

"Too late. Mama and Papi are dead. See that man, he comes to kill us."

Then, he noticed the form in the bright red dress crumpled in the yard and his father's body, half his head blown away, laying near a brown beer bottle in the sandy soil. The cactus and thorn bushes seemed to be sucking up the pools of blood like badly needed water. A big man, pale-skinned for a Mexican, headed their way with a long-barreled pistol by his side.

"Mama said, 'If bad men come, you must run and hide, Xochi'."

"I think your Mama was right. Let's get out of here."

"And go where? He see us run."

"Quick, stay low and run to the other side of the shop. I got an idea from when I was looking for you."

For once, Xochi cooperated with him. Mr. Gonzales paid no attention as they crept past. He waited on two gray-haired American tourists, a pot-bellied man and a thin, age-spotted stick of a woman, the kind that came from the U.S. to buy cheap, glazed clay pots for their gardens. Intent on accepting their American Express card, the proprietor did not notice the children climb into the rear of a dusty pickup truck with Texas plates and hoist a puppy with them. Two huge, thick-walled containers of deep blue edged with brown filled the bed. Tommy helped Xochi shinny into one of them and handed her Macho.

"Keep him safe and quiet for me."

He braced himself on the side of the other pot and

used the lip to pull himself up and over. Kicking practice had made his legs a lot stronger, and a good thing, too. Tommy settled into his hiding place. Moments later, the driver slammed the tailgate shut and revved the engine. With the windows of the cab rolled down, he could hear every word the couple said.

"Harvey, don't pull out too fast. I don't want my pots chipped. Drive nice and slow to the border, you hear."

"Yes, Dolores, but it seems to me we could have gotten the same pots at Lowe's, the price of gas being what it is."

"Not for twice this amount of money. Mr. Gonzales always gives me the best deals. Wouldn't have been such a bad trip if the air-conditioner hadn't run out of coolant halfway here. Then you had to go and eat that chicken burrito and beans for lunch and get a touch of Montezuma's revenge. I told you to stick to the fish tacos."

"All the more reason to drive faster, my dear."

"Well, at least I got my Mexican vanilla and that special Coca-Cola you like in the bottles before you got the runs."

Inside his urn, Tommy snickered. The sound amplified in the small space.

"Are you laughing at me, Harve?"

"Never, dearest. Only farting."

Behind them, the noise of pottery shattering and Mr. Gonzales shouting shivered in the warm air. "Good Lord, Harve! Look back there. We're in the middle of one of those Mexican drug wars. No wonder he can afford to sell so cheap. Pedro must deal on the side."

"Mind if I drive a little faster, my love?"

"Chipped pots be damned. Get us out of here!"

The ride got rougher then. Tommy prayed the urns wouldn't break, they rattled so. He'd have bruises for sure. Macho barked then stopped suddenly. The people in the truck didn't appear to notice. The vehicle veered suddenly, nearly toppling his pot.

"Hell damn, Harve, the driver of that red van thinks he owns the road. Louisiana plates. It figures. Well, he'll get his when he drives into that firefight."

Red van, could the daddy who raised him be coming to the rescue? Tommy was sorely tempted to rock his container over and stand up in the back of the truck to see, but he recalled the advice Knox Polk gave him when him and Dean played paintball. Stay low and don't give a good target. Not likely Daddy Joe would come here for him when Bijou sent a card saying he'd be home by Sunday. No, best to lay low until they reached the border.

Chapter Seventeen

Nothing but delays and frustration since the rescue party arrived exhausted in Laredo. Everyone agreed they should get some rest and food before going into Mexico. Joe wanted to plow ahead, but outvoted, they'd gotten rooms and slept half of Thursday away just wasting time. Knox said they'd best go in fed and refreshed, so he tried to wait patiently while the Rev wolfed down a huge enchilada platter for lunch. Then, the ranch manager insisted on taking a case of bottled water along, so they'd had to stop for that.

Joe hadn't counted on this being spring vacation for some colleges. Despite warnings not to play in Mexico, scantily clad coeds with tramp stamps on their backsides and young men in ripped jeans and snarky T-shirts clogged the border crossing. Why were the guards so slow, checking every car? Hell, the students would try to bring weed back into the States, not take it to Mexico.

When their turn finally came, despite all the licenses that cost two-hundred dollars each, *their* van got pulled aside. *Their* group got hauled inside while the authorities contacted the manager of the hunting rancho who had provided the documents. That man had gone out hunting peccaries of course. So they sat sharing the guacamole made in a blender by a woman who had tried to bring back a crate of uninspected avocados and wanted to get her money's worth out of them. Joe paid for bags of tortilla chips from the vending machines—his treat. Snacking passed the time until the game manager returned the call and cleared them with the guards. Unfortunately, he also made clear their identity. Before they could leave, a line formed for autographs. Cassie fumed, but Knox simply sat back and enjoyed more guacamole as the Sinners passed scraps of paper from Joe, to Connor, to the Rev, to Howdy to satisfy their fans.

Good they'd filled up on chips because dinnertime arrived before their crew crossed into Mexico, and Joe had no intention of stopping until he found Tommy. He paused for directions to Bijou's house and place of employment, then drove on, nearly being forced off the road by two near-sighted geezers in an old truck driving right down the center of the lane. Texans always thought they owned the right of way. He hoped those two big jugs in the back cracked on the return to their damned enormous state. Way they were driving, it was a good possibility.

"Slow down, Joe. We have trouble ahead. A house down there is on fire, and someone is shooting up a pottery shop." Knox removed the rifle by his side from its case and prepared it for use.

A rotund Hispanic man had his hands in the air. A steady stream of words issued from his fat lips under a thin mustache. Joe brought the van to a stop in the shelter of a lone shade tree and pressed the button to slide the windows down. Knox got out and took up a post behind the tree's trunk.

"Anybody know what he's saying?"

Silence, then Howdy spoke. "He's asking the man

not to kill him. Says he doesn't know where the children are."

"Impressive," the Rev said.

"Not so much. High school and college Spanish and a lot of spring breaks spent down here. We had a hired man who spoke the lingo, too. Do you figure the shooter is looking for Tommy?

"I don't believe you said lingo," Cassie sneered.

"We don't need the snark now, Cass," Joe reprimanded. "We need to find Tommy."

She sobered instantly. "Yes, sorry. Do you think he really means Tommy?"

The muscular man with the Mayan face put a pistol with a silencer under the potter's wobbling jaw, and then that timeless face shattered like an ancient artifact used for target practice.

"He ain't looking for Tommy anymore," Knox said.

The obese man, covered in gore, sank to his knees.

"Dear Lord in heaven be with us this day," the Rev murmured. "Did the other gun go off when you shot?"

"Nope," said Knox. "I think the fat man is just shittin' those white pants he's wearing. Close call."

Cautiously, Joe allowed the van to drift forward until they came up next to the kneeling Mexican. "Howdy, ask him about Bijou and Tommy."

"I speak English. *Gracias*, you save me. Miguel would kill anyone for *El Jefe*. The man called Bijou, he is dead down there. They burn his house. Miguel tell me so. The children, I don't know. They played here. Now, they gone. I must go *rapidamente* before the others come for me." Without stopping to change his brown-stained pants, Pedro Gonzales waddled to a truck packed with clay vessels and abandoned his business in favor of his life.

"We'd better go down to that house and check. Tommy might be hiding nearby. If he sees us, he'll come out. Could be Bijou is still alive." Joe drove on very slowly searching for red hair among the gray-green bushes.

Everyone got out at the burning house. "You sure that's Bijou?" the Rev asked.

"I'm sure. Look at those rings he's wearing. And the gold tooth."

Cassie agreed quickly with Joe before going behind a large cactus to puke up the guacamole.

"Pretty woman," Connor remarked, keeping his eyes on Pilar's less gruesome corpse. The flies attracted by any moisture in a dry land buzzed around the wound in her chest. One crawled over the crease in her red lips. "Seems like the killer didn't want to mess up her face. Sad, very sad."

"War always is," Knox remarked as if he hadn't shot a man minutes ago.

Joe glanced at the dead woman's face. "Jesus God, she's wearing Nell's earrings."

"You want me to get them?" Knox asked.

"No. I'll get Nell a new pair, a different kind. I don't want to remember this."

Cassie went to the van, cracked open a bottle of water, and rinsed her mouth. Keeping her eyes off the carnage, she leaned against the side of the vehicle. Howdy went to stand beside her and swilled half a bottle as if trying to keep his own barf down. Joe kicked the dirt.

"Shit, what do I tell Aunt Flo now? Always knew

my cousin would end up this way. I hope my not paying the ransom into his account had nothing to do with it. Anyhow, we have to find my boy. Could be he's at this Rancho Miro down that way. And damn you, Bijou, I'm taking my stolen truck back, too, you hear wherever in hell you're burning!"

"Easy, Joe," the Rev said. "No use in speaking ill of the dead. Only God gets to judge."

"Now, there you and I disagree. Look, if this fire spreads to the brush, it could be bad for all of us. I want you and Connor to go back into town and alert the police, the fire department, whatever. Howdy, you and Cassie go with them. I'll take my truck down to that ranch and see if they know anything about Tommy. Meet you at the border crossing. Knox, you're with me."

"I'm going with you, Joe. He's my son, too." Still a little shaky, Cassie made her way to the truck and climbed into the back of the double cab only because Knox had silently transferred the weapons from the van and taken the shotgun seat again before Joe finished talking.

"Count me in." Howdy slung himself in beside her.

The Rev climbed into the driver's seat of the van, adjusted it to his comfort, and leaned across to help Connor with his bad leg into the other seat. They set off on their humanitarian mission into the city with no more need for further instruction than when running a frequently practiced route.

Joe shaded his eyes. "Appears we won't have to drive down here. A black SUV is on its way from the ranch. We can wave them down and ask about Tommy. On second thought, they're coming on pretty fast and might not stop. I'm gonna pull across the road so we can get some answers. Would you look at all the crap on this floor?" The big engine roared to life. At least, God-damned Bijou had kept the engine in good condition. Joe drove the truck aslant across the lane.

"Wait a minute! They have guns. Automatic weapons. Get us the hell out of here, Joe!" Not a suggestion, but an order from Knox, punctuated by the rapid rat-tat-tat of bullets leaving a barrel and singing through the air

The quarterback swung the vehicle around as if he were executing a trick play and burned rubber back toward Laredo. In the back, a bulky package flew out from under the seat to join the other junk on the floorboards. Howdy snagged it with one long arm and peeled back the brown paper.

"Ah, Joe, I think I know what they might want. Looks like we got a kilo of cocaine back here."

"Figures. It just fuckin' figures. Anything Bijou could do to make a quick buck, he would do. Probably what got him killed, and now us."

"Maybe not." Knox took a careful aim leaning out the truck window but only blew a side-view mirror off the Escalade. "Shit. Howdy boy, climb across Cassie and try your luck on getting the driver." He handed over a second rifle. "Girl, you get your head down. They're getting closer."

Howdy showed the same coolness he displayed on the football field when attempting a fifty-yard field goal. He steadied the rifle as best he could, used the scope and squeezed the trigger, but a sudden bump in the road threw his aim off, the only casualty, the front windshield of the pursuing vehicle.

"I got another idea. Joe, if you can put some distance between us I'll send them what they want."

"Veer off! Don't take this into the city," Knox shouted. "Aim for that little outcrop of rocks."

Joe took the truck off-road and silently thanked God-damned Bijou for the huge, deep-treaded tires he'd purchased or stolen to outfit his rig. Doubtful the Escalade, all shiny and new, had ever left a paved road. It followed, but the space between the two vehicles increased as Joe churned the desert landscape.

Nearly at the mound of rocks, Howdy called, "Here is good."

Joe braked hard, and his kicker scrambled out with the sack of cocaine clutched tightly against him like a football recovered from a fumble. He sat it upright in the dirt and stepped back to go through his paces. One-two-three, the instep of his athletic shoe connected hard with the sack. It flew upward and arced, trailing a white tail like a comet from a hole punctured in the plastic. The SUV slammed to a stop when the bag landed a few feet in front of it. From the passenger side, a rider emerged and, using the door as a shield, the Escalade moved slowly forward until the sack could be easily retrieved and tossed inside the vehicle.

Howdy dusted his hands and headed back to the truck, smiling ear to ear. "That should do it."

Their pursuers didn't think so. Shots peppered the ground behind him.

"To the high ground," Knox commanded. Taking the rifles and ammo with them, they evacuated the truck, dashed for the outcrop, around its back, and up its side where the ranch manager quickly took up a prone position and sent two shots into the front tires of the Escalade. The SUV stopped rolling forward, but the men within again used the doors for cover and continued firing. Knox surveyed the terrain.

"There's a little arroyo back here. Probably carries water down to the Rio Grande in the wet season. It will make good cover and lead you back to the border. Get going, all of you. I'll cover and come along once I finish business here."

"No way. I got you into this, Knox. I stay with you. Howdy, get Cassie to safety." Joe took up a loaded rifle, aimed and put a sizeable hole in one Escalade door. The bullet might have punched through since one of the enemies fell back but got up again.

"I'm not going!" Cassie hunkered down behind a boulder with Howdy who prepared his own shot.

"See here, girl, you can't handle a rifle. You're a liability. Now go on. Get us some relief soon as you can. Howdy, carry her if she won't move. Leave the rifle," Knox directed. He squeezed off another round to keep the gunmen from advancing during a lull.

"I'm asking you to go, Cassie. I care about you. If this turns out badly, you tell Nell and the kids I love them." Joe stopped talking and aimed his rifle again.

"Same message to Corazon," Knox said. "Now get."

Chapter Eighteen

"I don't want—"

Howdy put his rifle on the ground, wrapped his arms around Cassie, and tugged her backwards off the far side of the outcrop. She dug her feet in when they hit ground, but he continued to drag her toward the ravine. It wasn't very deep, so he hugged her close and jumped off the edge, landed in a crouch, and continued shoving her along like one of the huge Sinners' linemen practicing on the tackling sleds.

"Stop it! Stop shoving me, Howdy."

"I will if you move along on your own. Joe and Knox are saving our lives. The least we can do is make sure their stand isn't for nothing."

"Joe said he cared about me. How can I leave him?"

"Darn it, Cassie. We don't have time for 'He loves me, He loves me not.' Move your sweet bippie."

"Bippie. Really?"

"You know what I mean." He shoved her forward.

Resentfully, Cassie started down the ravine. A few more shots sounded from the outcrop and more rapid gunfire answered.

"If we hurry, we might be able to get help."

Thankful for all that exercise on the treadmill she began to jog, and then run full out. Howdy stayed right behind though she suspected he could have passed her easily. His stupid cowboy code probably decreed he had to take a bullet in the back for her. She pushed herself harder. Her mouth went dry, damp strands of hair clung to her face, and she began to pant. Glancing back she saw Howdy coming along, silent and strong, his pale blue shirt with the sleeves rolled up plastered to his heaving chest with sweat. They'd run way more than the length of a football field.

The arroyo curved a little to the right, and they came up fast on a tiny pool of water, a patch of shade, and two grazing burros taking advantage of slightly greener vegetation than above the rim. The animals eyed them suspiciously, determined they were only loco humans, and went back to their meal.

"Finally, some luck. Looks like we got transportation." Howdy stopped her with a hand clamped on her sweat-soaked shoulder.

"Those tiny things?"

"Small but tough. My guess is like any domestic animal, they know where their barn is. Climb on one."

"What if they're wild?"

"They would have run away if they were wild."

"We don't have a saddle or bridle."

Howdy stared hard at her, clamped his hands on his hips, and splayed his legs wide like John Wayne without a weapon facing down a gunslinger. "Get on the burro, Cassie, before I throw you over one of them. I've about had it with your attitude, your mouth, and your sass."

"You just make me."

He did. Despite his lankiness, he had some muscle and it showed through that sweat-soaked shirt as he upended her and slung her over the back of the closest donkey. He swatted its rear and shouted, "*Andale, burro!*" rolling his Rs ferociously. The small beast of burden took off at a trot. The other followed. He caught up with it quick and used its mane to lever himself aboard. Cassie, meanwhile, had struggled upright and clung to the bristly hair on her donkey's neck. Behind them came a sudden shout of *ladron, ladron*! An old man with skin nearly the color of the clay forming the arroyo limped after them waving a thick walking stick every few steps. A plain straw sombrero toppled from his head and hung by its leather thong around his wrinkled neck.

Howdy called out over his shoulder, "No *ladron*, not thieves, just borrowing, *comprende*?"

But the accusations continued to follow them until they came to a narrow path leading upward. Once up on the rim, they could see a small farm in the distance: a white cinderblock house with a corrugated metal roof, a shed sheltering an old tractor, a corral and lean-to for the burros, all surrounded by acres of irrigated tomato and pepper fields. Ignoring their long-legged riders whose feet nearly bushed the dust beneath their small, sure hooves, the donkeys headed directly for the corral in short, choppy strides. Cassie's burro arrived first. She dismounted much more gracefully than she'd gotten on and opened the gate for the animal whose large brown eyes looked longingly at the vegetable fields for a moment before resigning itself to a manger with a few wisps of withered hay.

Howdy slid off as they passed the green door of the farmhouse and let his mount go on without him. He pounded with both fists on the sun-blistered wood and yelled, "*Se llama policia!*"

The door cracked open just enough to expose the double barrels of a shotgun. A youthful female voice hissed, "*Donde esta mi abuelo?*"

"The old man? He's fine. Our friends are in trouble. Some gunmen have them pinned down a couple of miles along the arroyo. *Comprende?*"

"*Si, sus amigos* anger Don Esteban. He the only one who kill people here. You get us in trouble. Go away, gringo."

"One phone call, *por favor*. Don't give your name. Say shooting is going on by a rocky outcrop near the arroyo." When the woman did not answer, Howdy played the celebrity card. "The men are American football players from the New Orleans Sinners. If they die down here, there will be a big investigation."

"Which players?"

"Joe Dean Billodeaux and a friend."

"I like Joe Dean, a handsome man with a smile like *El Diablo*. I will save him. Come in after you put the burros in the corral. They eat everything they see."

Cassie had already taken care of that and dashed over to stand by Howdy. Then, she saw the shotgun. "I don't believe this."

"It's okay, Cassie. She's going to help us."

The barrel of the weapon jerked upward. "Inside, pronto!"

The woman, quite young enough to be susceptible to the charms of Joe Dean Billodeaux or the movie stars she read about in Spanish language tabloids, gestured them to a set of chairs around a carved wooden table. They sat as she got her cell phone and made a call speaking so rapidly, Howdy had no idea what she said. For all he knew she could be notifying this Don Esteban of their presence in her living room. Sometimes as the Rev would say, you simply had to trust in God and the basic decency of people.

"Done. I have save Joe Dean. You want some coffee?"

"Any form of liquid would be mighty appreciated right now, ma'am. We ran a long way. Your burros came in handy. I'll gladly pay you for their use."

Their hostess gave him a beautiful, white smile. She wore her black hair parted in the middle and drawn back in the traditional bun but had on snug, white Capri pants and green rubber flip-flops. A yellow tank top worn braless allowed for a lot of jiggling from her small, firm breasts. Large, crescent-shaped earrings swung when she tossed her head. "I like you. I think I know you, no?"

"Well, ma'am, I do kick for the Sinners."

She clapped her hands and chanted, "Howdy, Howdy—Doody, Doody." Her bobbing breasts helped keep time.

"Yes, I wish folks wouldn't do that when I come out to kick. I especially wish they wouldn't shout 'doody, doody, doody' when I miss."

"You don't miss much. My brother watches the American football. He is far out in the fields today, but he be back in a while for dinner. I am not married, but I keep the house for him. I am called Carmelita Gomez." She sat a pottery mug before him and leaning very close, poured the coffee.

"If you two would like to be alone, I could go outside and talk to the burros," Cassie sniped.

"Pump some water for them while you out there, *gracias*," Carmelita said. She turned her shining, dark

161

eyes back to Howdy. "They are the pets of *mi abuelo*. He go into town and put on a big sombrero and a serape I make for him and pose with the burros for the tourists. He sell my weavings, *tambien*. You like to see my weavings? They are in the other room."

Cassie stood up. "I'd love to see your weavings. Howdy, you sit and enjoy your coffee."

"I think you want to visit the burros, no? I can give you a carrot for them."

"No, no, I'm much more interested in weaving. Howdy, stay put."

As Cassie figured, the large handloom filled half of a bedroom with celebrity pictures taped to the walls and a dozen bright pillows scattered across a single bed centered beneath a small window. She fingered through a pile of handwoven rugs and some colorful sashes draped over the back of a chair.

"Very nice work." She selected a rug with wide turquoise and terra cotta stripes and a vibrant fringed green sash with a metallic sparkle. "How much for these?"

Carmelita sized her up and said, "Hundred dollars American."

"Way out of my budget. How about forty?"

"Maybe seventy-five."

"Fifty."

"Sixty. Your boyfriend, he is rich football player."

Cassie started to deny that, but swallowed her words. "Done deal."

She threw the rug and sash over her arm and walked back to the table. She held up the rug for Howdy's inspection. "Won't this look great in your apartment? Pay Carmelita sixty dollars, honey. Honey, that's like *querido* in Spanish, right? I got a little something for myself, too."

Cassie wound the sash around her slim waist and modeled it by twirling around with her arms held gracefully above her head. Her hair might be stringy with sweat, her makeup gone and revealing her freckles, and she probably had raccoon eyes from running mascara and liner, but by damn, someone had to save Howdy from this Latina vixen.

"Pretty," said Howdy, carefully keeping his eyes focused on a space between the two women.

The door burst open. Carmelita screamed and ran for her shotgun, but the old man held up his hands. Gasping, he asked where his burros were.

"In the corral, *Abuelo*. We have a famous visitor, Howdy McCoy of the Sinners."

"*Es verdad*? Howdy Doody McCoy steal my burros?"

"No, only borrowed them. Look, I'm buying some of your granddaughter's weavings. How much for the time we rented those animals?" Howdy took a leather wallet molded to the curve of his butt from his hip pocket.

"Hundred dollars American?" Carmelita's grandfather answered.

"Seems to be the going rate for everything around here," Cassie snapped. "How about a hundred for the rug, the belt, and the burro rental altogether, and I'd still say you come out on top."

"Okay, sure." The man held out a wrinkled brown hand, but his granddaughter got to the offered sweat limp hundred-dollar bill first.

"You sign it for me," she asked Howdy. She found

a pen and handed it to him. He wrote on the greenback, "For Carmelita, Thanks for saving Joe Dean. Howard 'Howdy' McCoy."

Carmelita took the bill back, went into her bedroom, and returned with two crisp twenties for her grandfather. "Maybe I never spent it. Maybe I put it up on my wall," she said, slinking up to Howdy again. "You can come back someday and visit it, no?"

"Look, we have no more time for this. The autograph session and souvenir buying are over. We need to get into town and find the others. Can either of you drive us there?" Cassie, still wearing the sash, put her hands on her hips.

"For a hundred dollars American," the old man said.

"Oh, just give it to him if you have it, Howdy. I am worn out trying to save you money."

He peeled another big bill away from several others and shrugged. "I thought we might have to bribe someone so I hit an ATM when Knox stopped to get the water and you went in to use the bathroom." He offered the bill to the grandfather who nodded at the pen. He autographed it.

"I sell this on eBay, no?"

"Whatever you want. Talk about bribery. Do you have a car, or do we have to ride the burros again?" Cassie snapped.

"Carmelita drive you. My eyes are not so good no more."

The young woman dangled the keys from her fingers. "But I am a good driver. Come." She led the way behind the house and drew a tarp off a polished robin's egg blue, vintage Ford low-rider.

"Sweet," Howdy said.

"You ride up front with me. She go in the back."

"That's okay. You ladies ride together."

"Then, we not going anywhere."

"Howdy, don't argue with her. Just get in. We need to find out what happened to Joe, ASAP!" Cassie opened the rear door, tossed in the rug, sank way down on the seat, and slammed it shut.

Howdy took his place next to Carmelita who cranked up some lively Latin music before putting her foot on the gas pedal. Under the cover of the beat, he mumbled, "Sure, it's always about Joe."

Chapter Nineteen

"At least we got everyone else to safety. I wonder if we'll ever know what happened to Tommy?" Joe squinted through the sight of his deer rifle but decided the thugs were too well hidden to waste a shell on them.

"Where's the Billodeaux optimism? We ain't lost the game yet, *compadre*. They have rapid fire and lots of ammo. We have long range and accuracy. By their stillness, I'm thinking they might be running low since they didn't know they were running into armed men," Knox assessed. "Could end up being a standoff.

"Yeah, a Mexican standoff."

"We can always slip down into the ravine and make a run for it. I doubt those guys are in as good a shape as us. A man does want to see his baby born."

"I'm not against running. If they shoot up the truck, we might not have any other choice. Wait, is that a white flag?"

One of the enemies had tied a handkerchief to the nozzle of his weapon and waved it above the door of the SUV. Eyes shaded by mirrored sunglasses, he stood up very slowly. Blood on the arm his flowered shirt attested that Joe had winged him. The big man was no Mexican, just a white thug with a deep tan. Cautiously, he stepped out from behind his cover and moved closer to the rocks. "We got the package. You tell us where the boy and girl are, leave the truck, and we let you walk away."

"The boy and the truck are mine. Bijou stole them both. I don't know about any girl. I came here to get my son and go home. That's all," Joe answered.

The negotiator conferred with the second man still under cover. "Bijou said the boy is his son. Yeah, he probably stole that truck. We don't care so much about the truck. *El Jefe* wants the boy."

"You can have the truck. I won't give up my son. What have you done to Tommy?"

"Nothing. Wait, Bijou when he was drinking always said his big time football playing cousin stole his boy. You that guy?"

"Yeah, I'm Joe Dean Billodeaux of the New Orleans Sinners."

"I remember that Super Bowl when you asked for help to find a runaway girl."

"Bijou had her, left her pregnant. Tommy is her child, but I adopted him and want him back. My cousin was holding him for ransom. We came down here alone to bring the boy home, but the police back in the states know where we are. The FBI will come looking for us."

"Yeah," said Knox. "You don't want the *federales* in on this."

"I spit on the *fedrales*." For emphasis, the man did just that, but he answered, "The boy is missing. That is all I can tell you. You take the truck and go. *El Jefe* isn't going to believe this. Joe Dean Billodeaux right here, and that's his red-haired boy."

Knox spoke up. "Go back to your car. Throw out all your weapons. Shut your doors and stay still. If I see one muscle move, I'll put a shot through your head."

"Fine, but first, would you autograph my

handkerchief, Joe?"

The negotiator laid down his weapon, removed his white flag and moved close to the rocks. He tied a stone into the handkerchief to give it some weight and tossed it up to Joe.

"You got a pen?" Knox asked Joe.

"I always have a pen, brother." He stretched out the white cotton over a smooth surface, wrote "A pleasure to meet you. Joe Dean Billodeaux" and drew his trademark devil's tail heart beneath it. Usually, he used that for women, but he wanted to make the signature as authentic as possible to impress *El Jefe* and hope he would leave Tommy alone if he found the boy first. He weighted the cloth again and threw it in a nice, easy arc to the henchman who snatched it out of the air.

"I'll treasure this. Thanks, man."

"You're a good size and have pretty nice reflexes. You should change careers and try out for the football league." Slathering on the butter never hurt.

"You think so? If I need to change careers, I just might." The gunman left his weapon in the sand and walked back to the SUV with the shot-out tires. The other shooter tossed down his weapon on shouted orders from Joe's big fan.

Knox motioned for Joe to climb down to the truck while keeping him covered, then he followed, totally alert, forever the soldier, despite his short-cropped gray hair. He kept his eye on the SUV while Joe climbed in and started their ride out. Backing to the passenger door Joe opened for him, Knox jumped inside and immediately stuck the rifle out the side window.

"Drive along the arroyo, then veer for town. Don't backtrack."

"What about Tommy?"

"Nothing much we can do now, and no one is sorrier than me. If I don't come home with that boy, Corazon will never forgive me. Soon as we come to a road, take it into the city and head for the border crossing. We need to bring the FBI in now, though I doubt they can do much this side of the border."

Joe nodded. That famous smile of his seemed gone forever. He didn't spare the truck until they reached Nuevo Laredo and had to slow down. They crossed over the bridge again with no problems. On the other side, both noticed the red van parked at the building where they'd dined on tortilla chips and guacamole only a couple of hours ago. Seemed more like twenty-four had passed, but the setting sun only now cast long shadows as the day faded into twilight.

"The Rev and Connor got here safely. That's good," Joe said in a flat tone.

In fact, the Rev with a huge grin covering half his dark brown face moved their way, coming out of one of those shadows like an exceeding huge and friendly vampire. He reached their vehicle and towered over the guard as Joe explained that the truck belonged to his cousin so the registration wouldn't match his driver's license or the passport he dug from a pocket. Knox offered his I.D., withdrawn from a holder he wore around his neck on a string. The rifles he'd stowed under the seat safely out of sight.

"You make any purchases in Mexico?" the border guard asked, running through the routine while checking the passports.

"No. We came to find a lost boy."

"And we did," the Rev interrupted. "These are the

guys we told y'all about. Tommy is here, Joe, right inside swilling down orange pop and peanut butter crackers. You won't believe this, but the kid hitched a ride in an urn those two senior citizens who almost ran us off the road brought back. The guard found him and a few other little problems when he did an inspection."

"Nothing we can't handle," Joe said with his smile and his optimism coming back in a rush.

"I don't know about that. You better come see."

The guard told them to park next to the van until everything got sorted out, implying they had lots of sorting to do. As soon as Joe entered the building he saw one of the problems, a thin little girl wearing a sunflower-print, sleeveless dress he was fairly sure had come out of the twins' closet. Same went for the neon orange sneakers on her feet. And damn Bijou, she had Billodeaux eyes. His cousin really had fathered a child south of the border, a daughter who was now an orphan. Talk about complications. As he came closer he noticed she smelled of urine. No wonder if she watched her parents die. The way she pushed away from the table holding her snacks, stood up, and put her hands on her hips defiantly as he approached reminded him a lot of his own daughter, Jude, tanned and taller but very feisty.

Her first words to him, "I did not wet myself because I am afraid. His puppy peed on me." She pointed an accusatory finger at the seat Tommy had occupied a second ago. Now only a little yellow dog stood there with his white front paws on the table as he scarfed up peanut butter crackers with his black muzzle, the pup who lured his son away, the pup Tommy would want to keep. More trouble.

Joe felt the tug on his leg and looked down on that beloved red head, those freckled little boy arms hugging his thigh, and heard the small voice of his son say, "Daddy!"

He knelt to Tommy's level and took his boy into his arms. "Oh son, we were so worried about you. Never do anything like this again, you hear?"

Tommy nodded against his shirt and after a chest-spanning hug finally looked his father in the eyes. "Papi said we were going on a vacation, and I did have fun until—until today. I got us away in some big pots, and I remembered my phone number when the guards asked me. Mama Nell knows we're safe. I have another sister now and a dog. Can we keep them?"

Joe ruffled the red hair that set this whole business in motion. "I'm proud that you kept a cool head and saved everyone. I think we can keep that dog, but he might have to stay with a vet for a while to make sure he's healthy. It's not so easy to claim a little girl."

There she was, right in his face, still stinking of pee and entirely undaunted. "Why I not go home with Rojito? My name is Xochi Gracia Billodeaux. I am American citizen, born in Texas. Mama says so. I want to see America. I never want to go home because— because Mama and Papi are dead and my house burn down." And then she cried, those large brown eyes with the curly lashes overflowing with huge tears. Joe gathered her into the hug. What else could he do?

"Look, sugar, I'll make sure you never go back there." Another child and a forbidden puppy added to three babies on the way, Nell might not forgive him this time for making plans without her. He'd never cheated on her, not once despite many temptations. He knew he was a good father as he'd vowed to be, but all women had their limits. Had Nell reached hers with the entire Billodeaux family? Add that to the quandary list.

Connor lounged with one leg up on a chair by a window overlooking the Rio Grande and the setting sun. With a smile on his face, he said, "Looks like I need to take daddy lessons from you." The smile faded. "We did report the fire and the…what happened to Bijou and his wife."

"Thanks. Won't be the first thing you did for me or I do for you. Kids, go finish your food while I figure this out." Joe turned to a guard, a short, stout woman with a Latina face. "We have two other friends still across the border and maybe in trouble. Anyway we can get someone to search for them?"

Before she could answer, Connor called out. "Here they come now, walking across the bridge. I'd recognize Cassie's hair anywhere. Some ride they picked up."

Joe went to the window and watched the couple progress across the bridge. On the far side, an attractive Mexicana leaned against a robin's egg blue low-rider in pristine condition. She appeared to be blowing kisses Howdy's way while he waved to her without turning around. Joe stepped outside to greet them. The young lady with the jiggling breasts jumped up and down and pointed. "Joe Dean," she shrieked so loudly he could hear it across the water. "I save you!" He doled out one of his bone-melting smiles and shouted a "Thanks" her way, though he had no idea what she meant.

Two more of his kids were on their way home. That's all that mattered. He waited impatiently while Howdy presented a curled, damp passport to the guard and Cassie turned her back and withdrew hers from her bra. Howdy declared a rug he had tucked under his arm and the green sash Cassie wore around her waist. They'd gone souvenir shopping in the midst of a crisis? Young people, go figure. Who needed a rug to remember what happened on this trip?

He moved forward as they came through the checkpoint and embraced them both. "Tommy is here, safe and sound, with the Rev and Connor."

Howdy stepped back. "That's great. And look at you, not a scratch on you."

Cassie lingered in Joe's arms. She pressed against him, arms around his neck, and said, "I was so worried about you and Tommy. That girl called the police for us after a little persuading and drove us here. We had to buy one of her rugs."

"No, we didn't. She never asked us to, but her grandfather did want a hundred dollars for the ride and forty for the burro rental. Long story. We can tell you on the way home," Howdy said.

Joe unwrapped Cassie's arms and moved aside to clap Howdy on the back. "Nice work keeping Cassie safe and getting here. I'll pay you back for the—um, car and burro rental."

"No need. Happy to do it."

"Sure, he was. That Mexican hottie laid all over him! I had to save him from himself," Cassie exploded.

"Well, he is a nice looking young man, Cass."

"Not my type. Where's Tommy?"

"Inside."

She stomped off, but got over her mad as soon as she spotted her son running toward her. She lifted him in her arms and twirled around in happiness. "You're safe! I love you so much, Tommy, so very much. You and I and Joe can ride home in the truck together, just the three of us." She set Tommy down and noticed he frowned. "What's the matter? Aren't you glad we're together again?"

"Sure, but can my dog and my sister ride with us?"

"What?"

Joe joined their reunion. "Another long story. Cassie, I think you should go along with Connor, the Rev and Howdy tonight. Get a place to stay, a hot shower and a good meal, then go back to Louisiana in the morning. I have to figure out what to do about the dog and the new sister and even Tommy since he left and entered the country illegally. Knox has lots of law enforcement contacts. He'll help me work it out."

"Do I stink? Oh! I must look awful. But, I'm good with children. I'll stay."

"No, you go along with the guys."

"Tommy is my son, too!"

"And always will be. Don't be *tetu*, you. Do as I ask, please."

"Only because you asked me nicely. Come on, Howdy. You could use a shower, too."

Chapter Twenty

Despite giving in, Cassie burned like a sparkler on the Fourth of July most of the way home. The three Sinners listened without commenting until the least experienced with women spoke up. The Rev rolled his eyes, the whites showing the way they did in spooked animals. When Howdy weighed in, Connor sat very still as if they carried nitroglycerin in the back seat of the red van.

"Yes, Joe said he cared about you. He sent you to safety. He cares about me, too. He cares about the Sinners and about winning another Super Bowl, but caring isn't love. He loves Nell and his children. He'd die for them. You can't make your own little family by busting up his, or at least you shouldn't." There, he'd gotten it out of his system after miles and miles of remembering and holding it in—the sight of Cassie pressing up against Joe and begging to stay with him.

A deep "Ah-huhhh," came from the Rev's throat.

"That's not what I was trying to do. Tommy needed one of his mothers, and Nell wasn't there."

"Because she is at home pregnant with three of Joe's babies. Tommy gave the guards her number to call for help. Nell is who he talked to first. You have a cell phone. It didn't ring the whole time we were in Mexico. You're the young, fun mother, not the one Tommy turns to when he's scared. Get over it. Get over

Joe."

"My phone probably lost its charge." Cassie flipped open the slim instrument she took from her hip pocket. The bars lit up brightly. "I don't think it works in Mexico."

"Most likely not, but we're almost to the Louisiana border, and he hasn't called yet."

"Maybe Joe won't let him."

"I understood the deal was Tommy could call you anytime, but you had to stay away from Lorena Ranch until Thanksgiving."

"Joe didn't mean that. He couldn't possibly after what just happened."

"Look, I understand you wanted to help, but you horned your way into this trip and only got in the way! You could have been killed, Cassie."

"Got in the way! I saved you from that Mexican tramp. You would have ended up forgetting all about Joe after she lured you back into her bedroom to catch who knows what kind of terrible diseases if I hadn't scraped her off of you and bought a rug."

"With my money. I told you I've been to Mexico before. I know how to handle myself there. I didn't need your help."

"To fight off cheap women? Or don't you fight them off?"

"I'd say two-hundred dollars isn't cheap in Mexico. Maybe I gave way to temptation more than once during my spring breaks in college, but I didn't catch anything."

"Howdy, son, it disappoints me to know that," the Rev said.

"I'm not proud of it. I'm just saying I'm a man

who can take care of himself."

"That's good, Howdy Doody McCoy, because you have no family. You have no one who cares about you! I thought you were my friend." Cassie slashed at him with her words.

"Low blow," the Rev commented softly.

Howdy cleared his throat of something stuck deep down inside and said, "That's true enough. My mama left me on my grandparents' doorstep when I was three years old. While I sat inside their house having milk and cookies with Grandma, she drove off with her boyfriend. I don't think he was my daddy, but I can't be sure. Never saw her again. Now those good people who raised me are gone, but they built their house upon a rock, not on sand. No matter where I went, they waited for me with open arms. They left me their place, and I hope to make a home of it again some day with my own family."

The Rev couldn't resist an "Amen."

Howdy continued, "Cassie, the ones who raise you *are* your family. Would have been nice if my mother stayed in touch like you do with Tommy. He won't ever have to wonder if he wasn't loveable or not good enough to keep like I did. As for being your friend, well, in my mind, a friend tells it like it is to keep that other person from being hurt even more."

With a choked gasp and a flood of tears, the sparkler burning in the back seat went out. Connor kept his eyes straight ahead. "I saw that coming from way, way off."

Howdy moved across the aisle to the seats Cassie occupied alone. "Shoulder to cry on?" he asked.

"Uh-huh." She stammered out, "I'm sorry" before

burrowing into the fabric of another of his pale blue shirts, this one clean and smelling of fabric softer. She cried herself out and eventually fell asleep in the hollow right below his collarbone as if they were lying in bed together wrapped in each other's arms, his imagination running wild of course.

****

Joe looked at his son's bright head nodding against the truck window. The boy hadn't slept well, tossing and turning against him in the motel bed they shared next to Knox Polk who winked out as soon as the lights went off thanks to years of training. No wonder. He'd learned that Tommy hadn't viewed the actual killing or seen the bodies up close. Thank God for that. But still, he'd lost his natural father—who had treated him well for their short time together—and a new-found sister. Child services came and took Xochi away until her citizenship could be established. He gave the tired, rumpled woman who arrived after dark his contact numbers and his Aunt Flo's information, too. He assured her that Xochi's father had been a Cajun-American and she had relatives in Louisiana willing to take her and give her a home.

Last of all, he swore to Xochi she would have a new place with them soon. The child, dry-eyed now, answered, "I do not believe you." So much cynicism in so young a child broke his heart, but then she'd been raised by Bijou. Most likely many promises had been made and broken in that family.

The female border guard remembered Tommy from his last crossing and, very ashamed, apologized sincerely that she hadn't seen the Amber Alert and stopped the truck before they got into Mexico. She pointed out the fake passports in the glove compartment. That and a call from Sheriff LeDoux got them released to go home. She helped them find a veterinarian willing to open his place and take the pup into quarantine.

"But he's an American dog," Tommy protested.

Good at explaining the facts to children as many veterinarians are, the animal doctor told Tommy that Macho might have picked up diseases in Mexico and needed to have his shots, but he'd keep him safe until the day when the Billodeauxs returned for the dog. Still, the puppy whimpered and put his black nose up against the wire of the small cage when they left. Tommy held back his tears until the truck door shut.

"Is that why they kept Xochi?—because she might have diseases? Maybe I have them, too."

"Nope, you've had all your shots," Joe joked, trying to cheer his son. "With Xochi, it's more a matter of deciding where she should live."

"With us, don't you think so, Mr. Polk?" Tommy asked as he tried to gain the support of the taciturn ranch manager.

"You never know what the government is going to do," Knox Polk answered.

Intentionally, Joe selected another hotel far from the one where they'd stayed the night before their incursion into Mexico. Cassie might have been a comfort to her son, but she could be drama personified. The kid didn't need any more theatrics. He let Tommy sleep as long as he wanted in the morning, stuffed him full of waffles and milk at breakfast, and headed home to Nell who always knew what to say and what to do when it came to their children.

Showing a great deal of tact, Connor, Stevie, and the Rev had all decamped for their homes by the time the long-lost silver truck turned into the drive at Lorena Ranch. They knew he'd call if he needed their help again. With relief, he noticed Howdy's red truck gone, too. Didn't mean he wouldn't find Cassie inside waiting to come between him and Nell. Joe took a deep breath and got out of his vehicle. He came around to the passenger side and scooped the sleeping Tommy from his seat. A light rap on the side window immediately woke Knox who had stretched out for a nap in the backseat. Though dark had fallen, the kitchen door flew open and released a stampeding herd of women and children. Being more fleet, Dean and the twins reached them first.

Tommy startled in Joe's arms. He rubbed his eyes. "Hey, we're home."

Dean tugged on his brother's jeans. "We saved Easter candy for you."

"Thanks. I got us a dog. I mean he's my dog, but I'll share him with you.

"Where?" the little girls shrieked and swarmed to the truck.

"His name is Macho, and he's in Texas, but he can come home in a month."

"Oh." Their pretty, elfin faces showed their disappointment.

Tommy squirmed to get down, and Nell replaced him in Joe's arms. "You're home safe. Now what's this about a dog?"

Joe said, "Bijou gave him the puppy, not me, but I think the kids can take care of him. Right, team?"

"We'll feed him and brush him and give him

180

baths," the girls agreed.

Nell leveled her gaze on her children. "You'll clean up his poop and his piddles?"

"Oooh, yuck," the female half of the family replied.

"We will," Tommy and Dean replied in unison.

"Good. All of you inside and get ready for bed. It's way past your bedtime."

The herd turned and trotted away at this command from their leader. Tommy chattered about Mexico as they went. Corazon's sobs drowned out his words as the housekeeper stopped him at the door, knelt, and smothered him with kisses. "*Oh, mi Rojito, mi pequeno Rojito.*"

He resisted. "Stop it! I'm not small anymore. I escaped from a man with a gun, Corazon, so don't call me Little Red anymore."

"Ay, what you telling me?"

Knox raised his wife up and gently led her away. "I'll tell you all about it, *mi amor*. Joe, I'll clean those rifles in the morning. Looks like I won't get to them tonight."

"No hurry." Joe steered Nell to the house. "We have lots to talk about, you and me."

"I'd say so. I get a call from a border guard who puts Tommy on the line. I can't make any sense of what he's saying, but catch the words: sister and guns and giant pots. Then, Connor and Rev show up to stay with him until you arrive. They say Bijou and his wife are dead, but they don't know where you are. Cassie is with you, Knox and Howdy, too. Finally, I get that two-second phone call from you last night saying everyone is fine and we'll talk when you get home. Not good for my blood pressure, Joe."

"Sorry. Go settle the children. I'll put on some coffee. We can talk as long as you want."

"Better be decaf.'

"You got it. I don't need any jitters tonight. I shared a bed with Tommy last night and when he wasn't kicking me in the back, he stuck to me like hot glue." Joe eyed her belly. "How's the rest of the family doing? I swear you've grown an inch since I went away."

"Don't be ridiculous. You were only gone a few days. It just seemed like a lifetime. Of course, your mother came over every day and stuffed us with her cooking which is not exactly lo-cal. You know how she gets offended if you don't clean your plate and ask for seconds. Lizzie's boys did all the ranch work so none of us got any exercise except for a few long walks. No wonder if I do look bigger."

"But beautiful, very beautiful." He drew her in for a kiss, started out light on the lips, then went deeper and deeper until…

"Mom, you gonna tuck us in or not?" Dean said from the doorway. Tommy stood right behind him. The disgusted look on their faces said they'd caught their parents smooching again.

"Coming, definitely coming," Nell said. "Scoot!" She followed them out.

By the time she returned, Joe had the coffee made. She marveled how he'd managed to make decaf taste strong. Eating it right out of the pan, her husband dug into the half a pecan pie left from dinner,

"Mama does make a great pie," he said, licking the crust crumbs from his lips. "So you know about Bijou being dead. Some drug lord did him in, no surprise there, and killed his wife. You heard about the dog. There's one other little thing we need to discuss together. I know you like when I do that instead of making a family decision on my own."

"Yes, we've discussed this."

"Well, Bijou left a daughter behind. Her name is Xochi. She's a tough little thing same age as our girls. I wanted to bring her home with Tommy, but since we aren't sure of her citizenship, Health and Human Services people have her in Texas."

"Oh, no. Poor thing to lose both parents and then be left with strangers."

Nell had the softest heart when it came to children, at least unfrozen ones. She'd taken on the raising of Dean, his love child by another woman, then Tommy, and finally the twins conceived by IVF. He counted on that weakness for kids now.

"I sort of promised to come back for her. Tommy has already claimed her as his sister, but if you can't handle having another five-year-old daughter, you just say so. Aunt Flo and Uncle Hal would probably take her or one of my sisters."

"You think a five-year-old would be too much for me when I'm carrying three? It's taking care of a trio of babies that concerns me. No, Flo and Hal have raised a large family and deserve their rest, though they'll be delighted to have another grandchild. We should keep her, especially since she's Tommy's half-sister and a Billodeaux, too. Unlike that puppy, she won't pee on the floor or chew up the furniture."

"She claims she doesn't wet herself, but she might take a bite out of someone, none of my guar-an-tees there. I have three months to help you get her tamed before summer training starts."

"I'll hold you to that."

"Thanks for getting rid of Cassie so we could have some private time when I got home."

"I didn't. Howdy sort of prodded her my way. I could tell she'd been crying. She apologized for upsetting me in any way. She said she'd call Tommy in the morning. Then, he loaded her into his truck, and they went back to New Orleans. That young man is becoming much more assertive."

"If he expects to get anywhere with Cassie, he'll have to be. Say, this might not be a good time for a suggestion, but do you think we could have some very, very gentle sex tonight? I really need to de-stress."

Nell took a seat on his lap. She licked the sweet molasses of the pie from his full lips. "Let's see what we can do in the way of stress relief. I could use some, too."

Chapter Twenty-One

Only too happy to escape his dream of being pursued by gun-toting drug runners and dashing through that arroyo praying he didn't tread on any rattlers and lose his kicking foot to their poison, Howdy woke to the shrill buzz of his doorbell. Throwing on a terry robe over the boxers he slept in, he made his way to the peephole and glared out at Brian Lightfoot who held up a grease-stained white bag. He unlocked the door, and Brian breezed in with his offerings.

"I have returned. I bring beignets and café au lait for breakfast. My mother sent you an Easter basket filled with home-baked goodies. It's downstairs."

"Does she think we're a couple?"

"Possibly, but I think it's more the orphan story playing on her heartstrings. She says next time I should bring you home." Brian set the bag and grande-sized paper cups on Howdy's breakfast bar exactly like the one in his place except for the pebbled exterior, beige marble top, and the rush-seated stools.

"I hope you told her I had an invitation from a girl to go to her house."

"Why crush her hope that I'd found a nice guy to spend my life with forever?"

"Thanks a lot for that. So how was Easter at the Lightfoots?"

"Same old, same old. Baked ham, deviled eggs,

and Aunt Celia telling me she understood my lifestyle choice while Uncle Newt called me Ella's faggot son. Family, you don't get to pick them and have to take them as they are. How did it go with Cassie? Making any progress there?"

"Hard to say. We got called away from her hoard of a family. Must have been fifty people crammed in that house and most of them red-haired. I didn't have much chance to talk to her with her older brothers quizzing me on my intentions and asking if I played rugby and her mother and aunts pushing more food on me because I seemed too thin for a football player."

"Typical family holiday if you ask me." Brian lifted the lid on his coffee and took a cautious sip.

"Look, I appreciate the donuts, but I got in real late. Let me get some clothes on." Howdy pulled the sash on the robe tighter.

"Still afraid I'll jump you? Is that why we don't meet here more often?"

"Yes—and no. You make fun of my condo."

"It is so mockable. Your designer took one look at you and said, cowboy motif. You did not correct her. I do rather like the new rug, but shouldn't it be under the distressed oak coffee table rather than slung over the saddle leather sofa?"

"Got it in Mexico and if Cassie doesn't start seeing me as man rather than a friend soon, I might have to go back there and buy another one."

"I take it rugs are now a euphemism for sex? Interesting, go on."

"You got that right. We get this call from Joe Dean on Friday night. Tommy's natural father, a low-life called Bijou, made off with the boy. He tried once before but Knox Polk, Corazon, and Joe fought him off."

Brian bit into a beignet and scattered powdered sugar across the counter. Tidily, he cleaned it up with a paper towel ripped from a wrought iron holder. He swallowed and said, "I remember that. Joe took a knife to the shoulder, and the Sinners lost their first playoff game because he was out on medical leave. Tragic."

"You wanted to play for the Sinners even then?"

"No, dear boy. I wanted a grand lifestyle in a big - cosmopolitan city where my queer ways would not be questioned."

"Makes sense. Anyhow, I drive Cassie over to Lorena Ranch because she's too upset not to kill herself on the road getting there. Joe already has the Rev and Connor there planning a raid into Mexico to get Tommy back from this Bijou. Cassie refuses to stay behind with the rest of the women, most of them pregnant. I offer to go along—to keep her safe, but she doesn't seem to notice that."

"Ungrateful bitch."

"Language, Brian. She's too worried about Tommy to see what I'm doing. We get down there and find Bijou and his wife dead, Tommy missing, and some Mexican drug lord's goons gunning for us. We get far enough away so I can punt the kilo of cocaine they want their way, but they keep on coming, firing automatic weapons at us. I shoot out a windshield trying to get the driver. Knox takes out their tires. Joe wings a guy. He insists I take Cassie to safety, so I do. We end up in the house of this hot *chica* who makes rugs and drives a low-rider. She helps us get back to the border. Least I could do is buy a rug, but Cassie seems to think I need saving from STDs. Oh, what the hell."

Howdy sat on one of the rush-seated stools and gulped half his coffee. His robe parted over his knees, but Brian prudently kept his eyes on his friend's face even when sugar from the beignets powdered Howdy's chest hair.

"When we get together with Joe again at the border, we find Tommy made his own escape and brought a little girl with him, his sister, he says. Cassie melts all over Joe, wants to stay with him, drive home with him and Tommy in a stolen truck he reclaimed like one little, happy family. No way Joe is doing that. He ticks Cassie off, and the rest of us have to listen to her rant all the way home. I tell her off for her own good. She cries and messes up another one of my shirts. I make her go home and stop bothering Nell. The end, no sequels. I am still her friend, maybe even her BFF. I'd only take a bullet for her." He stuffed half a beignet into his mouth and let the sugar fall where it may.

Brian held up a manicured finger. "Wait, I see some progress here."

"Where?" Howdy shaded his eyes with a hand and pretended to search a wide horizon.

"First, Cassie was not trying to protect your innocent self from STDs. She exhibited jealousy. Second, you showed you wouldn't put up with her bitching in a very manly display. You shot out a windshield and dragged her to safety. That makes even my heart go pitty-pat."

"She didn't thank me. In fact, I had to reveal I'm not as innocent as I appear."

"The second part of that is good I think. This girl has a rather sordid past. Deep down, she may feel unworthy of a nice boy like you. And I do think she noticed what you did to save her life, hence the spate of jealously."

"Evidently, she feels worthy of Joe."

"We both know Joe has his own lurid past—all those women, the love child. He's not a clean-cut guy like you."

"Women like bad boys. I'm not one."

"Come on and tell Uncle Brian how you lost your innocence. In high school with a cheerleader under the bleachers? Am I right?"

"No, I had a girlfriend, everyone on the team did. We went to the same Baptist church. She wanted to remain a virgin until marriage, so she did."

"Ah yes, I remember those days. I had a high school girlfriend, too, and she also remained a virgin. College?"

"I got through freshman and sophomore year untouched, but then I became the ace kicker for the Sooners. I save a championship game with a field goal, and the rest of the team takes up a collection for a trip to Mexico to buy me a whore."

"You had no whores in Norman, Oklahoma?"

"We had a tough season. The team wanted to party down somewhere Coach wouldn't find out what they did. And they did it all, tequila and blow and the best whorehouse in town."

"You said, they. I take it you did not participate."

"Not in the first two. Well, someone had to be the designated driver. We rented a van. They gave me a load of bail money to hold just in case."

"Howdy, Howdy, Howdy, what can we do with you?"

He contemplated the last sugar-coated donut. "You know, Brian, sex is better than beignets, and that's saying a whole lot. By the times that *senorita* got done with me, I could hardly walk back to the rented van. Spent every weekend there I could after that."

"Same whorehouse?"

"Same whore. She taught me a lot. Like how to take my time, same way as I kick, as long as I paid for the minutes."

"Incredible. You were loyal to a whore."

"Until I graduated. Just told the guys and everyone else I had a girlfriend in Mexico. Got ragged a lot about that. I hadn't quite figured out that sex and love are not the same thing. But being a Sinner is full of temptations. I quit going down there because the way Joe sheds women since he married, there are plenty to go around the team. Most of them don't interest me much though. Next time I got to Mexico, Lupe had moved on and so did I."

"You do have sordid past. Wonderful! When do you see Cassie again?"

"No telling. I guess she'll call when she wants to see me again. The way I chewed her out that might be never."

"No, no, no. She has seen your gun-toting, Mexican whore lovin', I don't take crap from women side now. Do not fall back into being her nice guy friend. You call her. Make it clear you are asking for a real date. Act now!" Brian handed him the phone.

Howdy took it with sugar-sticky fingers and regarded the phone much like the rattlesnakes in his dream. He had the urge to run before he got bitten where it would hurt the most—in the heart, not the heel.

"Want me to dial for you?" Brian offered.

"No, I can do this."

Cassie answered as groggy as he had been an hour ago. "Howdy, what? Has something else happened?"

"No, it's just I think we should celebrate Tommy coming home safely. Just you and me. No Brian. We hit the clubs, tear up this town."

"It's pretty hard to tear up New Orleans. Happens nearly every night."

"Good. Is it a date?"

"I guess so. What time?"

"Seven. I'll pick you up."

Brian gave him the thumbs up sign, gathered the soiled, empty bag and paper cups, and headed for the doorway. He paused by a tall saguaro cactus in a red crackle-glazed pot. The cactus wore Howdy's cowboy hat. "I like the whimsical touch."

"Oh, I don't wear my hat much in the city. People stare and make comments."

"As would I if I didn't know you well. Wear it tonight. It might provoke a brawl. Then you could really impress Cassie with your manliness."

"Right. Punching another guy does that. Seems she might be worried I'd punch her one of these days."

"Oh, she already knows you better than that. Call anytime night or day when you get in and spill. Ta-ta."

****

The smoke lay like a fog bank inside the bar. While New Orleans restaurants had gone smoke free, no one seemed to care if bartenders or musicians got second-hand lung cancer. Despite the dim lighting, Howdy, hunched over his second beer, recognized the fruity scent of the cologne when the Brian took a seat next to him.

"I thought you were staying out of this. How did you find us?"

"You two always wind up here. I'm afraid I was too curious and too bored at home. I waited until Cassie left for the powder room to make contact, and I will silently slip away before she returns. How goes it?"

"Fine, I guess. The music is good. We did some dancing. Band is taking a break, so now would be a good time to talk, but I can't seem to spit out what I really want to say."

"Barkeep, this man needs a shot of whiskey for courage," Brian said to the young man behind the counter. He whispered in Howdy's ear. "He's new and kind of cute, don't you think?"

"No."

The slim young man in the tight black T-shirt revealing a Celtic tattoo around one bicep asked, "Jim Beam, Jack Daniels, Old Grandad, Old Crow…"

Howdy cut off the listing. "The first, I guess."

"Water, ice, straight up?"

"Ahhh…"

Brian winked at the bartender and waited a beat to see if he'd get a response. Nothing. "Straight up. Make his a double."

The drink appeared in a flash. Brian paid with a big bill and let the bartender keep the change. Howdy downed it in two quick swallows, coughed, and slapped the shot glass back on the speckled black granite counter.

"Okay, thanks Brian. I think I'm drunk enough now."

"Not nearly for what you have to do." His

luminous dark eyes followed the bartender's firm and shapely ass as he walked away to tend to other customers. Distracted, he failed to notice Cassie's return or Howdy's reaction.

The kicker shoved his cowboy hat to the back of his head and turned to watch her cross the barroom's checkered floor. She moved through the smoke like a siren in the mist, the pools of recessed lighting picking up the red in her hair, not the blonde streaks. Oh, the way she walked in that tight gold dress, sinuous, leading with her full breasts, heading directly for him. A red-furred arm with an anchor tattoo etched on its forearm waylaid her.

"Hey, Red. Wanna dance the next set?"

"Not with you." Cassie shook off the arm that locked around her waist.

"Why not, doll? We could make beautiful red-haired babies together."

"Smooth, Shaun," his table buddies razzed.

"Because you are a big, obnoxious, drunken jerk," Cassie answered. "And I already have a date." She pointed a finger at Howdy grinning at her from the bar.

The rest of the man emerged from the shadows and joined her in the puddle of light. He was truly big, very drunk, and definitely a jerk. "The cowboy? He's with that fag. Baby, I got what you need if you're dating him." He grabbed his crotch and gave it a squeeze in case she missed the point. Cassie slapped his orangutan arm away again when it attempted another possession of her waist.

"Now, Howdy, now!" Brian urged, pushing his friend away from his seat.

The bartender floated over. "He need another?"

"No, but I do. What time do you get off, handsome?"

"I thought you were hitting on him." He nodded his pretty head at Howdy.

"Howdy, no, he's straight as they come, though he does have a nice derriere. We're with the Sinners. He kicks. I punt long ones."

"Thought I recognized you. I get off at two."

Howdy heard Brian's banter with the bartender in the back of his mind like the buzz of a dying fluorescent light, not something he was concerned about as he approached Cassie and her rough admirer.

"Leave her alone." Okay, not very witty, but the only phrase he could come up with as his brain seemed to be going numb.

"Who are you, the guy in the white hat coming to her rescue?" Shaun knocked the Stetson to the grubby dance floor.

"Last time I checked, it was gray," he answered with a bit more wit. "My grandpa gave me that hat."

Shaun raised a steel-toed, work-booted foot to come crashing down on the crown of the Stetson, but it did not reach its destination. Howdy's punch to the jaw sent him sprawling into his mates' table, overturning their drinks and sending the free bowl of peanuts skittering underfoot. Outraged, his buddies raised up in anger as Howdy bent to retrieve his hat. Coming up, he took one sucker punch to the stomach, defeating the blow by hardening his muscles, but he stayed doubled over feigning injury and head-butted his second assailant.

A third approached him from the side, but Cassie caught the man with a full slam in the face from her lethal little purse covered in sharp, metallic disks and strangely weighty. With his face suffering from myriad bleeding small cuts, the guy staggered back clutching his bloody nose. "I think the bitch broke it!"

"Watch your language around her." Howdy gave him a strong, two-handed shove that set him on his butt among the peanut hulls. Unfortunately, the main cause of the brawl had gotten to his feet again.

"Oh dear, three against two and one of them is a girl," Brian remarked to his new friend. "Excuse me."

He took three running steps forward and with the elegance and accuracy that were his trademarks, placed a kick directly into the orangutan's nuts with his rather pointy Italian leather shoe. Three down, fight over—except for the two brawny black bouncers heading their way in a cloud of peanut dust through the maze of chairs and tables. The bartender gestured to him and his companions, pointing out a rear exit. "Two, remember," he said as Howdy pushed Cassie to the backdoor and Brian brought up the rear. Running into the bartender who feinted right, then left before they got by, the bouncers pounded after them

In the alley piled with reeking shells from the oyster bar next door, they made a quick decision. "You go left, we'll go right. Get in the first cab you find. I'll pick up my truck later," Howdy ordered.

Brian, light on his feet, rounded the corner and turned left without the tiniest hesitation. Howdy dodged the always-creeping traffic of the French Quarter shielding Cassie with his body. He tugged her, skittering on high heels, toward the bright lights of a hotel marquee where taxis in abundance waited to be signaled forward by the doorman and bypassed them all. At the entrance to the cream and gold lobby, he tucked her arm under his and entered.

Breathless, she said, "We don't have to wait on the doorman. Just take the last cab in line, and we can get out of here."

He spun her to face him. "Tonight. You, me, here. Let's get a room," he said, the two shots of whiskey and the adrenaline still pounding in his head.

Cassie considered the intensity of his blue eyes, the serious look on a face usually caught grinning, and found herself loving that sprinkle of freckles across the bridge of his nose. Joe had never looked at her in that way, never would.

"I think...yes," she said.

Chapter Twenty-Two

The desk clerk didn't so much raise a brow when the young man dressed in cowboy casual threw down a platinum credit card like the ace of spades in a poker game. Nor did the night clerk make any remarks about the swollen condition of the guest's right hand as he awkwardly signed the printout of the hotel registration. Obviously, he encountered odder guests staggering out of the French Quarter at this time of the evening on a regular basis.

"Upgrade that to a suite," Howdy said. "And send along a bucket of champagne."

"Certainly, Mr. McCoy."

As the clerk made the adjustment and phoned in the order to the bar Howdy glanced over his shoulder to make sure Cassie still sat waiting on the gold brocade banquette and had not changed her mind and gone outside to take a cab home. With her legs crossed and draw to the side the way fashion models placed their long legs, she hadn't moved. Men passing through the lobby from the bar eyed her as if she were a high-class prostitute. The red-gold hair down over her bare back and the short metallic dress worn with killer high heels might have given them that impression, but they shouldn't be staring at her that way. He felt an unfamiliar surge of possessiveness rise from his groin all the way to his suddenly jittery stomach.

"Your key card," the clerk said for the second time. "Enjoy your stay."

"Here we go then." He offered his arm to Cassie like an usher at a wedding.

She accepted his gesture with a funny little smile on her peach-painted lips. Whatever she used to cover her freckles tonight had a glitter to it, or the whiskey had affected his vision as well as his good sense. The dress draped down low in the middle. His eyes followed a sparkly trail to where her breasts came together held up by some kind of miracle bra that allowed her back to remain bare almost to the waist. The elevator moved them slowly and soundlessly upward without a single jolt. He wanted to crush her against its cool, stainless steel wall and slide his tongue between those peaches. That's what Joe would do and exactly the reason why he shouldn't, wouldn't, couldn't.

So, he stayed in his formal pose, her arm resting lightly on his until the elevator doors opened with a discreet chime. He led her to the suite, but fumbled with the key card putting it in upside down, then backwards until he finally got it right, and the green button lit. Inside, the place was vast, full of spindly chairs, draped with heavy curtains, and decorated with vases of tropical flowers so lush they put Brian's roses to shame. The king-sized bed must be behind the ornate paneled door to the right.

"Oh, Howdy, this is—this is so unlike you." Cassie moved to the swagged draperies and opened them. They looked down upon low-slung New Orleans, a city built for the most part on unstable swampland and so it spread out, not up. A cruise ship ablaze with lights moved down the Mississippi headed toward Cozumel or Cancun.

"You mean I'm kinda rustic. That's what Brian says about my place."

"I wouldn't know. You've never taken me there. We always seem to meet at Brian's condo or you pick me up."

"Guess I didn't want you to feel pressured by being alone with me—or to make fun of my cactus."

"Your cactus? Is that a euphemism for…?"

"No. I have a cactus, a really big one, a saguaro that hardly ever needs watering, the perfect plant for a man on the road a lot the decorator said."

"I'd like to see it sometime soon."

A brisk knock announced the arrival of the champagne in a silver bucket on a linen-bedecked trolley. Howdy tipped the server and said he'd open the bottle himself to get rid of the guy as soon as possible. He didn't do too badly peeling back the foil and getting prying off the wire. He worked the cork out slowly with his thumbs, though one was sort of sore, and released it with a jovial pop and no spillage.

"Nicely done, no waste," Cassie remarked, holding out her flute. "I thought you only drank beer."

"And wine with Brian. He taught me the correct way to open champagne. It shouldn't spray all over the place if you go at it easy. That's how I do most things."

"Really, you have to show me." Her brows, almost the same shade as her hair but darkened a little, arched.

"I will as soon as we drink some of this." Howdy poured, chugged his first glass, and suppressed a burp.

Cassie sipped hers. "Brian didn't tell you how to drink it though. Take your time. We have all night." She turned down the lights and returned to her seat on one of the spindly chairs across a tiny, bandy-legged table from Howdy.

They sat watching the glimmers on the river and slowly finished most of the bottle before Howdy stood, moved behind her, raised that red-gold hair, and kissed her neck. He felt light in the head and light in his heart. He moved his kisses down the curve of her spine to her waist and worked his hands under the bodice of her dress where he encountered something very rubbery.

"Ah, what's this?"

"That's what's holding my breasts up. Say, why don't I see if they have a spa robe in the bathroom? Bet they do."

"Sure." He watched her move off to the lavatory for the sheer pleasure of it. "Ply with champagne, be gentle, go slow," he repeated to himself. He was forgetting something.

"Durn it!" The words came out louder than he intended.

Showing only her head, Cassie peeked out of the bathroom. "Something wrong? Does your hand hurt? Put some ice on it."

"I forgot to bring some protection. I mean I didn't think we'd end up here." For gosh sakes, he bet Joe never forgot condoms in his heyday. "I have to go out."

"In my handbag." She closed the door again.

Howdy upended the small, bulging purse. Two lipsticks, a comb, tissues, a twenty-dollar bill, a driver's license, a credit card, and quarter of a brick fell out with two condoms wrapped in foil stuck to its bottom.

"You know you got a brick in here?"

"Sure." Cassie emerged swathed in fluffy white terry and nothing else as far as he could tell. "I took this self-defense course. You know a purse or a high heel can be a weapon. Look how well it worked tonight. As for the condoms, Nell told me always to be prepared when I left for college."

"Remind me to thank Nell next time I see her."

"You want to change, too? There's another robe in there and the most gorgeous bathtub I've ever seen."

"Later, I think." No way a terry robe would hide the hard-on he had right now.

"Should we go into the bedroom?"

She led the way. He scooped up the two condoms and followed her like a hound dog on a scent. She turned on the bedside lamp that gave a pink glow to the room, turned, and dropped the robe. "Well, what do you think?"

He had that goofy ear-to-ear Howdy grin on his face. Suddenly unsure, she glanced down at her body. "Are you laughing at my freckles?" They did spangle her everywhere not covered by makeup.

"Nope. My grandma didn't care for most of the children's shows on television. She gave me Biblical dot-to-dots to do instead. I'm real good at connecting dot-to-dots." He moved forward and ran a slightly swollen index finger from one freckle to another across her breasts.

"My tummy, then? It's not a flat as it should be because of having Tommy."

"I like the way it curves a little." He ran his hand down its slope and wrapped a curl of that red pubic hair around his pinky. She had a bikini wax but not one of those bizarre jobs he'd seen on some of the groupies only too eager to show him.

"So why are you smiling like that?"

"Because you're beautiful, and you're mine."

Cassie flinched. She closed her eyes and remembered her first time with a man, with Bijou and with no others since that foul man made her his. He'd sung that old song to her their first time together. *You're sixteen, you're beautiful and you're mine.* She realized now how sordid it had been, a man in his mid-thirties, scarred from bull riding, the moonlight glinting off his gold tooth, mounting her on a sleeping bag in his parents' old, deserted house. He'd said the flattering words that a skinny, freckled girl with carroty-colored hair wanted to hear. She'd survived cancer same as Nell and doubted she would ever be attractive, ever be able to have children. She certainly proved that last worry wrong. Bijou hadn't been rough, only insistent that they were meant to be together in this way because that's what people in love did. She believed him.

Bijou stroked her breasts and down between her legs. After the first few times, she'd come to enjoy his handling, but it got rougher as time passed. He didn't want the baby, had tried to get her to abort him, and sometimes, the way he pounded against her, she thought he was trying to make her lose the child. Then, he'd traded her services to pay his gambling debts. Thank God, none of those men wanted a pregnant teenager. One had even given her money for a bus ticket home.

"Cassie, am I doing something wrong?"

She opened her eyes. The vision of the gold tooth vanished, replaced by Howdy's slowly diminishing smile. They stood in a luxury hotel room, not some third-rate motel, the best Bijou ever got for her when they weren't sleeping in the truck. The young man who had stepped back a pace was as decent as they came. She wanted to bring back his goofy grin. Cassie stepped forward and crushed her lips against his. She fumbled with his shirt buttons and the aggravating buttons of his fly eager to make him smile again.

"Easy, Cass, easy. You like country-western music?"

"Huh? Not so much. I heard a lot of it when I was barrel-racing on the rodeo circuit."

He stilled her frantic hands. "Do you recall a song about a wanting a man with slow hands. Cassie, I'm that man. I take my time. I'm not all flash and dash like Joe, so get used to it."

"I think I can."

"Good." He lifted her onto the bed and gently spread her limbs, opening her to him, and worked her from the lips down and then from the bottom up, connecting all the dots, leaving none of them out.

****

The cell phone placed on the elegant night table by her ear blasted *When the Saints Come Marchin' In*. Cassie rolled over, checked the number. Mom. She cleared her throat and rubbed the sleepiness from her eyes before answering. "Hi, Mom. I'm fine, couldn't be better. Don't ask where or why. I am over twenty-one and entitled to stay out all night if I want. Yes, I had the brick and the condoms in my purse and got to use both. Am I trying to shock you? Yes. I'll be home in a little while. No, I won't be back in time for the eleven o'clock Mass. Yes, I'll go to confession this week. Stop worrying. Later, okay?"

Howdy, ready to go again, pressed up against her freckled backside and splayed his hands over the soft warmth of her breasts. He nuzzled her red hair aside and kissed her nape. She responded with a contented sigh and a quelling comment.

"Hey, it's ten a.m. We need to vacate the room at eleven. Besides, my mother is on my back."

"No, I am." He gave her a small nudge with his erection. "So, there is at least one good thing about having no family, a lack of interruptions." His cell phone rang, merrily spewing out the song, *Oklahoma!*

"A show tune. Really. If it weren't for last night, I'd still think you were gay."

"Brian's idea of a joke. He programmed it for me. And speaking of the devil... Hi, Bri. Yes, I'm with Cassie. No, not at my place so don't invite yourself upstairs. Yes, uh, yes and yes. How about you? Good. Look we need to check out of this place soon. None of your business. Yeah, see ya."

"Brian says hi. He hooked up with the bartender and is mighty mellow this morning."

"I could say the same about me. You know I have to go back to LSU tonight. My friends won't believe what I did on *my* spring vacation."

"Fleeing from Mexican banditos or sleeping with me?"

"Both are pretty spectacular. I'd say you scored two out of three field goals last night."

"Would have done better, but we only had the two condoms. I could kick my own rear for not bringing my own, but I didn't think…"

"I thought maybe and came prepared. I've been fighting off your cowboy charms for a while, but after that John Wayne act dragging me down into the arroyo and setting me straight in the van on the way home, I think you might be able to handle me."

"All I want?" He stroked her breasts and moved his hands southward.

"In the shower. I can take care of your early morning urges with my nice, soapy hands since we're out of protection. I don't know where you suddenly got attitude, but I like it."

"John Wayne, *The Quiet Man*. Grandma didn't approve of many recent movies, but she'd watch any John Wayne flick over and over. Have you seen it?"

"I don't think so."

"In this one scene Wayne, an American, drags his Irish wife off a train and marches her five miles back to their home when she tries to leave him. Very inspirational for a guy like me."

"I'll get the DVD to see how it turns out."

"They get married and stay married."

She tensed under his hands. "Too soon, Howdy, too soon to mention those words even in a movie context. Let's enjoy the moment in the shower and then go over to your place. You can show me your great big cactus. If I have to go to confession, I might as well make it a spectacular one."

Bumping her hips playfully against him for a second, she slid from the bed and sashayed into the first class bathroom. He followed the sway of her hips all the way to shower stall. Incredible what two people could do with some imagination, a bar of soap, and spray jets when they'd run out of condoms.

Afterward, Cassie dried her hair with a wonderfully powerful hotel dryer while Howdy put on his wrinkled blue shirt and jeans and settled his gray Stetson into place for their march of shame in the same clothes worn last evening through the ritzy lobby. No one took the tiniest notice. This was, after all, New Orleans, a city of sin long, long before Las Vegas rose like a giant phallus out of the dry desert sands. Howdy squared the bill at the desk and turned in the key cards.

"Beignets?" he suggested. "We can walk to the Café du Monde from here and still beat the church crowd from St. Louis Cathedral. Beignets are one of my favorite things about this city."

"Mine, too. Let's go."

"Say, I'll drive you back to Baton Rouge tonight. I know you have classes and all, but maybe we could get together next weekend."

Her peach-colored lips turned up at his uncertainty. "I'd like that."

"After finals, well, I want to take you to see my ranch in Oklahoma before I have to leave for training camp. It sits right near the Texas border and has its own spring that forms a little lake. We could swim and ride and do other things. The house isn't much, not like Lor—" No, he didn't want to mention anything having to do with Joe or her exile from the place where Tommy lived and ruin this day.

Whether she caught what he'd almost said or not, he didn't know. He only heard her answer. "Sounds great. Let's plan on it."

Cassie's hair flamed under the sweltering morning sun, mid-April and already eighty degrees. Her golden dress glittered and drew the eyes of men as they moved through the French Quarter. Howdy kept a hold of her elbow, partly to steady her heels on the cracked sidewalks and partly to show possession, complete possession, of the beautiful creature he'd finally gotten into his bed—thanks to an assist from John Wayne. He didn't hesitate to kiss the powered sugar from her lips right there at an outside table with all the tourists watching and the cameras clicking. Because he was no Joe Dean Billodeaux, the paparazzi never followed him, but today he'd made the final score and won the game for sure.

Chapter Twenty-Three

Cassie called in advance because Howdy said it was the right thing to do. She asked Nell if they could stop on their way to Oklahoma and say bye to Tommy. They wouldn't hang around and overstay their welcome. Nell gave surprisingly cordial permission for their visit without consulting Joe. She asked how finals had gone and when summer classes started much like the old days when she'd been Cassie's counselor at the hospital, all very friendly and interested.

"See, it's just good manners, and those will take you a long way, Grandma said." Howdy turned his red truck into the Lorena Ranch drive and the gates opened before them like the entrance to Heaven.

The sometimes-angelic Billodeaux children formed a circle under one of the ancient live oaks that had seen the Attakapas Indians and the Union Army come and go into history. Dean, using a pointed stick, drew something in the oak duff. They pulled alongside the group and got out.

"Figuring out new plays?" Howdy asked.

Tommy immediately detached himself from the ring and ran to hug his second mother around the waist. Howdy let them have their reunion in peace and distracted the other kids by looking at the scratches in the ground. "So what's this?"

"We're figuring out the balance of power," Dean

said. "I heard about that on TV. See here are the boys, Tommy and me. Here are the girls, Jude and Annie. Dad is on his way to Laredo right now to pick up Xochi and Macho. Xochi goes here with my sisters. Tommy says Macho should be counted with the boys, but I say dogs don't count in the balance of power."

"I think they could," Howdy remarked. "A good dog won't ever let you down. I had one once."

"Okay." Reluctantly, Dean drew another stroke for the dog in the boy's column. "See, Mama and Daddy found out we really are going to get three babies in the fall. One is for sure a boy. They could see his wiener. The other is a girl." Dean marked the appropriate columns.

"The third one won't turn around and show itself, so it's a mystery child." He made a question mark to one side. "That one could upset the balance of power. I mean the guys are already behind if we don't count the dog since Dad is bringing another sister home. What if number three is a girl. Then us boys will be way outnumbered."

Howdy nodded solemnly. "I see your dilemma. But, did you ever consider that your dad grew up with four older sisters and turned out fine?"

"Yep, but he said it was H-E-Double L and a good thing he was a *Dieudonne*, a gift from God to MawMaw, so he had all the saints looking after him or he never woulda survived."

"I think your dad might be joking. I'd give anything to have brothers and sisters, even annoying ones."

With her hand stroking Tommy's red hair, Cassie stood behind Howdy. When he made such statements, she always felt this little twinge in her heart. Throughout her leukemia treatments as a child, she'd never been alone, not one second. Open her eyes from a hospital bed and there sat her careworn mother, her hard-working father, an older brother reading a comic book, or an older sister painting her nails. The brother would offer to share his reading material even though he knew she loved celebrity magazines best, and her sister would go from embellishing her own hands to doing Cassie's toenails, all to cheer her up. If Howdy became ill or injured, he had no one to take care of him, except maybe the Sinners if they felt he could recover and play again.

"Tommy, Mr. Howdy and I are going to visit his ranch in Oklahoma for a few weeks. Then, I'll be back in Baton Rouge at LSU again. I'll take lots of pictures and bring you a nice present from there." Three other sets of dark Billodeaux eyes stared at her hopefully. "I'll bring all of you presents. We stopped to say bye and won't stay long. I guess I should say hello to your mama now if your daddy isn't home."

"I'm right here," Nell said, coming through the grove.

Cassie noted she'd already developed a waddle. "Hi, Nell, why don't you look…"

"Huge. Go ahead and say it. Into my fourth month and it might as well be my sixth."

Howdy leaned down and kissed her cheek. "You look beautiful, Miss Nell, glowing."

"Just Nell, please." She looked pointedly at Cassie. "I wouldn't let this one get away if he thinks pregnant women are beautiful. Howard, you are a keeper."

Tommy tugged at Nell's maternity top, pulling the

stretchy yellow knit tight across her belly. "Mama, can I go to Oklahoma with them? I'm outta school. I like to travel. I want to see Mr. Howdy's ranch."

Nell regarded the young couple. Her nostrils flared a little, and Cassie wondered if she could smell sex on them the way Nell had once told her Nadine could from a mile away. They'd been at it before beginning their trip.

"Not this time, Tommy. Xochi is coming home this afternoon, and you don't want to miss her welcome party, do you? You and your dad and Mr. Polk will be the only ones she knows. Maybe next time."

Cassie caught that she hoped there would be a next time. Nell's mood had softened with her pregnancy or maybe with the success of getting her together with Howdy. She suddenly realized that since arrival she hadn't once searched for a sight of Joe coming from the barn or doing some kind of ranch work with his shirt off and his chest bare. In the past knowing Joe was gone, she would have hinted for an invitation to stay until he returned. Now, she found she'd rather be on her way to Howdy's ranch for two weeks alone with a man she'd disregarded until recently.

Maybe because she hadn't pressed, Nell made an offer. "Would you like to stay to greet Xochi? The two of you could remain overnight, whatever kind of sleeping arrangements you want, and go to Oklahoma tomorrow."

Howdy blushed and stared at the toes of his boots. "Thank you kindly, Nell. Maybe we can stay for the party, but I'd like to get as far as Houston tonight."

Cassie's delighted laugh drew the eyes of all the children. "You've embarrassed him, Nell."

"Well, I'm not your mother or even MawMaw Nadine telling you what you can't do. Grownups do grownup things, and I think you two might have reached a new maturity since going to Mexico. Come on and help us finish getting ready for the party. Corazon made a Tres Leches cake and her special extra-cheesy enchiladas, plenty of chips, fresh salsa and dips, too. We got a great deal at the Party Place on leftover Cinco de Mayo decorations, streamers, big crepe paper flowers, a piñata, to make her feel at home. We could use a man to hang the streamers since Corazon and I are forbidden to get up on a ladder."

"Knox won't do it for you?" Howdy asked, a little reluctant to stay.

"He's hiding out to escape being pressed into service, though he says he's walking the perimeter and grooming the ponies before the onslaught of our summer guests in a few days."

"So Camp Love Letter is still going strong?" Cassie said referring to the cluster of cabins Joe had built to accommodate the families of seriously ill children and give them a vacation on his ranch.

"Bigger and better than ever. We have a handicap ramp going down into the pool now. Every cabin is booked all summer."

"Camp Love Letter?" Howdy asked.

"Joe's charity. It's a play on his name. In his carousing days he always told the ladies Billodeaux meant love letter in French. I suppose it is a corruption of the term. As long as he's not using that line on other women anymore, I'm happy." Like a Madonna giving them her blessing, Nell gazed benignly upon them with her hands clasped over her belly. "Stay for the party."

"Thank you, we will," Cassie said simply.

They swarmed to the house where Corazon trundled around the kitchen putting the finishing touches on the feast. "Here, you cut up some vegetables for the dips. The *senora* says always we must have something green. I say we already got guacamole." She handed Cassie a paring knife and pointed to a bunch of celery and a pile of green peppers lying on the cutting board.

Nell hustled Howdy into Joc's vast den that had become more and more of a family room since the birth of the children. She pointed to the ladder in the center of the room and a festive piñata in the form of a burro ready to hang from the ceiling fan.

"Tie it to the fan post, but let it drop fairly low so the children can reach it," she directed.

Once he had completed that task, Howdy moved the ladder to the corners of the room and fastened the streamers of red, green, and white to drape merrily across the cathedral ceiling. The girls scurried below him placing bouquets of gaudy red and yellow crepe paper flowers into any container they could find including several of Joe's trophies. The boys seemed to feel they were above decorating and started in on the bean dip and tortilla chips until Nell sent them outside again with an "If you can't help, go watch for your dad and Xochi."

Mission accomplished, Howdy folded the ladder. "I'll take this out to the barn and make sure the boys don't get into any trouble in the meantime." He hefted it with ease, but very nearly knocked the vegetable-filled tray from Cassie's hands as she entered the room.

She placed the platter filled with green pepper

strips and celery sticks flanked by mounds of grape tomatoes on either side of a bowl of Nell's yogurt dip on a vast, slate-topped coffee table where salsa and chips already resided. She pointed to a piece of furniture that didn't match the rest of the light oak and leather décor. The plain blanket chest, reddish-brown and patinated with age, scratched in many places, squatted before the fireplace.

"I haven't seen that since your wedding, the second one."

Nell nodded. "Rosemarie, the old *traiteur's* granddaughter, brought it to the celebration. She said her grandmother wouldn't live to see all our children born so Madame Leleux had worked ahead with her knitting and crocheting. You remember how Madame always had just the right baby blanket ready for a gift when she'd predicted a birth. Frankly, I always thought she had a hoard of them in her attic and simply picked out an appropriate one when the child came. When we opened it later, we found two fuzzy pink angora blankets for the girls right on top, but that didn't make Madame prescient. Everyone knew we were expecting twin girls by that time. It's the fact the chest contains eight more blankets that gives me the creeps."

"How come? They're only afghans in an old homemade box."

"Madame told Joe we'd have twelve children, this way, that way, all ways, and being the superstitious coonass he is, he believes every word of it."

Cassie looked at Nell's swollen belly. "Well, I'd say you have a good start on that prediction."

Nell shivered. "To think I once believed my bone marrow transplant made it impossible for me to have children, but Joe never gives up on anything he believes. First he implants twins, then triplets, and now brings home a Mexican orphan. What next? How can I cope? How can I complete with young women like you when I have a C-section scar on my belly after delivering these?"

Cassie steered her former counselor to the long leather sofa. "Sit. Don't panic. Joe will see you have every kind of help you need with the kids. And if it makes you feel any better, he never encouraged me in any way. That was all me wanting what you had, I guess because I knew Joe and felt I'd be safe with him unlike Bijoux."

Nell gave a tiny laugh. "Joe safe? Never. He'll always be a challenge. You simply have no idea. But he does keep his word, always, and that's why we are about to get a new daughter. He promised he'd go back to Laredo and get her."

The boys roared into the room. "They're here! Coming down the drive right now!"

The family flocked to the front entrance of the Billodeaux mansion. The children lined up before Nell and Cassie and below the immense and intricate brass chandelier that hung from the foyer ceiling and illuminated the sweeping staircase behind them at night. The entryway floor of deep burgundy tiles, so much more practical with children running in and out than carpet, gleamed beneath their feet. The grand double doors opened. Joe entered and set down a pet carrier. His hard glance came to rest on Cassie. "What's she doing here?"

"I invited her and Howard to the party. They are on their way to Oklahoma—together."

"Oooh in that case, great to see you, Cass. Tommy, remember this guy? He's a little bigger than the last time you saw him." He opened the latch and an ecstatic pup burst out, skittered across the tiles and collided with the mass of children who fell to their knees to give pats and accept sloppy dog kisses.

Nell looked on in dismay. "I thought you said he was a small dog."

"He was last time I saw him. Man, I could hardly squeeze him into the carrier. I should have known when I noticed those big feet."

"Where's Xochi?"

"She's right behind me."

She still was—hiding from all the eyes suddenly turned her way. Joe stepped aside. "Gang, this is Xochi, your new sister, or she will be once all the paperwork is done."

The girl took in the chandelier, the impressive staircase, and gleaming floor tiles reflecting her small form. "*Es un palacio,*" she murmured.

"No, it ain't. It's only a great big house, not a palace," Tommy informed her.

"Don't say ain't," his Mama Nell corrected automatically. "Welcome to your new home, Xochi."

"You're fat," the new daughter said.

Joe snorted. "I warn you, she calls it as she sees it. But sugar petite, your new mom isn't fat. She's full of babies is all, so you'll have three more brothers or sisters in a few months."

Xochi frowned as if this weren't such a great idea in her opinion. She regarded the tussle of children wrestling on the floor with Macho. "Do I get a room with a lock on the door?"

Nell moved forward and knelt before Bijou's daughter. "You'll have your own room, but in this family we don't lock each other out.

"Sure we do," said Dean who'd been knocked to the floor by Macho's exuberance. "Whenever you and Dad want some privacy, you lock us out."

Her pretty pink dress hiked up above her knees, Jude straddled the dog. She glared at the newcomer. "Hey, aren't those my sneakers, the ones I've been looking for all over?"

Annie, who held Macho by one silky bent ear, said, "I think she's wearing my favorite sunflower dress."

Defiantly Xochi answered, "The dog peed on it. You don't want it no more even if it been washed."

Annie cringed. "Yuck, dog pee."

Joe rolled his eyes. "I knew this would mean trouble. I swear to God I left money with that welfare lady to buy her new clothes, but she likes these things the best. Considering the temporary foster parents mostly bought her white underwear and some shorts and tops from Wal-mart, I can see why. But look kids, all Xochi's clothes burned up in a fire. You need to cut her some slack."

"I want my shoes back." Jude abandoned the dog, came in low, and grabbed one of Xochi's feet. The new sister kicked her flying back into Macho who yelped and ran down the hall with Tommy in pursuit. Jude regained her footing and charged back with her hand made into a fist. Xochi raised her dukes in preparation for a battle.

They got one punch in each before Joe grasped both of the fighting girls by the backs of their dresses and parted them. "Listen up. No hitting. You almost knocked Mama Nell on her keester."

"What's a keester?" Xochi asked.

"Her backside, dummy. You talk funny," Jude said only too happy to reply.

"Ay, her ass."

"We don't say dummy or ass or tell anyone they talk funny in this family," Nell insisted.

"Then, you don't say much. I gonna get the belt now for my smart mouth, right? 'Cause I don't care. I got the belt lots of times. I never cry." Xochi crossed her arms tightly.

Joe mumbled, "God-damned Bijou" under his breath for probably the hundredth time, but Jude's dark eyes widened in admiration.

"You're really tough," she said.

Nell tried again. "Honey, we do have lots of rules in this family, but no one gets the belt ever. We do have punishments though."

"Yeah," said Dean. "She'll think of a good one, too, like extra manure shoveling."

Xochi wrinkled her nose. "In Mexico I don't shovel shit. Papi did that."

Nell shook her head as if giving up word correction for the time being. Tommy shouted, "Macho piddled in the hall, and now he's eating the bean dip!"

Nell smiled, and Dean said, "Here it comes."

Nell pronounced their sentence. "For fighting, insulting your sister, and use of bad language, the two of you go to the kitchen and get rags and clean up after the dog. Jude, show Xochi the way. If that bean dip runs right through him, you'll clean that up, too. Join us in the den after you've finished."

"I don't think I like this place," Xochi announced.

Joe clapped. "Hop to it!"

"But it's Tommy's dog," Jude whined even as she took her new sister's hand and started toward the kitchen.

"You all promised to take care of it. Everyone else into the den." Nell marched them forward. They found Howdy and Knox already in place on the sofa, Macho restrained by Tommy's arm around his neck, and a desecrated bowl of bean dip.

"Dean, please take the dip back to Corazon and tell her to put more in a clean dish." Nell sank into a vast and comfortable recliner, closed her eyes and put her feet up. "Give me a few minutes to regroup."

The quiet Annie crawled up beside her and snuggled. "She can keep my dress, Mama."

"Glad I have one like you, Anna," her mother whispered.

Cassie, who had taken this all in and not said a word, took a seat beside Howdy and murmured, "Why did I think I was ready for a big family? Nell, how do you do it?"

"Never let them get the upper hand," Nell answered with her eyes still closed. "Patience, punishments to fit the crime, and consistency. Joe, I'll need more household help fairly soon. Corazon and I can't do it all."

"You got it, Tink." He reached over the high top of the recliner and massaged his wife's tense shoulders. "Thank you for all you do." She nodded. As a husband Joe Dean Billodeaux had come a long, long way for the better.

The two punished girls appeared in the doorway. Jude did the talking. "We're finished. We put the rags in the trash and washed our hands. Now can we have the party?"

"A party?" Xochi said.

"Yes, silly, for you. See it's supposed to look like Mexico to make you feel at home, Mama said." Jude gave her a little shove into the decorated den.

"*Por mi*? Maybe I do like it here."

Nell got to her feet. "Shall we eat first or do the piñata? Xochi gets to decide."

"The piñata! I go first." Joe handed her a plastic T-ball bat. Before they could do any blindfolding or turning the girl began to whale on the papier mâché donkey in a way that would have been considered cruelty to animals if the thing had been real. It burst on her fourth stroke. Xochi filled her upturned skirt with falling candy. Macho barked and pulled lose of Tommy to join the scramble for treats.

Dean hesitated a moment. "I want *her* on my team."

"You don't get her. You and Tommy have the dog. I need Xochi on my team to help protect Annie," Jude answered with her fists filled with sweets. Annie scraped up a small handful from the edge of the chaos.

"Okay, okay. Now pour everything into this bowl to be shared later. You can leave behind anything having dog slobber on it." Nell held out a big, glass sphere. Her children queued up and deposited their gains. Xochi came last and reluctantly.

"In this family we share," Nell prompted. Xochi dumped her catch into the communal bowl and sat down to sulk.

Corazon bustled in with the Tres Leches cake bearing a single candle. She set it in front of the angry child who refused to acknowledge her effort in any way. A flood of Spanish burst from the housekeeper's lips. The little girl hung her head and nodded. "*Gracias*," she said.

"Howdy, you catch any of that?" Joe asked.

"The gist is that this is a nice home with good people. She should behave and be grateful."

"Good advice for anyone," Joe answered, but he looked at Cassie not at Xochi. That young lady also hung her head and refused to meet his eyes.

Nell urged her new daughter to blow out the single candle representing her first day with her new family, which she did. "Now, this isn't a birthday party so we don't have lots of gifts, but Xochi, I want you to go to that chest and choose any blanket you want for your own. Each one of my children has one made by special old lady." Nell pointed out the battered box, and the girl approached it cautiously as if a *bruja* might jump out at her.

"Go on," Joe urged. "I guar-an-tee there ain't no *loup-garou* in there. That's a Cajun werewolf, sugar. You'll learn more about that later. That old lady was very holy. She could see the future and made one of those exactly for you."

Xochi raised the lid. She got to her knees and dug to the bottom of the chest but ultimately selected the one on the very top of the pile. Getting up, she wrapped it around her shoulders. Big enough to swathe a good-sized child and not a baby, Madame Leleux had created an afghan of multi-colored red, green, and white rosettes, the colors of the Mexican flag. "This one," she said.

Joe gave Nell a triumphant look. "I told you

Madame had the sight." He went over to the box and held up the next afghan, pink with a frilly white edge. "For our baby girl to come." He took out the next of deep cerulean. "For our boy."

Dean edged up next to him. "What's the next one, Daddy?"

Joe withdrew a small blanket of the palest blue threaded with silver. "Looks like it was made for another boy, son."

Dean punched the air. "Yes, yes, another boy! The balance of power is safe."

Joe smiled. "Seems like we only need one girl's name, Tink. You want to know what else is in here?"

Nell shook her head vehemently. "No, I do not. Close it and haul it back to the attic while you have Howdy and Knox here to help. Right now. Who wants cake?"

"No, no," Corazon corrected. "My enchiladas are ready in the kitchen. Sweets come last." She swatted Xochi's finger away from her frosting, then relented. "But you get the biggest piece after we eat."

****

Replete with Corazon's enchiladas and stuffed with other goodies and cake, Howdy and Cassie waved good-bye to the Billodeaux family and headed for Oklahoma by way of Texas. Cassie rubbed up against his shoulder, and he put his arm around her.

"You still want a dozen kids?" he asked. "I don't know about you but I was kinda overwhelmed back there."

"What was I thinking? I came in the middle of my family and always had older sisters and brothers around to help, but eight all under the age of eight. I know Nell can handle it if anyone can, but I pity her."

"Still, I wish I'd had siblings, only not so many. It's hard to be alone and worried about the old folks. I keep thinking if I hadn't gone off to play for the Sinners, maybe I would have been around to save Grandpa when he had that heart attack."

"You can't think that way. He lived to see you grow into a fine man, one he could be proud of, and maybe he was ready to go be with your grandmother. I've seen people in the hospital simply pass when they felt all their affairs were settled."

"Thanks for saying that. So, you'd want maybe two or three kids now? That's a lot less scary."

Cassie kissed his cheek. "Who knows what the future holds? Too bad Madame Leleux is no more, but I understand her granddaughter has the sight. Maybe we'll go see her someday, but right now it's a little too soon."

****

Nell brought the children down from their sugar-highs with warm baths and a session of bedtime stories, Joe helping her all the way, but she asked to put Xochi to bed alone tonight.

The girl, wearing a clean white nightie, sat crossed-legged on her bed in Corazon's former room. The walls glowed with bright yellow paint and a wallpaper border of garlanded red roses. The furniture, an intricately carved headboard and a massive Spanish chest of drawers with matching night tables seemed too out-sized for a child's room.

Nell sat down on the edge of the bed. She didn't touch Xochi's long, tangled curls or try to hug her because the girl seemed as wary as a stray cat that had been chased away too often.

"Honey, if you don't like this room, we can change the colors and the furniture. The girls want to take you shopping tomorrow for more clothes. I see all your underwear is white. They like panties in colors or with designs on them. Would you like that, too?"

"Yes. I must speak American now all the time."

"No, you should remember your Spanish, also, but you speak English very well."

"Papi says when he home we talk American, but if he not at home, I speak Mexican with Mama." Xochi's face crumbled, no longer fierce and defiant. "I want my Mama, but I know she in heaven now."

"Yes, dear, that's right. I think you won't want to call me mama for a long time maybe, but Tommy calls me Mama Nell because he has two mothers. Maybe you could call me that."

Xochi nodded, but a few tears coursed down her face and made little transparent dots on the thin white nightie. She looked up hopefully at Nell. "At night, my mama brushed my hair to help me sleep, she say."

"Well, it's all tangles now and very long. The twins have curly hair like this, but they wear it shorter so it's easier to care for. Would you like to get a haircut like theirs?"

"No!"

"Then you won't. Tomorrow, we'll buy a brush and comb set for only you to use and wash your hair with a cream rinse to remove the tangles. At bedtime, I will brush it for you if you will let me." Tentatively, Nell reached out a hand. "For tonight, we'll just do this."

The child curled beneath the covers, and Nell

stroked Xochi's black curls until the child fell asleep. Nadine and Joe felt the Lord never sent more than a person could handle, and both thought they could fix anything. Maybe they were right.

Chapter Twenty-Four

Cassie rolled over to get some sun on her front. She'd unhooked the under-wire top of the bikini to avoid tan lines and when she turned, her breasts escaped the boldly printed orange and yellow cups. Howdy, out deep in the small shining lake, noticed as she'd intended, and started making his way back to the flat rock where she lay on a beach towel. A total gentleman, he'd poked all around the slab of rock to make sure no rattlers hid beneath it before letting her stretch out to take a tan. Oklahoma certainly offered more than waving wheat and winds that came right before the rain—like a selection of venomous reptiles.

She watched him reach the shallows and rise up out of the water, the palest man she'd ever seen with just a touch of cowboy tan on his arms and neck. Unlike Brian, he didn't believe in tanning beds or creams. That was so Howdy. Still, the water slicked down his lean body, darkening the triangle of hair on his chest and making its way toward a very ordinary pair of blue swim trunks with white stripes up the sides. No Speedos for him. Below the trunks, his legs emerged long and muscular, full of the promise of strength and endurance.

He came to stand between her outstretched limbs. Not bothering to cover up, she propped herself on her elbows and let him look. He smiled with that big goofy grin she was beginning to find very endearing. "Shouldn't you cover those up? I hear redheads burn pretty easy."

"Oh, once I get a start, I tan fairly well. It covers up the freckles."

"Now that would be a shame. No more dot-to-dots. You don't want to swim?"

"Hey, I put a toe in there. It's freezing."

"Spring water. Gets warmer in the summer."

"And I was a little put off by the company." She nodded toward a few head of white-faced cattle taking a benign interest in them from the far side of the pond. "Except for my adventure on the rodeo circuit, I'm basically a city girl. We can see the bottom of our pools, and they are guaranteed cow slobber-free."

"Aw, come on, skinny-dipping is one of the best activities a country boy can offer. You're half-way undressed already."

He stared at her nipples, orange-tinged tan in color. They puckered as if he'd thrown a pail of cold water on her, but she didn't feel chilled at all, the very opposite. He leaned over her and shook his auburn hair like a dog right after a bath. The icy droplets showered over her, and she brought her knees up to protect herself.

"That position won't do you any good. It makes you easy to bundle." He scooped her up, leaving the bikini top behind, and after three strides, tossed her into the water. She floundered until she found her feet and splashed him in the face as she tried to escape back to her nice, warm rock. He caught her in retreat by hooking a thumb into her brief swimsuit bottom and towing her out to deeper water. Once he reached waist-high, he simply divested her of the rest of the bikini and lobbed it ashore.

"No fair! No fair! You still have your trunks on. Oh, cold, cold, cold. The bottom is all gooey."

"That's only mud, darlin', not cow slobber." He raised one knee, then the other, showed her his discarded swim trunks and threw them after her bikini. "Now we're even."

"Still freezing."

"You need to move around to get warm. Like this." He executed a prefect surface dive, his buttocks jutting up, his long legs following them beneath the water. When he came up, Cassie was laughing.

"Hey, I thought I did that pretty well."

"Not your dive. Howdy, you have the whitest ass I've ever seen."

He shook a finger at her. "We do not say ass in this family."

"I can't believe you're mocking Nell."

"Actually, I'm imitating my grandmother. I have the greatest urge to run inside the house and drop a quarter in the cuss jar. After she passed away, Grandpa and I had to go from using a quart container to a gallon size. We gave it all to the church in her memory once we filled it up."

Cassie moved into the deeper water where he stood. "I guess you're kind of religious. I noticed the Bible on the nightstand last evening. It made me almost too guilty to seduce you."

"Glad you didn't let the word of the Lord deter you. Nope, not as religious as I should be. That was Grandma's Bible. Grandpa kept it on that table near him at night as a comfort. He rarely opened it. Neither do I, but still it is good knowing we had something she cherished. In fact, I never got dunked into the Baptist Church as she died around the time I was supposed to seek salvation. Unlike you." He reached beneath the surface and up-ended her.

Sputtering to the top, she splashed him again making a wave with her arm as she spun around. "To think I almost asked you to warm me up."

"Happy to do that, ma'am." He brought her tight against his chest and lowered his head for a deep kiss. Her hands slipped to clutch his buttocks, pale-skinned but firm from kicking all those field goals.

"Hmmm," she said when they came up for air. "I expected a little more action down below."

"Like you said, it's cold in here. You want action we need to take this elsewhere."

Howdy lifted her into his arms and carried her from the lake. He paused to slip on a pair of lime green flip-flops left at the water's edge. Cassie stared down at them and giggled at the squishing noise they made as he strode along.

"Somehow your footwear makes this less romantic."

"As you pointed out, we are sharing this spot with cattle. Believe me, if I have to stop to wash my feet of cow plop, all the romance truly will be gone."

She conceded that point and gave him an extra one for getting her all the way back to the house without putting her down once. They wound up on the old-fashioned double bed with the white iron headboard and the worn log cabin quilt spread. Cassie reached over Howdy, her naked breasts brushing his chest, and placed the Bible into the night table drawer.

"There, now I can concentrate on you. I see we

have liftoff."

"Care to ride a rocket to the moon, darlin'?"

She did. The ride lasted a long, long time with Cassie at the controls. The landing came off perfectly. After a period of exploration, they were ready to blast-off for home with Howdy in charge.

"Warm enough now?"

"Yes." She nodded against his chest. "Howdy, I do not deserve you."

"Huh?"

"I insulted you, was mean to you, kept you at arm's length as my friend for the longest time. I have a smart mouth and too dirty a past for a nice guy like you."

"What brought that on?"

"The Bible in the drawer."

"Didn't bother you enough to quit last night."

"But now it's broad daylight. Forgive me for the way I treated you."

"Hey, that's one thing I recall from my Baptist upbringing. I'm big on forgiveness. As for your past, seems to me most of the dirt that rubbed off on you came from Bijou. Time to wash that away and forget it about, Cassie."

She hugged him tight. "I really, truly do not deserve you. I want to do something wonderful for you."

"Sweetheart, I think you already did," he answered, groggy from cold water swimming and very hot lovemaking.

"Something better than sex."

"Nothing is better than sex," he murmured on the edge of sleep.

"Shades of Joe Dean."

Howdy's blue eyes opened to two narrow slits. "Don't be bringing him into our bedroom."

"Sorry. Forgive me again. How about I find your parents for you? Then, you won't be alone."

He nuzzled her neck. "I'm not alone now, Cassie. Just let it be."

But, being Cassie, she could not do that.

Chapter Twenty-Five

Cassie sat in the bed with the log cabin quilt tucked under her arms, her naked breasts covered. They hadn't left the bedroom much after their swim, only long enough to rustle up some dinner and watch a DVD of *The Quiet Man* from the complete John Wayne collection housed on the shelves beneath the huge flat screen TV that didn't quite fit the modest, comfortable living room. The TV and the collection were gifts to his grandpa from Howdy's signing bonus. The old man hadn't gotten to use them for very long. Pushing that sorrow aside, they laughed at the comic fight at the end of the movie and acted out the struggle between John and Maureen O'Hara on their way back to bed which turned out to be a real turn on. She feigned reluctance. He played the dominant part. Good time had by all.

Howdy had been correct in calling his place small. The white frame house possessed only two bedrooms, one old-fashioned bath, a large kitchen, and the living room paneled in knotty pine and decorated in plaid. A generous porch overlooking the lake added a little more space for relaxing in rocking chairs. A barn with a corral sat far enough away to keep the flies from being a problem. An old, unoccupied bunkhouse leaned drunkenly on the other side of house distant enough for privacy. Instead of a windmill or an oil well, a homemade football goal stood out against the sky.

These and a few other outbuildings made up the spread called the Bar Mack after its brand, McC over a straight line. Howdy had given the caretaker, Emilio, the man who had helped him learn his Spanish, the week off. The man's wife had cleaned the house before their arrival, so they had the place pretty much to themselves except for the inquisitive cattle.

Pots and pans banged in the kitchen. The rich smell of perking coffee wafted back to the bedroom. She'd wanted to help with breakfast, but Howdy insisted she stay beneath the covers. The only trouble, now she was wide awake with nothing to do after a dash to the bathroom and a quick brush of the hair and application of makeup. She opened the nightstand drawer and took out the Bible, a King James Version with a cheap leatherette cover and the name Ruth Weems McCoy embossed in nearly vanished gold. Cassie found what she looked for between the Old and New Testaments, a page to record marriages, births, and deaths very sparsely written upon.

The first entry showed the marriage date of Ruth Weems and Howard Angus McCoy in 1947 with their birth dates in the late 1920's also noted. Ruth had inscribed only two births, her daughter's and Howdy's: Mary Mariah McCoy in 1967, a late in life only child, and Howard Angus McCoy II, born 1988. No other marriages helped fill the page. The name that made her eyes widen sat right above Howdy's birth date, Benito Rizzo, father, no other information given. The bedroom door bumped open. She slipped the Bible under the covers.

Holding a white wicker bed tray, Howdy backed into the room and turned to present her with breakfast.

A small cast iron skillet sat on a hot pad in the center of the tray. Two forks, two spoons, thick, white mugs of coffee and an equally utilitarian cream and sugar set flanked it. Upright bottles of ketchup and hot sauce added some color, but the touch that brought tears to her eyes was a vase crudely and joyfully decorated by a child and holding a few of the small sunflowers that popped up all over the ranch.

"I really don't deserve this."

"Well, it's the house special. See, you fry the potatoes in the skillet first, then dump eggs on top and after they cook, add grated cheese. I put jalapenos on my side, but I wasn't sure if you'd like that." Howdy noticed her watery eyes. "If you don't want this, we have cereal. Or I can get you a plate. Grandpa and I usually shared right out of the pan. It saved on dishwashing, but I can see how you might not like that. We got the fancy bed tray when Grandma was sick, but there's not a lot of room on top of it."

"No, I love all of it. I don't think I've ever had breakfast in bed before. I was always up helping Mom make it for the younger kids. When we were on the road, mostly we had fast food breakfasts in the morning. Did you make the vase?"

"Yeah, a cub scout Mother's Day project. Grandma said she liked it more than all the crystal in Waterford."

"I think I do, too. Let's eat. I am starving." The quilt slipped down as she reached for her fork. Howdy drew it up again. Fully clothed in jeans and another of the endless blue shirts, he sat down next to her.

"What, no topless eating in this house?"

"I don't want you to burn your bosom because that would be a real sin."

He upended the ketchup, put a dollop in the middle of his eggs, added hot sauce, and dug into the house special. Cassie did her best to eat a respectable portion, but he'd made a farmhand's breakfast, too much for any young woman watching her weight. She left the rest to Howdy and slowly sipped her coffee, strong but not bad with a little sugar added.

"Howdy, I thought you didn't know who your father was." She withdrew the Bible from beneath the covers. "It says here he's Benito Rizzo. Haven't you ever tried to find him?"

"I wouldn't put much stock in that. Grandma didn't. She told me when she pressed my mother for a name she said, 'then put down Benito Rizzo.' Could be made up for all I know. My birth certificate doesn't list a father. I sure don't look I-talian. No, I take after my grandpa. Everyone says so. My mom named me after him."

Cassie snickered. "Yes, Howard Angus McCoy the Second. Angus, really?"

"'A venerable Scottish name,' Grandpa said. He got that from *his* grandfather. See, I have family way back. It's not like I'm adopted. Sorry, I'm not putting down what you did with Tommy. It's great you keep in touch and he knows all the Thomases. Enough about me. Confess your middle name."

"Grace, Cassie Grace Thomas," she said smugly.

"As pretty as you are."

"See, you don't even retaliate when I make fun of you. No, that's not true. You did make me feel about an inch small when I bitched about not riding with Joe and Tommy. I deserved the put down, and I did feel your pain about your abandonment. That's why I think we should track down your parents and get the real story. Do you think your mom is still in Vegas? How far are we from there? We could leave this afternoon."

"Not what I had planned for us today." Deliberately, Howdy set the bed tray aside, peeled off his clothes and got under the covers with her. "I figured on a short ride inside and a long one outside with a picnic lunch."

His hands started working on her beneath the quilt. "Better put that Bible away before you start feeling guilty again."

She placed it back in the drawer, but didn't forget about the entries, not during the morning sex, not during the long horseback ride around the spread where Howdy pointed out the small orchard with peach and apple trees bearing tiny green fruits barely emerged from the blossoms.

"Grandma made the best pies and preserves from the fruit. After her death, we stretched that last jar of her peach jelly out for weeks because we knew there wouldn't be any more. After that, we only ate the fruit and gave lots of it away."

"Still, a wonderful way to remember her. How did she die?"

"Cancer got her."

For a minute, Cassie envisioned Ruth McCoy dying in the bed where they'd made love only hours ago. Made her feel guiltier than the Baptist Bible. "Did she die at home?"

"No, she passed at the hospice. In case it grosses you out, she had a hospital bed at home. Mine is a single bed, so we had to use Grandpa's, right? The sheets are new even if the quilt is old, and Grandpa had his heart attack in the barn in case you're wondering."

"I love the quilt—and the bed and what we do in it."

"Good, because I'm not getting rid of them or you."

They rounded the lake on the two horses remaining on the ranch, a wide-rumped Appaloosa mare named Dolly, mostly white but freckled all over with brown spots the size of dimes, and her offspring, a gelding called Mad Son, bay in front and blanketed with white in the rear. No one would call either mount terribly youthful.

"I don't know why you call him Mad Son. He's a docile as can be," Cassie remarked.

"Oh, I got to name him. We were studying American history in the third grade when he came into the world. I wanted to show off my knowledge and said Madison went with Dolly, only I didn't get the spelling or the pronunciation right. Grandpa thought that was such a hoot he wouldn't change it for the world."

They came to a fairly new fence line and Howdy pointed out how the Bar Mack once spread out for miles. "Grandpa sold it off to pay the medical bills and get me through college in case my kicking didn't pay off. He only kept a few cows to produce steers for table beef after that, the ones you saw across the lake. And he kept the water rights. You never give up water rights."

"I've always thought of Oklahoma as being dry and dusty."

"Not down here near the Red River. The McCoys knew a choice piece of land when they saw it. The Indians got sent to the dry and dusty part, the part with oil on it as it turned out. I want to put up a new place here someday, but I'll keep the old house for guests. It gave me shelter for a long, long time when I needed it."

"See, you do have issues. We need to find your mother. We don't know her reasons for giving you up."

"Doesn't take a psychology degree to figure out I messed up her life. She never returned, didn't call, or take any interest in me."

"Maybe your grandmother burned her letters or wouldn't take her calls. Sounds to me like Ruth McCoy was very stern."

"Not with me so much. She admitted she drove my mother away by being too strict. My mother wanted to sing and dance. They allowed her to take ballet because that is classy and sing in the choir, but none of that 'shake your booty' dancing or 'nasty songs.' She wanted to wait tables at the local café after school for spending money, she said. They let her. Hard work is character building. They went twenty year childless and wanted to raise a perfect daughter once they had one. Well, my mother used her pay and tips on voice and booty shaking lessons taken on nights when she wasn't really working at the café. Grandpa got her an old truck to drive back and forth, also character building, old trucks. When she graduated from high school, she drove that truck directly from the party to Las Vegas, called once to let them know where she ended up and only returned to the Bar Mack once to drop me off seven years later."

Cassie let the reins rest on Mad Son's neck and touched his arm. "Maybe she did what was best for you."

"Maybe." Howdy stared out over the land once part of the Bar Mack Ranch and did not look at her. "Let it be. How about a picnic in the orchard?" He turned his old mare and headed back the way they came.

They shared a simple lunch of ham and cheese sandwiches on rye, store-bought apples Howdy claimed weren't nearly as sweet and crunchy as the ones that would fall from the trees here in autumn, and cookies from a box that didn't hold a candle to his grandma's home-baked goodies, all that spread out on an old red and white checked tablecloth. After eating, the tablecloth served as a fairly good bedspread.

As Cassie toyed with his chest hair, stroking him into contentment like a well-fed cat, she said, "I bake a pretty mean cookie myself. My little brothers and sisters always needed some for school."

"You're showing me your sweet side again, though I have to say both sides of you are pretty tasty."

"Howdy, I have no sweet side. I've been called feisty, tough, and sassy. Sassy, that's my nickname in the family. My attitude got me through years of cancer treatments when other children much nicer than me died. I survived life with Bijou which was almost worse than leukemia after awhile. I believe you have to face life head on without ducking."

"The Sinners should recruit you," he replied with a lazy smile and a hand on her breast.

"I think you're ducking by not finding and confronting your parents. A real football player would do that—but you're only a kicker."

"Hey, I thought we were past the insults." He dropped his hand and his smile.

"Whatever it takes to get you to go to Las Vegas tomorrow."

"Jesus, okay. There, now I have to put a quarter in

the cuss jar for blasphemy. Las Vegas tomorrow. Shit. Another quarter. Might as well be going to Sodom and Gomorrah when we have Paradise right here as my grandma would say."

Chapter Twenty-Six

They didn't get to Vegas in one day but arrived early enough on the second to see the losers and the drunks still sleeping on the curbs and benches. A group of waitresses in green uniforms and a man in a shiny tuxedo sucked on their smokes outside a breakfast buffet. "Do your job, Arnie," one of the women prompted as they passed. "They look like fresh meat."

Arnie tossed his cigarette aside and swung into action, running around to get in front of them. "Best breakfast buffet in Vegas. We got shrimp morning, noon, and night. Loose and easy slots in the rear. How's about a discount coupon—two for one this morning only." He waved a slip of paper in their faces.

Howdy shrugged. "Why not? I really could use some coffee."

He pinched the coupon and steered Cassie inside. The place looked clean enough and the buffet fairly standard with a steam table offering overcooked scrambled eggs, undercooked bacon, and little, gray sausages. The promised pile of shrimp of the tiny, pink variety looked like they might have come from a can, but who ate shrimp this early in the morning? Waffles, pancakes and French toast sticks fanned out on warming trays like winning hands in poker right next to cups of yogurt and cubed fruit in bowls sunk into crushed ice. All this for a mere twenty dollars a head, orange juice and coffee extra, but they had the half-off coupon. He'd never been a picky eater, but he asked Cassie, "This all right?"

"Sure. Let's ask the waitress for a phone book. We can start our search."

"Your search," he corrected.

Their waitress brought a pitcher of orange juice over to their table and held it enticingly over two upturned glasses. Howdy nodded for her to pour. Cassie asked for a telephone directory, and their server padded away on sensible shoes, delivering the request shortly like she'd gone to a lot of extra work. The woman brightened a little when Howdy wanted coffee, too, adding to the tab and the tip.

"No Mary McCoy or Benito Rizzo listed."

Howdy raised his eyebrows at her. "You thought it would be that easy?"

"We'll do a Google search as soon as I can find a wi-fi hot spot."

"We could find a room after driving all night. I'll get us a suite like the one in New Orleans, champagne again, maybe a marriage license once I get you liquored up enough."

"Quit joking. We have a mission to complete. A couple of Rizzos listed, but no Benitos."

The waitress, creeping up behind them in her crepe-soled shoes, served their coffee. From behind, she had a slim body and showgirl legs shored up by support hose, but the facial lines of a heavy smoker dragged her tired face down. The stench of her cigarette breaks clung to her long red hair, most definitely colored a brighter shade than Cassie's since the woman had to be in her forties or older. She wore it drawn back at the nape of her neck with a cheap hairclip. A nametag branding her "Mariah" perched on one of her unnaturally large breasts straining the buttons of the green uniform and offering a view of a vast cleavage. Her hard, emerald eyes regarded them and showed she'd reached some momentous decision as she retrieved the phonebook.

"Everyone in Vegas knows Benny Rizzo. He won't be listed in the phone book, but you can find out plenty about him on Google. He owns Nero's Lounge and Casino. You look like his type, sister, if you want to get into show business, but you'll need to get a private appointment with him. Have your agent here make one and get lost. You audition for Benny alone." The waitress said agent as if the word were synonymous with pimp.

"Not me. It's my friend who wants to see him."

"Last time I heard, Benny didn't do guys, but in Vegas you never know. You look like nice kids right off the farm. Why don't you go home and forget about meeting Rizzo?"

"We think he might be Howdy's father," Cassie blurted out.

Howdy ducked his head and turned red in the face. "Not my idea to meet him, ma'am. Hers."

"I had one of those private appointments with Benny Rizzo years ago. I can tell you that you sure don't look anything like him. If you have to see for yourself, I'd make an appointment for the girl. He likes 'em fresh. Then pull a switcheroo to get yourself into his office."

"Thank you, Mariah. You've been a big help. Howdy, give her a nice tip."

Obeying, he handed the waitress two twenties.

"My, my, anything else I can do for you, sweetie?" Mariah shot out one hip and posed a hand on it. Clearly, she did not mean the "sweetie" for Cassie.

"No, ma'am," he mumbled, staring at the cutlery. "We'll just have the buffet. Thank you."

"I do like a boy with manners," she said with a sly, full bronze-lipped smile. "After you meet with Rizzo, you hurry back to the ranch or farm or wherever you came from before this town tosses you to the white tigers." She moved away to pour coffee at another table and flipped one of the twenties to another waitress as she passed. The other bill disappeared into her substantial cleavage.

"Howdy, she could be your mother. Mariah was her middle name."

"Heaven forbid, Cass. I'd know my own mother. I have pictures of her from high school, even in her ballet tutu. Dancers don't have huge breasts like that. Her hair is four times as red as mine, and my mom had blue eyes, not green. That much I remember."

"Look at me, Howdy. Do you see a single freckle on my face today? Do you think I was born with blonde streaks in my red hair? And I think in Vegas all dancers have huge, fake tits because they don't dance, they only strut around poking them out at guys like you. Twenty would have been plenty for a nice tip by the way."

"That's another thing. I don't think my own mother would hit on me."

"She hasn't seen you all grown up, and you are kind of cute. There, I finally admitted it."

"Thank you, thank you very much," he said, doing a creditable Elvis imitation. "You having eggs or a pile of carbs? Personally, I think I could use both after that gas station burrito we shared at two a.m."

He stalked off to the buffet and filled two plates with some of everything, dumping a pile of the tiny, pink shrimp on top of his eggs.

"Thank you," Cassie said as he plunked down the two plates.

"Get your own," he growled.

She got up to do exactly that. "At least now I know you're grouchy after pulling an all-nighter and not always so polite and goody-goody."

"Eat, and let's get this meeting with Rizzo over so we can go home."

Nibbling on French toast sticks dipped in syrup, Cassie took her good time eating while Howdy wolfed down his two plates of chow. Earning that forty-dollar tip, their waitress returned again and again to refill their coffee cups and slip them more orange juice free. She gave them directions to Nero's Lounge, not too far distant, no need to hunt for another parking place. Howdy ate up the sidewalk with long strides in his haste to get there and get out. Regretting her early morning decision to switch from sneakers to heels in order to look more sophisticated and suffering from the tightness of her jeans, Cassie wobbled along beside him. They turned in between two faux Corinthian columns. A chubby man wearing a toga wrapped around his tubby body and a laurel wreath on his bald head materialized from the perpetual twilight of the club.

"Welcome to Nero's Lounge and Casino. We hope you will stay and fiddle with us all day long. Free cabaret show at nine and midnight. Summon one of our charming Vestal Virgins for drinks at your table or step into the Golden Room and indulge in our decadent round the clock buffet."

Howdy got right to the point. "Ah, thanks, but we haven't come to gamble. We want to make an appointment to see Mr. Rizzo."

"Difficult, very difficult to see the emperor at this time of day. However, if you take one of the elevators to the top floor, you may request an audience from his personal assistant."

The greeter bowed away and disappeared between a row slots. They found the elevators and climbed aboard the first to arrive. A large poster set into a frame on one wall touted a performance by an aging jazz musician who cradled his horn like a babe in arms. Exiting, they stepped directly up to a large, circular glass-topped desk staffed by a leggy, bleached blonde with thinly plucked eyebrows. She raised those eyebrows at them now. "Yes?"

"We want to see Mr. Rizzo on a matter of business," Howdy said.

"Mr. Rizzo is solidly booked for the day. Why not check into our adjoining hotel and enjoy the casino. I'll see if I can work you into his schedule tomorrow. Is this an audition for the young lady?"

"No."

"Yes," Cassie corrected, giving Howdy an elbow sharp enough to drive home Mariah's advice on how to get Benny Rizzo's attention.

The second of the elevators opened and disgorged a short, thick man clad in a gold, yes, gold tuxedo with the bow tie unraveled around his neck. He scraped a hand over his black stubble and said, "Christ, I need some sleep."

With eyes darker than Joe Dean Billodeaux's, he caressed Cassie from her peep toes to her tits encased in that snug turquoise top, lingering in that last area until he finally raised his gaze to her face. "But, baby, you are an eye-opener. You here for an audition?"

Putting a cautioning hand on Howdy who seethed beside her, she replied, "I am, but I understand you have no openings until tomorrow. Is there any way I could see you sooner?" She fluttered her eyelashes.

"Make her my three o'clock today, Darci. Comp them a room." Benito Rizzo slicked back both sides of his ebony hair and licked his thick lips before entering his office and shutting the door with a definitive click.

Darci flicked her red fingernails over her computer keyboard and asked their names. "Be on time and wear something easy to slip out of. Mr. Rizzo likes to examine the whole package."

"You tell Mr. Rizzo to—"

Cassie stopped Howdy again. "That we'll be here at three. Come on, McCoy, let's take advantage of that free room."

She dragged on his arm before he could say anymore and led him into the elevator used by Rizzo moments ago. It still reeked of the man's heavy cologne.

"Stinks in here," Howdy remarked.

"But it stinks expensively. Would you look at that? It's our waitress." Cassie pointed to another framed poster advertising singer, Mariah Coy, looking far more youthful and glamorous than she had in her green uniform at the breakfast buffet.

"Mary McCoy, Mariah Coy—it's her stage name,

Howdy. I tell you, that's your mother. She saw you walking right toward her this morning and got that barker to lure you inside so she could feast her eyes on you after all these years."

"Hogwash! That is not my mother." He caught Cassie's smirk. "Go ahead and laugh at how I express myself. This is her."

He fished out the same curved wallet stuffed with hundred dollar bills he'd had in Mexico and flipped it open to a set of small opposing photos, one black and white, obviously taken from a dance recital program, and the other a high school graduation portrait. En pointe on willowy legs, long graceful arms extended in a classic ballet position, the young woman in the picture wore a serious expression and her hair pulled back in the traditional bun. Her costume completely flattened her meager breasts.

The other offered a full color shot of long, smoothly curled hair the exact auburn shade as her son and wide blue eyes. Not anything like Howdy's, her mouth, sitting small and pouty above a stubborn chin, already showed signs of discontent in its unwillingness to smile for the camera. The white graduation gown fell in straight folds down her front and its matching cap crooked at a defiant angle. A pretty girl who couldn't wait to get out of Oklahoma, Cassie judged.

She paged to the next set of pictures, Howdy's grandparents. She recognized the white-haired old man in his grandson. They shared the same generous grin, the same mellow blue eyes, even a smattering of freckles across the bridge of the nose, though Howard Angus McCoy the elder's had faded with time. His wife, Ruth Weems McCoy, stared straight at the photographer with cool, gray eyes and small, pursed lips, her chin just as stubborn as her late born daughter's. Gray hair, short and severely styled close to the head, did nothing to soften her image. No padded bras for Grandma McCoy, either. Her navy blue dress with its prim white collar sported no unseemly erotic bulges above the waist. She was what she was, take it or leave it. Hard to believe Howdy's grandfather had taken it.

"I guess she wouldn't have approved of me," Cassie wondered aloud.

"Not in those tight jeans, but I like 'em," Howdy said as he reclaimed his wallet and they left the elevator. "Let's get a room."

"I believe Nero's Palace Hotel is right next door."

"We aren't going there. I want to take you to the Bellagio. That's where Joe took Nell the first time they married."

"But the Palace is free."

"I can afford something better, as good as anything Joe would do."

Cassie linked onto his arm as they left the gloom of the casino where colorful machines pinged and dice rolled from the fingertips of those who'd never gone home. They moved into the already hot desert morning. "You don't have to be jealous of Joe anymore."

"Good, then let's get hitched. I know what wedding chapel Joe and Nell used, too."

"Howdy, have you ever been in love before? Don't you think you're rushing things?"

"I thought I was in love with a Mexican whore once. I can see I had a bad case of lust now. Heck, she went off with someone else, that's how pitiful I seemed to her. I really do love you, Cassie. Maybe if we get married now, you won't get around to leaving me later." He said the last with a slight smile.

She wasn't fooled by his making a joke of it. "Abandonment issues, Howdy, you have them big time. That's why you have to deal with your parentage before you can move on to other decisions."

"If you say so. Will you give me an answer once we're through with this? If you want a big engagement ring, we can pick one out right now. I'm sure this place has a jewelry store on every corner like Starbucks in Seattle. Joe got his rings right at the hotel."

Red hair flying, she shook her head. "Ever since Bijou, I've had an aversion to big, gaudy rings. Look, we both have our problems. Let's handle one at a time. First, we find out if Benito Rizzo is your father."

Howdy took a turn at head shaking. "I don't see it."

"Second, we find out if Mariah Coy is your mother."

"More hogwash."

They returned to the truck and drove to the Bellagio with its dancing fountains and ceiling of glass flowers. Howdy insisted on a suite. She insisted they make love before sleeping away the rest of the day until that looming three o'clock appointment.

Chapter Twenty-Seven

They arrived promptly for the appointment with Benny Rizzo because Cassie had set the suite's alarm clock for two, giving her enough time to primp and cover her freckles with makeup. Riding up in the Mariah Coy elevator, she posed seductively in front of the poster. "What do you think?"

Dressed as his plain ole cowboy self, Howdy frowned, so unlike him but he found he did it more and more since meeting Cassie. "How come you brought a dress like that to the ranch?"

Not that he didn't like what she wore. It had one of those halter tops that went behind the back of her neck and held her breasts up without a bra. The back ran low, and he'd done up the short zipper for her not long ago. The skirt, very short, way above the knees, poufed-out in swirling layers of green and blue. High heels of metallic gold made her almost as tall as himself, and she wore no stockings on the legs she'd tanned at the ranch. She'd put her hair up in a messy, just got out of bed suggestive style he didn't care for at all. Dangly earrings of tiny iridescent beads pretty as a peacock's tail swung from her ears. As usual, her lips were the color of ripe peaches, but she'd ramped up the eyeliner, mascara, and green shadow. Men stared at her on the street, and addicted gamblers took their eyes off their cards for a moment when she passed through the casino for the ride to the top of the building.

"I always bring along one good dress. You never can tell when you might need it. Do I look the part?"

"Of a showgirl wannabe or an expensive call girl?"

She acted a little hurt at his assessment. "I had to dress the part to get us inside the office. Look, I wore panties because you insisted."

"I'd hardly call what you got on under that dress panties, more like a thong, and Mr. Rizzo won't ever have the pleasure of seeing it if I have my way."

"But you will have that pleasure after we clear up the paternity issue."

His face still burned at the thought of taking off that thong as they got out of the elevator and approached the desk. The blonde raised those thin, penciled brows again. "My, you did clean up nicely, Miss Thomas. Go right in. Mr. Rizzo awaits. Mr. McCoy, take a seat."

"I don't think so." He advanced to the door and turned the knob, allowed Cassie to strut in first out of sheer habit.

The first words his supposed father uttered were, "Out! Only the girl stays. Don't make me call security." The man, clad in gray monotone mafia chic, rapped his knuckles against an inlaid mahogany desk to emphasize his order. "You, Cassie, take a seat on the couch."

Howdy didn't like the looks of that couch. Both ends scrolled up but the divan had no back, plenty of red cushions though, and a double-wide tufted width that reminded him of a mattress. Cassie sat down, folding her legs the way supermodels did. Rizzo's black eyes followed her all the way. Without removing his glance from those long, tanned limbs, he repeated, "Get out, kid."

Howdy stood his ground, the sheriff ready to draw on the villain. "Sir, we aren't here for an audition. I have reason to believe you might be my father. My mom put your name in the family Bible."

The black-eyed stare whipped back to Howdy's open, pleasant face, his wide grin gone missing. "Not the first time I've heard that. I don't see any resemblance. Who's your mother?"

"Mary McCoy."

"Means nothing to me."

Cassie piped up from the casting couch. "How about Mariah Coy?"

The casino owner shrugged. "Now her I've fucked more than once, but not lately. She's getting kind of long in the tooth. But you, you could have a career in Vegas. You sing, dance?"

"Not very well. I'm a psychologist helping Howard McCoy find his father. It's vital to his mental health." She rose to stand by Howdy's side.

Rizzo barked out a laugh. "You're off my hook. I can't stand a woman with too many brains. They always want to talk instead of getting down to business by which I mean…"

Howdy moved close to the desk and leaned over it. "We know what you mean. Answer the question, Are you my father? and we'll leave."

"I doubt it, but if Mariah is your mother, maybe." He opened a drawer and sent a business card skidding across the polished top of the desk. "My doctor. He has my DNA on file for cases like this and other possible mishaps. When you deal with gambling, you never know what might happen." He shrugged his nicely padded shoulders. "If you are mine, I can give you a position in my establishment. Otherwise, don't try to shake me down for nothing."

Howdy stepped back a pace, hands on hips, ready to draw. "I have a job, a very good one. I'm a kicker for the Sinners and don't need your money. In fact, I don't want you to give me anything, not even a DNA test."

He folded the card into a triangle and flicked it like a paper football back toward Rizzo. A quick hand with peach-colored nails intercepted it in flight. Cassie smoothed the card out against the desk's slick surface. "Thank you, Mr. Rizzo. We'll let you know the results."

Benny Rizzo smiled, his teeth glaring white against his olive complexion. "Hey, I'd like to have a kid in pro football. What do you think the odds are of Billodeaux taking another Super Bowl?"

Howdy answered before he could stop himself. "Not this year. The team is rebuilding."

"But sometime down the line, a missed field goal could change the outcome of the big event, right?"

"I always do my best, sir. I'd never throw a game."

Rizzo found that statement and Howdy's solemnity hilarious. He laughed until tears ran down a jaw already blue-black with early beard shadow and blotted his face on a pale gray pocket square. "See, I tell you, no son of mine. Get outta here. But I just gotta ask—you have panties on under that getup, honey?"

Cassie hitched her hip on the edge of the desk and swayed close to Mr. Rizzo's prominent nose. "You'll never know."

"Sassy," Rizzo said. "I do like sassy."

"That's what they call me. Come on, Howdy, we

really are outta here." She put an extra sway in her walk that both men could appreciate as she went to the door.

"If you can't handle her, son, send her to papa."

"I think I'll manage without your help."

Howdy rushed to block Rizzo's view of Cassie's backside and closed the door with a slam that startled the secretary and made her muss the red nail polish she applied. "I guess you won't need a second appointment?"

"No, we'll just leave a message." Cassie summoned the elevator.

Once safely inside the metal box, Howdy slammed his hand against the wall, leaving a palm print behind on the immaculate space. "I don't want that man to be my father. Give me the card so I can tear it up."

"No way." Taking a cue from Mariah Coy who vamped at them from her poster, Cassie shoved the card deep between her breasts.

"Cassie, give me the card or I'll go in after it."

"No, you won't. You're too much of a gentleman. Besides, we need to know who you are really." She gazed at herself in the glass covering the picture of Mariah. "I may not sing or dance, but I think I could be an actress. I played the role of sultry slut fairly well."

"Stay a psychologist because if Benny Rizzo is my dad, I'll need a shrink for the rest of my life."

****

Since this was Vegas, the nurse who took the sample showed no surprise at their request for a DNA test. Must happen all the time. Expect the results at the end of the week, she said. Mr. Rizzo had phoned ahead and would pay the bill. By five p.m., Howdy and Cassie stood before the white medical building flanked by two palm trees and wondered what to do next.

"Since you're all dressed up, you want to take in a show? Celine Dionne, maybe? Or Donny Osmond. My grandma liked him," Howdy suggested.

"I'm more in the mood for cabaret. Let's get some dinner, then go see Mariah Coy. Even if she isn't your mother, we can go back and say we were served breakfast by a celebrity."

"I really don't want to do that."

"Come on, Howdy. We're in Vegas. Let's gamble a little, stuff ourselves with lobster, and watch Mariah perform."

He humored her. They went back to Nero's Lounge, played the slots and won a paltry number of coins compared to the ones they put in the machines, but broke even at blackjack. The Golden Room had small, chilled lobsters on the buffet and shrimp almost as large. Howdy ordered a bottle of Dom Perignon at one-hundred fifty dollars a popped cork with complete panache thanks to the lessons received from Brian Lightfoot.

"Is this where you get me liquored up?" Cassie asked, smiling at him over the rim of a bubbling flute.

"Yep. We could get married between Mariah's acts. Maybe she'd agree to be your bridesmaid."

"Sorry, I did rash and impulsive with Bijou. Never again. Besides, my mother made it clear after that fiasco I must marry in the Church with every Thomas alive in attendance to make up for her embarrassment."

"You think she'd accept a Baptist? I know she likes me. She saved me extra dessert on Good Friday, hid it from the ravenous hoard of your family."

"Being used to Joe, Connor, and the Rev, she

thinks you're too thin for a football player, but yes, she does like you."

"You couldn't marry Joe in your church. He'd be a divorced man."

"In my childish fantasy, I thought he'd buy an annulment."

"And make his kids illegitimate. I don't think so."

"Me neither, not anymore. Nell has the life I thought I wanted, and I was willing to go after Joe to get it. I feel almost as ashamed as the day the two of them rescued me from Bijou."

"Be glad Joe turned you down, or you might be implanted with his triplets right now and not sipping champagne with me in Vegas." Howdy gave her one of his broad, loopy grins.

She raised her glass and clinked it against his. "To us."

"Right, to us."

They finished off the bottle because Dom Perignon was not a wine to be wasted and made their merry way to the lounge to get a front seat for Mariah Coy's act. When the lights dimmed over the audience and brightened on the stage, their waitress appeared sitting atop a white piano with an accompanist wearing the de rigueur tuxedo and a drummer and bass player filling out the stage.

Creative makeup and kind lighting softened her lines and removed ten years from her face. A tight black gown so low cut it barely covered her nipples helped distract from her age by luring the eyes of male viewers elsewhere. She had her long, showgirl legs crossed, a backless stiletto high heel dangling from one toe. Making love to the mic, she crooned a selection of steamy songs, then slid off the piano to do a red hair tossing Tina Turner strut around the stage on a couple of faster pieces. Clearly winded, Mariah returned to lounge against the baby grand for a smoky version of *Fever* to close the show. Adequate applause rewarded her performance, but she did not return for an encore song. Instead, the band slid into a blue note, the cue to bring out the aging jazz trumpeter who waited in the wings.

"Not great, but not bad," Howdy evaluated. "Let's go back to our room. I think I can give you a fever." He tickled the back of her neck with a single finger.

"First, we pay our respects to the chanteuse." Cassie headed for a hulking white-haired guard, whose once broad shoulders hunched with age as he protected the backstage and dressing rooms. She assumed Howdy would follow. He did.

"Um, Billy…" Cassie read the name embroidered in red thread on his uniform pocket. "We'd like to meet Ms. Coy and tell her how much we enjoyed her act." Attesting to her acting ability, she inflected her words with a breathless admiration

"Been some time since Mariah had any fans ask to see her, and I've guarded her since she started years ago. Let me check. Be right back."

They watched Billy lumber on stiff, arthritic legs down a dimly lit corridor where he raised his large, big-veined fist to rap on a door bearing one dingy silver star. He turned the knob, poked his head inside for a moment, then shambled back to them.

"You go right in, but you better not be making fun of her. Youngsters sometimes do. I won't have it, you hear? Toss you out on your ears if you do." He hardly looked like he could carry out the threat, but they reassured him.

"We won't be doing that, sir," Howdy said. "We only came to talk."

As they walked along the corridor, he whispered to Cassie, "Why do I feel like I'm walking the last mile on Death Row?'

"I think it's the lighting. Courage, Howdy. Get your John Wayne on again like you did in Rizzo's office."

"Enter," the seductive voice called when they rapped on the star, flaking off even more of its silver paint. In the short interval since the show, Mariah had shed her slinky black gown and a body stocking that lay across a chair like a broken cocoon and the damp creature that had crawled out of it. Kicked into a corner, her shoes interlocked their killer spiked heels. The red hairpiece that augmented her thinner tresses perched on top of a Styrofoam head in one corner of the dressing table. A single coral-colored rose in a crystal bud vase adorned the other.

Mariah, clad in a black dressing gown made gaudy with Chinese red dragon embroidery and not covering much of her overblown chest, sucked in a lungful of smoke from her cigarette and blew it out again. "Saw you in the first row. So you came to see your waitress sing. Want an autograph?" She flicked the ash into a handy coffee cup, no better receptacle in view.

"No," Howdy said and could not go further.

Before he got them thrown out by Billy who would probably need their help to do so, Cassie answered. "We did enjoy your act, but what we really wanted to know is if Howdy is your son, yours and Mr. Rizzo's boy."

"You're a sharp young woman, cheap-looking, but sharp. I'll give you that. So they call you Howdy now. I knew that, but to me you were always my sweet, little Howie. I named you for my father, the most decent man on earth. One day, I knew you'd come to find me. When I saw you moving along that sidewalk looking like you'd driven all night in search of me, I recognized you right away. I goosed Arnie into giving you the discount coupon and paid off Doris to take her table."

"See, see?" Cassie said triumphantly. "I was right."

"Could I sit? I feel a mite dizzy in here. Maybe it's all the smoke." Howdy sank into the chair holding the discarded gown and settled on the body stocking.

"Yeah, Benny doesn't like anyone smoking back here so I have to keep the door closed. He thinks not providing ashtrays will keep a person from taking a drag. Ha! Splash some of that air freshener around, hon." Mariah gestured toward a can of lilac-scented spray.

Cassie obliged, but the artificial aroma only made the air thicker and more cloying. Howdy looked ready to hurl. She eyed a nearby waste can filled with makeup-soiled wipes just in case he needed it quickly and moved closer to rub his tense shoulders.

He raised his drooping head and asked his mother, "I didn't know you. How did you recognize me?"

Mariah opened a drawer in the dressing table and removed an album bulging with playbills and clippings. The pale pink cover glittered with tiny gold stars, something a teenage girl might purchase to hold pictures of her movie star crushes. A clear pocket displayed a current publicity still with her facial lines air-brushed away. Since Howdy made no move to take it, Cassie brought the album to him and laid it open on his knees.

Turning page after page, they watched flat-chested Mary McCoy morph into busty Mariah Coy. The first photo displayed a very young woman in a long draped gown designed to hide her lack of assets. Wide blue eyes gazed at them hopefully, wanting their approval. The small rosebud mouth smiled tentatively. Gradually, the breasts grew larger and larger, the small lips fuller, pumped up with collagen. The auburn hair burned to the brightest shade of red, and the blue eyes suddenly turned to emerald green.

"Not that stuff. Look in the back," Mariah prompted. She ground out her expired cigarette with its filter ringed in bronze lipstick into the coffee cup and lit another.

Cassie flipped over a substantial section and stopped at a baby picture of a toothless infant with a wide smile and a shock of auburn hair. A succession of school pictures followed, then news clippings of Howdy's rise as a kicker, his receipt of the Lou Groza Award for top college placekicker, his signing with the Sinners.

"Dad sent me stuff behind my mother's back. The deal when I left you in Oklahoma was I'd stay away, keep quiet, and my folks would raise you, Ruth's idea of course. They did a better job with you than me. My mother bound me so tight I just had to bust loose. Maybe with your being a boy, Dad had more influence." The more she talked, the more she became the Oklahoma girl again rather than the sultry songstress.

Howdy, his innocent blue eyes bloodshot and blinking, managed to choke out, "So Benny Rizzo is my daddy."

Mariah shrugged. "Ruth pressed me and pressed me for a name to put in the Bible. I wanted you to have a rich, powerful father who might help you out in the future. But, I don't know. It could have been Benny. He was my first lover, then on and off again for years. Not much finesse there. I hope you do better by women, Howie."

"Oh, he does!" Cassie blurted.

Howdy sank his face into his hands and mumbled through the spaces between his fingers. "Who else could it be?"

"Might be Lionel Lowe, my agent. He bought me my first breast implants—to enhance my career, he said. I always hoped you belonged to Chet Lovell, a big real estate man in Vegas. He was my sugar daddy for a while. I thought I'd be his fourth wife, told him the baby must be his. Bless his high blood pressure he pre-paid the obstetrician and the hospital for my care before stroking out on the ninth hole while playing golf. Said we'd be married as soon as I got my figure back. Chet financed my second set of boobs, huge ones, the way he liked them, before I wound up pregnant."

"Anyone else?" Howdy asked without raising his head.

"Maybe I should include old Billy. I stayed pretty active around that time flushing out all the Baptist in me, and Bill adored me."

Howdy moaned. "Old Billy, too. Didn't you ever hear of birth control?"

"Look, twenty-four years ago, Billy acted as my

bodyguard because I needed one back then. You talk about a hunky older man, but after sixty men slide some. He still looks out for me. As for that birth control crack, the pills made me nauseated and bloated. I used a diaphragm, but must not have got in sucked in just right. I did lots of drinking back then and maybe forgot a time or two. And I won't sugar coat it for you either. If I hadn't been five months along and wearing Chet's engagement ring when he died, I would have gone for an abortion. My career peaked right around the time I got knocked up. After I had you, it all went downhill."

"Yeah, blame the baby. It's a wonder I wasn't born with fetal alcohol syndrome," Howdy retorted, coming out of the shell of his hands like a snapping turtle. He unfolded from the chair and scraped the clinging body stocking from his butt as if he'd sat in shit. "Come on Cassie. I can't take anymore."

"Well, you asked. I want you to know I stayed off the sauce and the ciggies for the duration. I didn't want a cretin for a child either." Mariah blew smoke in his direction. "If you really want an answer, I know Billy would be willing to take a test. Chet is long gone, but he has a son about twenty years older than you. He runs Lovell Real Estate now. I always liked him, and he was very taken with me. I think he wouldn't mind."

Howdy froze the doorway. "Could he be my father, too?"

"No. I wouldn't have done that to Chet. I have my standards. Too bad he didn't provide for me in his will. His three ex-wives bought me off and for a while, Lionel and I lived the high life. The money ran out, and I had to let the Mexican nanny go and get back on the stage. Li and I dropped you off in Oklahoma. He recreated me as a green-eyed goddess. Damn, back then, I only needed the contacts to tint my eyes. Now I need them to see fine print. Billy, you out there?'

The door burst open with surprising force missing Howdy's freckled nose by an inch as the kicker jumped back. "You need me, Mariah? These kids giving you trouble?"

"No. This is my son, Howie, and his girlfriend, I guess. You might be his daddy. You willing to take a paternity test?"

"Sure. If he's mine, will you marry me?"

"Now you know that won't ever happen, darling. Could be Lionel, too, and I never would marry him either."

Cassie withdrew a notepad pad and pen from her small, kicky purse. "Let's see.

What's your last name, Billy?'

"Ruggles. I hope he's mine." The guard's watery blue eyes, nestled in two deep pouches of flesh, lit with hope.

"Thank you. So, we have Benito Rizzo, Billy Ruggles, Lionel Lowe, and Chet Lovell as suspects. Where can we find your agent?"

"In his office tomorrow or hanging around the bus terminal handing out cards to possible clients fresh off the bus, but he usually slithers in after my last show hoping for a little free nooky—like I have the energy when I need to get over to the restaurant by six. Stick around if you really want to meet him. I'll give him a heads up on the situation if you don't. Chet's son you can find at his place of business. The real estate market is crap in Vegas right now. Tell him you want to buy a house, and he'll see you, no problem."

"Thank you for your help, Ms. Coy." Cassie closed the note pad and put it away. "We'll set up a time for all the daddies to get their DNA test and let you know."

"Yeah, I always wondered."

Howdy, face ablaze, glared at Cassie. "What are you, my personal assistant? Maybe I don't want to know. It's bad enough finding out *she's* my mother."

He found a big, wrinkled fist thrust at his chest. "Don't you talk to her that way. You should have seen Mariah when she first came here, all fresh and pretty, before Rizzo and Lowe got their hands on her. I had to protect her from lots of guys, but I couldn't save her from them." Billy Ruggles ran out of steam and lowered the fist as if it were too heavy to hold up much longer.

"Billy, you've always been my hero. Howie, I did right by you taking you back home. You grew up straight and tall like my daddy. I see him in you every move you make, every sentence you say without a single word of cussing. I don't see how it matters who your father is because you turned out fine, really fine." Mariah plucked a tissue from a box on the dressing table and dabbed at her eyes careful not to smudge her lavish makeup.

"The lawyer called me when Dad died, part of his instructions so I'd know, along with a letter saying he'd left the ranch and what little he had to you. I stayed away from the funeral. I kept my word, and I didn't come running when you signed a big contract with the Sinners. My singing career is pretty much over. Benny lets me have this gig for old times sake, then I go to work at his cheap breakfast buffet to pay my house note. I have a little place of my own and live there alone. You may not be pleased by the mother you found, but I'm not asking anything of you either."

Howdy nodded and walked out the door. Cassie said, "We'll be back to meet Lionel and get this all cleared up."

"No, we won't." Howdy's voice sounded from the hall.

"Yes, we will. Interesting meeting you, Ms. Coy."

Mariah pointed a long acrylic fingernail her way. "Right back at you, sweetheart."

Chapter Twenty-Eight

Walking her dazed man up and down the dazzling Strip as if she were attempting to sober him up, Cassie kept up a constant chatter. She might as well have been saying, "Stay with me," like EMTs did to patients who were bleeding out.

"Really, she's not so bad. I admire how tough she became to survive in this town. She never once broke her word to your grandparents. She has the McCoy sense of honor, wouldn't you say?"

Howdy declined to answer. She steered him into a bar, ordered a whiskey, neat, and held it to his lips until he swallowed.

"It burns all the way down," he said.

She wasn't sure if he referred to the liquor. "I favor Billy over Benny Rizzo for your father. I'll bet he was an athlete in his youth, and you both have blue eyes. He seems like a nice guy and loves your mother."

"My mother has blue eyes, or at least she did. But yeah, I'd take Billy over Benny any day if I had to choose a father. Except I don't get a choice."

"About time to go back to Nero's Lounge and catch Mariah's second set. We need to check out this Lionel Lowe."

"I have the feeling I won't like him any better than Rizzo."

Cassie put on a happy face. "You won't know until

267

you meet him," she said cheerfully, but the misery she'd caused him weighed her down like the sacks of coins most people traveled to Vegas to win. She'd told him she'd given up impetuous acts, but she had dragged him here without any preparation for what they might encounter. Now he knew his mother slept around, would have married a man for his money, might have aborted her son if it didn't work out. She'd never be that blue-eyed sylph in the tutu for him again, a terrible loss. He bled from the soul if not from the heart.

She got him another whiskey and coaxed him to drink, then took him outside into the refreshingly chill desert night to pace some more. No sense in making him watch his mother prance around with her enormous boobs hanging out again. She got him back to the lounge as the aged trumpet player blew his first note.

Billy escorted them directly to Mariah's dressing room. "He's in there, Lionel Lowe. She always calls him Li, and it fits. How many times did he promise her a better career if her tits were bigger, her hair redder, her eyes greener like she had no talent to offer at all? She never smoked a butt or a joint, took a drink or slept with a man before he nabbed her. He picked her up by the side of the road when her old truck broke down just outside the city limits on her way from Oklahoma. Ruined her, ruined that pretty young thing with a voice like lark on a sunny morning. It's gone now, that voice, all because of him."

The guard rapped on the door harder than necessary. "Come," Mariah answered, but Billy got in their way. "I want to say I don't think Lowe is your father, Howie, because he'd only breed belly-dragging snakes like himself and you seem like decent guy." He stepped aside and let them enter Mariah's smoky domain.

Adding to the funky air in the small room with his own cigarette, the agent sat backwards in the only spare chair and leaned his arms across its top. Mariah, hairpiece discarded and lying on the table like a dead fox but still in her costume, removed her stage makeup with cold cream and wipes, each swipe adding the years back onto her face. Lionel Lowe had been watching her, but now his eyes, a muddy mix of green and brown, fastened on Howdy. A lean and hungry look is how Shakespeare would have described him, Cassie thought. His cheeks sank in as he took a drag. Unlike Rizzo who might be dying his jet black hair, Lowe had allowed two silver wings to sprout over his ears and another to grown down the middle of his dark brown hair. Skunk came to mind, not angel.

"So you might be my kid. Always thought you belonged to that old geezer, Chet. But hey, I think this is great. Only now does Mariah shows me all those clippings about you she's been hiding. You're kinda famous. You got an agent?"

"A sports agent," Howdy answered, his face gone blank.

"You turn out to be my son I could take you on, keep all that income in the family so to speak. Always wanted to try my hand at representing athletes, but it didn't work out."

"Because naive young women are easier to con," his mother said.

"She's always joking. I love that about the *old* gal. You tell me where and when for the DNA test, and I'm there. Here's a card with my numbers." Lowe held it out between forked fingers.

Howdy made no move to take it, but Cassie did. "I'll try to get an appointment for late tomorrow afternoon if everyone can get there."

Through the small crack left in the doorway, Billy answered, "I can come then."

Lowe laughed like a jackass issuing several strong "hee-hees." "You took so many steroids in days gone by, I doubt if you ever came. I'm amazed you haven't died of testicular cancer by now."

Billy slammed the door fully open and, pulling back his stooped shoulders, loomed over the chair where Lowe lounged. "Tell him that ain't so, Mariah. You and me were good together." The agent rose to face him, a slender reed compared to a gnarled oak.

"You were a sweet lover, Billy. I hope the boy is yours."

"See. She doesn't want him to belong to you. You made her give the kid away. She cried in my arms one night right here in this room because of what you done."

"Shut up, Billy. All of you, out of here. I need to change and get some shuteye before the breakfast shift. Leave and don't come back until you get the results." Mariah stared into her mirror and swiped hard at the makeup beneath her eyes.

Howdy moved across the small room in two quick strides. He bent and kissed her cleansed cheek. "Goodnight, Mama."

If he expected a soft reply, he received none. "Is that hard liquor I smell on your breath, Howie McCoy? You know your grandma would not approve. Don't you turn into a drunk on me now that we finally got together again."

He straightened. "I won't. I promise, and McCoys keep their promises."

"Yes, yes they do. Now get out each and every one of you."

****

Howdy slept in late the next day, though it wasn't as if they'd torn up the sheets last night after returning from Mariah's dressing room. He wasn't in the mood, didn't feel like it, wanted to be left alone. Cassie ordered room service and ate stuffed French toast topped with fresh strawberries along with her coffee while she organized the DNA test for four p.m. and informed Billy and Lionel about time and place. She did hope Howdy woke soon so they could track down his possible brother, Robson Lovell, and get him to attend as well.

He stirred in the suite's bedroom. A shower blasted on and ran for a good long time. Finally, he appeared freshly shaven and wearing his usual cowboy gear. Cassie looked him over with a critical eye.

"Didn't you bring any khakis or maybe a golf shirt?'

"Brian says this is my look. It's the only one I brought along. I didn't figure we'd be staying more than a few days. Exactly how much did you pack for a stay at the ranch?"

Cassie glanced down at her full-skirted dress with the blue floral print, little capped sleeves and modest scooped neckline. She wiggled her peach-painted toes in their white sandals. "Well, you've seen the size of my suitcase. I thought we might have to go to your church and this would be okay."

He relented. "You do look pretty this morning, but nothing like last night."

"I wasn't pretty last night?"

"You were scary, sexy gorgeous last night, but I think I prefer pretty in the morning."

That warmed her heart. She cut off a corner of the French toast she'd saved for him and impaled a small strawberry on top of it. Holding out the loaded fork, she said, "You have to try this. It's amazing—bread stuffed with a cream cheese filling, then dipped into eggs and fried. So good with the strawberries."

He pushed the fork away like a petulant toddler. "Not hungry. Got any coffee?"

"Yes, I made a fresh pot in the kitchenette while you showered. You'll feel better if you eat. If I finish both pieces, I'll put on five pounds before noon." She wiggled the fork at him again.

"I said I do not want any!" he replied with each word cut into a small piece like the French toast.

"Champagne hangover? They're the worst. I shouldn't have made you drink those two shots afterward, but you seemed to need fortifying, and beer wasn't going do it. How about if I order some dry toast and tomato juice for you?"

"I'm not hung over. My selection of daddies is making me sick to my stomach. Why don't we just go over to Rizzo's breakfast buffet and have my mom wait on us again?"

"If you want, but I'm stuffed. Besides, it's nearly noon. I think they might be closed. I hoped we could find Robson Lovell and invite him to the DNA test party. See, I'm dressed like a newlywed looking for her first home. I guess she married a cowboy if that's all you packed."

"Cassie, I was being sarcastic."

"No wonder I didn't get it. Sarcasm is new for you. I don't think I like sarcasm before noon."

"Right now, I don't much care what you like." Howdy fixed his coffee, gulped it down, and poured another. Grudgingly, he pulled the plate holding the last of the berries and French toast toward him and ate for the energy he'd need to get through another miserable day in Vegas.

He'd barely swallowed the last bite when Cassie grabbed an elbow and steered him to the elevators and out into the glare of the noonday sun. The dancing waters of the Bellagio's fountains made him wince. Maybe he did have a tad of a hangover, another first for him along with sarcasm. A dynamo of determination, Cassie already had the address and directions to the offices of Lovell Real Estate. Reluctantly, he drove his truck there to ruin Robson Lovell's afternoon, too.

They got past the receptionist and into the owner's domain because of another premier performance by Cassie. Hanging on Howdy's arm, she gushed, "My boyfriend and I are thinking of settling in Las Vegas after we get married. He's Howard McCoy, kicker for the New Orleans Sinners. We can live anywhere he wants in the off-season. I'd like something really nice and roomy. Could we deal with Mr. Lovell directly?"

Not trusting this news to the intercom, the motherly, middle-aged woman, wearing comfortable gray slacks topped with a silk blouse under the company's red blazer, hustled down a long hall to the end office, rapped, and entered. She returned with alacrity.

"Mr. Lovell will see you immediately. He's canceling his afternoon tee time for you." She beamed as she delivered her message.

They walked along the corridor decorated with framed photos of fabulous estates both sold and still on the market. Robson Lovell met them at his door, escorted them inside like a well-trained butler, and offered seats in two deep red leather chairs facing his desk.

"Would you like something to drink, anything at all? I'll have Linda bring it."

"No, thank you, sir." Howdy, uncomfortable in the well-padded seat, gripping the armrests like he might sink in too far, glanced around the office—at the half-paneled walls of light oak and matching desk, the shelves of golf and real estate trophies, photos of the agent with famous clients, the view of the desert beyond the large plate-glass window.

"Such a pleasure to meet you, young man. I am a huge Sinners fan. I think you're going to help the team to another Super Bowl. I'll put my money on that," Lovell said with the easy way of the born salesman softening up the client with chitchat.

Finally, Howdy took a good look at the man, scanning for any family resemblance. Both were tall and blue-eyed, though Lovell wore stylish glasses, hiding his behind a slight tint in the lenses. Fortyish and graying, the real estate agent's hairline receded deeply leaving only a small patch on his forehead, a little island holding out against an encroaching bald spot. He might once have been an athlete, but the beef had turned to lard and hung over the alligator belt cinching in a red golf shirt with another reptile emblazoned on the pocket. Noticing his patter fell flat, Robson Lovell turned to Cassie.

"I can imagine this stunning young lady sunning herself beside her very own pool with a built-in Jacuzzi and fire pots to illuminate nighttime parties. Wouldn't she be superb in a setting like that?" He brought his vision back to Howdy.

"Actually, we don't need a house. I have a ranch in Oklahoma and a condo in New Orleans."

"A man of your stature can always use another place to relax. Maybe a penthouse. Vegas can offer whatever you want. Why, your quarterback, Joe Dean Billodeaux used to come here to unwind all the time. He got married right here."

"Yes, I know." Joe hadn't been back since because Nell didn't consider it a good place for children, but why bother to rub that in when Lovell was about to hear worse news. "Do you recall your father dating a woman named Mariah Coy?"

"I could hardly forget. Being twenty-one at the time, we were close to the same age, decades closer than my father. I had a little crush on her, you could say. I thought she'd be Dad's fourth wife, but his golf game got the best of him. One good tantrum after a bogey, and he dropped dead on the green just like that." Lovell snapped his fingers, obviously not suffering from years of mourning for his daddy.

"I finished my business degree and took over the company. Those were the days, yes, they were." Lovell steepled his fingers as if imagining skyscrapers rising from the desert soil, all of them paying off in huge commissions for land. "Hard times now, but we've branched out into billboards and signage. Las Vegas always needs billboards. Lovell Real Estate is doing fine. You can put your trust in us if you are looking for an investment."

"No, I came here looking for my mother, Mariah Coy, not an investment."

"Well then," Lovell sighed in disappointment. "She went away after Dad's death. The ex-wives weren't about to share the wealth anymore than they had to. Dad followed a pattern, you might say. He kept each wife around ten years, then traded them in for younger, bustier models. Had a child by each one. I've got two half-sisters. He left me the business and my sisters other assets, mostly cash and stocks. Old Chet always said not a one of his ex-wives would remarry as long as they could continue to soak him for alimony. Maybe Mariah went on to better things. She had talent. In fact, I heard she's singing again in one of the places downtown. I should look her up. I'm divorced myself, maybe…"

"Mariah was pregnant with me when your father died. He paid for her hospital expenses in advance and did intend to marry her. She says I might be your half-brother." Howdy stood, preparing for outrage, anger or insult, but that is not what he got. Instead, Lovell's face lit with elation.

"I always wanted a brother instead of those two harpy sisters, gold diggers exactly like their mothers. My brother is Howdy McCoy, ace kicker for the Sinners. How great is that! I played a little football in college myself. Must run in the genes." Lovell sucked in his gut and pushed out of his chair.

Before Howdy could prepare for the onslaught, his maybe brother surged around the desk and embraced him in a comradely hug. "Bro!" Robson Lovell said.

The unexpected contact dried the spit in Howdy's mouth and prevented the rest of the story from passing through his lips.

Cassie, so quiet up until now, rushed in to assist him. "There is more to the story, I'm afraid. Mariah isn't certain you and Howdy share the same father. We'd like you to participate in a DNA test today to make certain you are really brothers. He doesn't want anything more from you than to know his parentage. Would you do this for him?"

"Have the Sinners won a Super Bowl? Tell me the time and place. In fact, let me take you both to lunch at the country club. Before we go for the test, maybe you'd like to take a look at a few secluded properties where you could keep horses. I see you have a sort of western flair, Howdy."

"We'd love that, wouldn't we?" Cassie nudged his arm, and Howdy managed to free himself the well-padded belly hug of Robson Lovell and nod.

His possible half-brother ricocheted off in another direction and snatched a photo from the wall. "This is Dad. Look, we have the same eyes. Unfortunately, not the same hairline. I'd give much to have a mop like yours. He's old in this picture and used to be taller. He could be your father. Yes, I see a resemblance to both of us."

Howdy didn't, but he went along with the enthusiastic outburst, as he did to lunch at the country club and a tour of ranches, one of which used to be a bordello, outside the city. It filled the time until four p.m.

Chapter Twenty-Nine

The candidates for most likely blood relative of a Sinners football player showed up promptly, all a little astounded by their number and diversity. Already in his uniform for his night's work, Billy, the most eager, volunteered to go first. Robson Lovell followed, pumping Howdy's hand before giving his sample and saying, "However this turns out, a pleasure to meet you. Give some thought to which one of those ranches you'd like."

Mariah's agent greased his purported son's hand with another of his cards. "In case you lost the last one." He made the "call me" sign and offered up his spit for consideration in the Who is Howdy's Daddy contest.

As the men filed out, each shook Howdy's hand again—Billy with a hard but shaky grip, Robson offering the natural salesman's glad-hand, and Lionel, the sweaty palm. Cassie gave Howdy a jubilant hug and hung on his arm as they left the doctor's office for the second time.

"The hard part is over. What would you like to do while we wait for the results? We could ride horses at one of those ranches or go see Boulder Dam. I'd love to get Celine Dionne tickets if we can. I guess Donny Osmond would be okay, too, if you want."

"I don't feel like celebrating."

"But why? You found your mother and are about to discover your father. This is great. You'll know who you truly are."

"I knew who I was before you dragged me here. Now I'm not so sure. Get in the truck. We're going back to the room."

"Sure, if you want. We can celebrate that way, too."

"Shut up, just shut up."

He maintained silence all the way back to the Bellagio. She did as well until the door to their suite closed behind them. A complimentary bowl of fresh fruit replaced the breakfast dishes. Cassie selected an apple and bit into its crisp, white center.

"I shouldn't be hungry after that lunch Rob treated us to at the country club. I think he'd make a great brother. He doesn't need your money. You could golf together."

"I don't play golf, and I'll have to buy a place in Vegas if it's him. Not sure I ever want to come here again."

"Even to get married?" Cassie said with a coy smile and another bite of the apple.

"Do I amuse you? Do you get a kick out of dragging me down to your level with dirty, nasty secrets from my past? Last week, I knew I came from good, caring people. Now I have a whore of a mother and a whole bunch of fathers, none that I want to have as family. Jesus, Cassie, you have destroyed me!"

She'd gone pale but kept a playful façade. "Uh-oh, that's another quarter in the cuss jar for blaspheming."

"Yeah, make fun of my morals. At least I haven't had a kid out of wedlock unlike you and my mother and

Joe Dean. You all have that in common." He ripped open the mini-bar door, took out a miniature bottle of Jim Beam, unscrewed the top and swallowed the contents in two gulps.

Two red spots appeared on Cassie's cheeks, and she struck back. "Each of us did what was best for our child. Joe is raising his, I gave mine up for adoption, and your mother took you to a safe place to grow up. Imagine what you would be like if Lionel Lowe helped raise you? Didn't you hear what Billy said? She cried over that decision."

"I heard. That's why I kissed her, but you're whores, you're all whores, Joe Dean, too!" He selected a tiny bottle of tequila and downed it.

"Yesterday you wanted to marry me. Now I'm a whore, but I'm no different than I was when we came here. Neither are you."

"The scales have fallen from my eyes, yes, they have. I thought I loved Lupe, too, but she was only a fickle prostitute from south of the border. You gave yourself to that piece of filth, Bijou, and I don't know how many other men. I only have your word there was no one else between him and you throwing yourself at Joe Dean. You sure seemed to know your way around a man's body when we got together."

Cassie slung the half-eaten apple at him hard as she could. He deflected it easily with one hand and chose a little bottle of rum with the other.

"Stop drinking and listen to me, Howard Angus Howdy McCoy. Bijou seduced an innocent teenage girl and made her do all the things he liked best. So, yes, I knew what to do. What I didn't know was how good those acts could be with someone I truly love."

"Right. Now you say you love me, but you wouldn't marry me yesterday when I wanted to give you a ring. All you can think about is celebrating with sex like my mother, exactly like her, and she's a whore, a God-damned whore."

"Stop saying that!" Her hand met the side of his face with a sharp slap that made the mouthful of rum he'd swilled spurt from his mouth.

He rubbed his cheek. "I'm taking you to the airport. This is never gonna work. We're never gonna work."

"You are so right about that. I'll take a cab. Why should I risk my life with a drunk?"

She stomped into the bedroom and slammed the door. He finished the rum and a bottle with two servings of red wine while she packed. His stomach roiled with the mixture of drinks he'd consumed, but he cracked open another, Jack Daniels maybe. His eyes weren't focusing so well. When Cassie rolled her over-stuffed bag from the bedroom and headed for the door, he found himself unsteady when he followed.

"You're right. I can't drive. Here, here."

Taking out that wallet molded by his hip, he handed her a spread of five hundred-dollar bills like she was exactly the kind of woman he'd accused her of being. Howdy remembered her story about the gambler who'd won a night with her from Bijou in a card game. A decent guy, that man had given her part of his winnings for a bus ticket home and never collected on the sex. Did all her relationships end this way—with a ride back where she came from?

He could tell she wanted to throw the money in his face, but knew she'd foolishly maxed out her credit cards on a wardrobe to impress Joe. Her teaching assistant's salary after rent and food made only a small dent in that debt each month. None of her cards had enough of an open balance to get her to New Orleans. Unless she really wanted to earn her way there as a streetwalker, she had no choice but to take his cash.

"I guess you were right about me," she said as she took the bills and stowed them in her bra where they wouldn't be stolen. "I hope I showed you a real good time, cowboy."

Then she left, striking out hard and fast for the elevator another man held open for her. Howdy swayed in the doorway watching her until she got aboard, smiled a taut thanks to that other man, and pressed the down button.

"I didn't mean it that way. For plane fare. The money is for plane fare. Should go after her." His belly heaved. He wasn't going anywhere, not tonight. Not for another week when the test results arrived.

Hurling his stomach contents and maybe a bit of the lining into the toilet didn't keep his mind off Cassie or his possible parentage. He spent the night between bouts bent over the commode imagining Cassie had stayed in the hotel, gone with the stranger to another room because the nice guy she'd trusted had kicked her out and made her feel cheap. As for his potential heritage, Howdy dreamed of himself as the son of a mafia don being gunned down at a tollbooth or a bodybuilder swollen with steroids and rage, a junior agent waiting at the bus station to rake in new, unsuspecting talent, and the most innocuous, a golfer playing double with Robson Lovell.

In the morning figuring he needed that hair of the

dog everyone talked about, he made an excursion to a liquor store, bought a gallon of rye whiskey, and hauled it back to the suite where he downed as much as he could stand. It came right back up. He made coffee with a shaking hand and sipped it slowly, black and hot. That worked better. After a while, he ordered scrambled eggs and toast and kept that down. Exhausted but afraid of his dreams, he had another shot or two from the giant jug of booze and laid down to sleep away the afternoon after posting the Do Not Disturb sign on his door.

No one bothered him. He ordered a large, loaded pizza and found it went down well with rye. As the lights burned up the night sky of the city and obliterated the stars, he had no desire to quit his room and wander with the crowds coming out in the darkness—if the Strip could ever be considered dark. He stayed in bed where the sheets still smelled of Cassie and sex because he'd refused maid service as he continued to do all week. Food and liquor, easily ordered in. Time passed, staggering by with bleary, bloodshot eyes and whiskey breath.

The pounding on his door in late morning woke him from a great dream where he and Cassie lived at the Bar Mack Ranch and never went to Vegas. He untangled himself from the sheets and staggered close to the suite's entrance when the drumming continued. "I don't want my bed made up. Leave me alone. Can't you read? *No leer*?"

"Howie McCoy, this is your mother. You open up right now, or I'll scream loud enough to bring the guards."

Reluctantly, he flipped the security latch, unlocked the bolt, and turned the knob. Mariah Coy stood before him bulging out of the top of her green waitress uniform. She padded in on the same kind of shoes nurses wore and took a good look around.

Kicking pizza boxes and dirty dishes out of the way, she said, "This would be a pretty nice place if a pig didn't live here. What would your grandma say about a man who didn't pick up after himself? Huh?"

"That I'm going to hell in a handbasket."

"Damn right. Good Lord Jesus, you're knee deep in pizza boxes and liquor bottles. Ruth is turning in her grave right now. The doctor said he couldn't reach you at the number you gave him. Where's your phone?'

"Somewhere," he said vaguely.

Not a bit shy, his mother pushed into his bedroom and found it lying on the night table right next to the dented pillow where he slept. "Dead. You'd think with important news on the way you'd remember to keep it charged. Where's that girl of yours? Seemed like she had some sense—unlike you."

"Gone."

"Walked out? Can't say I blame her." She sniffed at the stale sheets spotted with spilled whiskey and bits of pepperoni.

"I sent her away."

"Then you *are* an idiot. Anyone could see she was crazy about you. So, not even interested in the DNA results? No desire to know who your real daddy is?"

"I don't think I can handle the news on an empty stomach."

"Well, man up because I am your wake-up call. Billy cried—when he found out it wasn't him. Li shrugged. Them's the breaks. He's still trying to figure out how to make money off of you."

Howdy had to admit his mother had a flair for the dramatic, drawing out the suspense. "So is dear old dad Rizzo or Lovell? Just tell me."

"Chet, Chet Lovell, the only old dude I ever knew who could get it up without little blue pills. He was surely a phenomenon. I hope you inherited that ability. When did you shave last?"

Mariah squeezed his cheeks and ran a thumb along his stubble. "You'd give that gal of yours a bad beard burn—if she'd stayed. Still, makes you look tougher. You could use some tough. Have you changed your clothes in a week? You been sleeping in them? Phew! Get yourself into the shower right this minute."

She gave him a shove in the right direction. Before he got that far, Mariah had the house phone to her ear. "We need maid service, pronto! Send a whole damn cleaning crew. Howie you have six messages on the hotel phone. How could you sleep with this red light blinking all night long? Drunk, that's how. I answered my own question. Get in there and come back presentable, you hear me, boy?"

Jeez, she sounded exactly like his grandmother. He decided against telling her that. He lingered in front of the bathroom, no more sanitary than the rest of the place with its smell of barf and heap of dirty towels where he'd tried to clean up his mess. "Any word from Cassie?"

"Very first one. She says she arrived in New Orleans just fine, not that you'd care, and she will be returning one-hundred fifty dollars right away and the rest as soon as she can manage. I have to say you don't have the same touch with women as Chet did. He knew how to treat a girl, never asked for any change or his jewelry back. Learn from the man, Howie."

"Yes, ma'am. What about the other calls?"

"Mostly from today. Billy weeping. A 'congratulations, bro', from Robson and two panicky calls from his sisters saying you won't get a dime from them. The last one is from me asking why in hell you don't pick up your phone. I came over here soon as I got off work."

"Thanks, I guess. Look, Mom, you don't have to work anymore. I make a good living. I have a condo in New Orleans with lots of extra bedrooms. You can stay with me. I'll take care of you from now on."

"Who says I want that? Singing is my life. Unless I can sing in New Orleans, no sense in going there. Besides, I make my own way. I see what you're thinking." She shook a finger at him. "Don't! Yeah, I slept with Benny Rizzo to get my big break, but I gave money to Li and never got a cent in return. The best Billy can do is put a coral-colored rose in my dressing room every night. As for Chet, yes, I took from him and made him happy in return. I would have married him. No harm in giving gifts to your fiancée is there? Anyhow, you owe me nothing."

"You gave me life. You left me in safe hands."

"You're still drunk. Get in the shower and sober up. Either go hug Robson, and I know he loves to hug, or get on back to New Orleans now that you found out what you wanted to know."

He didn't repeat this was all Cassie's idea. Crude and outrageous as Mariah Coy could be, he still thought saying he hadn't come to seek her might break her stone cold heart to pieces as if he'd poured hot water over it. He didn't have it in him to injure the feelings of another woman so soon after Cassie, and that had been wrong, so wrong.

By the time he emerged with a towel wrapped around his hips, his mother had left, but a bevy of maids giggled as they shoveled out the mess in his suite. He raided his suitcase for clean clothes, called Robson, got talked into lunch, and ignored his new sisters' calls. He'd never wanted to leave any place as badly as Vegas. Checking out, he went to bond with his brother. Then, he planned to head directly back to Oklahoma and figure out on the way how a guy going to hell in a handbasket could get back into paradise.

Chapter Thirty

Joe Dean Billodeaux watched Brian Lightfoot punt the football deep. His return squad formed a protective V around the punt returner and ran the ball back into the wall of the defensive line. Good, they looked good—all except for his placekicker who shanked one field goal attempt after another no matter what the distance. How could a guy who won the Lou Groza award and made ninety-seven percent of his kicks his rookie year go so sour? Howdy McCoy sat on a bench icing his leg as if that would make his performance better.

Joe answered his own question. Woman trouble, the same kind of crap that caused Connor Riley's slump half a dozen years ago, and now he'd have to deal with it again. Sure, when Nell broke up with him during their courtship, he'd been down, but he'd gone out there and done his job on the field just the same. His own fault, he never should have pushed Cassie on that nice kid to solve his own problems. Howdy couldn't handle her. Now, he had to fix the situation.

Coach Buck whistled for a break. The men trotted in to suck down water and athletic drinks of choice, take off helmets that sometimes seemed more like saunas for the brain than necessary protection, and mop the sweat from their faces with cool, damp towels. A few of them threw glares Howdy's way. The kicker had cost them a couple of pre-season games already, made the team look bad, and the players weren't very forgiving. They expected better from last year's top kicker in the league.

Joe signaled to Lightfoot to join him. "You're Howdy's friend, but nothing else, right?"

Amused, Brian replied, "That's right. He is so not my type." He gave Joe a salacious grin.

Joe did not return it. "Glad to hear that. You need to talk to him. I've tried. Nell has tried. He won't open up about what happened in Las Vegas. I mean we know he broke up with Cassie, but there has to be more. It's killing his game. Coach Buck is thinking we might have to call Ancient Andy Mortenson out of retirement and see if he has any kicks left in him if Howdy can't straighten himself out. Failing that, the boy might be traded early in the season if anyone will make an offer."

"I'm no psychologist, but I know Cassie is who he's missing. She caused a big mess with his family and walked away, I presume. However, I get the impression that's not the whole problem. Ah well, let me get out some of my magic fairy dust and sprinkle it on the situation," Brian said, probably to make Joe wince. He got the desired result.

"Whatever it takes. Now is a good time. Go get 'im."

Brian sauntered away and took a seat next to Howdy. "Hey, bro, what's with the shank-itis? Hate to bear bad news, but Joe says they might bring Andy back because you can't do the job. Worse things will happen if you don't shape up. How about spilling to Uncle Brian?"

"I don't have any uncles. Turns out I have a half-brother who wants season tickets to our games and two half-sisters, who once they found out I didn't want a share of the family fortune, would like to be introduced to some of the players, even though one is divorced and the other is still married. My father is a dead Las Vegas real estate magnate, and my mother looks like the kind of women Joe used to date. I want her to move here so I can take care of her, but she says she won't do that unless I find her a singing gig because she earns her own way. I shouldn't do anything for her because she never did anything for me—except give me life and settle me with a decent family, my words, not hers. I want her to break with that slimy agent of hers and the guy who owns the lounge where she works. No dice unless she can work here. Is that enough to distract me from the game?"

"Might be, but I sense there is more." Brian put two fingers to his forehead as if he were a swami divining the thoughts of his friend.

"Brian, I don't deserve my good fortune, to be on this team. Not after the things I said to Cassie, words I can't take back. Football players might break bones, but words can maim, too. I tried doing good deeds all summer. Thought she might notice, that Tommy might say something when she called, but she never asked to talk to me. I think she'll hang up if I call her, but I'm afraid to find out."

"Ah, so you are punishing yourself by kicking that ball so hard, so off center, it always shanks. I noticed that."

"That obvious?"

"Only to those of us who know you well. Don't Baptists believe in forgiveness?"

"Sure, but we also believe in hell for those who have hurt others. Hell is where I'm located right now."

"Maybe it's only purgatory, and your friends can pray your way out. Oh right, Baptists don't believe in purgatory. I'm not sure I do either, but I'll bet Joe believes. Let's see what we can do to put you back in paradise. And by that, I mean in Cassie."

Howdy punched Brian's arm hard enough to hurt but at least didn't kick him in his punting leg. A good sign, Brian thought, that his friend wouldn't hear anything low about the woman he loved.

"Ease up, Howdy. You know when you hurt yourself, you hurt the team. Besides, if the management trades you, Ancient Andy will refuse to room with me on road trips. He thought I lusted after his shriveled old shanks during our short acquaintance. Not so, definitely not so." He returned the punch with a pat on the back and trotted back to Joe.

"Well?" the quarterback said.

"We need to get his mother a gig in New Orleans. You still have some influence at the clubs, right? I seem to remember you got that comedienne, Tabby Johnson, her start."

"Yeah, and I didn't sleep with her either. I'm still proud of that. She sends me tickets to her shows. Most times I give them to charity auctions. But, if I guar-an-tee I'll show up for the opening and bring some of the team, I guess I can get Howdy's mama a show."

"See, everyone is able redeem themselves. We also need to get his newfound brother season tickets and introduce his half-sisters to the team."

"Easy."

"Next, we bring him and Cassie back together.

Evidently, he said some pretty foul things to her and drove her away."

"Howdy doesn't know how to be foul. After he came back from his ranch, he spent all of June and July helping us with Camp Love Letter. I cleared a field and put up miniature goal post for the kids. Even the ones in wheelchairs played flag football, and he taught those that could how to kick. He stood in as lifeguard at the pool since Nell wouldn't put on a swimsuit. Said someone might mistake her for a beach ball. I could tell he was down, but he never took it out on the children, even when Tommy and Macho followed him around non-stop."

"Evidently, what happened in Vegas, stayed in Vegas. He seems to think that town brought out the beast in him and what he said cannot be forgiven when it comes to Cassie."

"That's the trouble with Baptists, no confession to make them feel better. They have to stew in their guilt. Hey, if I can be saved, Howdy should be easy. Let me talk to Nell. She always has an opinion about how to handle Cassie."

****

Nell Billodeaux spent the afternoon soaking in the round, black platform tub in Joe's New Orleans condo. Big enough to accommodate four, she certainly took up at least two places, maybe three. The bubbles slid down the sides of her pale, mountainous belly like snow in an avalanche. Being in water alleviated the weight of her pregnancy and two jets aimed at the small of her back relieved some of the ache. In one of her grouchy moods, she'd complained to Joe about his wretched taste in choosing ebony fixtures and dark mirror tiles veined in gold during his bachelor years. Big mistake.

"I despise bathing in stygian gloom," she had to say when she really meant she hated being on extended bed rest, loathed the size of her baby-bloated body, and could not stand Nurse Wickersham installed by Joe in his pale blue Madame Pompadour bedroom to watch over her for the duration. While Joe probably had no idea what "stygian" meant, he got the general idea.

The next day while Nurse Wickersham coaxed her to stuff more applesauce into a stomach pushed up against her esophagus by the triplets so she always had heartburn, an electrician arrived. He installed a blazing gold chandelier hung with little teardrop crystals exactly like the one in the ranch's bathroom over the black tub. Now, she could see every pink stretch mark veining her engorged stomach with extreme clarity.

When Joe asked her how she liked the new fixture, she replied, "Perfect," trying very hard to keep the sarcasm out of her voice. Like most men, her husband tended to take her words literally, and he did mean well. Her long baths gave her respite. She listened to music, read escapist literature in the now glaring light, called her children when they came home from school and listened to each and every one tell about their day. She missed them so, even knowing two of Corazon's cousins of which there seemed to be an endless supply took good care of them.

Corazon did not have this luxury. Carrying only one child, she remained on her feet bossing the others. Gestational diabetes had set in and with many of her favorite foods now forbidden, bossing took over as her favorite pastime. Knox probably wished she'd spend time in the pool instead.

Until Joe insisted his wife come to stay in New Orleans in order to be closer to Ochsner Hospital in case she "popped", the one good part of bed rest had been time shared with Xochi. Despite her origins, the child showed intelligence and an eagerness to learn. While the other children ran wild and free outdoors for the summer, Xochi tucked in against Nell's belly and read from primers designed to improve her English. She used a small iPad to learn her kindergarten math and glowed at every correct answer. In the fall, she would go the Episcopal day school a few miles from Chapelle where the girls attended. Tommy and Dean endured the rigors of Ste. Jeanne d'Arc Parochial in the town because Cassie wanted her son to have a Catholic education. As for Dean, don't get her started on the pressure brought to bear by his MawMaw.

Though Nadine made an argument to send Xochi with the boys since the child had been raised Catholic, Nell held out for a more liberal environment. On the single visit they'd managed to the day school before the doctor sentenced Nell to bed rest, the principal treated Xochi more like an interesting exchange student than a kid who couldn't speak English perfectly. In fact, when they talked on the phone, the child delighted in telling her she'd been asked to teach her class a few Spanish words a day. Nell only hoped the teacher vetted the words in advance. She could only imagine Xochi standing before the group and saying, "My Mama used to be a *puta*. Repeat *puta* after me. It means whore." Joe's investigator found that much out when untangling the child's place of birth and her parents' marital status. Surprisingly, Bijou had married the woman.

A heavy, masculine knock sounded on the door she

was forbidden to lock. Could be Nurse Wickersham or Joe, back from practice. "Sugar, I'm home. Can I come in and talk to you?"

Joe, then. Nurse Wickersham would have rapped hard once, bulled her way in, and told Nell she had to get out now and eat her snack or take a vitamin. "Sure, how did practice go?"

Her too-gorgeous-to-be-legal husband entered and sat on the edge of the tub next to the bidet where a green and yellow pothos vine thrived in the formerly dim light from the tiny windows above the tub. Even Joe couldn't kill it because all he had to do was turn on the little spigot to create a small fountain to water it. She hoped the brilliant new lighting scheme would not do away with the hardy plant she'd installed during the first weeks of their marriage.

"*C'est bon,* pretty good. Everyone looks ready to take on the Falcons in the opening game except Howdy. He's still shanking his kicks, distracted by his new family and the loss of Cassie. That's our fault. We need to fix it."

"Now he knows the dubious joys of having relatives. You can't fix that. I tried to get him to open up all summer about what happened in Vegas once he found his family, but he'd only tell me he'd said some unforgivable words to Cassie. When I suggested I invite her to the ranch so they could talk it out, he turned pale and said he couldn't look her in the eye ever again."

"Kickers. No guts," Joe said with disgust.

"Come on. He went into Mexico with you and showed quite a bit of bravery as I recall. It's women he can't handle. I had no better luck with Cassie. I called and invited her to celebrate the Fourth with Tommy, but she said she'd stay away until Thanksgiving as agreed. When I said that ban had been lifted, she told me she'd dragged a nice guy through the mud and couldn't face him again. Howdy was right about her being dirty and pushy, so right, but she swore she'd never slept with anyone but Bijou. Then, she apologized again about hitting on you and hung up. I gather finding his family was her idea, not his, and the stress caused him to throw Bijou in her face. In a way, her interest in you showed a sign of healing, being ready to trust another man. This has set her back again, I'm sure."

"Always the psychologist." Joe kissed the top of her head. "I can handle Howdy's family demands, but I have no ideas on how to get him and Cassie back together."

Nell's hand tapped a stack of celebrity magazines stacked by the tub. "Got an idea. You recall how Cassie loves the tabloids and gossip sheets? You tried to use them to get Connor and Stevie back to together."

"Yeah, what a disaster."

"You still have the number of that editor you tried to intimidate when his rag focused on me?"

"Sure, I have it stored in my phone. You never know when you'll have to kick someone's ass again."

"Like that worked the first time. Gimme. Let me try something."

Joe handed his cell phone to his bathing beauty. She held it carefully above the bubbles as she scanned the list of names. "You know, you could erase some of these women now. This the one?"

"That's him. I didn't want to keep all those names, but they transferred them over when I got the new phone."

"Remind me to show you how to delete after we're through here." Nell punched the number, and the signal winged directly to the source.

"Yeah, what do you want, Billodeaux? No retractions. No retractions ever."

"This is not Joe Dean. I lifted his phone. I'm an informed source." Nell lowered her voice into conspiracy mode. "The Sinners rookie kicker, Howard McCoy, is in a slump and hurting the team over breaking up with his girlfriend. She's a grad student at LSU. Her name is Cassie Thomas. This is where you can find her in Baton Rouge." She rattled off Cassie's address and disconnected. "That should get her attention."

"In a big way. Can't wait to see the headline. How is this going to help exactly?"

"It will let her know how much he needs her in his life. Now, can you get us skybox tickets to the first game? We'll make sure he knows Cassie is up there cheering for him."

"Us—who is us? I'll be down on the field. You will be in bed watching me play. Think of it this way, sugar. Only six more weeks to go. You've done a great job of carrying these babies. You don't want to blow it now."

"I want to go to the game. If Cassie gets to go, I do, too."

"Tink, you know pregnancy makes you irrational."

"I'm not irrational. I'm stir-crazy. I'll go in a wheelchair. Nurse Wickersham can come along to watch me. I swear I'll only sit there overflowing my seat like Jabba the Hut. Please, please, please."

She stood up and all the bath foam dribbled off the

crest of her belly. Joe helped her out of the tub and put his arms around her from behind or tried to. He had to admit, only to himself, she'd gotten so big he could hardly lace his fingers over her stomach anymore. Just below her navel that stuck out like an air tube on a beach ball, one of his babies kicked beneath his hands. He kissed his wife's neck. "I'll see what I can do, but only if your doctor allows it. Say, is Harry Connick, Jr.'s number still in my contacts?"

Nell checked. "Yes."

"Good, after we get you dried off I'll give him a ring and see if he can get Howdy's mom a place in Musician's Village down in the ninth ward. No matter what the boy says, he does not want to live with his mother."

"Amen to that. Hand me my muumuu."

"It's not a muumuu. This is a plus-size piece of lingerie I bought for my sexy wife. Let me towel you dry. You know it's been a long time for me, too, and I have more than another six weeks to hold out. Add more for your recovery time." Joe took a heavy towel from the heated rack and began stroking it over her body. "That you are full of my babies is kind of a turn on." He pressed his erection hard against the curve of her back as he reached around and wiped the bubbles from her belly, lifted each swollen breast and gently patted them with the soft terry, making sure no soap remained on the sensitive nipples by going round and round them.

"I can tell. I'd love to invite you in, but that's a big no-no right now."

"Not inside, can't do that, no. Maybe this?"

He draped the towel over her shoulders in order to

unzip his fly and probe between her legs from the back where her stomach would not get in the way. Warm and thick, he slid back and forth between her thighs. She grew wet and not from the bath. He moved his hands beneath her bulge and found her most sensitive spot. No stopping him or either of them now.

A single sharp wrap on the bathroom door made them freeze in position. A deep, authoritative female voice said, "Mrs. Billodeaux, you really need to get out of the tub now. I have a lovely cup of custard for your snack. Do you need help getting out?"

"No, Joe is helping me. I don't want any custard."

"She wants cream," Joe answered. Nell snickered.

"Ice cream? We have several kinds."

"No, just cream. I want to satisfy her cravings, Nurse. Say, do we have any rocky road?"

"I don't think so, sir."

"Great. Why don't you go out and find us some because everything is under control in here, completely under control.

"Very well. I might be gone for half an hour."

"Sounds about right. Better get going."

Nurse Wickersham walked away and closed the front door to the condo quietly.

Nell tightened her thighs and moved her hips back into their former rhythm. Joe's hands got busy again beneath her belly. Nell pressed her head under his chin and arched for him. "So you're in control."

"Sugar, I lied. This ain't gonna take half an hour. And just think, we can get our strength back with a little rocky road."

Chapter Thirty-One

In her high-heeled white sandals, Cassie strode across the Louisiana State University campus. Never wear white after Labor Day—who cared anymore? The early September weather remained sweltering hot. She wore a pale gray pencil skirt with a significant slit up the back to free her long legs and topped it with a buttoned, short-sleeved white linen jacket over a silky, bright yellow chemise, more of her "impress Joe Dean" collection. She'd be paying the clothes off for the next two years and might as well enjoy them. While going into debt, she should have gotten a better bag to tote her laptop and papers than the old, battered one she'd used all through college.

Passing the student union, she unbuttoned the jacket. She'd taught her Psych 101 class and attended another she needed to graduate in December before noon. Her afternoon opened before her with no demands other than to work on her master's thesis, the one she had second thoughts about now. Entitled *The Need to Know: The psychological necessity for adoptees to find their heritage,* she'd intensively interviewed fifty adults adopted as infants or very young children. Her findings urged more people to accept open adoptions and government and religious agencies to loosen the restrictions divulging parentage once the child reached twenty-one. Most of her subjects wanted to obtain this information if they had not already. Some gave up after meeting many roadblocks but remained unsatisfied, incomplete. A rare few stayed content, happy with the families who raised them, wanting nothing more.

Honestly, she thought she'd done right by pushing Howdy to discover his mother and father, not simply as names in a Bible but in person, flaws and all. She had no idea how great those flaws would be or the devastation that would cause to the world's nicest guy. Doubting her ability to counsel anyone anymore, she would finish the degree she'd by started by emulating Nell and ended hoping to help troubled young women, only to discover she was still one of those girls herself. What a mess she'd made.

The aroma of pizza and expensive coffee tickled her nose as one of the lower union doors opened and closed revealing some of the selections available at the small restaurants and cafes inside the building. No money for five-dollar iced mochas or tempting pastas, she'd be better off financially making a sandwich back at the apartment. She kept on walking, considered cutting across the parade ground and taking a shortcut back to grad student housing, but the extreme heat of the day convinced her to stay on the sidewalk in the shade of the massive live oaks lining the way.

As she approached her place, she bundled her long hair with one hand and held it up off her neck to let the slight breeze dry the sweat trickling down her back. With the chemise clinging tightly to her breasts, she thought only of getting out of her stylish getup and into something cool and comfortable. A young man with a thoroughly professional looking camera stepped from beneath the staircase leading to her apartment, said, "All right!" and snapped her picture.

"What are you doing?" she challenged.

"You are Cassie Thomas, right?"

"Yes."

"Jackpot!" he shouted and took off running in excellent athletic shoes.

She considered pursuit, but too hot and tired to care what student prank was afoot now, made her way up the stairs and into her unit where the air conditioner blasted out a significant amount of cold. She only hoped she wouldn't find herself plastered all over FaceBook or some other media outlet with her head attached to a nude body. This close to finishing her Master's Degree, she could not afford to lose her job.

Her roommate, Kim Wong, glanced from her computer as Cassie breezed through the living area on her way to the bedroom. Resembling a little China doll with her small stature, black bangs and short bob, Kim laid claim to being third generation American but still had the Asian work ethic driving her toward a medical degree.

"Hey, Cass, some guy, not that sweetie, Howdy, came looking for you. This jerk bangs on the door and takes my picture when I open up. Says 'You Cassie Thomas?' I say, 'Do I look like a frickin' Cassie Thomas?' and slam the door in his face. Anyhow, someone is out to get you."

"Yeah, and he did. Who knows what's happening the way my life is going. Not that I don't deserve everything that comes my way."

"You lay more guilt on yourself than my Chinese grandmother could, and she's really adept at it. You should call your honey and talk out your problems. I bet he still loves you."

"When a man says you have destroyed him among other choice accusations, I doubt he ever wants to hear from you again."

"Well, you're the psychologist. The human mind is messier than a heart transplant. I'll stick to healing the body. At least you know if a wound heals."

"We have anything for lunch?"

"Half a cold pizza, some Ramen noodles, iced tea, beer, a couple of apples and a bag of salad past its expiration date. If you avoid the mushy stuff in the bottom of the sack, you can probably get your greens for the day. We do need groceries."

"I'll go on the weekend. It's too damn hot to shop today. The eggs will boil in their shells. So, cold pizza and expired salad it is. Good enough to keep me going until Saturday."

****

If she'd stayed on campus and not ventured to the Winn-Dixie, Cassie might never have seen herself plastered on the front page of a tabloid at the grocery store as she waited to check out. She always chose a long line in order to get a free read of her guilty pleasure while waiting. But, there she was looking right at herself. The photographer hadn't focused so much on her face as her breasts straining that chemise. He'd caught the curve of her arm holding up the mass of her hair like a model posing for a sensuous picture, but someone had Photoshopped her battered laptop case into oblivion. With her lips partly open from sucking in the hot air on her trek across campus and her startled blue eyes wide, she did look every bit like a woman the magazine could dub Howdy's Hottie.

Howdy's Hottie Causes Sinners Slump

A reliable source told this reporter that ace kicker, Howard "Howdy" McCoy, has not been able to split the uprights since his breakup with LSU graduate student, Cassie Thomas. Last season, McCoy led the league with a ninety-seven percent success rate in kicking field goals and PAT's. His golden toe lifted the Sinners into the playoffs but could not keep them there.

During the off-season, informants say McCoy fell hard for the voluptuous psychologist, a frequent visitor to quarterback Joe Dean Billodeaux's ranch where she visits her son, Thomas, adopted by Joe and his wife, Nell. Presumably, the couple met there and only months later were spotted at the Bellagio Hotel in Las Vegas. Friends suspect an elopement gone awry. Bellagio maids who do not wish to be named confirm that Thomas abandoned McCoy in their luxury suite. The kicker secluded himself in the room and emerged only after being routed by his mother, well-known cabaret singer, Mariah Coy. He left behind a shambles of empty liquor bottles, pizza boxes, dirty dishes, and sheets.

The blunt-spoken Coy offered us this quote, "I wish the hell my boy would get over her or go after her because he is a damned mess right now. Howdy, if you read this, get up off your ass and take care of it."

Returning to Louisiana, McCoy spent the summer volunteering at Camp Love Letter, Billodeaux's retreat for seriously ill children and their families. Even this distraction failed to end his obsession over the fair Miss Thomas with whom he has had no contact since their parting. Since returning to the Sinners summer camp, Howdy has been unable to score, dare we say, because he cannot score with Cassie. His pre-season PATs stand at zero. Cassie Thomas, what must a guy do or not do to get your attention?

"Oh no, oh no, oh no," she whispered. An inset picture of Howdy in his black and red uniform only made her heart squeeze harder. He smiled directly at her with that wonderful, loopy grin of his, certainly the most innocent Sinner that ever lived, and she'd ruined him. The article had the story completely wrong, naturally. She hadn't left *him,* exactly the other way around. He'd made no attempt to get in touch with her, to apologize, but for what? Everything he said rang true, except for her being a whore of course, and she couldn't disprove that. Lots of college girls slept around during their four years on campus, and he'd lumped her in with them. As for the cause of his slump, Mariah and his new found family shared the blame.

"Lady, move it," a harried mother said as the toddler in her cart strained small hands toward a pack of gum in the impulse purchase racks.

The checker asked, "You gonna buy that?"

She shoved the tabloid onto the moving belt and unloaded her groceries after it. Once she returned to the apartment, she'd have to figure out a way to help Howdy without doing further damage. But how, but how?

Opportunity called before Cassie got the containers of yogurt and fresh bag of greens into the fridge. "I saw that tabloid story about you and Howdy," Nell said. "Having been their target when Joe and I were seeing each other, I know how you must feel."

"Awful. I don't know what to do. It's his family situation causing his problems, not me. He made it clear he never wanted to see me again. I stayed away from Lorena Ranch all summer because of that when I wanted to see Tommy so badly, wanted things to be the way they were before Vegas. I still don't know who his father is."

"A fellow named Chet Lovell who left him a brother and two sisters, all sort of grasping."

"Believe me, Nell, it could have been worse."

"Joe is taking care of the family problems. I do think you two need to talk. Say, I have skybox seats with some of the team sponsors at the opening game. Want to attend? You can stay with us over the weekend. Nurse Wickersham is in the Madame Pompadour room, but we still have plenty of space since the kids are in Chapelle. Howdy lives a few floors down, you know."

"I've been there."

"Who knows, you might run into each other in the elevator, or possibly one of you could bring yourself to knock on a door."

"I could see that happening if you think that door wouldn't be slammed in my face."

"I'm fairly sure he regrets his rash words, Cassie. But men, they don't know how to say it. So, get yourself down to New Orleans right away, okay?"

"Absolutely. Thank you, Nell, for this and for forgiving me about going after Joe. You have a big heart."

"That's not all that's big about me right now. Wait until you see."

Chapter Thirty-Two

Cassie waited nervously by the entrance to the skybox. Several middle-aged men and a young guy, some carrying laptops, entered, giving her the eyeball in passing as if she were an item on the buffet spread out in the back of the room. They took the seats up against the glass overlooking the field. A latecomer with their group slowed as he approached her and said, "You want to sit with us, honey?"

"No, thanks. I'm waiting for friends." She hadn't dressed this way to pick up businessmen on vacation, but for Howdy. He should be able to see her form-hugging, scooped neck scarlet top from the field— maybe. Her low-slung skinny jeans were black of course, to carry out the Sinners' color theme, and belted with a wide studded leather band. Black high heels ramped up her height. In the crook of her arm she carried one black and one red plastic thunder stick, the promotional items for the opening game of the season.

A little too eager, she'd arrived early and gained easy access to the luxury level with the ticket Joe left for her at the box office. Finally, the elevator at the end of the corridor opened to reveal a stout woman overflowing a wheelchair and her gray-haired, hatchet-featured nurse. Cassie took a moment to recognize the patient as Nell bloated beyond belief and covered in a tent-like black dress worn in a vain attempt to look smaller. The red scarf tied jauntily around her neck failed to distract from the sheer size of her belly.

Behind them, the ever stunning Joe Dean Billodeaux moved along nervous as a nanny with twins at a water park. He passed the nurse who wore the old traditional white uniform, cap and shoes rather than the more comfortable and friendly scrubs and came alongside of his wife. His lips moved a mile a minute, and Cassie heard his lecture as they came into range.

"You have one pain, your water breaks, you go to the ambulance, quick, quick. No foolin' around, Nell, no waitin' till the end of the game, you hear you me. The EMTs know where you are. All you got to do is call this number, and they be ready for you, *cher* heart."

Though Nell seemed a little pissed over his concern, Cassie smiled. Anxiety brought out the Cajun in Joe big time. She didn't run to him for a hug as she would have earlier in the year. Instead, she waited and accepted that he would only give her a nod and a tense smile as they entered the skybox together. The nurse parked Nell in front of a guardrail on the top level.

The businessmen left their seats and lined up to meet Joe and get his autograph. He thanked them profusely for sharing their box with his wife and her friends at the last minute. When asked if he felt he could beat the Falcon's young quarterback, he replied, "For sure, we're gonna win."

"Even with Howdy Doody McCoy off his game?" the guy who had hit on Cassie asked.

"He'll be on his game today. Just you let Cassie, here, up by the window to provide a little inspiration for him."

With a leer in her direction, the fellow answered,

"She could inspire me to do lots of things. If it gets too crowded, she can sit on my lap."

Joe frowned darkly as if debating whether to beat the guy up or not, but evidently decided he didn't have the time. He only replied, "She's Howdy's girl. Don't you forget that."

One of his cronies, a pencil-necked geek type who had been engrossed in something on his laptop, suddenly took an interest in his surroundings. "You mean we're sharing our box with Howdy's Hottie? I Googled her. Sure, we'll make space for her."

"To you, she is Miss Thomas. Got it?" Joe said, his expression going from cordial to dangerous in a second, giving them a close up view of the Billodeaux game face.

The geek paled. "Sure, right. Miss Thomas. Great to meet you in person, Joe."

"This is my wife, Nell. I expect y'all to take good care of her."

"Jesus, what's wrong with her?" the less than diplomatic laptop guy blurted.

"Since you mention it, she is great with child like the Virgin Mary, only we're having triplets, you see."

The lean and lecherous one shouted, "Way to go, Joe!"

"Thanks. Look, I have to get to the locker room. Enjoy the game."

He kissed Nell and left the box, but they heard him greeting others as he made his way to the elevator. The commotion in the corridor increased and headed their way. In burst two of the team wives, Precious Armitage, the plus-sized and then some wife of nose guard Calvin Armitage, and the slim and slinky

Sharlette Dobbs who belonged to the tight end, Asa. They arrived with a festoon of pink and blue balloons centered around three big Mylar storks proclaiming, "It's a boy, It's a girl, It's a boy."

Precious tied the balloon bouquet to the railing, "Look at you, girl. You're bigger than Fats Domino at his fattest."

Lovely mocha-colored Sharlette leaned over to kiss Nell's cheek. "Don't mind her. You'll lose that weight and then some running after three more. I certainly did after giving Ace his son."

"You look great as always. How is your boy doing?" Nell asked.

"As well as any child whose father named him Prince."

"Others have done that before Ace, so he is in good company. I do wish I could wear animal prints the way you do, but right now I'd only look like an obese tiger."

"Yes." Precious smoothed the jacket of her red satin pants suit over her tremendous thighs. With her dark brown skin, she could make it work. "Big, beautiful women should stick to solid colors. But, I don't know. I'm still wearing the weight I gained with Calvin's number four around my hips. Fortunately, Cal appreciates a woman with a little heft to her. He'd crush anyone else when he got on top. Joe probably feels the same way with you being so tiny—usually."

"Don't upset her! Honey, we tried to visit when we heard you were in the city, but your watchdog over there wouldn't let us in. She said you couldn't have any excitement."

"And we are exciting, yes, we are!" Precious proclaimed. "But, Joe gave us the heads up. Here we are to keep you company during the game. Wait till you see what we got for you. Sharlette, bring it in."

Sharlette, nimble even in high heels, returned to the hall and came back wheeling a stroller made for triplets. "Our present to the new babies."

"That is so great! Thank you." Nell teared up a little. "Sorry, hormones. Ah, Nurse Wickersham, why don't you help yourself to some of the food while I visit with my friends? Try the barbecued shrimp." As soon as her caretaker moved away, she whispered. "She's a former nun from a nursing order. Nadine found her. At least with that face, she's no temptation for Joe."

"Not to mention her age, but what about that one? She still giving you trouble?" Precious asked, not bothering to lower her voice. Cassie, hanging out nearby, blushed the color of Sinners' red.

"No, we're good. She's Howdy's girl or will be again soon."

"I sure hope so. Calvin says the kid can't kick an empty beer can across a street right now he's so tied in knots over her and his family, but Joe is working on straightening things out."

"Hel-looo! Is this the right box?" The figure of a woman posed dramatically in the doorway. Her huge breasts led the way as she made her grand entrance. The geek goggled. The lecher gave a low whistle of approval.

"Who the hell is that?" Precious asked.

Cassie spoke up at once trying hard to redeem herself in the eyes of Nell's friends. "Let me introduce Mariah Coy, famous Las Vegas cabaret singer and Howdy's mother." Her voice rose above the pre-game noise like the emcee of a floorshow. There should have been applause.

With a toss of her bright red mane in full bewigged splendor, Mariah moved to crush Cassie against her chest. "You can shill for me anytime, girl. I am so glad you could come today. Joe Dean Billodeaux got me the most fabulous gig right here in the French Quarter and the cutest little bright blue cottage in Musicians' Village to use during my stay. You know, my boy is just too good for this cruel world and needs you to protect him. I told him he threw away the best thing that ever happened to him when you broke up."

"She's available, then? How about you, babe?" the lech said.

"For you, not at any price. Come on, Cassie dear, we need to sit near the window where Howie can see us together cheering for him." She tucked Cassie's arm under hers.

"First, you need to meet the other ladies. This is Nell, Joe's very pregnant wife," Cassie said, stating the obvious. "And Precious Armitage in the red. Then, Sharlette Dobbs."

Mariah, her own leopard skin print dress stretched tightly over breasts and hips, nodded. "It takes real women to bring off the tigress look or wear red satin. Pleased to meet you."

"I like her," Precious said. Sharlette agreed.

Putting one leg before the other in a model's strut, Mariah moved down the steps to the front row with Cassie in tow, possibly holding her up on her impossibly high stilettos. "Young man, you look like a gentleman and um—very intelligent. How about giving Cassie your seat?"

"Sure." The geek snapped his laptop closed and

tripped into Mariah's breasts in his haste to move. "So sorry."

"Not the first time that's happened to me. Won't be the last. Now you, lover boy, make way for Mariah." She pointed a one-inch acrylic nail painted black with a tiny Sinners' red devil mascot decal attached to it at the mouthy guy. He made no move to get up and relinquish his prime spot.

Mariah snapped her fingers, no easy feat with nails that long, and a hulking figure no one had noticed after her startling entrance came to her side. "Meet my bodyguard, Billy. Billy, remove this man."

"Oh, don't hurt yourself," Cassie gasped.

"He's stronger than he looks, honey."

Billy grabbed the guy under the arms and hauled him into the second row. "Hey, hey," the man protested. "My company pays for this box. You have no right to…!"

"Are we late? Have they kicked off yet?" Two tall, fashionably bony bleached blondes with tennis court tans walked into the box. Both wore smart black sheaths and red devil earrings purchased from the souvenir stand. They carried their free thunder sticks like odd accessories. Between them, big, balding and paunchy Robson Lovell surveyed the room. "Cassie, great to see you again! Is there room up front?" Before Billy could act, three more businessmen removed themselves to the second row.

"Howdy's half brother," Cassie announced to the group in general.

"What is this—a baby shower or a fucking family reunion. We came to watch the game," Billy's victim complained.

"Shut up, Les," one of his more mature companions said. "This is priceless. Wait till I tell my wife and kids I met a famous singer and all the rest of Howdy's family. My teenage daughter has a crush on the kicker. Loves his freckles."

"So do I," Cassie murmured.

"These are Howdy's half-sisters, Meredith and Mimi. Meredith is from Dad's second marriage and Mimi from third," Robson continued as if no interruption had occurred.

"Making her the older one," Mimi pointed out needlessly.

"Only by six years," Meredith added. "And I'm divorced. She's still married."

"Les Webster at your service. You ladies interested in clubbing after the game?" Mariah's designed lover boy asked. "Divorced, no kids." He glanced at Nell. "Thank God, no kids."

"Take me down there," Nell growled.

Nurse Wickersham dropped her plate of hors d'oeuvres into a trashcan. "Absolutely not! You must stay in your wheelchair and not get excited."

"Precious, Sharlette, haul me down these steps."

Nearly as big as her tackle of a husband Precious did most of the work, depositing Nell where she pointed in the third row right behind Les Webster. Gently, she raised an arm between two of the seats to make sure Nell had enough room to be comfortable. Nell beckoned to Cassie.

"Let me have one of those thunder sticks you've been carrying around."

Cassie handed over the black one. Nell waved it experimentally, slashing the air close to Les Webster's head. He ducked. "Look, Les," she said.

"His real name is Leslie," the geek offered. "I'm Simon." He looked sidelong at the two blondes as he said so.

Nell chortled. "Leslie, I love it. I won't be naming any of my children that, but I kind of like Simon. Okay, Leslie. You are an asshole. If you say one more ugly comment about women, babies, or pregnancy, I will bop you with this thunder stick."

Cassie offered her the other one. "Clap them together over his head. They make lots of noise."

"Then, we should all have some," Mariah declared. "Billy, go get a bunch of them. For as much as this box costs they should have put them on the seats for us."

"It's not your box!" Les insisted. Nell hit him with the thunder stick, then clapped them together above his quarter-sized bald spot for good measure. He cringed while his companions hooted.

"Yeah," said Precious as she settled herself beside Nell in another double-wide seat. "This little lady gets real feisty when she's pregnant. I wouldn't mess wit' her."

"Bitchy is more like it," Les retorted.

Nell bopped him again. Billy returned with a dozen pairs of thunder sticks and distributed them among the women. He offered Nurse Wickersham a set, and she stared at it as if he'd presented her with a naked penis. "No, thank you." The remainder, he gave to the men who wanted them with Robson eagerly accepting his.

"Billy, where's our bartender? I want one of those hurricane drinks everyone keeps talking about. First, give me a cigarette and a light," Mariah ordered.

"No smoking! No smoking around Mrs.

Billodeaux," Nurse Wickersham decreed. "That goes for all of you." She fixed her former nun's eye on the group, and they recognized her authority, even Mariah.

"Shit, I guess I can hold out until halftime if I can get a drink. See about it, Billy."

The game announcer's voice intruded into the skybox. "Let's hear it for the New Orleans Sinners!"

The music in the dome ramped up. Thunder sticks boomed together making a stadium already known for its noise even louder. Joe emerged leading his team from the inflatable devil's head, its maw seething with dried ice. The camera captured the entrance, then panned around picking out honey shots of the cheerleaders wielding their black and red pompoms and fans in the stands to flash on the big screens circling the dome. Stevie and Connor Riley appeared in the survey, stood and waved from their seats in a box on the fifty-yard line.

"Jeez, she still looks like a movie star," Nell grumped, "and she's due in two weeks."

Standing beside Howdy, Joe pointed to their skybox. The camera followed his directions. Mariah rose and pulled Cassie with her. She pressed herself and the girl against the glass and waved deliriously. "Come on, honey. Show Howie we're here for him."

Cassie plastered a smile on her face and fluttered her fingers. The camera got an amazingly good shot of Mariah's cleavage through the glass as the announcer said, "Welcome to our special guests, Mariah Coy, mother of Sinners' kicker, Howard McCoy and Cassie Thomas, his fiancée, as well as our visitors from sponsor, Hartz Technology."

Cassie held her smile until the camera panned

away. "Oh, Mariah, we aren't engaged. Someone made a terrible mistake. Howdy will be so upset."

"In my book, my son is the one who made the big mistake so he has nothing to be upset about. Let him think on it and come to the same conclusion. You can sit down now."

"I believe I'll stand until the kickoff." Hoping her presence would make a difference, Cassie remained pressed again the window.

"Down in front!" Les called. Nell hit him with a thunder stick, and he quieted.

The Falcons won the toss and elected to receive, perhaps counting on Howdy's weak performance in the pre-season games, but with the chant of "How-dy, How-dy, How-dy" coming from the stands, he sent the ball sailing into the end zone with a slight curl. The receiver took a knee, and the game began on the twenty-yard line.

From the first quarter on, anyone could plainly see Joe's head wasn't in the game. His passes failed to connect, and he appeared to have developed a tick in the direction of their skybox.

"I should have stayed home," Nell muttered.

"That is correct," Nurse Wickersham said as she waved away a tray of hurricanes gratefully accepted by the other denizens of the box.

"Don't you worry, Nell, my hubby and his line won't let them score," Precious promised.

Her faith in the man often called Curse 'Em and Crush 'Em Calvin did not quite pan out. Despite a ferocious effort, the Falcons got one by him, scored, and made the extra point with ease. As the clock dwindled toward the end of the first half, Joe finally connected with one of his long, long passes into the end zone. The crowd took up the Howdy chant, and the troubled kicker walked out onto the field to attempt the extra point.

In the relative quiet of the box, the voice of commentator Al Harney spoke from the speaker of Simon's laptop where he watched the game rather than look at the field. "Can you believe it? Quarterback, Joe Dean Billodeaux, is going to hold the ball for Howard McCoy. After a stunning freshman year with a ninety-seven percent completion rate on his kicks, McCoy has slumped in his sophomore season giving a disappointing performance in the pre-season. I'd say that's true leadership when the head honcho risks a broken finger or his whole hand to steady a shaky player."

"Well done, Joe. Well done," his companion, Hank Wilkes replied.

"Oh, Joe," Nell whispered. She took a deep breath, as deep as the babies would let her. If Howdy choked and injured him, her husband could be out for the season. Joe knelt to receive the snap. Howdy took his place. Whistles sounded. The opposing team used their last timeout to freeze the kicker. Joe stood up and clapped Howdy on the back.

"Ice, baby, ice," Nell muttered. Cassie, who dropped into a seat next to her by climbing over the back of the chair rather than go around Precious or the grossly pregnant belly, took her hand and repeated the same words with a twist, "Ice, ice, Howdy."

The game resumed. Joe crouched to receive the ball from the center and place it for Howdy. The kick soared, shanked to the left, hit an upright and bounced back onto the field. Cries of "Doody, Doody, Doody" filled the stadium, none louder than Leslie Webster's voice chanting the same. Nell rose half out of her seat and hit him with the thunder stick on one side of his face. Cassie pummeled him on the other side. Hurricane-fueled Mariah wobbled over on her spike heels to smack him directly on the nose with her red plastic stick. Over the sound of their swats, Nurse Wickersham yelled, "You are upsetting my patient, sir. I will have you ejected from the box."

Al Harney's voice sounded from the computer. "There is a flag on the play—encroachment on the neutral zone by the defending team prior to the kick. Howdy gets a do-over."

The mayhem in the skybox ceased. Total quiet ensued as Joe Dean said a few short words to his kicker and prepared to hold the ball again. Howdy took his three steps, easily, loosely, hit the football dead on and sent it sailing over the center of the goal post.

"And that, my friends is how it's done," Hank Wilkes remarked. "The Sinners go into the locker room tied at the end of the first half."

Cassie and Nell hugged. The men headed for the buffet, bar, and bathroom. The door to the skybox opened and a server wheeling a trolley bearing a large white cake decorated with pink and blue icing roses entered. In frosting script across its center were written the words, "Good Luck, Nell."

"Cake for everyone!" Precious shouted her invitation.

Nurse Wickersham tapped Nell's shoulder. "Bathroom first, then cake. I know you need to go after sitting for so long, Mrs. Billodeaux."

"Do not."

"Any woman pregnant with triplets needs to void frequently. We don't want those kidneys to back up, do we? Now, let me help you up the stairs and into your wheelchair, and I will take you for a nice tinkle."

"Bring my cake down here."

"Let's not be stubborn." The nurse moved into the space vacated by Precious when the cake arrived and grasped Nell's elbow to tug her upright. She budged Nell only enough to catch sight of the soaking rear of her patient's dress. "Did we wet ourselves?"

"No, we did not. I guess my water broke when I laid into Les. Don't make me go to the hospital. I want to see the second half."

"I am calling EMTs. We must go now, Mrs. Billodeaux, for the sake of your babies."

"Honey, we'll save y'all some cake," Precious promised. "You know you gotta go take care of this. We'll be over to the hospital right after the game." She lent her bulk to getting Nell back into the wheelchair.

"Don't tell Joe," Nell pleaded. "It will throw off his game even more, and besides he'll just say I told you so."

Cassie bounded up the steps after her. "Do you want me to go with you since Joe can't be there? You shouldn't go through this alone."

"No, stay here for Howdy. See him after the game. Promise me."

"I will. Stay safe, Nell, you and the babies."

Nurse Wickersham placed herself behind the chair and began pushing it from the suite. "You will not be alone, Mrs. Billodeaux. I shall be with you every step of the way."

"Wonderful," Nell answered glumly as they exited.

Les Webster sauntered up the stairs careful to avoid the dribbles Nell left behind on the carpet. He insinuated himself between Meredith and Mimi who nibbled on the celery sticks accompanying the platter of hot wings. "Great, that bitch is gone. Can you believe how she treated me and everyone let her?"

Meredith arched an eyebrow at him. "Pregnant women deserve some leeway. I have a six-year-old daughter myself. You cannot imagine the pain of birth. My pelvis is narrow, you see."

"Looks fine to me," he said, ogling her crotch. "How about that offer to take on the French Quarter after the game? I extend my invitation to both of you lovely ladies.

Mimi dipped a celery stick into the ranch dressing and held it up. "Do you think this is lo-cal?"

Les answered her. "This is New Orleans, sweetheart. I doubt it."

Mimi shook off the dressing and dried the celery stick with a napkin. Still considering if she had wiped away all the calories, she waved the vegetable in his face. "I don't think we'll be available after the game. Joe Dean promised to take us to the victory party and introduce us to his friends. We're practically family. Our new half-brother is nearly engaged to his adopted son's mother."

"Hey, the way Joe is playing, there won't be any victory party. So how about it?"

He found himself standing in the considerable shadow of Precious Armitage. "Joe says there's gonna be a victory party and he will take these ladies to it, you better believe it. Now, step away from the chicken wings if you don't plan to eat none."

Les slinked back to his seat as the players returned to the field. Cassie went back to her post by the window for all the good it did. The third quarter passed scoreless with Joe still off his stride, Brian Lightfoot called upon to execute a couple of well-placed punts, and no work at all for Howdy. So far, Nell wasn't missing a thing.

Chapter Thirty-Three

The EMTs met the wheelchair bearing Nell Billodeaux at the base of the elevator. They lifted her onto a gurney, placed a pad beneath her hips and elevated her head with a pillow. Unfortunately, the half-time crowd milled in the corridor. Lacking a siren or air horn, the techs shouted, "Make way, make way!" calling all the more attention to Nell who felt as mountainous in size as Rev Bullock.

"Poor thing," one female spectator bearing a baby bump the size of a small cantaloupe said. "Say, isn't that Joe Dean Billodeaux's wife? I heard it's going to be triplets."

Instead of dispersing, the crowd closed in to gawk. Nurse Wickersham growled, "Back off!"—and they did.

As they levered Nell into the ambulance, she waved to the crowd and put a finger to her lips. "Don't tell Joe until after the game, okay?"

The gawkers made a murmuring mass promise and one shouted, "Good luck, Nell." Still, she worried about the fans wearing Falcons shirts who kept their lips shut tight as the white doors closed and the siren blasted an opening in the traffic.

They went up one highway ramp and down another, pulling into the emergency bay in short order. The obstetrician she'd been seeing weekly since her arrival in New Orleans arrived at approximately the same time and rode up to the labor room with her. As he had promised, no way would he miss the delivery of the Billodeaux triplets. Beneath his white coat, he wore game day red and black.

"Any labor pains?" he inquired.

"Not really. A few twinges, lots of drippage."

"Good. Let's get you prepped for surgery and attached to the monitors. We'll see how those kiddos are doing."

"Remember, we're doing this with an epidural. I want to see my babies born."

"I haven't forgotten. We'll set that up as soon as you're prepped. A couple more questions first. Have you eaten today?"

"Not much. Some tea and cereal for breakfast around eight. I have no appetite anymore, but they are saving me a piece of my baby shower cake."

"That's nice. How about bowel movements?"

Nurse Wickersham answered for her. "At eight-thirty-five a.m."

"Still, we should do an enema."

"That should take care of your need to void as well," Nurse Wickersham said with some satisfaction.

"I don't need to… Oh, never mind!"

Nell endured the necessity of having a nurse shave her pubis and the cramps of the enema, obeyed all of the anesthesiologist's instructions as he inserted a tiny tube into her spine and began feeding the numbing drug into her system. As soon as they finished, she asked, "Could someone put the game on the TV while we wait for this stuff to kick in?"

Nurse Wickersham turned on the set. The doctor

checked the monitors and drips. "Okay, Nell, I'm going to scrub for surgery. See you in a few minutes. Nurse, will you be joining us? If so, get your gown and booties on and do the same."

"Absolutely, doctor."

Nell, her eyes fixed on the screen mounted above the examination table where she lay, commented, "Still tied, but the Falcons have the ball."

"On the count of three," an orderly said, and they transferred her to a gurney, trundling her down the hall to the delivery room where Dr. Stewart waited in his pale green scrubs and light classical music played in the background. "Could someone put the game on?" she asked as they lifted her on to the operating table, hooked up the monitors, and checked the drips again.

"I wouldn't mind that myself," said the doctor. "But no getting your blood pressure up or off it goes."

"I promise I will not get excited."

The nurses arranged a drape over her nether regions, now numb as a log, and the doctor made his incision while the game distracted Nell despite the awful suctioning sounds occurring now and then. Early in the fourth quarter he lifted out the baby girl and held her up for her mother to see. Puny as either of Nell's premature twins at birth, she made a tiny mewing sound like a newborn kitten.

"So small," Nell murmured.

"Good size for a triplet, over four pounds, I'd say. Now let's go after her brother."

And the Falcons scored with a field goal. Nell's blood pressure rose, and suddenly she became aware of Nurse Wickersham at her shoulder taking her hand and saying calmly, "Breathe in through your nose and out through your mouth, now again. I am quite sure Mr. Billodeaux can handle the situation, but he will not be able to cope with your loss or that of the babies. Breathe again. We are calm. We are serene."

"Yeah, right, serene," Nell said, but she did the routine and felt her pulse slow.

Midway through the fourth quarter, the first of the boys left the womb. Once free of the birth fluids, he expressed himself with a few sharp cries before settling into the arms of the waiting nurse who brought to him Nell for a quick peek before hustling the baby off to the preemie nursery. Joe was missing all this. He would be so ticked off with her.

Dr. Stewart nodded behind his mask. "Looking good. Nearly as big as his sister."

"I'll take your word for it that they aren't just tiny mutants," Nell joked, still alarmed by their size.

The game clock ran down to the two-minute warning. The commentator gave the welcome news. "Billodeaux has moved his team into field goal range with that last short pass. Forty yards to tie the game and go into overtime, well within the abilities of kicker, Howdy McCoy."

Nell groaned. The anesthesiologist asked if she felt any pain. "Only mentally," she answered.

Nurse Wickersham patted her shoulder. "I have every faith in the young man, and you should, too. Such a polite boy. Unlike your lady friends, he never argued if I told him you were resting, simply left his flowers and little gifts and went back to his place."

"I do. I believe in Howdy. Doc, how's it coming down there?"

"Getting ready for number three. Hang in there a

few more minutes."

"It appears Billodeaux will hold the ball for McCoy the second time in this game. Falcons call a time-out, their last one."

"Aw, why do they always do that?" the anesthesiologist griped. "It never works."

"I hope it doesn't work this time," Nell answered, fearful again for her husband's very talented hands.

The well-known voice of Al Harney filled the cool, sterile air of the operating room. "And the ball is snapped. I do not believe this. Billodeaux receives and tosses it to kicker, Howdy McCoy. The Sinners line goes into a V-formation. The kicker is running the ball, trying for a touchdown, eating up the ground with those long legs of his. He's at the thirty, the twenty, his protection is breaking down. One good hit and the defense will smash him to the ground. He's at the ten-yard line. Look at Howdy go! Here comes the tackle attempt, but it drives him across the goal line holding the ball out in front, not sparing himself for the sake of the score. When did you last see a play like that, Hank?"

"Al, not since 1984, the Seattle Seahawks under 'Ground Chuck' Knox. The man did love his trick plays—and they worked. My guess is the Sinners won't be using this one again for the rest of the season. Howdy looks a little shook up on the play. Appears someone took a cheap shot at Billodeaux, too. The Falcons will get the ball back with a fifteen-yard penalty attached."

"Who's going to go for the extra point? The punter, Brian Lightfoot, is coming onto the field. The reserve quarterback will hold." There was a short delay.

Finally, the announcer said, "And the point is good."

The operating team cheered quietly along with Nell. Nurse Wickersham prompted, "Breathe in, breathe out."

"I'm fine. I'm sending my baby lots of happy endorphins right now. Doctor, doctor, I didn't hear him cry with all the noise in here."

"Oxygen," Dr. Stewart said. She watched the rapid motion of his arms as if he were pressing life into small lungs.

"I can't see him. You let me see the other two."

"The Falcons are going for it on the first play with a Hail Mary pass," Al Harney informed them.

"We can't lose it! We can't lose it!" Nell insisted.

"The attempt fails. Game over. The Sinners take it 14-10."

Chapter Thirty-Four

Cassie waited by the gate for the victorious players to emerge. They came out in groups, laughing, joking, still hyped over the trick play. None of them paid any attention to her standing there alone while Mariah and Billy held back the rest of Howdy's family. Finally, he appeared with Brian Lightfoot at his side among the last of stragglers with the sole exception of Joe Dean, held back for post-game interviews as always. Brian noticed her first.

He said, "Man, you got some righteous bruises, Howdy. I hope they never ask me to run the ball. Looks like you have some company." He merged with the group waiting for the kicker and left his friend to confront the woman he'd helped Howdy to woo for better or worse. Howdy dipped his head and stared at his valuable toes while a red flush climbed up his neck.

She spoke first since he didn't. "Howdy, you were right. I pushed and pushed you to do something you weren't ready to explore. I caused you harm. Can you forgive me?"

"No."

"What the fuck is wrong with that boy?" Mariah shouted and started forward, but Billy tucked her arm under his. "Not now, darling. Let them be."

"I understand I hurt you. I can't prove no one else came between you and Bijou, either. But, I hoped we could be friends for Tommy's sake. He adores you."

Howdy raised his eyes. "I can't forgive you because the fault is mine. I said words—terrible words—I can never take back. I want to blame the shock of finding out about my family, but my grandpa would say that was no excuse. A man should think before he opens his mouth. I didn't. And the money I gave you, only for plane fare. I didn't mean it any other way. So, I'm asking you to forgive me if you can find it in your heart."

Cassie took his hands and gazed into those troubled baby blue eyes. "Yes, I forgive you because I love you."

"Howie, kiss the girl!" Mariah coached from the sidelines.

"He's slow about a lot of things," Brian informed her. "But you, my dear, are fabulous."

A sharp slap caught the kicker between the shoulder blades and propelled him forward into Cassie's embrace. Joe Dean Billodeaux, fresh from the showers, grinned and said, "Yeah, kiss and make up. I need to get to the hospital. Some asshole told me Nell went into labor when I came out of the tunnel for the second half. Didn't know if that was true or not, but no way could I let us go into overtime. We worked on that trick play all week in case Howdy felt he couldn't make a field goal. Sure came in handy. See y'all later."

"But Joe, you promised to take us to the victory party," Mimi pouted.

Joe shot two fingers at Howdy's half-sisters. "I will. Pick you up at your hotel at seven. I'll introduce you to the players, and then you are on your own. I need to get back to Nell and my babies for the rest of the night. You two can come up for air now. Me, I'm a gone pecan."

The couple broke off their kiss. "Give Nell our best, Joe. Happy endings for all, I hope," Cassie said, but she spoke to his back as he sprinted for his Porsche.

****

Precious and Sharlette arrived at the maternity ward before Joe. They bedecked Nell's suite with the balloon bouquet and placed the cake on a side table. The new mother had a piece in hand when her husband entered. He kissed the icing from her lips. "Good to see you eating again, Tink. I could use some of that myself." Precious carved off a slab and handed it to him on a napkin.

"Suddenly, I'm ravenous. Shammy says I need to eat to get my bowels working again. Oh, sorry everyone. Gross."

"Shammy?" Joe asked, his words muffled by frosting and crumbs.

"Nurse Wickersham. She was wonderful in the delivery room, held my hand the whole time. Did you see the babies yet?"

"No, I came here first. Sorry I wasn't the one there to hold your hand."

"I'm the one who's sorry. The babies came too soon. If I'd stayed home and quiet the last wouldn't be so small and sickly. We almost lost him in delivery. If he dies…"

"Nell, I pushed you into having three babies. I won't do that to you again. Now you feel bad about their size. Let's not do the guilt trip the way Cassie and Howdy did. Hey, good news on that. Last time I saw them, they were smooching. Besides, I know Trinity

331

will make it. He's got Billodeaux blood. That makes him a fighter. Your sister is pretty aggressive, too, as I recall. Might take a while, but he'll be fine."

Resembling a float in the rose parade, Rev Bullock entered the room with three vast bouquets of flowers, one red, one pink, one yellow. "Sorry, no blue roses, Joe. I tried. Trinity, now that's a fine name for the tiny guy."

Joe nodded. "My mother would say he's got the Father, Son and Holy Ghost on his side. We decided the last born would be called Trinity whether it turned out to be a boy or a girl. The girl is going to be Lorena Renee after my great-great-grandmother, the namesake of our ranch."

"What about the other boy? You know, no one has named their kid after me, and mine are Connor, Riley, and little Joe." His broad, black face filled with hope.

"Your name is Revelation Jeremiah Bullock, fool. No one is going to call a defenseless child that," Precious said. "Am I right, Sharlette?"

Sharlette held up her hands and shook her head. "I have a boy named Prince. I cannot take sides on this."

Two more people crowded into the room. Connor Riley headed for the cake while Stevie kissed Nell's cheek and handed her an envelope. "It's the usual, a gift certificate for baby pictures. I cannot believe you beat me to the delivery room. I still have two weeks to go. I'm huge and so uncomfortable."

"You call that huge. I reached the size of a blue whale."

"You're about killer whale size now," Precious added. "That's an improvement."

"About that name," the Rev pressed.

Stevie smiled his way. "We're calling ours Jack Haile Riley for our mutual friend."

"You'd name a boy for a lesbian golfer, but not Revelation Jeremiah?"

"Yes, the lesbian golfer who brought Connor and me back together. Jackie promised to be here for the birth. She thought she'd still be in the area to hold Joe's hand when your time came, but it looks like she missed her shot."

"Can't wait to see her. Somebody, give me more cake," Nell pleaded.

Nurse Wickersham strode into the suite. "I'll take those." She divested the Rev of his flowers. "Everyone out in the hall except the father. Mrs. Billodeaux's parents are here and a line is forming behind them."

"Can't they stay? I feel wonderful," Nell protested.

"Yes, new mothers always do. By day three, you will be in pain and feel quite miserable after a section. I suggest you start resting soon."

"Thanks for telling me that. Something to look forward to besides bringing the babies home."

"That won't be for quite some time, but I shall remain to care for you and them when the time comes. Now, everyone out."

"If you are going to be a fixture in our household, may I call you Shammy?" Nell asked with a mischievous smile.

"I believe I would like that. Come now, out. Allow Mr. and Mrs. Abbott some time with their daughter."

Ann and Gary Abbott stayed only long enough to be sure their daughter had come through her travail well. Then, they left for the nursery along with Joe Dean who warned as he backed out of the room, "My mother is on her way and about one hour out. You might want to take a sleeping pill before she gets here."

"No one can get on my nerves right now." Perhaps, she spoke too soon because Cassie, Howdy, and Brian Lightfoot entered. She sincerely hoped they left their troubles in the waiting room.

They came bearing pink and blue teddy bears and yet another bouquet of roses. Brian Lightfoot set down the impressive silver vase. "Are those blue roses?" she asked about their unusual shade.

"A shade of lavender, actually. I had my florist arrange them with baby's breath. He wasn't too keen on opening the shop on a Sunday, but I'm a big account. You can have the vase engraved with the babies' birth date and names later. It's an antique I picked up some time ago."

"Brian, your gifts are always unique and tasteful."

"I'd like to think so."

Howdy offered the two blue teddy bears and Cassie handed over the pink one. "Not very original, but the gift shop downstairs didn't have much else. We'll do something better later," he said modestly.

"Joe tells me you are back together. That's all I could want. Cassie, don't let this man go. He's the real McCoy. I've been waiting months and months to say that!" Nell laughed.

"I think that term came from meaning a fine brand of whiskey, and he really doesn't hold his liquor very well."

"No argument there. I'm back to beer and wine only. The hard stuff brings out my mean side."

"As if you have one," Cassie said with a fond smile.

"I beseech you to let Cassie pick out her own engagement ring. For certain, the man has no taste on his own," Brian interjected.

"Not only back together but engaged? I am so happy for you."

Howdy colored a little. "Well, I asked her to marry me a bunch of time in Vegas, but she always put me off. I finally got a yes out of her on the way over here."

"Make way for the daddy!" Joe barged to the head of line in the hall and came to his wife's side. "They let me in the nursery, and I sat down beside Trinity and gave him a pep talk. His pulse rate went right up. I'll do that as many times as it takes to convince him to fight for his life. When I get home, I'll put a bug in St. Jude's ear, and everything will be all right. Our Lorena is a strong-willed girl, I can tell already, coming out the biggest, shoving her brothers around before birth. No need to worry about her."

"Just what we need, another one like Jude and Xochi, but it's good, really good that she's strong."

"Now, about the other boy. I been thinking we need to commemorate that trick play. What do you think about McCoy Billodeaux?"

"I think it sounds sort of strange, no offense, Howdy."

"None taken, but I would be honored."

"Okay, how about Mack Coy Billodeaux? Mack Billodeaux, good name for a running back or wide receiver."

"Your mother would say he has no saint's name, Joe. You know how she is." Nell flicked a glance at the doorway afraid her mother-in-law might be bearing down on them with preternatural speed and hearing like a super-hero.

"We'll throw a Christopher in there. Mack Coy Christopher Billodeaux, I like it."

"Hasn't St. Christopher been kicked out of the Catholic church?" Nell asked.

"Only demoted to holy martyr. Shows what you know. He'll still look out for the kid. It's a great name."

"Won't Rev be disappointed you didn't name the baby after him?"

"You do know what his real name is, huh? He's a man of God. He can handle the disappointment, but this play, it was a once in a career deal. Unless you want to try it again sometime, Howdy."

"Let me heal first. As it is, they'll be gunning for me now, expecting me to take off with the ball."

"Yeah, we can get some great penalties if they rough you up a little. This is going to be a fantastic season. I can feel it."

Nurse Wickersham put her head in the door. "Time's up. Game over. Everyone, go home."

Epilogue

A perfect Christmas Eve, thought Nell Billodeaux, incredibly now a mother of eight. Joe home, not on the road. The children tucked into their beds after attending the Rev's Christmas Eve service and church social complete with a black Santa who looked suspiciously like him, a few good friends gathered around the fireplace drinking a good merlot sent by Brian Lightfoot, the CD of Mariah Coy singing *Have Yourself a Merry Little Christmas* playing in the background. No onslaught of relatives until tomorrow.

A twelve-foot tree covered with tiny white lights, shining balls, and children's handmade decorations sat in the corner towering over an avalanche of presents. The stockings on the fireplace hung empty because only Santa could fill those. Jude had questioned the AME Santa closely when she went to sit on his lap to receive an orange and a candy cane, making sure he would be able to get to their house tonight. Dean didn't believe anymore, and he had told Tommy, but both kept quiet for the sake of their sisters and the babies.

Howdy and Cassie snuggled together close to the small fire even though they had to run the air conditioner to enjoy it on this warm, holy night. With all the bedrooms now filled with children, they would stay over in one of the cabins, enjoy watching Tommy and the others open their presents in the morning, then after an enormous family brunch, take Cassie's son to celebrate with the Thomas family, Mariah, and Billy in New Orleans. Bijou's parents, anxious to get to know Xochi better, planned to have her visit at Toledo Bend with them for a week's stay.

"I'm pretty sure my mom and Billy are livin' in sin," Howdy remarked as his mother's smoky voice moved on to *Blue Christmas.*

Cassie massaged his shoulders. "Loosen up. So are we until the wedding." Her two-carat princess cut diamond ring flashed in the firelight.

"Yeah, but I don't think they plan to get married the week after the Super Bowl like we are. Maybe I should ask Billy his intentions."

"Leave them alone, sweetie. Unlike us, they grew up a long time ago. A wedding on Valentine's Day, perfect for a bunch of redheads like us." Cassie sighed the way every bride-to-be should. Her thesis done and defended, her second degree already framed, for the time being she had nothing to do but plan her wedding and enjoy New Orleans with Howdy.

Corazon trundled in with a last tray of snacks. "If it's okay by you, I go home now. Knox, Jr., he wants to eat again. Ay, a twelve pound baby. Who knew they came so big? Mine is a giant, not like the triplets, always hungry."

"A lineman, that's what Junior will be," Joe predicted.

"Don't you dare plan on working tomorrow. Let your cousins fetch and carry," Nell said. "You know Nadine and Joe's sisters will bring more food than anyone can possibly eat and clean up, too."

Also delivered by C-section, but a week overdue,

unlike Nell's children, Corazon still carried much of her baby weight. Nell marveled that Knox, Sr. did not mind, nor did Joe ever remark about the scar that now crossed her own belly even though she'd trimmed down fast with all the children needing her attention.

She'd gone daily to the hospital to sing and read and hold the triplets even for brief moments. If Joe could, he came along to give Trinity another pep talk. The baby always made gains afterward. When he finally came home to share a room painted a soothing green with his brother and sister, they did notice he responded more to Joe's voice and Nell's singing than in any other way. One had to get close up to his tiny face to elicit a smile, though he produced a grand one when they did. The pediatrician suspected he had vision trouble and to date, they kept Trinity on a monitor to alert Nell and Shammy in her cottage to any problems with his breathing.

Joe never mentioned that either. He simply remarked that not everyone could play football. As if reading her thoughts, her husband said to Connor Riley whose own bald-headed, blue-eyed son slept upstairs with his brood, "You miss the game, Con?"

"Not as much as I thought I would. I enjoy doing motivational speaking and setting my own hours. I have an offer to be commentator next season if I want it. We need to talk about getting our barbecue sauce company started, Connor's Mild and Joe Dean's Red Hot. I'd like to have another child."

Stevie, sitting on her husband's lap in one of the big recliners, bopped him. "Not right away."

"Sure, I know that."

"We can use the sauce proceeds to build more

cottages for Camp Love Letter. With Corazon and her family in one, the maids in another and Shammy in a third, we're running out of room. In fact, I think we should add a wing onto the house just in case," Joe Dean said.

Nell sat up abruptly from where she lounged against Joe's shoulder and spilled her merlot down her festive red sequined top. "Why?'

"You know Madame Leleux said we'd end up with twelve children, this way, that way, all ways. Never wrong, that old *traiteur,* no. Their blankets are already in the chest."

"Not possible. Only superstitious nonsense."

"We'll see. I think we should be prepared."

The trouble with Joe, he was so often optimistically right. He said he would take care of the Cassie problem, and he did as unerringly as he threw passes. He swore the triplets would be fine, and mostly they were. Now, she could not imagine being without them.

"I'll call an architect in January." Nell blotted her stained top, glad to see the sequins had repelled much of the mess, and leaned against Joe once more. A future with him would always be an adventure. Time she got used to the idea and made it her New Year's Resolution.